The Rebel Queen

Other Books by Lexi Blake

ROMANTIC SUSPENSE

Masters and Mercenaries
The Dom Who Loved Me
The Men With The Golden Cuffs
A Dom is Forever
On Her Master's Secret Service
Sanctum: A Masters and Mercenaries Novella
Love and Let Die
Unconditional: A Masters and Mercenaries Novella
Dungeon Royale
Dungeon Games: A Masters and Mercenaries Novella
A View to a Thrill
Cherished: A Masters and Mercenaries Novella
You Only Love Twice
Luscious: Masters and Mercenaries~Topped
Adored: A Masters and Mercenaries Novella
Master No
Just One Taste: Masters and Mercenaries~Topped 2
From Sanctum with Love
Devoted: A Masters and Mercenaries Novella
Dominance Never Dies
Submission is Not Enough
Master Bits and Mercenary Bites~The Secret Recipes of Topped
Perfectly Paired: Masters and Mercenaries~Topped 3
For His Eyes Only
Arranged: A Masters and Mercenaries Novella
Love Another Day
At Your Service: Masters and Mercenaries~Topped 4
Master Bits and Mercenary Bites~Girls Night
Nobody Does It Better
Close Cover
Protected: A Masters and Mercenaries Novella
Enchanted: A Masters and Mercenaries Novella
Charmed: A Masters and Mercenaries Novella
Treasured: A Masters and Mercenaries Novella, Coming June 29, 2021

Masters and Mercenaries: The Forgotten
Lost Hearts (Memento Mori)
Lost and Found
Lost in You
Long Lost
No Love Lost

Masters and Mercenaries: Reloaded
Submission Impossible
The Dom Identity, Coming September 14, 2021

Butterfly Bayou
Butterfly Bayou
Bayou Baby
Bayou Dreaming
Bayou Beauty, Coming July 27, 2021

Lawless
Ruthless
Satisfaction
Revenge

Courting Justice
Order of Protection
Evidence of Desire

Masters Of Ménage (by Shayla Black and Lexi Blake)
Their Virgin Captive
Their Virgin's Secret
Their Virgin Concubine
Their Virgin Princess
Their Virgin Hostage
Their Virgin Secretary
Their Virgin Mistress

The Perfect Gentlemen (by Shayla Black and Lexi Blake)
Scandal Never Sleeps
Seduction in Session
Big Easy Temptation
Smoke and Sin
At the Pleasure of the President

URBAN FANTASY

Thieves
Steal the Light
Steal the Day
Steal the Moon
Steal the Sun
Steal the Night
Ripper
Addict
Sleeper
Outcast
Stealing Summer
The Rebel Queen

LEXI BLAKE WRITING AS SOPHIE OAK

Texas Sirens
Small Town Siren
Siren in the City
Siren Enslaved
Siren Beloved
Siren in Waiting
Siren in Bloom
Siren Unleashed
Siren Reborn

Nights in Bliss, Colorado
Three to Ride
Two to Love
One to Keep
Lost in Bliss
Found in Bliss
Pure Bliss
Chasing Bliss
Once Upon a Time in Bliss
Back in Bliss
Sirens in Bliss
Happily Ever After in Bliss
Far From Bliss, Coming 2021

A Faery Story

Bound

Beast

Beauty

Standalone

Away From Me

Snowed In

The Rebel Queen

Outlaw: A Thieves Series, Book 1

Lexi Blake

The Rebel Queen
Outlaw: A Thieves Series, Book 1
Lexi Blake

Published by DLZ Entertainment LLC

Edited by Chloe Vale
ISBN: 978-1-942297-54-3

Acknowledgments

It wasn't until I was almost through with this book that I understood what it's truly about. That happens often when I'm writing—especially a Thieves book. I think I'm writing about a fantasy world where every story is about kings and queens, and at some point I realize the whole story is really about me. Writing is often the way I process my thoughts and emotions. Never before was this more true than with The Rebel Queen. This book was written in 2020. If you're reading this at a time when 2020 is no longer a curse word, then I salute you for surviving. For many of us 2020 was the year when time seemed to stop and fast forward all at the same time. It was the year we lost an unimaginable amount of people to a virus that shut the whole world down. And it was more than the pandemic. 2020 was the year a lot of us realized the world wasn't the place we thought it was. What had seemed safe and comfortable and fair to many of us flat out wasn't for our brothers and sisters. It was a year of anger and hopelessness, and it was absolutely a year where I wanted to go back to a time when I understood things, when I was in control. I also turned fifty this year, and somehow I looked in the mirror and didn't recognize the face I saw because I remember myself as so much younger. All of this made 2020 a roiling ball of misery.

But there was good in it, too, and that is what I learned while writing this book. I worked so much out through writing this part of Zoey's story. 2020 was a precious time. I spent a year getting to know my kids without the constant running I'd done before. 2020 was the year I learned how to be still, and that is important. I learned who my friends are and how much I love them. We found ways to keep close, to not allow the storm that raged to force us apart.

As this book is published, there's hope and the world is starting to open up, but I won't forget the lessons I learned. When the doors open, the world we walk into will be forever changed. But if we reach out and hold on to the ones we love, we'll make our way. We'll walk together the only way we can—forward.

Thanks to my whole team—Kim Guidroz, Maria Monroy, Kori

Smith, Stormy Pate, and Riane Holt. Thanks again to Karen Cox who has an encyclopedic knowledge of this world. Thanks to Liz Berry and Jillian Stein. Thanks to Jenn Watson and Social Butterfly for the publicity help. As always thanks to my husband who makes my writing life possible.

This book is dedicated—as it should be—to my children who grew up far too fast.

For Dylan and Lindsey and Zoey

Sign up for Lexi Blake's newsletter
and be entered to win a $25 gift certificate
to the bookseller of your choice.

Join us for news, fun and exclusive content
including free Thieves short stories.

There's a new contest every month!

Go to www.LexiBlake.net to subscribe.

Chapter One

"Zoey, are you all right, sweetheart?"

I was aware of my husband moving in behind me, knew he was touching my shoulders and that his voice had gone soft. But I couldn't feel Devinshea. All I could feel was a numbness descend because this couldn't be happening. Not to us.

I stared at the poster in my hand and the ones in neat stacks on the desk in front of me.

"Of course she's not all right." Kelsey Owens stood by the door as though she was waiting for it all to go wrong.

The day had already gone firmly to hell.

This was supposed to be our homecoming. We'd been away from the Earth plane for days, trying hard to find our way back. We hadn't meant to leave. Devinshea had been missing, along with our long-time friend Marcus Vorenus. We'd sent the *Nex Apparatus* to find them. It had been the day after Kelsey's wedding, and she'd had to put her honeymoon on hold.

She'd gone missing, too.

In our search for them, Daniel and I had gotten sucked into a magical painting and sent to a far-off plane with no means to get home to our children and the supernatural kingdom Daniel reigned over. Yeah, it's that kind of life, but it's ours. And as so often happens, getting sent to another plane had ended in something wonderful.

Daniel and I had found our daughter Summer. Our first child. She was happily married to Marcus now, and it turned out she'd been born to balance the outer planes. She was a powerful source of energy, and with her king at her side, she would ensure the outer planes stayed powered with her unique magic.

As we'd left that incredible place, I had mourned the fact that it could be years before we saw our daughter again, but I was eager to see our other children. Rhys and Lee are our twins, and Evangeline is our sweet daughter. They're eleven and five.

At least they had been when we left. The posters in my hand—the wanted posters—showed my children all grown up.

Wanted for crimes against our good King Myrddin
Lee Donovan-Quinn, outlaw, traitor and thief
Dead or alive

My baby boy. My human child. He was staring at me from the poster with his one good eye. His left eye was covered in a patch, a jagged scar crossing his face. He wasn't a boy anymore. He was a man. A grown man.

Twelve years. Somehow we'd lost twelve years. Only four days had passed for us, but twelve years had gone by on the Earth plane, and it seemed Daniel's old mentor, the wizard Myrddin Emrys, had decided to use that time to take his crown.

The wizard, who was also known as Merlin, had been the power behind all the kings who wielded the sword most famously known as Excalibur. Now he'd taken the crown himself, and it was obvious he had a problem with what was left of the royal family.

"I think we should move out as carefully and quietly as we can." Kelsey put down the poster that proclaimed Trent Wilcox was wanted for sheltering enemies of the king. "We need to get out of this building and try to find our people."

Our people. Our families. Our children, who'd been on their own for twelve fucking years. Who'd apparently been on the run for a while.

"We need to figure out what's happened here," Daniel was saying. "We know we're in the Council building. In what used to be the armory. We've apparently been gone for twelve years, and something's happened with our kids. Could it be a misunderstanding?"

"Do you mean could Myrddin have tripped over your crown and oops, it's on his head and he can't get it off and wouldn't it be fun to play a prank and put a bounty on the royal kids and their friends?" Kelsey kept her voice down but every word dripped with sarcasm. "I thought we got the thrall stone out of your head. How about you, Quinn? You want to march up to Myrddin and ask him if he wouldn't mind giving you back your kingdom?"

One of the good things that had come from our journey had been figuring out how Myrddin had easily manipulated my husbands for years. He'd planted thrall stones in their brains, and they had allowed him to influence both Danny and Dev.

"I know exactly how dangerous Myrddin is," Daniel growled back. "I'm merely saying maybe we shouldn't overreact. Maybe we should figure out what happened. Twelve years is a long time. We have to ask ourselves some questions. Are we on some alternative plane?"

"We've obviously come to the wrong place," Devinshea was saying. "Something went wrong when we came back through the painting."

"Or this was exactly what Myrddin wanted for us." It seemed to me he'd done everything he could to get rid of us. This could have been his fail-safe.

"I don't think so." The newest member of our party was standing beside me, looking down at the poster of Lee. "I dream about him at night. I think this is exactly where I'm supposed to be."

Dean Malone was a twenty-three-year-old wizard we'd picked up along the way. According to Kelsey, he had something to do with the prophecy about Myrddin. Kelsey was carrying a book that she claimed held the prophecies of the witches of Arete—a plane where witches ruled. It was in the pack on her back, and she'd vowed to do anything to keep it in her possession.

This particular prophecy foretold that two people in all the planes held the power to kill Myrddin Emrys. Myrddin had avoided one by having his pregnant mother kidnapped and sent off plane. If Kelsey was right, that young man was Dean Malone. Myrddin had manipulated the other man into a situation where he'd been killed.

Where I'd held him as he lay dying. Kelsey's father, my guard, Lee Owens. He'd been the one who the prophecy identified.

Myrddin didn't know that the Heaven plane had offered me a gift—Lee's soul in my child's body, the chance to give one of the best men I'd ever known an easier life.

Fucking prophecy.

"Is there any way to use the painting to get back to where we came from?" Dev was asking. "If we can get back, we can talk to Summer. She might have a way to get us to the proper time."

"I can't go back." Dean stood up taller. He was a young man with stark white hair and crystal blue eyes—a sure sign that he wasn't entirely human. The magic he wielded was another clue. He was at least a foot taller than me, almost as tall as my faery prince husband. "This is where I'm supposed to be. The wizard has conquered the supernatural world—the world I was born to defend. I need to find Lee Donovan-Quinn."

"But you don't," Daniel said in that annoyingly soothing tone he used when the world had exploded and he was trying to keep everyone calm. "If we go back to the proper time, I can end whatever coup Myrddin was planning. I'll know what's happening going in, and I'll kill him myself."

Danny might be using a calm tone, but his fangs were out. The King of All Vampire took his crown seriously. After all, we'd fought a war for it once. We could take care of a minor battle this time.

I was all on board with this plan. I let the poster drop from my hand. I never wanted to see it again. I wanted my sweet little boys and girl. I wanted Fenrir, Kelsey's son, to be the baby werewolf he was, the kid who didn't like to wear pants. "Let's do it. Dean, Dev is right. If we can get home, we'll take care of the problem and then you won't have to do anything but enjoy the Earth plane."

It was that moment that I was reminded I hadn't come through the painting alone. There was a butterfly attached to my hair, a ruby-red pixie, the queen of her kind. She had been a constant companion for years, as I was also known as Her Grace when I was in Fae society. Devinshea was the High Priest of Faery, and I his acknowledged goddess.

Arwyna fluttered her wings and flew for the door Kelsey guarded.

"That's not what the prophecy says," Dean replied stubbornly.

I didn't care about prophecy. Prophecy had gotten us into this clusterfuck in the first place.

Kelsey looked at me, a grave expression on her face. "*The world will fold and bend in on itself and you will be left on the wrong side.*"

I felt anger rise quick and true. She wanted to throw that at me now? "I don't want to hear anything about a trick or a trap. Gray's been peddling that nonsense for years. I'm not going to let it stop me from trying to fix this."

Grayson Sloane was one of two prophets who walked the Earth plane. He was also Kelsey's other husband. Like me, she had two. Trent, one of the strongest werewolves in the world, and the dark prophet, Gray. For the last several years he'd warned us of a coming evil—a trick and a trap.

I was not going to allow myself to be trapped here.

"I know this one by heart," Kelsey continued. "*Years will pass. Your wolf will howl but he will remain steadfast.*" She pointed to the wanted poster featuring Trent. "My wolf has protected your pack. This is the event Gray foretold, and we now have parts to play. You know Gray's prophecies can't truly be altered. They can only guide us."

Arwyna was flying around the room, seeming to look for something. We stood in the room that used to be the armory. It was in the lower levels of the building, under Ether, the club my Fae husband ran. Now it seemed to be some kind of office and storage area.

Daniel paced the floor, his jaw going tight even as he spoke. "Wasn't there something in that prophecy about a magician?"

Kelsey nodded. "*The magician will rule but you can win. Take back the plane.*"

I didn't want to take back the plane. I wanted to go home and be with my children. I wanted to be their mom and have fun with my husbands and…

I was pregnant. I was pregnant with Daniel's child.

While we'd been on that distant faery plane, our daughter's magic had taken my vampire husband and turned him briefly human.

It had been a terrible change since we'd been in danger and Daniel had been the vulnerable one for once. But we'd taken the chance we had, and our faery prince had overseen fertility rites for us.

I was pregnant. Kelsey was pregnant. She had to understand. "Kelsey, if this is true, you've been away from Trent and Gray for twelve years. Fenrir is grown now. You lost all that time with your son. You have to want those years back."

"Of course I do, but I don't think that's going to happen, and we need to consider the fact that we're now standing in enemy territory. We need to find a way out," Kelsey insisted.

For the first time in our acquaintance, Kelsey's steadiness bugged me. "How can you be calm? Your son is on a wanted poster."

"Yeah, but he's wanted for something I would do too, so I can't judge him." Kelsey opened a metal cabinet and quickly went through the contents. She sighed and closed it again, not finding what she wanted. "I'm calm because I have to be. I have to get us out of this building. And honestly, that freaking prophecy has been haunting me for years. Now I understand it. There's a little peace in that."

I shook my head because I didn't get her logic at all, but the painting was nothing but a blank canvas now, and none of us understood the magic behind it. We weren't going to be able to jump back through it and get a do-over. Dean wouldn't be willing to do it even if he understood how.

Kelsey was right. We needed to move.

Arwyna flew up and disappeared into the air vent.

I went on my toes because I couldn't scream at her. "Hey, we don't know that's not dangerous. Come back."

Daniel went still. "Devinshea, maybe you need to see if that sonic weapon you stole is working."

Kelsey shook her head. "If it's anything like the one I stole, it's out of charge. It's the first thing I checked."

Dev had a small sonic gun in his hand. He'd taken it from some vampire mercenaries we'd had a run-in with on the outer planes. "Mine's dead, too. But it had a full charge when we came through. How could both of them fail?"

Daniel moved to the door, cocking his head and likely opening his preternatural senses. "Are there plants you might be able to use? Someone's coming. I don't recognize the scent."

Dev brought his hands up, sending his power outward. Devinshea is a Green Man, and in addition to his fertility powers, he could call all things green to our aid. It might seem like a soft power, but Dev could do a lot of damage with vines and roots.

Kelsey picked up the nearest object she could find. It was a stapler.

"What are you going to do with that?" Daniel asked, his brows rising.

Kelsey shrugged. "I'll probably throw it and then use my fists, but I feel better with a weapon."

"Zoey, I think you should move to the back." Daniel was tense, his shoulders straight and claws out.

I didn't want to move to the back. I wanted to go through that painting again and restart the damn day. Once it had been a slow-moving scene of a beautiful woman running through a field. Summer. Now she was in her rightful place and the painting was empty.

"Now, Z."

Dev moved at Daniel's barked order. He placed himself in front of me, and I could practically feel the frustration rolling off him. "I can't use my magic. Something's blocking me."

Dev crowded me, sending me further back, and I caught sight of another stack of wanted posters.

Wanted for Espionage and Sheltering Enemies of the King
The Vampire Known as Sasha
Bounty paid only on a live recovery

Sasha. His real name was Oleg Federov. At least that had been his human name. He was the only new vampire to rise in the last few years, and Daniel had turned him on the night of his death in Munich. He'd stayed in Europe. At least he had been in Venice at Marcus's home when we disappeared.

Sasha had once been a spy, a member of Russian intelligence, and then he'd worked with a group of former military men for a long time.

Where would my children have fled in those early days? Would they have gone to Venice, hoping it was safe? Was that where they'd found the Russian warrior? I glanced around and discovered whoever ran this office loved to make wanted posters. "Sasha has a poster, too. And Albert and Hugo and Henri."

"What about Eddie? And Gray?" Kelsey asked, and I could hear the worry in her tone.

Because at least if there was a poster, it meant they were probably still alive. "I don't see one for them."

Daniel held up a hand, a sure sign that he wanted me to be quiet. I took a long breath, trying to picture where we were in the building. If it hadn't changed, we wouldn't have a ton of choices for how we would escape. There was a stairwell and the elevators. Those were our options, and by options I really meant we would need to take the stairs. If they were guarded, there would be no way out of a fight.

Dev tensed in front of me, and I held my breath.

That was when I noticed Dean. He was standing to the side, his hands up and head down. There was a bluish tint to the air around his hands, a sign of the power he was funneling through them. After a moment, his head came up.

"There was a male coming down the hallway. He's coming this way. I can easily get in his brain. He's remembered something he forgot," Dean explained. "Or rather, he thinks he did. He's going back to his apartment." He stared down at his hands. "I'm more powerful here."

"And I have no power at all," Dev complained. "Something is blocking me. I can feel the plants beneath the ground, but I can't call them."

Dean looked around, moving like he could see something the rest of us couldn't. "The whole place is warded against certain magic. Fae is one of them, and very likely it is warded against you in particular, Your Grace. There's also some dampening magic. It's against death magic." Dean frowned. "I would bet it dampens the power of vampires."

Kelsey moved beside her new ward. "How can you tell? I don't see any wards."

Dean placed a hand on the wall. "It's not a simple ward. It's the building. It's in the paint, I think. It feels like it's everywhere."

"You can use your magic," Daniel pointed out.

Dean shrugged. "My magic is based on witchcraft. I don't feel anything that would dampen spellcraft from a witch. If anything, I would bet there's something in the building that magnifies our power."

"Myrddin had a dark temple built," Daniel explained. "It's a direct portal to the Hell plane, and it does magnify the darker magic. It feeds that side of his nature and anyone practicing black magics. Dean, I'm going to need you to be ready to do whatever it takes to get us out of here."

That temple had been built shortly before we'd disappeared through the painting. I had known nothing about a portal to Hell being built in my home until it was already completed. It only struck me now how much Myrddin had prepared for his moment. He'd done it behind my back and with my husbands' help, since Daniel had known exactly what was going on. I would assume Dev had as well. He'd likely helped pick out what curtains went best with the Hellscape and never once mentioned it to me.

I couldn't even yell at them because now I knew it was the thrall stones that had influenced them. I was sure that under the influence of those stones, Myrddin had convinced them a dark temple would be a lovely surprise for me.

I grabbed the painting. Well, the canvas. It wasn't a painting now, but I couldn't leave it behind. It had been a portal once, and perhaps it could be again. Perhaps it could take us where we needed to go because I didn't intend to lose twelve years with my children.

"Zoey, you can't take that." Kelsey was frowning my way. "It's too big. We're going to have to try to make our way up to the street level and then over to the eastern wall of the building. There's a window we can use. That canvas is too wide to fit. I'm honestly afraid the king is too wide."

Daniel's brow arched. "You want us to try to make it out of the laundry room? Is that how you got out of the building that first time?"

When Kelsey had first come to live in the Council building, she'd gotten good at evading any attempt at Daniel monitoring her. I'd long thought she'd had help in the form of the only other person who was as good as Kelsey at dodging security.

Lee. My son had a deep connection to Kelsey, and they'd both felt it even before they'd known Lee's soul was recycled. Lee Owens had been Kelsey's father. His soul—despite the fact that it was now housed in my son's body—still reached out for his daughter.

"Yes," Kelsey replied. "There's a window we should be able to get through. It leads us to the street outside, and from there we run until we get to a safe place. I'll find a phone and call Trent."

"Kelsey, it's been twelve years," Dev pointed out.

Kelsey shook her head. "He won't have given up his phone. He might not keep it on him, but it will be someplace where he can access it. He'll have a way for me to reach him. He'll have a plan. We just have to get out of this building for it to work."

Because her wolf was faithful. "I do believe that Trent would have a plan in place. If he thought there was a chance for us to come back, he'll have prepared a way. And we have to know that Myrddin will likely have a way to block him as long as we're in this building. He'll have it on lockdown."

"He might even have a way to know we're in the building." Dev looked around as though still praying for a weapon.

Daniel nodded. "Which is precisely why we should get out of here as soon as possible. If Myrddin's had years in this building, he'll have all sorts of alarms and security. Zoey, that canvas won't fit through the window Kelsey's talking about."

I held on to it like it was a lifeline. "Then I'll find another way out."

Dean stepped in front of me. "Your Highness, there is no magic left in this object. It's served its purpose and it's dead now. There is no reason to bring it with us."

I couldn't believe that. The idea made my gut churn and my heart threaten to seize. "It has to work. There has to be some way. It brought us here. It has to be able to take us back."

"No." Dean's tone was not without sympathy. "It was a tool that's burned out. I've studied magic for years. There is no more magic left here. We can leave it behind and try to find another way. I'll look for you, Your Highness, but for now, we must run. I sense a dark presence coming toward us. I sense anger and hate and so much rage."

That got Daniel's attention. He pulled the canvas from my hands and picked me up before I could protest. "Kelsey, take the lead. Dean, can you persuade whatever is coming to go another way?"

"No. I won't be able to influence this one." Dean had gone even whiter than normal. The kid was fair skinned but usually had an odd luminous quality to him. Now he turned the slightest bit sallow.

"Are you all right?" I didn't fight Danny. He could overpower me, and honestly, in that moment I was so overwhelmed I wasn't sure I could move on my own anyway. All I could think about was getting through that painting, making it come back to life so it could return me to mine. But something about the way Dean had paled broke through that need.

Kelsey eased through the doorway.

Dean seemed to try to shake something off. "Her presence is quite overwhelming. It's unlike anything I've felt before. I don't even need to get into her head to read her intent."

"Her?" Daniel asked as he approached the door.

"The hallway's clear," Kelsey said quietly.

Dev took our back, with Dean behind him. "Turn to the left and we can skirt around the edge of Ether to get to the stairwell."

"Yes, I sense a female witch." Dean's eyes had gone a bit glassy, though he continued to move with us. "She's filled with dark energy. She's given up much to gain her power, and she won't let anyone take it back. She's been powerless before, and now she's a queen. She's projecting quite loudly. I think she wants me to know she's here."

"She senses you?" Kelsey picked up the pace, starting to jog down the long hallway.

It had to be Nimue. She was certainly a queen, and I knew there had been times when she'd felt powerless. I was almost certain she also had a thrall stone in her head. It was the only thing that could explain the change in my once dear friend.

"She senses all of us," Dean replied. "She's stalking us. We're her prey, and when she brings us all to her master, she will be able to take her proper place at his side. She knows I can sense her. She likes my fear. It makes her feel powerful. Wait. There was a moment. She felt one of you and she had a moment of weakness."

"Nimue and I were close once," I explained. Maybe I could get to her. The thrall stone should only influence her. It shouldn't cause her to throw out all of her morality.

"She cares about one of you. She never thought she would see you again. God, she doesn't want you to see her like this." Dean put a hand on his heart, like it ached and he could ease it. "But she is resolved. She chose this path and she will see it through no matter what. She belongs to the darkness now."

Kelsey had turned down the second hallway, the one that would lead to the stairwell we needed, and she stopped.

"Olivia?"

Standing there, blocking our path, was Kelsey's best friend, Olivia Carey. Liv. Once she'd been one of the kindest souls I'd known. She'd been a witch who used earth magic to help her friends.

The woman who stood in front of us only vaguely resembled the woman we'd known. Now she was all witch, and she was going to kill us.

"Welcome home, Your Highnesses," she said, the air crackling around her with power.

It was not the homecoming I'd been expecting.

Chapter Two

"Olivia, what the hell is going on? First off, what did you do to your hair?" Kelsey asked.

There were several physical changes to the woman we'd known, the one who used to teach English in the school our kids had attended. Her hair reached her waist, and it was a pitch black that didn't look natural with her skin. She'd had a warm brown color before. There was something lovely and cold to her appearance now.

"Really? Twelve years and that's what you say to me?" Liv rolled her brown eyes and for a second her lips started to tug up in a familiar grin.

"Dude, it's been like four days tops for me. What's going on with you, bestie? And when did you start to love the leather?" Kelsey took a step toward Liv. "It doesn't matter. Can you help us get out of here?"

"Kelsey, stop," Daniel ordered.

Kelsey turned slightly. "It's Liv. She might look weird, but she's still my best friend. What are you doing here? Are you spying for Trent?"

Daniel set me on my feet but kept a firm hold of my hand as though he expected me to take off on my own. I wasn't planning on doing anything of the kind. I shoved my heartache to the side because we were in full-on survival mode now. Kelsey was wrong. I believed Dean. Something had happened to Liv in the years we'd been gone. I'd seen the beginnings of this change when she'd used Arwyna to prove her powers to Nimue and Myrddin.

I looked around, trying to figure out where the pixie queen had gone. I didn't like the thought of her flying around a place that had been warded against Fae magic. Anything could happen to her.

"Of course," Liv replied. "Trent knew you would return this very day. He sent me here to save you. The canvas that held the portal went blank years ago. The wizard thought he was safe. But Trent knew you would return. He sent me here after the wizard declared himself king."

"She's lying," Dean whispered.

"And who might you be?" Liv's eyes lasered in on Dean. "You're new. And quite powerful." She frowned. "Your magic…it's familiar to me. Like a wine I tasted once and never again, but it lingered on the tongue."

Kelsey stepped back, her eyes going wide. "Okay, who are you and what have you done with Liv? Because you were not this douchey before."

"Where did you find him?" Liv asked, ignoring Kelsey, but then she shook her head. "It doesn't matter. We should go. I'll take you out a back way and then we'll call Trent."

"You're lying." Dean sounded stronger now. "You're going to try to trick us into a cage. You want to present us all to your master who will execute us. Can you do it? Can you watch him kill her? There's still a spark of love in your heart, and it has to do with her. And one other. Casey. You still feel for Kelsey and Casey."

Daniel squeezed my hand and I turned, seeing what he'd been wanting me to see. There was a group coming up behind us, blocking our path. Three men and a woman. The men all dropped to their knees and in seconds there were two wolves and a panther growling our way. I didn't recognize any of the men, but the woman had been a witch in the Dallas coven.

"I feel nothing," Liv snarled back. "I made my choice a long time ago, little boy, and nothing will take me off my path. Now that my friends are here, perhaps we should go upstairs and have a chat.

Daniel Donovan, you are named outlaw by the true king of the supernatural world, King Myrddin. You and your consorts have been sentenced to death. Kelsey, your status has not yet been determined. There's still time for you to accept your place in our court. As the king is not in residence, you will all be taken into custody to await his pleasure."

"Liv, this is not you," Kelsey said, but I noticed her arm had changed. Kelsey is a specialized supernatural creature known as a Hunter. When she's in a fight she can change her dominant arm. Normally she would get a wolf claw, but circumstances had led her to developing something much stronger. Kelsey gets a handy, hard to hurt demon limb when she needs it. She's got the strength and speed of a werewolf, but with none of the wolf's normal weaknesses.

As Daniel proved.

He held out a hand, and I felt the power come off of him in a gentle, cool wave.

The wolves stopped snarling and sat back on their haunches, tilting their heads in that doggy way that always made them look all cute and curious.

"Let us go or I'll have them attack." Daniel's eyes had lost their whites and were pure blue orbs now.

"I thought King Myrddin spelled the compound to dampen vampire strength," the other witch said as she moved away from the wolves.

"There is only one king, and even if you take a portion of his strength, he'll still win the day." Dev was a good cheerleader. "Now, Olivia, if you allow us to leave, there might be a pardon for you at the end of this. Daniel will take back his throne. Make no mistake about it."

"You're really working with Myrddin?" Kelsey stood between us and Liv.

We still had to get through Liv, her witch friend, and the panther, who wouldn't be affected by Daniel's ability to call wolves to his side. Then there was the fact that we were in a building that could house five hundred or so people, and I would bet they hadn't kept our allies in their homes. Everyone in this building would have sworn an oath to Myrddin, and that meant we had to view anyone who lived here as the enemy.

"I'm a witch. Of course I follow the legendary Myrddin," Liv replied. "For too long the vampires have ruled our world. Myrddin helped me reach my full potential. He helped me when all any of you would do was tell me to be patient. You have no idea what it means to be vulnerable."

"Are you kidding me? Did he teach you to rewrite history, too?" Kelsey asked.

"I'll explain it all to you later." Liv held up a hand. "*Rigescunt indutae*."

Every bone in my body locked into place. I couldn't move, could barely breathe. Daniel seemed to be in the same position.

"*Eximo*." Dean did not have the same trouble. He spoke a single word and I could move again.

Liv's eyes widened. "Who the hell are you?"

"I'm the spellcaster who's been up against way better witches than you," Dean replied. "Meaner, too. You have nothing on the witches of Arete, but I did learn a few of their tricks."

"Here's one of mine." Liv thrust out a hand and suddenly Dev began to choke. "Let the wolves go and I'll think about allowing the prince some oxygen. Deanna, if you don't mind helping."

That was the moment I felt all the oxygen leave my body. Sometimes it sucks to be the king's wife because what I really am is the king's weakness. Dev has some superpowers of his own, but as a companion, my only true superpower is my power to attract vampires. It's a shitty power, if you ask me, and it did nothing to protect me from Liv's magic. I could feel that magic like a tight fist around my throat.

I looked to Dev, reaching for his hand. He was calm, patiently waiting for Daniel to do whatever it was he was going to do. He squeezed my hand, as though he could lend me strength.

I needed breath. Breath for me. Breath for the baby growing inside me.

Dev's eyes changed, and I knew I was in the presence of Bris, the god who shared my Fae husband's body. Bris was an Irish deity who'd brought his unique magic to our lives years ago. He amplified Dev's fertility magic, and I felt him try to send me a pulse of it.

It wouldn't come. The wards worked on gods, too, it seemed.

I felt something shimmer around me and I could breathe again.

Dean stood in the middle of our group, his hands held out as he shielded us.

"Aren't you the smart one? I can try harder. Let's see how long you can keep it up on two fronts," Liv challenged.

Dean braced as though he'd been hit hard.

"Protect Zoey," Dev managed to say. "I can hold my breath for a long time."

Before I could shake my head, Daniel was holding his hands up in the universally acknowledged sign of *I give up*. "Stop, Olivia. I'll go with you. We'll all go with you."

Dean sagged as the magic was turned off and we were left with three growling werecreatures.

"I'll get us out of this," Daniel promised.

There was a low growl, a deep, full-throated sound that hadn't come from the wolves coming toward us. It had come from the hallway we'd turned down to get here, the one that formed the long end of the T-intersection. I couldn't see what was coming our way, but I could hear it. A wolf of some kind, and it had the other wolves whimpering.

"What the fuck is that?" Kelsey moved toward Dean as though she was ready to protect the young man who seemed to have used a lot of energy in the last few moments. Dean's hands trembled.

I turned and watched as an arrow slammed into the panther from the side, and the witch screamed as another pierced her chest.

Arwyna flew in, her ruby wings pumping hard as she made a beeline for us. She landed on Dev's hair and seemed to hold on as though she knew this was about to be a fight.

Then the largest wolf I'd ever seen prowled into sight. Dark fur and with eyes that glowed with power, there was no question who the alpha was. He attacked the panther, easily biting into the big cat's neck and breaking it with a crunch.

The other wolves took off running, the witch right behind them. When I looked back, Liv was gone as well.

"Fen?" Kelsey had tears in her eyes.

"Hey," Daniel began, "we don't know who that is. Stay back."

Arwyna was shaking her body, her wings fluttering as if to express her disagreement with the king.

That mega wolf's tail had started to wag like a puppy's, and despite the fact that he was covered in blood, he ran straight up to Kelsey and rubbed his face against her leg.

Kelsey dropped to her knees and wrapped her arms around the wolf. "My Fen."

I stared as a young woman in all black stalked into the hall, an arrow notched in her bow. Her auburn hair was back in a braid, and she looked so much like Summer my heart hurt. "Evangeline?"

"Evan," Daniel whispered her name.

She turned and stopped, a shocked smile lighting her face. "I can't believe he was right. You're here. You're really here."

"I told you, sister. I told you this was the correct time and place. Trent and Sasha were being too conservative." Rhys looked like his father. He was dressed in tactical gear and had a familiar gun in his hand. It was my old Ruger, the one Daniel had modified to hold specialized rounds. And he looked like he knew how to use it. "Mother, Dad, Papa, we need to go. Lee is waiting for us in Ether. Liv and her lackeys might have run, but it won't take them long to regroup. The pixie queen found us. It's how we knew for sure you were here."

"Rhys," Daniel began.

He shook his head. "No, Dad. You can take charge when we get back to base, but for now this is my mission and I'm calling a retreat. I'm going to get my ass kicked by Sasha and Trent as it is. Fen, do not even think about changing. I know you want to show off how grownass you are, but you'll have to do it back at base. Kill anyone who tries to stop us."

Rhys turned and started back down the hallway.

"Rhys, there's no way out if we go that way," Dev complained, holding his ground.

Fen growled, an obvious warning that he could herd us if he wanted to.

"I think we should follow the kids," Kelsey offered.

"Papa, we know what we're doing," Evan said encouragingly. "Please follow Rhys. Lee and Eddie are waiting, and the sooner we get out of here, the faster we can explain."

"I need to get the painting." I clung to hope that I could find a way out of this nightmare I found myself in. My children weren't children. They were fighters, warriors, when I'd promised them an easier life, one where I protected them.

The walls started to rattle, the ground beneath us trembling.

"She's coming back," Dean warned. "And she's not alone. I won't be able to stop them all. There are so many witches here, and I don't think they're all from this plane. And I sense others. Demons, Your Highness. There are demons here."

It was everything I'd feared about that fucking dark temple. It would allow demons easy access to the Council building, but then it wasn't the Council building anymore.

Evan moved behind me, Fen coming to her side. "Momma, there's no reason to get the painting. It's dead. Do you think we haven't spent a decade trying to figure it out? Again, I'll explain it when we're safely back at base. Hurry."

Kelsey nodded. "Move it or I'll pick you all up and carry your asses. I want to see Trent. He'll fill us in on everything."

Daniel turned and jogged to keep up with Rhys, Devinshea moving in behind me.

"Evan, stay close to me," Dev said, reaching out to take his daughter's arm.

Fenrir growled, his hackles coming up.

"Stop it, you jealous wolf. He's my father," Evan said, rolling her eyes. "He's not trying to take me. Sorry, Papa. You have to forgive his bad manners. Fen has trouble with his animal instincts when he's in wolf form. And he has a lot of animal instincts. You better be nice to my papa or I won't give you any treats."

"She won't give you any treats at all," Dev swore under his breath. "She's a child."

"Fenrir is, too," Kelsey shot back.

Fen made a grumbly sound like he wanted to argue all those points.

I was numb again, jogging through the halls I'd once known so well, following the children I'd born and now barely recognized. It was a dream. It had to be. There was no way that Olivia Carey had used her powers to try to choke the life out of me, no way my home had been taken over by my worst enemy. No fucking way I'd missed my children's formative years. They weren't warriors. They were coddled and protected.

Rhys was an eleven-year-old with a cocky grin who wouldn't

ever think to order his parents around. Rhys was a good boy who followed the rules. He was every teacher's pet.

Evan played with dolls, not bows and arrows.

I was going to wake up. I had to. I would wake up and be safely in our bed at Summer's palace. I would be in between Dev and Daniel, and I would tell them all about this awful dream and they would laugh at me. I would go through the portal again, but this time we would find ourselves back in Danny's office and everyone would be so relieved to see us. We would take down Myrddin and move on with our lives.

I didn't have to believe that prophecy. I could control this.

If I could only wake up.

"Evan, to your left," Rhys yelled as he moved by a connecting hallway. He didn't even look back. He simply tossed the words over his shoulder as he jogged along.

Evan zipped past her fathers and was firing down the hall before either could protest. She had two arrows off and landing in her targets as Fen leapt to her side. He growled and the third shadowy figure who'd been coming down the hall took off running. But not before Evan got off another shot, and I watched the last attacker go down even as Kelsey hustled me along.

"I think the kiddos know what they're doing," Kelsey assured me. "Let's follow their lead. This is their world. They know it far better than we do."

It was their world. Not mine. It couldn't be mine.

We ran, the ground still rumbling under us, and suddenly we found ourselves moving through familiar doors into a dark place. Ether. But not Ether.

"What the fuck did he do to my club?" Dev stopped and stared at the changes the years had wrought.

Ether had been a high-tech nightclub where all of the supernatural world came to play. It had a light-up dance floor and a sleek bar. It had been modern and energetic.

Someone had decided to give the whole place a Hell makeover. It had been redone in shades of red and black.

"I win!" A muscular man walked from behind what used to be the bar. It had been exchanged for what appeared to be some kind of shrine. I didn't have a chance to really look at it because Lee was right there. He held every bit of my attention.

He was so changed, but when he high-fived his brother and then grinned my way, I could see my little boy.

"I bet Rhys that Papa would be way more upset about Ether than he was about how old we are," Lee admitted.

"I assure you, Rhys wins that bet," Devinshea promised. "I'm upset about many things. The atrocity they've done to my beautiful club is merely one of them. I don't want to see the penthouse, do I?"

"According to our spies, you do not," Rhys replied. "Get in a circle. Olivia's going to try to overpower the bomb we deployed, and if I'm right about it, we've got maybe three minutes before our window closes."

"Bomb?" Daniel asked.

"Think of it like an electromagnetic pulse for some very specific wards, Your Highness." Eddie stood in front of one of the walls that was now draped in black and red velvet. They'd covered the ultramodern dance floor with heavy hardwoods. "My mistress, it has been such a long time."

Eddie was Kelsey's butler, a small, red-skinned demon with the cherubic face that marked his particular class of demons. He was a satan. Normally they were the Hell plane's lawyers, the keepers and arbitrators of contracts, but Eddie had chosen a different path.

"You, too, Eddie." Kelsey was wiping away tears, her hand on Fenrir's back, smoothing his fur down.

Lee started to come my way, but Rhys put a hand on his twin's chest. God, they weren't even close to identical anymore. Rhys's face was still perfect, and Lee had so many scars.

"No, brother. We have to go. Now," Rhys said.

Lee gestured my way. "Come on, man. It's Mom. We've waited forever."

"And we can wait a bit longer. There was something we didn't account for. We've got extra passengers." Rhys nodded our way. "I don't know who the male is, but he's not the only one. I just sensed the others. Pregnant women. We need to move."

I put a hand to my stomach. Rhys had come fully into his power while I'd been gone. He was a Green Man now if he could tell Kelsey and I were both carrying children. He hadn't even come close to us.

Lee's eyes went wide and his mouth dropped open as he turned to the wolf. "Fen, you fucker. You said you would wait until she was eighteen. We had a deal."

Fen was suddenly a broad-shouldered young man with dark hair that hit well below his shoulders and a body that…well, it had changed since he'd been a baby boy running around the Council house without any pants. He needed pants now. Extra-large pants. "We cuddle. That is all."

"I'm talking about Mom," Rhys corrected. "Mom and Kelsey."

Lee made a vomiting sound. "But she's old. Sorry, Mom. I thought maybe you and Papa would get over that. And Kelsey? Trent is going to be heartbroken. He's been faithful all these years, and he's had some good shots. There was a really hot mermaid on this one plane we went to, and she was all over him."

"Lee, I didn't cheat. I've been gone for four days," Kelsey complained. "And I want to know where that mermaid is. I know I'm not supposed to have sushi in my condition, but I'll make an exception."

"I want to know what the hell you're doing with my daughter that my son would think she could be pregnant." Devinshea didn't care that Fen had a large man part out in the open.

"Dev, maybe we should have this family session somewhere else." Daniel was trying to be the reasonable one.

Fen's eyes narrowed, his body going predatory. "What have I been doing with your daughter? I've been protecting her. I've been bleeding for her, watching over her. Never abandoning her. And she's my mate. Get used to it, Your Grace. And if that vampire is still planning on coming for her, you should know I'll pull his heart from his chest."

Evan moved like she intended to get in between her father and the wicked, dangerous wolf who seemed to have laid claim to her.

"We will get used to nothing if we're dead." Rhys took over, cutting off that fight. "Eddie, can you handle us all?"

"We need to leave." Dean had gone tense again. "She's almost here, and she's brought reinforcements."

"I shall do whatever it takes to protect my king and queen and my mistress," Eddie said with a light of determination in his eyes.

The doors flew open and Liv floated in, her feet not touching the floor. "You're not going anywhere. I should have known you would bring the traitor. Little demon, step away from them and the king might be satisfied with merely killing you."

"Come around me. Put a hand on me," Eddie bade.

The room was starting to fill up, and yes, there were a whole lot of demons.

Fen had changed again, and he stood before the whole group. It was obvious to me that they had worked together before. They were a team, and Fen was the front line.

"Mom, I need you to touch Eddie." Lee's voice was steady even as we were being surrounded.

"I'll get that ward back up," Liv promised. "He won't be able to teleport you out of here. Not all of you. Who are you going to leave behind, Danny? I'll take the newbie. I'd like to see what makes him tick."

"I'll stay behind," Daniel said. "Son, get your mother and Kelsey out of here."

"And I win the martyr bet." Rhys shook his head. "Eddie, do what you need to do. Fen, we're going now."

I felt a bubble go around us, and it was like the world's volume had been turned down. I saw Liv shout something and then the whole crowd rushed our way.

But it was too late, and for the second time that day, I found myself in another place entirely.

Chapter Three

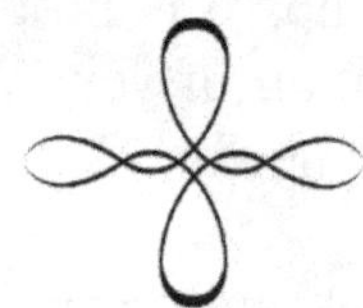

I stood in the middle of mountains, though they didn't look like the ones I'd been to in the Rockies. These were gentler, more rounded, as though age had softened them. We were by a stream, flat emerald green land spreading as far as my eye could see.

It looked a bit like the northernmost parts of Faery.

We seemed to be at the base of a mountain, and I could smell the salt of the sea, hear the crashing of waves, though they seemed to come from below us.

I should have worn a coat because it was cold and there was a soft twilight, though I'd thought it was still day. When we'd come through the painting, I'd glanced at the clock in the office and it had read a bit after one p.m.

"Is everyone here?" Eddie had fallen to the soft earth. He looked up at us with weary eyes.

Rhys bent down and picked up the small demon, cradling him in strong arms. "We're all here."

"Even…" Eddie began

Rhys nodded. "Even the unborn. They're fine. As always, you have served us with strength and honor, my friend."

Devinshea moved in behind me, his hand covering my belly as

though he wanted to ensure Rhys was right. I felt him sigh in relief. Arwyna had made it, too. She clung to Dev's hair.

"You did great." Lee gave Eddie a thumbs-up. "You should take a nap and when you wake up, I'll have a hunk of meat for you."

"But I must get our domicile ready for my mistress," Eddie argued.

Kelsey was right there, taking his clawed hand in hers. "All I need is to be here with you and Trent and Fen and Gray."

Eddie looked away. "I am afraid Master Gray is not in residence at this time, but we expect him soon."

Oh, something was wrong there. I feared Kelsey was handling the entire situation far better than I was, but now I worried things were about to go wrong for her. Twelve years. So much could happen in twelve years. Where was everyone? This valley we were in looked empty. Would we jump again? Was that where I would find Neil and Sarah and my dad?

How old was my dad now?

Twelve years. Those two words sent panic through me.

"And Trent's not here either," Evan said.

"Dad's on assignment back in the States." Fen was stepping into jeans that looked to have come out of the backpack Evan had been carrying. She pulled a sweater out and handed it to him. "When Eddie's had a chance to rest, I'll take you to him, Mom. I can't tell you how happy he's going to be to see you. And he's going to be relieved the ritual worked. Dad told me about it. He wasn't sure, but I knew he had hope. The baby is Gray's right?"

Kelsey nodded, worry plain on her face. "Yes. That was the plan. Gray and I would have a child, and then Trent and I. Where is Gray?"

Fen pulled the sweater on and ran a hand over his mass of dark hair, pulling it back and tying it at the base of his neck. "I think Dad should explain that to you. Gray's alive. He's not a prisoner or anything. Having you back might help."

"Why do you call Trent Dad but Gray is Gray?" Kelsey got to the heart of the matter.

Evan put his boots on the grass, a move it looked like she'd done a thousand times since Fen didn't even have to look down to shove his feet inside.

"Again, I would rather talk about it with Dad around. Mom,

we've waited twelve years. You can be patient about this," Fen said in a calm voice. "I don't know everything. Dad should be the one to talk to you, and he's in Atlanta right now."

"I'll have you there in no time at all," Eddie promised though his voice shook.

"In the morning," Rhys corrected.

"But, I can…"

"The morning is fine," Kelsey interrupted. Her voice was calm, though I could see her clear frustration in the way her jaw was tight. "You need your rest. You're not used to transporting so many. You did great, Eddie. But where are we?"

Dev had moved away, his hands on his hips as he took in the landscape around us. "I suspect we're in Huldrefólk country."

Lee moved in, a huge smile on his face as he held his arms open. "Hey, Mom. Long time, no see."

I was still numb as he enveloped me. I'd promised him I would see him in the morning. I told him not to worry and called him my darling, and then he'd been left on his own. He'd been left to fight and suffer and bleed. He'd lost his eye. I hadn't been here to protect him.

I had to fix it.

He seemed to realize I wasn't responding and stepped back.

Daniel moved in and pulled Lee into a bear hug. "It's good to see you, son. I want all the stories, but first we should get your mother somewhere warm. Where are we?"

The smile was back on Lee's face. "Papa's right. We're in Iceland, at the northernmost tip. We should get inside. It's much warmer in the mountain."

Dev had Evan wrapped in a hug, Fen watching carefully.

I had to get it together. I wasn't going to allow this timeline to stand, but that didn't mean my children didn't deserve their mother's love. I reached out to Rhys, who still carried Eddie. "Hey, baby."

He went still and took a long breath, as though fortifying himself. "Hey, Momma."

He was trying to be strong. Lee's scars were on the outside, but it was obvious to me that Rhys had been through a lot, too. Rhys was fully Fae. Any wounds he'd taken would heal, but that didn't mean he wouldn't feel them all in his soul.

"I'm sorry," I whispered.

He looked into my eyes and nodded slightly. "We should get inside." He seemed to shake off his emotion and he lowered Eddie to the ground. The small demon appeared to be recuperating quickly. "But first, who is this? Why is he traveling with you?"

Dean. He was talking about Dean. And Rhys didn't seem to feel the cold the way I was. Dean's shoulders straightened as he realized all eyes were on him.

"My name is Dean Malone. I'm here to kill the wizard Myrddin."

Lee's laughter seemed to bounce off the mountains.

Evan slapped her brother's arm. "Lee, manners."

"He has none, sister." Rhys's lips had quirked up, the first sign he was anything but serious. "And you have to admit it's pretty funny. Thank the goddess. Dean Malone is here. We are saved. Who the fuck is Dean Malone?"

Fen moved around Dean as a light snow began to fall. "He smells like a witch."

That pronouncement had Rhys and Lee both going predatory.

"You brought a witch?" Rhys asked. "You do understand we're at war with the witches. I know you haven't been back long, but I assumed Olivia Carey had brought the point home."

"Dean isn't from this plane," Kelsey explained.

I had to stop this argument. It seemed my boys had turned dangerous. "He's a friend."

My teeth were starting to chatter.

"He's the baby Myrddin sent off world." Kelsey didn't feel the cold the way I did. "Trent has to have explained this to you."

A brow cocked over Rhys's eyes, an expression so like his father's that it made my heart clench. "The one with the power to kill Myrddin?"

"It's more complicated than that," Kelsey replied. "But the important thing is Dean is trustworthy. If he's the reason you've brought us here instead of to your home base, then he and I will make our way to the nearest village. We'll find a way to Atlanta ourselves."

Eddie's black eyes looked endless as he stared up at Kelsey. "No, my mistress. You can't do that. It is too far."

There was nothing that Eddie feared more than one of his charges being uncomfortable. It kind of made me wish Albert was here since he likely would have made me a coat by now. He would have hunted down some furry creature and I would feel guilty but warm. I was okay with that in the moment.

Dean was pointing to the base of the mountain. "No, we're here, Kelsey. There's some kind of doorway, right there. It's good magic. Is it Fae?"

"It's supposed to be undetectable is what it is," Rhys complained. "I'm going to have a long talk with our guardians."

Dev had stopped staring down Fenrir and had me cuddled against him. Arwyna had burrowed under Dev's shirt. I wished I could do that, too.

"Is it warmer inside?" Dev asked. "Or do you plan to freeze your mother? We need to get in out of the elements. We have much to talk about."

And we had to plan how to get out of this timeline.

"Rhys's putting off the moment when he has to face the music." Evan shook her head and strode forward, waving her hand.

The air around us shimmered and the entrance to what appeared to be a cave was suddenly in front of us. I could see torches lighting the way inside.

Rhys frowned. "Or I'm making sure we don't invite the enemy into what's supposed to be a secret base of operations."

Evan tossed her braid over her shoulder. "Momma wouldn't bring the enemy with her, and you know all about the prophecy concerning Lee. If they've found the other half to that prophecy, then good for them. It means we have two chances instead of one. It might make the years we've lost worthwhile. You're afraid of what Sasha is going to do when he finds out where we've been, and he should be awake by now. Come along, brother. He'll be less likely to murder us when he realizes we were right."

"I doubt that." Rhys stepped up to the doorway. "He was clear about us not going today, but damn it, I was right. And hey, Dad's back. Dad, don't let Sasha kill me. Dad is Sasha's king no matter what Myrddin says. Goddess, it's good to be the son of a king again."

"A king without a crown," Lee said as he gestured for us to move through the doorway. "We're outlaws. It's a bit more fun, don't you think?" He stopped Dean before he could enter. "You should know that if you betray my family, I will kill you. I don't care what kind of magic you have. I have rage and hate, and they will win every time."

Dean stopped and stared at him. "You aren't full of hate, Lee Donovan-Quinn. You should be. You should be a ball of misery, but you still have light. You're everything I dreamed you would be. It is good to meet you."

Despite the fact that I could feel the warmth coming from inside, I stopped and watched because this felt…important.

Lee had lost that devil-may-care look on his face, and he stared down at the hand Dean was offering him.

"We truly believe he's the child Nemcox talked about. Did Trent ever tell you about the two people on the Earth plane who could kill Myrddin?" I didn't want Lee to turn down that hand. Since the moment I'd realized what Dean might be able to do, I'd wanted him to take Lee's place, to be the one with the burden. But it felt wrong. It felt like they should be in this together. Against all odds, against every machination of the world's wickedest wizard, they were here together. They were the same age, seeming opposites of each other. Lee's looks were dark like his father's, while Dean was white as the snow that fell around us.

They seemed like pieces of a puzzle finally falling into place.

Dev's hand slipped into mine, as though he felt the moment, too.

"He told us what Kelsey learned from the demon known as Nemcox." Evan was watching Dean now.

Lee finally reached out and took Dean's hand. "If you are who they think you are, then we can work together. But you need to understand that I will kill that wizard."

Dean's lips curled up as he took in my baby boy. Turned up in a way that made me wonder just what had been in those dreams he'd been having. "Then I shall help you, Prince Lee."

Lee shook his head and took his hand back. "Just Lee. I was never a prince. But I would be glad for someone with magic who doesn't attempt to kill me. Come inside and I'll buy you a beer. No one makes ale quite like trolls can."

The electricity between the two was palpable. They had chemistry, those two men.

Like Danny and Dev had from the moment they'd met.

It was odd because I'd always thought he would end up with Mia. As children, Lee and Sarah's daughter had clung to each other, been the best of friends. I'd worried because Lee was human and Mia both a witch and a companion. She'd gotten her magic from her mother and that glow that vampires loved from her fallen-angel father. "Where is Mia? Is she still with you?"

Lee's expression shuttered. "Mia died along with her parents. Myrddin killed them, and I shall have his head for it. Grandfather is dead as well, and at the wizard's hand. Though Grandad still manages to be a pain in my ass. Welcome home, Mother."

Chapter Four

"Lee!" Evan strode up to her brother in the torchlight. "How could you tell her that way?"

My world seemed to be reeling.

My father was gone?

Dev had moved me into his arms, giving me his strength.

"Yes, I would like to know the answer to that question as well, son," Daniel said, his voice cold as the snow outside.

Even in the gloom I could see my son had paled. "I'm sorry, Momma. I…I'm rattled and I didn't think I would be. You asked me about Mia. She's a sore subject for me. I'm sorry I said it that way."

"We don't know Mia's dead." Rhys looked like a ghost in the torchlight. The shadows played over his face. "We never found a body. Any of their bodies."

"They told us," Lee replied quietly.

"Olivia told us, and Liv lies now. If Myrddin killed them, he would have made sure we saw the bodies." Evan moved in front of me. "Momma, we don't know that Aunt Sarah and Uncle Felix didn't get out. And Granddad wants to see you. He's been waiting so long."

I breathed a deep sigh of relief. He wasn't dead. Lee must have been using a euphemism. Like my going missing killed my dad. "I need to see him."

I heard Dean saying something in Latin and then the torches flared, and I could suddenly make out where I was far better than I could before. It was warmer, too. Dean stood near where Kelsey held Eddie's small hand in her own. The butler looked up to Dean and nodded.

"Thank you," he said quietly. "The cold gets to me when I'm tired. It is warmer inside."

"I'll leave you to explain to our mother," Evan said to her brothers. "I'm going to take my punishment and get it out of the way."

"Like Sasha punishes her." Fen rolled his eyes as he started down the long tunnel after Evan. "She starts to cry and then he's the one apologizing. Meanwhile, when I screw up, I end up running laps and chopping wood for hours. It's better to be a girl." Fen turned, walking backward with no effort at all. He pointed to Dean. "If you're responsible for the light and warmth, thanks, man. You'll have to come by our place. No matter how well I get the fire going it's still chilly."

Dean nodded his way. "It's nothing more than a warming spell."

"It works and I'm grateful." Fen turned and jogged after Evan.

"Rhys, it looks like the whole village is waiting on us," Evan shouted from the end of the tunnel.

"Our place?" Dev asked. "Tell me he isn't living with Evan."

"We've all lived together for years," Rhys said. "And you should go easy on Fen. He protects Evan with his life. He would give it for her. I promise they're good together or I wouldn't have allowed the relationship at all."

Lee snorted. "Like you could have stopped it."

"If I thought the relationship wasn't good for her, I would have found a way. Like I did with you and the barmaid in Oslo." Rhys walked along and I found myself walking after him.

So no one was one hundred percent sure dead. It was good. I clung to that as we made our way toward the light at the end of the tunnel. I could see it now, light and green grass. Fen reached Evan, and his hand found hers as they walked into that light.

"I wasn't serious about her," Lee argued.

"You said you were going to marry her," Rhys shot back.

"Well, she served stout mead and had very large breasts. I was distracted by them," Lee replied. "I say crazy things when I'm drunk."

He shouldn't be drunk because he was eleven.

"Well, that answers one question. Lee turned into me," Dev said with a grin.

Daniel's eyes had that glow that let me know his vampire senses were open. "Oh, don't think he's not my son, too."

Daniel moved ahead of us, not bothering to explain what he meant.

"I want to see my dad." I felt Dev's hand squeeze mine. "Lee was joking, right?"

"I assume something's happened, but he also said your father was still a pain in his ass. So it sounds to me like Harry is fine." Dev stopped, allowing Kelsey and Dean to move ahead. "Are you all right, my goddess?"

I shook my head. "No. I'm horrified. We left them for twelve years."

"And now we're here," Dev replied. "I know it's a shock, but we have to remember that they're still our children. They still need us, and they've missed us. You hurt Lee when you wouldn't hug him."

"I hugged him." I had. Hadn't I?

Daniel had stopped up ahead, staring toward the entrance.

"He felt your lack of enthusiasm," Dev told me. "I know you want to get out of this timeline, but we're here now, and we must make the best of it. We're about to walk through that door and into whatever coalition our kids and Trent have built. For now this is our army. They cannot see the depressed and horrified mother. They have to see Daniel's queen. Do you understand me?"

It wasn't fair. "I don't get an hour to mourn?"

"I'll give you many hours to mourn, my goddess, but this will not be one of them. Our mourning must be done in private." Dev smoothed back my hair. "This is our return. This is history."

"It won't be when I find a way back," I vowed.

"Then it shouldn't be hard for you to put your chin up and be the queen we need you to be." Dev was excellent at turning a situation around. "Our children have worked hard. They've been at war for years, preparing for this time. We must give this moment every bit of attention it needs. Pomp and circumstance have their place."

As it had in the beginning. I did know this game. We'd been forced to play it before, and Devinshea had been the one to guide us through.

"Hey, are you two coming? Z, you need a moment?" Daniel had made his way back to us.

Dev looked to him. "I was explaining that we need to go into royal mode. I know that the two of you are processing…"

"Processing the fact that Myrddin stole twelve years of time with my children?" Daniel's tone had gone glacial. "That he stuck a stone in my head so he could control me? That he took my crown and our home? I do not need to process that, Devinshea. I understand there is some prophecy out there that claims Lee or Dean will kill the wizard, but I'll make that bastard wish for death. I will make him beg my son for the killing blow. Make no mistake of that. You're going to ask me to hold my head high and walk into whatever we're walking into like the King of All Vampire should. I am more. This is my plane. He might hold it for now, but his time is running out. I remember how to play this game. You taught me well. When I walk out there, they will see a king."

Dev was practically drooling. "Is it wrong to say I find you extremely sexy right now, my king?"

Daniel's hand went to the back of Dev's neck, tangling with the hair he found there. He tugged and got into Dev's space. "I will process this later in a very physical way."

"I look forward to it." Dev took a long breath, and the lust that had taken over was replaced with the smooth politician he became when we needed it.

I had to find my will because they were right. I couldn't walk out there like the shell-shocked mother I was. I couldn't cry and beg for someone to take me home no matter how much I wanted to.

"Put it aside, my queen," Dev whispered. "You don't have to think about it right now. This evening when we're alone, we'll talk about what there is to be done."

Daniel took my hand. "But for now I need you. The children need you." He brought it to his lips, kissing my skin. "I know you have a thousand questions, and we'll find the answers."

"Do I look all right?" It was ridiculous but Dev was correct. Appearances mattered. We would need allies, and that meant giving them confidence in the crown.

We were the crown.

"You look beautiful." Daniel leaned over and brushed his lips over mine. "You remember how to do this. We haven't been formal with the exception of ceremonial functions for years."

He stepped to the side and held out a hand. I placed mine in his. Dev moved to Daniel's left. I straightened my shoulders and we began to walk.

We emerged from the tunnel to find a whole vibrant village under the mountain. A village filled with Fae and supernaturals.

There were trolls and brownies and *sidhe*. I thought I recognized a few werecreatures from the Council. There was a crowd of them, and they seemed to hold their breath as we walked through the entrance to this magical realm. Faery lights gave the place a soft glow, and Arwyna took off from Dev's shoulder, joining the large kaleidoscope of pixies fluttering in excitement at the return of their queen.

There were hushed whispers, and then a great shout went through the crowd.

"Long live the king!"

"The king has returned!"

"Down with the wizard!"

I looked over and Evan was grinning, leaning against a tree, with Fen by her side. Rhys and Lee stayed close to them, Lee's eyes trailing over to where Dean stood with Kelsey. They both looked like they were happy to stay out of the spotlight.

A familiar face rushed through the crowd toward Kelsey.

"Casey's here," I whispered Daniel's way as I waved to the crowd. "I pray that means the academics made it out all right."

The academics were a specialized group of vampires. Marcus Vorenus had been the leader of the academics and Daniel's greatest supporter. We trusted the academics always, and any war would be hard for us to win without their support and wise counsel.

Sure enough, I caught sight of Hugo and Henri at the back of the crowd. Henri's companion was beside him. Kimberly Jacobs had a smile on her face as she joined the crowd in their cheers. Diana Spelling had an arm locked through Hugo's, and I was so glad they'd all managed to get out.

I let go of my fears for the moment because they needed hope, and we represented that to every being in the crowd. How much had they gone through? How hard had these years been on our friends?

Out of the corner of my eye I saw another familiar face, this one making my blood chill. The elegantly dressed vampire stood at the edge of the crowd, leaning negligently against a fence.

"What the fuck is Alexander doing here?" I breathed the question, not expecting an answer.

Alexander Sharpe was a vampire I always stayed away from. He'd been around for more than a hundred years. The Victorian-age vampire had played an interesting role in history, an infamous one. He'd been Jack the Ripper, and despite his knowledge in the medical area, I wished the Council had never welcomed him into the fold.

Of all the vampires I knew, Alexander is the one I would happily have left behind.

But he was here. Here with the resistance. Here with my children. I didn't like that idea at all.

"Rhys Donovan-Quinn!" A deep voice boomed over the crowd, and everyone stopped as though they did this man's will.

I looked back and Rhys had stepped up, his shoulders going straight and chin coming up as though standing at attention. They'd all done it. Lee and Evan and Fen formed a line next to Rhys. Good soldiers. That was what the last twelve years had turned my children into, soldiers, and the big vampire striding toward them was obviously their general.

Sasha.

He wore jeans and a dark sweater, combat boots on his feet. He looked to be in his mid-thirties, with dark hair and harsh features that somehow worked together to form a starkly attractive face. I'd spent a few weeks with Sasha the previous year… Well, in this timeline it had been thirteen years ago. We'd taken a couple of weeks to help Sasha through his transition. I liked the man, though he'd been quiet and contemplative when I'd known him. At that time, I'd wondered if he would ask to walk into the light. He'd learned his wife was dead and his daughter lost to him. He'd made some hard decisions, and one of them had been to live.

Now this man stood in front of my children, his hands on his hips and a frown on his face. "What did I tell you? Has your hearing gone, Rhys Donovan-Quinn?"

I started to walk toward them but Daniel stopped me. He had to stop Dev, too, because my faery prince clearly had the same reaction I did. Neither of us liked the idea of our kids being dressed down by someone who wasn't their mom or dads.

"Don't. He's been their leader for years," Danny whispered.

"No, sir." Rhys's expression had gone stony. "I heard you, sir."

"Then why did you defy me?" Sasha asked the question on a low growl, his Russian accent thick.

"Because you were wrong, sir," Rhys replied.

"We had four different dates, and we decided on one." Sasha loomed over Rhys despite the fact that they were roughly the same height. "We agreed that summer of next year was the most likely date for the return of the royals. We only had enough magic for one attempt at rescue."

"We don't need another," Rhys replied, his eyes coming up. "We don't need another because we saved them. I know you and the academics and Trent used logic, but sometimes we have to go on feeling, on instinct. I felt them coming. I felt it in my soul. You thought that feeling was hope, but I knew it was right. I accept any punishment you feel you must dole out, but my siblings and Fen are blameless. They were following orders."

Evan snorted. "As if I would follow your orders blindly. We all agreed."

Sasha shook his head. "Lee has never followed orders once in his life, and you could not make Fenrir do something he did not wish to do. Even for all the beef jerky in the world. Only Evan can control him."

"She makes really good jerky," Fen said with a grin.

All of the kids had relaxed, as though they knew they'd gotten through the worst of it.

"Yes, that's the reason," Sasha said with a shake of his head. He put a hand on Rhys's shoulder. "You followed your gut. You are a true leader, Rhys Donovan-Quinn. I wish you would have fought with me, made me understand, but I also know I am a stubborn ass much of the time. You brought your parents out and you lost no one. You are everything I trained you to be."

I watched Rhys's jaw tighten as he fought the emotion that had to well inside of him.

My baby was a man and a soldier, and he seemed to have a wonderful teacher.

Sasha turned and the whole village released a collective breath. "Your Highnesses, you have no idea how happy I am to have been wrong. Welcome to our village. We named it Frelsi, which is Icelandic for freedom. I'm more than pleased to turn it all over to you, as well as the primary care of these soldiers of mine. They are the best, the finest I have ever had the pleasure to train." He turned to the crowd and raised a hand. "The king is not dead. Long live our king!"

A cheer erupted, and the happy chaos began again.

Sasha strode up and held a hand out to Daniel. "My king, tonight we will feast and drink and celebrate. Tonight is for reunions. But in a few hours, we'll meet in the great house and I will answer all your questions. Our plight is grave, but the war will turn now. Thanks to your children."

Daniel dragged the vampire in for a manly hug. "I want to know everything, but I cannot thank you enough for taking care of our kids."

Sasha bowed his head formally. "It was my honor to do this for you, to have the chance to shelter the children as mine has been all these years."

Sasha's daughter had found a family to love and care for her, and he'd paid it back by loving mine. I could see it clearly in his expression and in the way my children looked to him. He might have been their general, but they adored him.

Sasha greeted us all with handshakes and hugs as the villagers started to set up tables and the ale began to flow.

"I must go and inform Trent of what has happened." Sasha turned to Kelsey. "Would you like to come with me? He's waited all these years to hear your voice again."

Tears in her eyes, Kelsey nodded and followed after him, Eddie walking with her and promising to make her as comfortable as possible.

Dev put an arm around me as Daniel moved through the crowd,

greeting all of them. "It's going to be all right, my goddess."

I didn't know about that. It wouldn't be all right until I held my children in my arms again and saved them from ever having to become soldiers at all. Still, I leaned against my husband and let his affection soothe me.

Lee approached with a young woman. She looked to be in her mid-twenties and had dark skin, her hair a curly crown that topped a lovely face with wide warm brown eyes.

Was I about to get another shock? Had Rhys saved Lee from the busty bartender because he had a girlfriend here in the village? I'd lost the chance to see love bloom between Fenrir and Evan.

"Momma, Papa, I want you to meet Shahidi. We call her Shy, though it's a misnomer. She's not really shy," Lee said with a grin.

"I am right now," the young woman corrected. She was dressed in jeans and an emerald green sweater, boots on her feet. "I'm going to be honest. I didn't think I was ever going to meet you. Do you prefer Your Highness or Your Grace? I've been told you go by both. Rhys teaches a class in royal etiquette. I am not his favorite student."

Lee snorted. "Yeah, he can't stand you."

"He complains often enough," Shy replied.

"It's not you he's complaining about." Lee turned back our way. "We met Shy when she showed up outside the mountain seven years ago. She camped out until we let her in."

"I don't like camping, but your grandfather wouldn't let me do anything else. Stubborn old man," Shy complained, but there was affection in her tone.

My dad? Relief poured through me. "Where is he? I would love to see him."

I missed my dad, and it had only been a few days since we'd talked. He'd been one of the last people I'd seen before we went missing.

"Maybe we should go sit down." Lee looked around. "This could be a bit of a shock."

Shy's eyes changed, going all black, and her whole body seemed to shift, shoulders softening, the expression on her face becoming something oddly familiar to me. "Hello, me darlin' girl. It's been so long, and I've missed you. Devinshea, you still need a haircut. You look like a girl."

Her accent had become a deep Irish.

"Harry?" Dev asked.

I barely heard the question because the day had been way too much for me, and my peripheral vision started to fade.

Dev caught me even as I heard Lee sigh.

"Told you we should have eased her into it, Grandad."

I let the darkness take me and prayed this was all just a dream.

Chapter Five

I came to on an unfamiliar bed, candles lighting the room. Someone had moved me here, covering me in a soft quilt. For a moment I tried to convince myself that it had all been a dream and I was back in Summer's palace.

But the smallness of the room, the scent of something cooking, all told me I was exactly where I thought I was.

"Hey, Mom. There's water next to you," a soft voice said. "Should I go get Papa? Dad is still out talking to the vampires we have here, but Papa is in the kitchen with the boys."

I sat up and Evan was in a chair by the bed, a fire glowing softly in the hearth. She looked like her sister. Not exactly, of course. She was shorter than Summer, her body more petite and lithe. She wore the same tactical clothing her brothers wore and I could tell she was fit and muscular.

From years of training when she should have been playing.

"I'm sorry Lee hit you with Shy that way," Evan began. "Lee doesn't get that you have to be eased into things. He kind of steamrolls his way through life. I should explain."

"My father is dead and he found a way to stick around." I forced myself to sit up. "Did Myrddin kill him?"

Evan nodded shortly. "Yes, though we didn't know exactly what had happened for years. He was there that day. He was there when Myrddin came for us."

"Tell me about it."

"You should rest. I'm sure Rhys will give you a full debrief."

"I want to hear it from you. I think Rhys has become a leader, and he'll leave emotion out of it. I want to know what it was like. How did my father die? How did you end up with Sasha? He was in Italy at the time. How long was it between when we disappeared and you were forced to flee?"

"It was the morning after you went missing. From what I understand Myrddin waited until the warrior vampires were sleeping before he made his big move. It was early enough that I hadn't woken up yet. Albert came in and woke me up and handed me a bag. He told me I had to put some clothes in it and I could take one stuffed animal. It's the only time I can ever remember seeing Albert flustered. Granddad was there, and he came in and helped me. He promised me it would all be okay, and he let me take two stuffed animals. He also slipped a picture in my bag. I didn't find it until later. It was a picture of our family. He had to fold it up, but I still have it."

My heart ached with every word she spoke. "Why didn't he go with you?"

"Because Myrddin showed up before we were ready," my daughter explained. "He rushed in and we were in our rooms. Granddad held him off. Held all of them off. He bought us time with his life. He'll have to tell you that part. He doesn't talk about it past that. Anyway, Eddie managed to get us out of the penthouse. He can only teleport to places he's been to before, so we ended up in Italy on the island of Poveglia. From there we made our way to Venice and Marcus Vorenus's townhouse there. Sasha was in residence, and he and Trent took control. For the first several years, we moved around a lot. Even from plane to plane when they found someone who could teach us."

They'd gone from pampered kids to fugitives overnight. "Teach you how to fight?"

"Yes, and some magic. I'm not that great with it, but Rhys has been able to funnel some of his Fae magic into powerful Earth magics," Evan explained. "Sasha was insistent that we all train to our capabilities. We found a ridiculously cold plane where Fenrir was taught by a werewolf mentor. There was some discussion about leaving him there while the rest of us learned our own skills, but we rebelled. The kids, that is. We wouldn't let ourselves be broken up, so we all learned new skills."

How hard had it been for them to stand up to their leaders and keep themselves together? Even I could see the benefits of breaking them up and placing them with mentors and guardians who matched their talents. Rhys needed to be around other Fae, and Fenrir was a wolf king. He would long for others of his kind, but it seemed he wanted his family more. "I'm glad you stayed together. Lee mentioned that you didn't meet Shy until a few years ago."

"Yes, after we settled in here in Frelsi." By the firelight my daughter's skin was warm toned, her eyes flashing with intelligence. "We came back to the Earth plane often, and this last time we met with Ingrid and Halle, and they'd found this place for us."

My godparents. Ingrid and Halle were trolls who'd lived under the bridges of Dallas for all of my life. I'd spent most of the summers of my youth with them. Daniel and I would get out of school and head for the bridges, searching until we found them and then walking with them all summer long. "They're okay?"

It was terrible, but I would have to make a list of everyone I knew to find out if they were alive or dead or had been taken to the other side.

"Yes," Evan replied. "They prefer the bridges to the mountains. There are lots of bridges around here. I can help you find them when you're ready. We've hidden here in Frelsi for years now. It's good to have a home. We still run raids and prepare for the time when Dad will lead us into war, but it's given us some normalcy."

I was smart enough to not say what I wanted to say—that her father wouldn't be leading her into anything like a battle because we would find a way to erase this timeline. I would give her normalcy again. I would give her the childhood she'd been denied.

I sat up and glanced around. There was a small window, and it looked like darkness had fallen. Though shouldn't it always be dark since we were under a mountain? "Are we in a *sithein*?"

A *sithein* was a piece of Faery, a bubble attached to the Earth plane with its own sun and moon and time. There were two attached to the Earth plane—the Seelie and the Unseelie. Devinshea was the High Priest of both. His children were the grandchildren of the Seelie Fae queen. It made sense that they might be granted a piece of Faery for their own.

"No," Evan replied. "It's a pocket world the Huldrefólk have used for centuries. We came here eight years ago."

"Why aren't you in Faery with your grandmother?" Devinshea's brother, Declan, should have come for his nephews and niece. Rhys was a powerful Green Man. The idea that Prince Declan wouldn't protect him was ludicrous. With Devinshea gone, Rhys would have been needed. Even as a child, his power would have helped the Fae. "Your uncle should have taken you straight to the *sithein*. Come to think of it, Albert should have taken you there himself. You shouldn't have been dragged across the planes."

Evan stood, her expression shuttering once more. "You'll do much better if you somehow manage to not sound outraged at every decision that was made, Mother. I understand from Papa that it has only been a few days for you, but we have dreamed of this reunion for years. I'm willing to make allowances for the shock you've had, but so far I have to think that the stories my brothers told me of you have been exaggerated."

It was hard to deal with the fact that not only was my baby girl not a baby, she was standing up to me, challenging me. "Stories?"

"Yes, they told me how much you loved me, and I'll be honest, I don't feel that at all. Papa shows up and all he cares about is my relationship with Fen. Dad…well, Dad has much he must do. I understand that, and at the very least he's pulled me aside, given me a hug, and asked if we can spend time together after he's done his duties. The only one of you I don't share biology with and he's the one who seems to care."

I was screwing this up. "Evangeline, of course I care. You're my daughter."

"But I'm not. While you've slept I've given this some consideration. You need time. I had this vision that you would walk in and we would be a family again, but it's going to take longer. I'm not the baby you left behind, and honestly you're not the parent I made up in my head. So perhaps we should begin as queen and…advisor." She moved for the door. "Are you hungry? There's stew and Albert's brown bread. I heard he was talking about making potatoes for you. He claims you eat a lot of potatoes when you're pregnant."

I felt oddly vulnerable against my daughter's steady confidence. She said I'd hurt her, but her expression was unfazed. When she'd been a child she'd cried readily. It hadn't been an annoying thing. It had been because she was open and unafraid to show her emotions. She'd obviously changed because the look on her face reminded me of Devinshea when he had to deal with a particularly tricky political situation. He dropped all emotion and navigated the person or situation as carefully as he could.

As carefully as Evan was navigating me now.

"Albert's here?"

Evan nodded. "Of course. He would never leave us."

I didn't want to do this. I wanted to lie back down and sleep and pretend this wasn't happening, but it was obvious I was already having a negative impact on my children. It wasn't fair. I was a ball of emotions, but I was their mother, and we have to shove down our own needs in times of crisis. Or times of their need. I forced myself to sit on the edge of the bed and hold a hand out to this beautiful creature I didn't know at all. She was my daughter. It was time to start getting to know her and giving her the same courtesies she was giving me. "I'm not hungry right now. I would rather talk to you. Please, Evan."

She hesitated for a moment and then moved back into the room. "All right. You should know that I'm going to Atlanta with Kelsey in the morning. Trent has to finish up his visit with the primals, and Kelsey doesn't want to wait for him to come home. Fen wants to go with her, so I'm joining them."

"You're leaving?" But I had just gotten here.

"It's best if I stay close to Fen. He can be reckless. We've been told he'll settle once we're properly mated, but until then, my presence can help to calm him. It helps so he doesn't wipe out whole packs when they come for him."

"What?"

Evan sighed. "Some of the packs don't like the thought of a wolf king being in existence. Fen can bend them to his will. He doesn't, but he can if he likes. So they try to assassinate him. It's been explained to us on many occasions that if Fen would take his place at the head of the great pack, he could quell these sorts of rebellions, but then he would have to leave us, and he won't do it."

My heart ached because I thought I understood what she was really saying. I had been around wolves long enough to know what is expected of the alpha. "They would want him to take a she-wolf mate."

"A *proper mate* is the term they use," she explained shortly. "According to the Alpha Council, I'm only good for vampires. I believe they called me a nice meal they couldn't enjoy properly. Well, one of them called me that. I had to stop Fenrir from killing him. Needless to say, we don't go to pack meetings anymore, and it's best I stay close to him. I have to ask. Is Marcus Vorenus dead? Is that why he's not back with you?"

Marcus. I hadn't even thought about the fact that everyone on the Earth plane believed Evan was Marcus's fated companion. Marcus had been promised that a daughter of my line would be the companion to match his soul. It could be hard to be "claimed" by a powerful supernatural. I knew all about that. In the beginning, though I loved Daniel, I'd worried what it meant to be his wife. Was Evan having the same questions about Fenrir? Did she think Marcus could come in and save her? I didn't understand the situation, so I had to ask. "Sweetie, are you okay with Fen? Has he hurt you?"

Our world had never known a wolf king. His powers could be unstable for all we knew. The only specialized wolf I'd ever known had been the original Lee, and he fought his nature. Kelsey was a kind of wolf, and she'd required a lot of training to tamp down her killer instincts.

"Fen? Hurt me?" Evan rolled her eyes. "Momma, Fen would throw himself in front of a bullet for me. He freaks out if I get a paper cut. And yet he also allows me to do some crazy shit. We had one discussion a long time ago about him smothering me and now we're fine. Our main issue is Fen promised my brothers he wouldn't sleep with me until we're married, and I find that highly annoying. Well, that and the fact that he worries Marcus Vorenus is going to show up and try to take me away from him. If Vorenus is here on the Earth plane, he needs to understand that I'm in love with Fen, and I don't care what some prophet said a million years ago."

"Marcus didn't come back with us." I stopped myself from trying to tell her that she was seventeen and how could she know if she was in love. The question was dumb given that I'd known I loved Daniel long before the age of seventeen. "He's married to your sister now, and he's staying in her kingdom."

Finally, my youngest showed some shock. "My sister? Momma, were you with Summer?"

"You know about Summer?" I knew Lee had some inkling that he had a sister, but Evan had been so young I'd never discussed Summer with her.

She nodded. "Granddad talked about her. After he managed to find his way here, he spent a lot of time keeping our memories of you alive, talking about you and Dad and Papa. I know way too much, probably more than I would have if you'd been here with us."

And now my brain hurt again because I remembered my father was dead and somehow he was still here in the form of a young woman.

There was a knock on the door and Evan went to answer it. I couldn't see from my vantage point, but Evan was whispering, and then she turned back.

"Momma, Shy is here, and she would like to explain if you're up to it," Evan said.

I nodded, ready to face the young woman. She walked in, carrying a tray of what looked to be tea and some of Albert's madeleines.

"Hello, Your Highness." She set the tray on the table near the hearth. "Albert asked if I would bring you afternoon tea. The Fae keep proper British hours, and it's tea time."

"Oh, like you don't love it," Evan teased.

"Well, it is nice to have a schedule. God, I sometimes wonder if that's me or Harry," Shy said with a frown as she settled in on one of the two chairs there. "You staying? I brought three cups."

"Does he want me here?" Evan asked. "It might be easier for him to talk to her on his own."

Shy chuckled. "That old man hasn't been on his own since the day he died. He's good. He's thinking it might be easier on her if you're here. She's going to be…difficult. She always struggled with change."

I frowned. "I do not."

Shy's lips turned up. "Maybe you should talk to him."

I had so many questions. "How did you…just how?"

"I'm a medium. It runs strong through my family line. That's probably why Myrddin had them all killed." Shy pronounced the words with no emotion. She merely gestured to Evan, who took her seat and the cup of tea Shy poured for her. "I didn't realize that the fire that killed my mother and grandmother all those years ago was set by Myrddin. It was shortly after he took the throne by force. I pieced it together over the years. Fifteen fires set in the States on the same night. All unexplained. All killing powerful psychics and mediums. I wasn't home that night. I was at a friends, and then I got lost in CPS. I think that's the only reason I'm still alive. Anyway, I was a kid at the time, and I ended up in a psych ward because I came into my powers and had no one to explain how to handle them. I talked to dead people. It scared the shit out of any foster parent I had, and they finally decided that the best way to go was to drug me until I didn't complain anymore."

"I'm so sorry." What else had Myrddin wrought?

"And then one day a few years in, I met Harry. He showed up and asked if he could stay. He talked to me for hours, and not in the way the others had. He actually seemed to care about me. And I started caring about me again. He told me all these crazy stories about a whole world that is hidden from the human one. A world I belonged in. He told me about you and the king and Devinshea and his grandchildren. I wanted that world, so we made our deal."

Now that sounded like my father. "Deal?"

"I gave Harry some space in my brain. It's a bit like what the prince has with the ancient god Bris. I can share space with him and not lose who I am. Oh, if Harry was a different man, he could have easily taken over in the beginning. I was a mess, and I wouldn't have fought him even if I'd known how. Instead, he strengthened me. He talked me through how to get out of the hospital, coached me on what to say. Then we decided to come here. The wards make Frelsi undetectable to the living, but Harry knew where his grandkids were. He made me camp. It was terrible."

Evan laughed, the sound sweet and familiar since she sounded like her sister. "She was not an outdoor girl, to say the least. Or a cold weather girl. It was so sad. She showed up outside the mountain, and we all felt so sorry for her that we sent someone to talk to her."

"You sent a brownie," Shy said with no small amount of accusation. "I'd never seen a supernatural creature before and then this tiny withered thing is talking to me. Although I probably scared her more than she did me. And then she fixed my tent and offered to wash my clothes and I loved her." She smiled fondly. "It took them another week to finally believe me, and every day Liesl would come and help me. That little brownie gets all the cream."

I stared at the beautiful young woman. "So he's inside you."

"Yes. Like I said, we share space. Harry's in what I like to call mid-transition. If he hadn't found a soul space, he would likely would have ended up with the sluagh. He heard them call to him." The smile on her face had faded. "He couldn't leave. He knew you would be back and that you would need him."

My father had almost become sluagh? They were the restless dead, the ones who couldn't move on. "I thank you for finding him. It can't be easy for you."

"I would do anything for Harry. When everyone else abandoned me, he was there. I never knew my own father. He died when I was young. Harry…well, I don't want to get too emotional. The old man can't handle it," Shy said. "He's ready to talk if you are."

I took a deep breath. "I'm ready."

Shy turned and her eyes went black. "Hello, me darling. Don't pass out on me this time. After all, we've got a war to fight."

I moved to the end of the bed and took Shy's hand, took my father's hand. "Hello, Dad."

Chapter Six

Shy's chest sighed, the movement so familiar though the body was different. "You haven't changed at all. Is it true it's only been a few days for you?"

I was talking to my dead father. He was dead and hiding in another body. I forced myself to let that sink in. It wouldn't stand. I would find a way to fix all of this, but I had to start handling things better. "We were gone for roughly four days. I don't understand what happened. The painting was enchanted."

"The painting was meant for Marcus. It was spelled specifically for him," my father explained. "I know all of this because I spent the first year of my death in the Council building, following Myrddin and learning about his plans. He never meant for Daniel to go through that painting. He was perfectly happy to lose Devinshea and you and Kelsey, but he wanted Daniel around and properly under his influence."

"Under the thrall stones."

Shy's head nodded. "Yes. He knew where he was sending Marcus to, knew that if you went through too they would likely figure out what he'd done. The stones are much more easy to obtain on the outer planes. It's where he got them. When Devinshea disappeared, he knew he couldn't keep Daniel. That was when he allowed the two of you to go through. He knew Daniel would never stop searching for Devinshea. The trap was for Marcus and Kelsey. Devinshea was what he hadn't counted on. The wizard came in and quickly assessed the threats to his absolute control over Daniel."

"Marcus and Kelsey. I'm insulted I wasn't on that list."

"Ahh, but he never gave you enough credit, my darling girl. He thinks you're nothing more than a wife and mum. He doesn't understand the most dangerous of all creatures is a mum whose kids are threatened."

"Why go after the kids?" I asked. "They couldn't challenge him. Why not allow Declan to come for them? Miria would have taken them and they wouldn't have been any trouble at all."

"When he came for the children that day, I think that's what he might have done. The hours after you went missing were quiet. No one had a clue you were gone because Danny was supposed to help with the locator ceremony."

Myrddin had planned to hold a ceremony in the dark temple at midnight that night. Danny and I were going to attend, and it could have gone on for hours. "He told everyone we were in the temple?"

"That was what I believed," my father agreed. "I stayed over because I wanted to talk to you when you got back from the business with Daniel. When you didn't come back, I went to look for you. I overheard them talking, and Myrddin decided the best way to deal with the situation was to lock down the crown very quickly. Honestly, I think he panicked a bit. He's not used to his plans being upended. I know he came into the penthouse that morning and fed me a line of bullshit about how you and Danny had been attacked and he needed to get the children someplace safe. Albert was already on the move, getting the children ready. Trent had spent the night with Fenrir, so he was back there, too. I held him off as long as I could."

"How did he kill you?" I wanted to know everything, every single reason to punish the wizard when the bill came due.

"When he realized I was giving Albert and Eddie cover, he stormed back into the kids' rooms. He quickly discovered that Eddie had transported them, and he took it out on me. The great Merlin packs quite a punch when he wants to. I'm not sure if he was trying to kill me or trying to hurt me and send me a message, but when that bolt of lightning from his hands hit me, my heart gave out. The world went dark and when I came back to consciousness, it was several weeks later and Myrddin had done his worst by then."

"His worst?"

Evan took that one. "He'd consolidated his power by killing everyone he could. He put out the story that the royals had been killed by a rogue group that had embedded members close to the royal family."

"Let me guess. Trent and Sasha," I concluded.

"And Marcus," Evan added. "He used Marcus's disappearance to make the vampires look particularly bad. Not that there aren't a subset that work with Myrddin now, but it was a good way to sway the supernaturals who don't like the vamps."

"It was a good way to get rid of all of our allies." The political situation had been tenuous at best. It always was in our world. Daniel's coalition had held, but there were always factions fighting, millennia of bad will and betrayal among the different tribes. The wolves didn't trust the vampires, and the witches are wary of the Fae. There was often some sort of rebellion to put down. "I take it he invited the demons in."

"Yes. By that point he'd brought in the demons, and the witches had taken over the Council," my father explained. "I had no idea where the children had gone then. I stuck close to Myrddin and learned a lot about his plans. In those first months, he simply struggled to secure the throne. He didn't bother to go after the children. He tried to figure out why the painting hadn't worked the way he thought it should. It went blank after it took you and Daniel."

I had so many questions about that. "Did he enchant it himself?"

Shy's hands expertly poured the tea as my father spoke. "He painted it himself, but the enchantment was commissioned. It was a particular form of magic that wasn't of this plane. He feared if he used his own, one of the witches would have sensed the purpose. He couldn't use demonic magic since there were wards against it at the time. So he was forced to use a witch from another plane."

I had to laugh because I knew what had happened. The trick had been on freaking Myrddin. "He tried to lay a trap for Marcus and perhaps Kelsey, but Marcus was needed by the outer planes. Twelve years ago did anyone sense a…" What to call it? "A disturbance in the force?"

Shy's head shook but the expression was pure Harry Wharton. "My daughter the geek. What do you mean?"

Evan had a thoughtful expression on her face. "Are you talking about the days when the veil thinned? I don't remember it well but Albert talks about it. It was how we moved so easily across the planes for a while. Even when it settled down, there were still places where it thinned from time to time. Albert thought Myrddin was doing it."

So they'd felt the convergences on the Earth plane as well. "No, it was because the Night King was dying and the Day Queen needed her successor to take over the job of fueling the planes. The outer planes exist basically on top of one another. Like Shy explained your relationship, those planes share a space and they require a unique magic to keep the walls up and the planes separate. Summer is made from that magic. She is that magic. But as with all things in our universe, she works best with a balance. Night to her day."

"Marcus Vorenus," Evan said with a sigh. "She was Marcus's mate. The prophecy wasn't about me."

"Not you." I had so many thoughts on how the universe would do its will, and nothing we do could thwart it. Myrddin had tried so hard, but someone had tricked him. "So someone from the outer planes found a way to get their Day Queen the king she needed. Summer couldn't take her place without Marcus at her side, and Myrddin gave them a perfect way to tempt him through."

What I didn't say was I doubted Summer took her place at all unless things had gone the way they had. Daniel had been the one to convince her to unleash her power. Without meeting us, I don't know if she would have found the peace she needed to finally come into her destiny.

And if we hadn't gone through, we wouldn't have been able to bring back Dean, who Kelsey now thought was absolutely essential to taking down Myrddin.

"Perhaps the painting went blank because it had done its job. The outer planes were saved when Summer and Marcus took their crowns," Evan mused. "But the academics came to believe that the object itself wouldn't close until someone came back through. They thought it was a fail-safe in case someone got trapped by accident. A way to keep the portal open so Marcus could still go through. Even though it went blank, we still believed you could return."

"Why didn't Myrddin destroy it?" I asked.

"Because I stole it, of course," my father admitted. "Well, I tried to. I wasn't good at the ghost thing at that point, so I convinced someone else to steal it. It wasn't hard. She was looking for a way to kill the man. I convinced her to be a spy instead. Turns out my little love is pretty good with death magic. She was trying to contact me shortly after I died, and she didn't stop until she called me to her circle. She's the one who found Shahidi for me."

"Christine?" Was he talking about Christine? Christine was my father's girlfriend for years. She was a witch of medium power, and she was roughly my age. My father might have gotten older over the years, but his taste in twenty-year-olds had never changed. Christine would be almost fifty now. Was she still loyal to my dad even after he'd died? I'd kind of always thought she'd go to the dark side in a heartbeat. Way before I would have said Liv would go all Dark Willow on us.

"Yes. I know you never liked her much, but she was a good woman. She still is. She's been in the Council headquarters for years now, quietly working with the rebellion," my father announced with obvious pride. "She's the one who saved the canvas from being stored on the Hell plane when they couldn't destroy it. She worked with a Planeswalker, who smuggled it back out."

"A Planeswalker?" I asked the question, startled that they even knew that name.

Evan frowned. "Those are creepy dudes."

The fact that my daughter knew what a Planeswalker looked like scared the crap out of me. I'd never seen one until I went to the outer planes. What had Evan and the boys been exposed to? What had they been forced to survive?

Shy's head nodded. "Yes. He said he owed the royals and that we should tell you his debt is now paid."

We'd encountered those specialized demons when we were in the outer planes. They were like the bees of those far-flung worlds. They helped spread the energy by walking the planes in regular rotations. When the old queen's magic had started to fail, so had the Planeswalkers' magic. We had protected them, and then Summer had taken her place. Now it appeared they'd returned the favor or we might have come through the canvas and straight onto the Hell plane.

"We've been trying to figure out when you would come back for years." Evan reached out and grabbed a cookie. "Trent's consulted with all kinds of psychics, and Christine gave us the dates the dark coven came up with. As we approached this first date—today—we realized how much magic it would take to get through all the wards and into the building. We stored magic for years."

"We also tried to take the canvas out of the building, but that didn't work. It wouldn't make it through the wards. The best we could do was store it, and then when we thought you might come through, put it someplace you would recognize and we would be able to get to." Evan sat back. "We knew we would likely get one shot. There was some disagreement on which date to try."

"I knew it was today," my father said. "Shy did, too. We felt it deep in our bones. Her bones. Rhys did, too. He'd seen some signs that convinced him it was time. Sasha is a good male but a bloody stubborn ass. Russians. Trent is honestly every bit as bad."

"I thank you for trusting your instincts, Dad." It was easier now to look past the oddness of my father speaking to me through another body. I reached out and took Shy's hand. "And I thank Shahidi for giving you a place to stay."

"Thank Shahidi for convincing Rhys, Momma." A glint came into Evan's eyes. "I doubt he would have been confident enough to go against Sasha if it had just been Grandad talking. But he'll do anything for Shy."

Shy's eyes narrowed. "Don't you tease them, girl. You know it's hard on your brother."

"Yes, every time he starts flirting with Shy, Grandad shows up," Evan pointed out.

"It was only the one time," my father said.

"It was enough." Evan chuckled. "I can't help it. He deserves it. Rhys acts like he's my dad. He's the one who made Fen promise not to touch me."

"Evan, you're only seventeen," I pointed out.

A brow rose over Shy's warm brown eyes. It was an expression I knew well. "And what were you and Danny doing when you were seventeen?"

"Is there anything stronger than tea?" I groaned. "Damn it. I can't drink."

"You're really pregnant?" Evan asked. "I thought you and Papa decided to not have more kids."

We had. We'd decided the three we had were enough, but then we'd had a chance I never thought we would. "It's not Papa's."

My father gasped. "What happened to you, girl?"

"It's what happened to Danny. I won't explain all the weird magic that went into it, but for a while on that odd faery plane, Danny was human and he was capable of having children." It had been a magical night and one where the three of us had been closer than we'd ever been before. "It's okay. He's a vampire again, but I did get pregnant."

"You're having another child with Dad?" Evan seemed to let that sink in. "Well, congratulations, Mom. I'm going to go find Fen. We need to get ready to go in the morning. This is my room. I'm sure Albert's gotten yours ready. Like I said before, there's supper for you when you're hungry."

She left before I could get another word out.

"What did I do?" Evan hadn't been happy with news of my pregnancy. Except she had when she'd thought this child would be with Devinshea.

"You didn't do anything at all." My father settled back in his chair. "Evan hides her insecurities well most of the time, but I think you touched a sore spot. She's always been closest to Daniel. I'm afraid even though you weren't here, those divides still held. You loved Lee most."

"That's not true."

"You all worried more about Lee, and in a child's world that translates to love," he explained. "You think back to how you felt about me and Danny after he turned. How I worried about him and took his side in most things. You were an adult and you were still wounded by it. I didn't mean to hurt you, but I did. In Evan's mind you were Lee's, Dev belonged to Rhys, and Daniel was hers. Now you've told her she's got a rival. She lost twelve years with you because you were with Summer, Daniel's child. Now you're giving him a biological child who will likely replace her."

"That's not true." Had I favored Lee? I hadn't meant to. I loved them all.

"Of course it's not, but it feels that way to her. Part of this is Shy talking. She's close to Evan. We're both worried about her. Not because of Fen. I know Evan will talk about how reckless Fenrir is and how she's got to keep him in check, but she's every bit as brash as he is. She's not wrong about Rhys trying to take her father's place. They've fallen into roles as they've gotten older. Rhys has gotten more serious. Lee is Devinshea's near twin, from what I can tell, and Evan, well, Evan's had to fight for her place. She's the only girl here, and the boys are overly protective, to say the least. It was good when Shy showed up and she had someone to talk to."

She should have had a mother figure with her. And a sister. "What happened to Sarah? I can't believe she would leave my kids."

Shy's shoulder shrugged. "I don't know. I wish I did. Like I said, I died and by the time I came back to consciousness, most of it was done. Sarah and Felix and Mia were gone, and Christine doesn't know where they went. She believes they found a way to flee the plane. She thinks if Myrddin had killed them he would have made a show of it. I wish I had a better answer for you. Now ask me what you've been afraid to ask."

Tears sprang to my eyes because he was right. I was afraid to ask, terrified at what I could have lost. "Is Neil dead?"

Neil, my best friend. He'd been at my side through everything. I didn't think he would leave my kids.

My father stood and sat beside me. "No. He's alive and well. He still works with us whenever we need him, but after the Council fell, some of the wolf packs went back to their old ways. The worst of the packs turned on what they considered weak members."

Weak meaning any member who didn't hold the reproduction line. With Dev gone, they would have spent years struggling with fertility again, and that meant attempting to force mating within their packs. "He's really okay? Chad's okay? What about Zack?"

Chad was Neil's vampire husband. Zack had been a part of our family since almost the beginning. He was Daniel's "servant" and had been for years. He was Kelsey's uncle, and I trusted Zack with my life and my family.

"Chad is with Neil, and so is Zack and his family. They're a few miles away in a small town on the coast. They welcome all wolves who've been abused by their packs. Neil and Chad have two children now. They adopted two wolves who'd been shunned by their families."

My tears were for another reason now because all Neil had ever wanted in life was to have a family, to love and be loved without conditions. "I can see him."

"Yes," my father said. "You should go tomorrow because Zack needs to see Daniel. He's…unwell."

I didn't like the sound of that. "Unwell?"

"He hasn't had vampire blood in years. You remember how much weaker Neil was when he stopped taking Danny's blood? Well, Zack was on it for far longer. He's never gotten his strength back, and it's gotten worse."

"We can go now." I started to stand.

Shy's hand reached out and stopped me. "Tomorrow is soon enough. I assure you they've been informed that the royals have returned. They'll be here in the morning. You need to stay in Frelsi. It's safe. You need to work on your relationship with the kids. Now that you're back, things will heat up, and we'll have that all-out war I've feared for so long. You know what we need to do, right?"

"Yes, I need to find someone who can get me back to the day we went missing."

"Why would you do that?" my father asked.

"This is wrong. This whole place is wrong, and we can fix it." I already knew who I needed to talk to. "Summer can help. She's so powerful, and she can find a way to get me back to that moment. I'll change everything. I'll save you."

My father stared at me. "I don't think that's possible, and even if it was, it wouldn't turn out the way you want."

"I'm the nexus point. I make reality." I'd learned long ago that I was different. I am the odd being who has no written fate. I can change the fate of the people around me. I intended to change all of our fates.

"No. You don't make reality." My father's tone had gone harsh. "You make choices, and this one could have hard consequences. You don't know that you wouldn't fuck things up more."

"I'm willing to take that chance. Can't you see that the kids shouldn't have had to go through this? I have to try."

"No. What you have to do is find a way into the Council building and take what we stole all those years ago," my father said. "Myrddin's grimoire is still missing, but he comes closer to finding it every single day. When he does, he'll have more power than you can imagine. He'll have his book of spells and he'll have the Sword of Light, and he'll be able to do what he's been planning for over a decade, maybe longer."

"And what is that?"

"He's going to permanently close all doors between the Earth plane and all Heavenly planes. He's going to give Earth to Hell."

Well, it looked like I had a job to do.

Chapter Seven

I sat at the big table in the house my children had lived in for the last several years, Devinshea at my side, while Daniel had taken the seat at the head of the table. Sasha sat at the other end, the king and his loyal general leading the discussion.

Kelsey had joined us, though she'd explained Dean was sleeping. Apparently fighting off a bunch of witches had tired him out. Fen sat next to his mom, practically glowing when he looked at her, while Evan had chosen the place next to Fen and would barely look at me.

Kelsey talked with Casey and ate at least fifteen sandwiches. Eddie kept bringing them one after another.

I'd barely touched the stew Albert had brought me. There were kind-eyed trolls serving the food this evening and making sure glasses were kept full. The home was warm thanks to the fire in the hearth. It was a cozy place to be, and I still felt numb.

Kelsey was doing so much better than I was, and I had no idea how she was holding it together when she didn't even know where Gray was.

Or maybe she was doing it for Fen, who was smiling like he'd won the lottery. My kids were treating me like I would break if they touched me. Probably because I'd acted that way. I'd noted they were all laughing with Daniel and Dev as I'd walked in, though Evan was still standoffish. She'd kept close to Fen.

I didn't belong here. None of us did. But I had to pull it together because if I couldn't find a way out of this mess, I would be stuck here, and my kids needed me. Devinshea had been right when he'd told me to shove my pain down and be the queen. Or in this case, be the mom.

"Before we get to the heart of the matter, I'd like to know what happened to Faery," Dev said. Dinner was winding down, and we'd promised to talk business after. "I always assumed if anything happened to all three of us that Declan would come for the children, or Albert would take them to my mother. That was the plan we had in place."

Devinshea always had a plan, though in this case it was one we'd all agreed on. If something happened to all three of us, the future king of the Seelie Fae, Dev's brother, Declan, would come for his niece and nephews. If he couldn't come to Dallas, he would show up to open the door to the *sithein* for them.

"Eddie was our best way out of the penthouse, and he had never been to Faery. He'd been to Italy and the base Marcus Vorenus kept there." Rhys was sitting at attention, as though this supposed family meal was a high-level war council. Which in all honesty it was. I noted that Shy had taken the seat across from Rhys. She was back to being herself, though she'd promised if my dad had something to say, he would take over.

"By the time we felt comfortable enough to reach out to Faery, they had closed their borders," Sasha explained.

"And that's that." Rhys had a mug in front of him, and I was almost certain it was filled with the same beer Albert had placed in front of Dev.

Lee snorted and rolled his eyes. "Sure it is. You'll learn Rhys likes to ignore the stuff he finds distasteful. Papa, Albert tried to follow your orders. When Sasha and Trent decided it was safe enough, they reached out to Faery. The Seelies wouldn't take in me or Fen."

"What?" That had me sitting up. "Your grandmother refused you entrance?"

"Yes, though she apologized. She's had trouble since Papa

disappeared. My human ass wasn't welcome, and Fen was considered too dangerous," Lee replied. "Apparently the last time werewolves were let in there was a war or something."

"It was more complicated than that." Rhys stared down at his mug.

"You mean they thought the human was unlucky, and my disappearance proved it," Dev said, every word dripping with bitterness. He'd been raised mortal in the world of the Fae. It hadn't been until he'd ascended that they truly accepted him.

"The Unseelie would have taken us in, but I decided against it." Sasha's color was up, proof that he'd fed this evening. The last I'd seen him, he was living off animal blood because the thought of taking a human female was distasteful to him. He'd lost his wife and been forced to send his daughter off to another family. I hoped he had someone who comforted him. "It was too rough a place for a human and a companion. So we sat down, Trent and I, and we decided to walk the planes for a while. It allowed us to stay off the wizard's radar while the children were young and in training."

"How did you walk the planes?" Danny asked. "It's not an easy feat."

"Albert's mother is highly placed in the demonic world," Sasha explained. "Through her we were able to obtain a map of the doors and how to open them. The map was spelled to work for several years, and then we made the choice to come back to the Earth plane and fight. But those years out there on the planes were important."

"We went to a dinosaur world. Rhys nearly crapped his pants," Lee said with a snort.

Rhys's eyes rolled. "And you took that time to say fuck as often as you could."

"Well, we were allowed to use it in case of a dino attack. Or stepping in a massive pile of dino droppings." Evan was grinning again as though those terrible, dangerous times had also produced good memories. "Fen had to bathe for a week before we could stand to be around him."

"We didn't stay long," Sasha said. "The UV light was too much for me there. We spent much more time on a werewolf plane."

Evan shivered. "It was cold. Fen spent a lot of time in his wolf skin."

Fen's lips went up in a wolfy grin, and he leaned over to kiss Evan's cheek. "I did that so you could cuddle up and stay warm."

I put a hand on Dev's thigh, a reminder to not make an ass of himself. It was obvious the kids had connections we couldn't understand yet. Although I could understand Evan and Fen. When I stopped feeling sorry for myself and looked at the situation, I could remember what it felt like to have that one person in the world I could count on. I'd had Daniel. And then I hadn't.

I didn't want that for Evan. I could start healing by supporting her.

"I'm glad," I said. "Evangeline was always cold as a kid. She carried around her blanky. Is the wolf plane where you learned archery?"

"Some of it," Evan allowed. "But most of it I learned here on the Earth plane. Sasha found a tutor for us. I took to it better than the others."

"You come by it honestly." Dev's voice was still tight, but I could see he was trying to shove down his anger. It wouldn't be directed Evan's way. It would be all about his family. The Seelies hadn't always been kind to my husband. "Your uncle was the best archer in Faery."

"I don't remember much about him, but I do miss Sean from time to time," Evan said.

"Well, given what we know about how time moves in Faery, our cousin is now younger than we are." Rhys took a drink. "He wouldn't recognize us."

"Certainly not me, since I used to have two eyes." Lee grinned my way.

"I'd like that story, son." Daniel, like Sasha, didn't have a plate in front of him. "I'll have all the stories, but our time is running short. I'll start taking meetings tomorrow and all through the week. We have to rebuild our coalition and convince a bunch of supernaturals who hate each other to work together. Hugo and Henri brought me up to speed on what they know about Myrddin's plan. Why does he think he can close the doors between Earth and Heaven? Shy, if you please? I've been told Harry knows the most about this particular subject."

"Of course, Your Highness." Shy took a breath and her eyes shifted. "Hey there, my Danny."

Daniel's jaw tightened, emotion plain on his face. "Hey, Harry. I…"

Shy's hand came up. "Don't even try, son. There's nothing to apologize for. I would die a thousand times to save my grandchildren. And I don't regret a bit of staying here to wait for you."

"Shy and Harry have done more for the resistance than anyone," Sasha explained solemnly. "Without them we would have very little intelligence. We would still be blind. Our spies have worked well for the simple fact that Harry was able to put a structure in place, and Shy was able to get him to us so we knew about the work he'd done. When we came back to the Earth plane and made Frelsi our base, we put up strong wards. Harry had been looking for us forever. Through his network of informants, he and Shy found their way here. Those assets formed the base of my own network."

"Christine is on our side." Dev's hand was on his mug but he didn't drink. "Who else do we have on the inside?"

Casey sat up straighter. Casey was a young vampire, but he was an academic, so his mental powers were already strong, and he had control most young vampires didn't possess. He was on Kelsey's team, and once everyone had thought he would end up with Olivia Carey. I couldn't help but think about what Dean had said. He'd read Liv's intentions and found some small hope there. She still felt for Kelsey and for Casey. Her heart wasn't completely hardened. "Christine is our main source of information on the inside of the coven. Making contact with us is dangerous. All magic is controlled by Myrddin, so she can't do what she would normally do and use a mirror or a spell to send us what we need. We use a courier system. We have a werewolf and a vampire who are trusted by Myrddin's court. Our vampire is here in Frelsi now. He recently brought us information from Christine about Myrddin's movements."

Well, that explained why I'd seen Alexander. "If you're talking about Alexander Sharpe then the reason he's trusted by Myrddin's court is because he's working for them."

Daniel sighed. "My wife doesn't have any faith in Alexander. Neither do I, but I would point out that he did not betray us to the old Council when he could. Alexander will be useful as long as he's getting something out of it."

Sasha nodded. "That was my assessment as well. He's been our vampire spy for years. I keep close watch on him, though. Right now Myrddin treats him like an errand boy. If that changes, or if I believe he might turn, I will execute him myself."

"And how would you know? If Myrddin sniffs out Christine, then none of your information is good," Dev pointed out.

"Christine is not the only witch asset we have." Sasha put his elbows on the table, his hands steepling together. "I have a network across the supernatural world. Some of them know who they are working for. Some of them do not. They do not know who the others are unless I need them to know, Your Highness."

"I don't know half of them," Rhys complained. "Sasha only trusts Trent with the whole of his network."

Sasha started to say something but Devinshea interrupted. "That's because if you don't know, you can't talk. He's protecting his network and you, son. Sasha knows what he's doing. He's former KGB."

"We called it SVR at the time, but your papa is correct. About my history and my reasons," Sasha conceded.

One of the things I'd seen in the armory made sense. "That's why your bounty is payable only if you're brought in alive."

Sasha nodded. "And that is why I carry this." He pulled a small device out of his pocket. "This is UV light spelled into a liquid form. I assure you, they will not take me alive."

"I've stolen it a couple of times," Lee admitted. "He brings out another one. I can't figure out where he keeps them."

"He has the troll who spells it put something on the container so I can't sniff it out." Fen sighed. "I keep trying to explain that I'll find him and get him out."

"He doesn't want that. He wants to protect you all and his network. He's a good spymaster." Daniel stared Sasha's way. "You have done well, my friend. I'm sorry for the circumstances, but damn I'm grateful for what you've done over the last twelve years. I would like for you to work with Devinshea, but I leave it to you how much you reveal. I want that network of yours protected as much as possible. Is the intelligence about Myrddin's plans reliable?"

"It comes straight from Christine and Harry, so I consider it truth," Sasha explained. "Though you should know it's been verified by my higher-level assets. The pretender king has made a deal with the Hell plane. Power for ability to populate the Earth plane."

"Populate? That sounds icky." Kelsey had a way with words.

"By *populate* he means demons could walk among us, live here in the open." Rhys lifted his hand slightly and one of the trolls hurried forward, refilling his drink. He glanced the female's way. "Thank you, Gedda. Please let the kitchens know the meal was delicious. We appreciate how quickly they put it together."

Lee gave the troll a thumbs-up. "It rocked."

Oh, they were both sides of their biological dad. Rhys, the thoughtful, cautious prince, and Lee, the decadent, charming rake.

When Gedda walked out, Rhys continued. "According to Grandad, Myrddin made this deal years ago."

"I believe it was in the weeks after you disappeared." My father seemed to draw in on himself, or rather on Shy. Like they were having a silent conversation. He finally smiled and reached for the glass of whiskey in front of Shy's place. She'd ignored it utterly but seemed to have given my dad permission to enjoy it. He took a quick sip and sighed in obvious pleasure before getting on with it. "They were chaotic, and Myrddin had to put down several factions that rose to take over. The wolves tried. The academics led a vampire rebellion. The Fae retreated. I didn't have a body for those first years. I was a wraith clinging to the shadows and learning Myrddin's secrets. He often disappeared into the dark temple where he met with the demons. Roughly two years after you disappeared, he had his deal."

"The demons gave pro-Myrddin witches power, and he promised to deliver the Earth plane to them," my vampire husband concluded. "When the witches had the full backing of dark magic behind them, they could put down the rebellions."

"He still doesn't have the power you had, Your Highness," Casey said. "There is no Council. All he's done is sent the separate supernatural groups back to their own homes. He can't count on any of them. Still, he's dangerous, and we've had a hard time finding any large group who's willing to join us. We have some wolves, some werecreatures, earthly Fae. We don't have an army."

"We don't need one." Daniel sat back. "This isn't the same as the first time we took over the Council. The way Sasha and Trent have been running this war is smart. I need to reconnect with our allies, let them know that we will take care of the problem, and then come together to solve any differences we have after I've taken back my crown. How bad is the political situation?"

The table went quiet and then Sasha turned Rhys's way. "He's talking to you."

Rhys's hand came off the mug. "He is?"

"He is," Dev agreed. "Rhys, are you or are you not the leader of your little army? The king is correct. This isn't the same war we fought before, but everything I've learned today leads me to believe that you and your siblings and Fenrir have been the heart of the resistance, certainly of the physical rebellion. Do you or do you not have thoughts on the political situation we're facing with the various factions of our former coalition?"

I saw the moment my son realized his fathers were taking him seriously. He sat up straighter, focus coming into his eyes. "I believe the pretender has attempted to make inroads with certain factions, but he isn't the politician he thinks he is. He's fumbled quite badly with the wolves. The alphas might never admit it in public, but they enjoyed the peace they had when you were king. They liked being able to refer certain problems to the Council rather than making decisions that could hurt them politically. They enjoyed the cover the Council gave them. I think they would welcome it again. The earthly Fae are with us. They come to Frelsi every week."

"They come to be close to Rhys," Evan said.

"They come to be close to all of us," Rhys corrected. "Dad, I believe that you should make the rounds. Quietly, of course. Let Sasha arrange the meetings for you through his contacts. While you're handling the political situation, Fen and Evan will escort Kelsey to Trent. He's been working with the primals, who are the one group we absolutely have on our side."

"Should Evan be going into a group of primal vampires?" I had never been to their underground Atlanta home. Primals were vampires who reverted to their primeval form. Whoever made Nosferatu had definitely met a primal vampire. I couldn't see Evan's glow, but I knew it had to be as bright as mine. She would shine for every vampire who saw her, and being underground, it might be hard for her to get away.

"I agree." Dev looked to Daniel. "Evan shouldn't be exposed to a large group of vampires. She should stay here. She and Rhys can go with us when we visit the Fae. We're fairly close to the Unseelies. From there I have questions to ask my mother."

"Evan comes with me." Fen's voice had taken on that low growl I'd come quickly to associate with his possessive nature.

"I come with you because I choose to, not because you make me," Evan said under her breath. "If you wish for me to keep choosing you, you'll allow me to handle this."

Kelsey's lips quirked up in a satisfied grin. "You go, Evan. Daniel, I'll look out for her."

"I'll take the time to teach the *Nex Apparatus* a few tricks with a bow." Evan tipped her head Kelsey's way.

"All I'm saying is we're here now and you no longer have to put yourselves in danger, and you walking into a nest of primals is putting yourself in danger," Dev replied.

I was starting to believe that Evan could handle herself. I understood why Dev was worried. I was worried, too, but she'd survived and thrived all this time. Perhaps what she needed now were supportive parents, not ones that still treated her like she was five. "It seems to me Evan knows the primals better than we do. We should listen to her."

If Evan heard me, she ignored it, preferring to stare her papa's way. "I've been visiting the primals since I was barely a teenager. They're some of the kindest souls I've ever met, and not one of them would hurt me. I've spent months underground with them and all they've ever done is teach me how to protect myself and share their knowledge with me. Unlike some of the warriors we've encountered. And the Fae. You want me and Rhys to go hang with the Fae?"

"Evan," Lee said, sounding more serious than usual.

Evan shook her head. "No. They waltz in acting like they understand what's happening. Taking charge of us without bothering to acknowledge that we're adults now. You want to know how Lee lost his eye? Lee lost his left eye when a group of Fae tried to kidnap Rhys and take him to the *sithein* where they would force him to perform as their Green Man. After they knocked Rhys out, Lee fought them all off. Lee gave up his eye and a good portion of his blood to defend his brother from your family, Papa. So no. We will not go to the Unseelie with you. I am going to Atlanta tomorrow. The primals might be able to help Kelsey with her book. They might be able to decipher the prophecies found there. Kelsey thinks we've got part of it wrong. She thinks there's a third part we've been missing."

"According to what I've read in the book I got from the outer planes, I definitely think we've got it wrong," Kelsey said. "I've studied their words, and I think Myrddin's interpretation is off. He thinks Dean and Lee are the only ones who can kill him, but these prophecies seem to point to them being the only ones who can wield the weapon that kills Myrddin. Wield or prime or something like that. I'm not great with languages but the primals are, and they're excellent with prophecy. Between the academics here and the primals, I hope we can crack it. If I'm right, I need to find that weapon."

"Hence, we're off to see the primals," Evan said. "The wonderful primals of Atlanta. I can work on my not tan since I'll be underground."

"Underground, where you could easily be trapped," Dev pointed out.

Evan stood, pointedly ignoring her papa. "I need to pack. Fen."

Fen hopped out of his seat as Evan swept from the room. He shrugged Kelsey's way. "Sorry. I know everyone thinks I'm the alpha, but I pretty much do what Evan tells me to. Let me know if you need me."

Lee shook his head. "What does she need to pack? She doesn't own anything."

"Our sister knows how to make an exit," Rhys said with a shake of his head. "Papa, don't even try with those two. It won't work and you'll alienate her. If you make us choose between you and our sister and Fen, you won't like our decision."

"That wasn't what he meant." I reached for Dev's hand because I knew he'd just taken a punch to the gut. "He's worried. You have to give us a few moments. You were babies yesterday. Our babies. And now we're so worried for the world you're in. We feel guilty for leaving you."

"You didn't leave us, Mom. We know that. You didn't want this for us," Lee said. "But it's where we are. I wish we could shut everything down and have a happy family reunion, but we're in the middle of a war. The only thing that has kept Myrddin from fulfilling his contract with the demons is what we did the day you disappeared."

"You mean the fact that I stole his grimoire? I took back Gladys, too." I could confess to that particular crime now that my husbands were no longer under the wizard's influence.

"Your mother didn't mention that she'd stolen Myrddin's book of spells. Harry, did you help her?" Daniel looked grim, but he always got back to business.

Lee grimaced and raised his hand. "That would be me. Granddad was the lookout. Oh, and Dannan helped. He dealt with that nasty cat of Myrddin's."

The little pixie sat on Lee's shoulder, and his wings fluttered as though to say *good times*.

I hadn't mentioned the heist in the beginning because I didn't trust Daniel not to run right to Myrddin and give both the sword and the spellbook back. After we got the thrall stones out of my husband's heads, well, we'd been running for our lives and then making a baby and running again. Let's just say it had been a crazy week.

"Myrddin has Gladys?" Kelsey's jaw had gone tight. Gladys was Kelsey's name for the sword she carried as the *Nex Apparatus*. The Heavenly plane called it the Sword of Light. It was the sword given to the companions before recorded history. Long ago when we'd been known as the Amazons. It had only found its way back to us when Kelsey had been made the *Nex Apparatus*. Once in female hands, Gladys's powers had hummed to life again.

"Had Gladys," I corrected. "Thanks to my father and Lee and Dannan, the sword and Myrddin's grimoire are safely in a bag of holding in my closet at the penthouse."

"But he lives in the penthouse," Sasha pointed out.

"Yes, but I'm the only one who can see the bag." The bag had been my father's gift to me on my wedding day. My dad had been the supernatural world's greatest thief, so I hadn't asked how he'd gotten his hands on the incredibly rare object from the Heaven plane. The bag of holding had been fashioned by angels during their wars with the demons. "Once I placed the grimoire and Gladys in the bag, it disappeared and can only be opened by the owner. Dad primed it with my blood. I'm the owner."

"Myrddin could burn the place down and he still wouldn't find it," my father said. "It should be exactly where she left it. He can try any number of locator spells, but they won't detect the objects he's looking for. The bag itself is a small pocket universe, so the objects aren't actually on the Earth plane."

"That explains why he hasn't found them." Sasha was making notes on a pad of paper. I'd noticed he'd walked in with notebooks and pens. He was an old-school spy master, but then I rather thought he didn't trust Myrddin wouldn't have hired hackers. "But they're in danger if they're still in the penthouse."

"The bag of holding isn't one hundred percent foolproof," my father mused. "But since he hasn't found a way to close the doors to the Heaven plane yet, we have to assume he doesn't have the objects he needs."

"I remember his office had a lot of books about the Heaven plane." Lee pushed his empty plate back. It was mere seconds before one of the trolls whisked it away. "I particularly remember one was called *Closing the Veil*. I think he's been planning this for a long time, and that was why he was examining Gladys. Given that Gladys is an ancient sword forged on one of the Heavenly planes, it could be helpful in whatever magic he's going to use to try to close the doors."

I remembered that day well. Lee and I had stolen the grimoire and Gladys by using the Mantle of Arthur—an invisibility cloak that had once helped Daniel flee the old Council. It had been one of Lee's favorite forbidden toys. That had been the day I'd realized how much Lee wanted to be in this world and how far he felt from it. "Have you kept up with your Latin?"

A smile split his handsome face. "*Studui dura per annos*. I'm fluent in Latin, ancient Greek, Aramaic, and Sanskrit. I'm good with modern and ancient Hebrew as well. And fuck the Seelie Fae, but I speak Gaelic better than most of them do."

"Of course you do." Daniel was studying Lee carefully. "You pick up languages quickly?"

"I don't know how," Rhys said with a huff. "He's got a thick skull for everything else, but he's better than all of us with languages. He was fluent in Icelandic a couple of months after we got here. Lee likes to study as long as it has something to do with the supernatural world. He spends a lot of time with the academics."

"I bet he does." Daniel said the words in that "I know something you don't know" way of his. "Have you figured out how bad it will get if the doors to the Heaven plane close? It's not like we're bombarded with angels."

Oh, how quickly he forgot. "Just because you don't see them doesn't mean they're not here. If the doors close, guardian angels cannot watch their charges. Or they'll be stuck here, and we don't know what that will do to their powers. We also have to consider that the dead who should ascend to Heaven will be stuck here, too. Like my dad."

"I'm not stuck, darling," my father corrected. "I see the door. It's there for me. I didn't exactly refuse it, merely told the angel who invited me through that I had work to do. She warned me about becoming sluagh, but with Shy's help, I managed to avoid that fate. The door is ready when I finish my work here."

"The door to Heaven?" Dev had a brow raised.

The softest look came over Shy's face. "Yeah, I was surprised, too. Turns out the old guy isn't as harsh as we make him out to be. Turns out we don't have to forgive ourselves to earn his." He seemed to shake off the emotion. "But my work isn't done, and if Myrddin gets his way, that door will close. It will close to all who die. We will be stuck here, and bitterness and anger and confusion will turn the dead into sluagh. Millions of sluagh."

A shudder went through my Fae husband. "That will change the plane."

"A few million demons won't help." Daniel sat back. "So while I'm playing king and possibly bait to draw Myrddin away from the Council building, I assume my wife is coming out of retirement."

I wouldn't stop looking for a way to fix things, but I did have a job to do, and I would need some help. "Lee is the only one who can see the grimoire when it's outside the bag of holding. I'm going to need him. Please tell me you stole the Mantle of Arthur."

Lee shrugged as though that was a forgone conclusion. "I was told I could bring one toy. It was my favorite. Cool. Me and Mom and Grandad. The band is back together."

And we would be playing one last gig.

Chapter Eight

I watched out the window at the bonfire going on in the distance. I didn't question the magic that gave this place under the mountain a night sky and allowed the fires to warm us without choking every creature with smoke. The Fae had some strong magic, and it was enhanced by being here in the land the Huldrefólk had called home for thousands of years. The mountain itself was magic. It was the birthplace of elves and trolls and brownies, one of the strongest Fae places on the Earth plane.

I had to pray it stayed that way now that we were here.

My sons were out there, sitting around the bonfire and drinking with their friends. Likely finding someone to bed down with for the night. Perhaps not Rhys. He seemed to tiptoe around Shy, his eyes on her when he thought she wasn't looking. There was a connection between them that couldn't be denied, but I understood it must be hard to be interested in someone who could turn into your grandfather at any given moment.

Lee, on the other hand, flirted with everyone who came into his space. I thought I'd seen an odd connection with Dean earlier, but Lee seemed to have forgotten him and moved on to trying to seduce a pretty *sidhe*.

"Do you want to join them, my goddess?" Big hands found my shoulders, drawing me back against a muscular chest.

I sighed and leaned against Devinshea. "I think my presence would put a damper on the celebrations."

Though the party was supposedly to celebrate the rescue of the royals, I felt the awkwardness any time I talked to one of the participants. The younger ones, at least. I'd had a lovely talk with Kim Jacobs and the academics, who were old friends. They hadn't seemed to have changed, but everyone else had. Especially my children.

Dev's arms went around me. "I decided the same thing. Daniel said he had to speak to the children before he joins us. It's been a long day."

It had been a day that lasted twelve years.

Sure enough, I saw Daniel walking back toward the house we were in. He had a grim look on his face, and I realized he hadn't fed.

"I'll take care of him." Dev always could read my mind about some things. Or perhaps it was simply that we'd been together for so long, and worrying about Daniel had given us connected minds in some ways. "Why don't you take a bath? Albert said the bathrooms here have tubs, and I assure you he won't mind heating water for you."

I shook my head and moved out of his arms. "No, I think we should talk."

"I think we should do more than talk." Dev was gorgeous by firelight. The shadows played over his features, sharpening some and softening others. His eyes were green jewels in that low light. "We had a terrible day. And a good day."

"What was good about it?"

"Our children are alive," Dev said firmly. "Our children seem genuinely all right, despite the fact that my family failed them entirely."

The door came open and Daniel walked in. "Oh, I disagree. Parts of your family might have failed, but Albert did a wonderful job. Albert saved them. He didn't hesitate. Harry did everything he could, and even held on after death to protect his grandchildren. Trent and Sasha raised them well. The family we put together functioned beautifully. They're good kids."

"I didn't say they weren't good. It's just not fair. They shouldn't have had to flee their home," I argued. "They shouldn't have had to become a paramilitary unit. They should have had their parents with them. Instead of worrying about setting this place right, shouldn't we be trying to find a way back?"

"Back to where?" Daniel stared at me like I'd said something crazy.

Shouldn't he have thought about this, too? I couldn't be the only one who wouldn't accept this loss. "Back to the night we fell through that painting. Back to where we belong."

"And do what?" Daniel sat down on the big bed and pulled his boots off. "Not fall through the painting? Not save Devinshea?"

"Fine, then we go back and we don't let Dev fall through." My frustration was building.

"So we leave Marcus alone?" Daniel asked. "If Dev doesn't go through, Marcus might never meet Summer. We definitely don't meet Dean and bring him back to the Earth plane. Kelsey doesn't get the book. The outer planes fall, and then the inner planes contract in on themselves."

I was sick of all the *ifs*. We could fix this if we tried. "Fine. We go back to a time before and I'll leave a note about what has to happen, but Daniel, they're our children. We lost twelve years with them. We can't allow this to stand."

Daniel looked to Dev. "And what do you think, Devinshea? Should we sneak out of here and go searching for a magical spell that will correct all the injustice we've recently suffered?"

"She needs time. She hasn't been through the things we have. This is a tragedy, and she needs time to process it," Dev said quietly.

"Tragedy means something else to me." Daniel reached for his boots again. "Maybe I should go."

"Maybe you should if you're willing to give up twelve years with our children so you can play the rebel again." It wasn't fair, but it irritated me that Daniel didn't seem to need time. Daniel was handling everything beautifully and with a grace I didn't feel.

A brow rose over his eyes and I could practically feel his anger. "Play the rebel? My love, we *are* the rebels now." He stopped and took a long breath, and then he was in my space, looming over me. "Zoey, this is not the time for us to fight. They need us. I know you think there's got to be some way to get back, but there's not. Even if we understood the mechanics of time travel, there's too much at stake to risk it."

Tears pulsed behind my eyes. "We have to fix it."

"We did." Danny moved into my space. His head dropped to mine, and there was pain in his voice. "We did what we were supposed to do. We helped our daughter take her place. We helped her find a male who will protect her and love her forever. And you feel that loss, too. I know I feel it. It will be a very long time before Summer can walk the Earth plane and come to holiday parties with us and meet her siblings. She might never be able to. We don't know how her position works. We lost so damn much in what felt like a second, but they need us. I'm not merely talking about our kids—though they do. I'm talking about every creature on the plane. If Myrddin succeeds, the Earth plane changes. Every human will be made slaves to the demons. Every supernatural will be in chains or twisted to serve the demons' will."

Why couldn't he see what I wanted to do? "He won't have a chance if we fix things."

"Some things can't be fixed," Daniel replied. "We don't get do-overs. We deal with the hand we've been given and we move on. I've known this since the day I died. Maybe longer. Maybe since my father died, or before that when my mom died and I was shuffled around. That's what Dev is talking about. Despite everything you've been through, you've never really faced a loss like this."

I stepped back. "I faced losing you. I assure you those years of my life weren't fun."

"And you had your dad to help you through it," Dev pointed out. "Daniel came back, and he watched over you, too. Yes, Daniel died, but it worked out in the end. You've never had to face something you couldn't fix. We can't fix this, Zoey."

"You're not even willing to try."

"I'm not willing to waste time on something that has to fail," Daniel corrected. "You know as well as I do that there is a balance to be kept. If we change something in the past, the effects on the future could be unimaginable."

I didn't want to hear about effects. The effects I felt now were unimaginable, but they were getting through to me. No amount of time with my children mattered if Summer doesn't take her place. If we don't fall through that painting, Marcus likely dies. Dev dies when the outer planes fall, and then we die.

The baby inside me is never conceived.

And the payment for all of that, the bill that came with survival, had been paid in full by Rhys and Lee and Evan and Fen. By my father.

"It's okay to mourn now." Dev had moved in behind me. "We're alone. I know I feel it. I feel every year we lost with them."

Daniel reached for me. "Please, we need to be together on this. I know I need you now, Z."

I needed them, and I was letting my anger and fear keep us apart. I'd lost so much time with my kids. I couldn't lose more because they didn't agree with me. We'd all had a rough day, had rough days in front of us, and we needed to be together.

I let the tears roll down my cheeks as Daniel brushed them away with his thumbs. I stared up at him. We hadn't lost each other. Our children were still alive, and there was another growing inside me. It might have to be enough for now. I wasn't giving up on finding a way to change things, but for tonight I let it go and let myself be with them.

Daniel's mouth found mine, bringing us together as Dev's magic started to pulse through the room.

Daniel kissed me long and deep, his tongue sliding along mine even as his hands did the same to the curves of my body. I felt Dev behind me, felt the hard line of his erection against the small of my back. His hands moved around to cup my breasts as he kissed the nape of my neck.

Goddess, I needed this.

"I know this wasn't the way you thought we would come home," Dev whispered. "But it ends the same. No matter where we go, each day ends with me loving you. Me loving you both."

No matter what happened, we were here together.

I let Daniel pull the shirt over my head and toss it aside. Before it even hit the floor, Dev had my bra off. His warm magic stroked over my skin, and it was easier to shove aside all my worries because they had no place here. This was a place for the three of us, a safe space where we expressed what we felt. Love. Passion. Need. Comfort.

We'd come so far from those first tentative days of sharing, those days when we skirted the edges of what we have now. I moved to the side, toeing off my shoes, and Danny moved right in without hesitation. His hand gripped the nape of Dev's neck and he hauled him close, their bodies bumping against each other before settling in, as if they needed that tiny bit of conflict before they made the choice to be together.

But then Danny's hand slid down Dev's back to his waist, where he held him tight as their mouths played against each other, tongues tangling. I love to watch them kiss. So often we're all together and they're focused on me. But I like the reminder that while we're a threesome, we have our own unique relationships with each other.

Danny and Dev needed each other as much as they needed me. They needed each other emotionally, and they'd come to need the physical act of sex together to feel complete. When they made love to me, even when they were rough, there was a delicacy to the act. When Dev and Daniel got it on, it was primal. Sometimes it was almost a fight between the two of them, and they needed it.

A low, sexy growl came from Daniel's throat and his eyes had bled to blue, the vampire inside him coming out and wanting dominance.

And probably dinner. He hadn't eaten all day.

Sure enough his fangs were out, and my arousal shot through the roof as I watched them drag across Dev's skin. Daniel forced Dev's head to the side, giving him full access to his neck. They should have been naked. Then I could have watched their cocks play against each other because there was no way they weren't hard and wanting. The very nature of the feed was sexual. It was why vampires almost always had sex when they fed.

I was pregnant, and Daniel would be gentle with me even when I wasn't. But Dev loved how rough Danny could be. Dev craved that kind of dominance. The sex god in my faery prince loved all sex, and Daniel and I could provide it for him. I would let Devinshea indulge his dominant side while he would lovingly submit to his king.

Dev's whole body tensed before Daniel struck, sinking those magnificent fangs deep. Then Dev relaxed and it was Danny's hands that held him up. Dev became a doll in Daniel's grip, riding the wave of pleasure that accompanied feeding him.

After a moment, Danny released Dev's vein and picked him up, moving him to the bed. It was small compared to what we were used to, but in some ways that would be a comfort. We would have to cuddle, have to be reminded that no matter what happened we had each other.

Daniel pulled his shirt over his head and tossed it aside, his eyes focusing on me.

That was all it took to get my whole body to go gooey, every part of me softening and ready for him.

Those sapphire orbs drew me in, and I went willingly. This was the best place in the world, the one place I could forget about everything and concentrate on what mattered—them.

He pulled me against him, our chests coming together, his arms wrapping around me. "Z, it was awesome making love to you as a human, but this is what I was born to be, who I am. I spent so much time longing for the past. This is all the time we have. Here and now. And I wouldn't be anywhere else but here with you."

He didn't give me a chance to reply, to argue that there was a better place for us if we only tried to find it. He knew how to blow past all my defenses.

He kissed me, dominating me with his mouth. His hands sank into my hair and I suddenly wasn't a queen on the run anymore. I wasn't anyone's royal highness. I wasn't anyone's mom. In those moments, I was simply his. Simply theirs.

Daniel's hands found the cheeks of my ass, bringing me close and letting me feel the hard line of his erection.

I felt another erection against my back and knew Dev had recovered and gotten out of his clothes. Warm skin pressed against mine, his hands coming up to cup my breasts. I was between the two men I loved most in all the planes, and it was the best place to be.

Daniel turned me around, letting Dev kiss me while he got out of his pants. Dev took the time to pick me up, let me wrap my legs around his waist while he kissed my breasts, sucking on each nipple in turn until I was crazy with longing.

Somehow I found myself on the bed, my back against the soft blankets and Devinshea in between my legs. He spread them wide and kissed his way down my torso.

Daniel climbed on the bed next to me, his hand going to my breast as he cuddled close. "I love watching him work."

Dev's head came up, a sweetly lascivious grin on his lips. "It's my favorite job. And since our love is pregnant, I can see a lot of this in her future. Or one of us in the middle, Your Highness."

Danny winked his way. "We'll find a way to take care of her."

They always did. I didn't take this chance to point out that I was only pregnant and not fragile. I suspected they would treat me like fine china for the next nine months. I would let them for the most part because this was probably my last pregnancy. I would do this upcoming job and then happily hide away.

I would definitely let them take care of me this way.

Dev put his mouth right over my pussy, and I couldn't think about anything but how I felt.

Really damn good because that magic of his pulsed through my body.

"Devinshea, this feels amazing, but we need to think about how it affects the others," Daniel said, his voice deep with desire.

Dev didn't bother to look up. He merely worked a finger inside my pussy. "There are wards. Bris can feel them. He says we're safe. They were likely put up for Rhys. I can control it, but the wards will keep my magic inside this room. So enjoy it."

Dev's magic was a drug. It took away anything but the love between us. It heightened pleasure, softened pain, made us warm and happy.

I welcomed it as I welcomed Danny's kiss and Dev's tongue on my clitoris. I welcomed the orgasm that came shortly afterward.

"Come on, baby. I want to feel your mouth on me." Danny urged me to turn over, to get on my knees.

I did as he requested, my body relaxed, but already Dev's magic was working on me, getting me ready for more. I rode that warm, happy wave as Danny moved in front of me, stroking that big cock of his with one hand while Dev moved behind me.

"I love that I don't have to wear a condom. I love feeling you like this. Nothing between us." Dev's cock stroked against my core. His hands gripped my hips as Danny pressed his dick to my mouth. They would treat me like a toy they shared between them, and I was all up for that. A sex toy.

I licked the head of Danny's cock and sucked it into my mouth, gasping when Dev thrust inside me.

He filled me, stretching me in the most delicious way. No matter how many times I'd been with these men, there was always a moment of wonder that came with it, that came with being caught between them.

I moved, paying attention to Daniel as Dev drove me higher and higher. I worked Danny's cock deep, letting my tongue whirl around and loving the taste of him.

I felt the moment his hand tightened on my hair. It was a sure sign that he was close. He stopped letting me play and started using my mouth, fucking in and out as Dev did the same to my pussy. A pulse of magic washed across my skin, pushing me over the edge as surely as the cock deep inside me.

The second orgasm hit me as Danny filled my mouth and Dev stiffened behind me.

We fell together, rearranging ourselves. I was gently pushed and pulled until I was safely tucked between them, warmed by their naked bodies and the soft quilt that covered us.

I let myself revel in the moment. Sleep I thought would elude me was starting to take over thanks to the warmth and relaxation. I was safe for now. I would deal with all the other problems in the morning. I could make decisions then. Tonight was for rest.

Daniel hugged me close, my head on his chest. "Sweetheart, there's something we still need to talk about. I should have told you I suspected it a long time ago, but I didn't want to worry you. Now there's no doubt."

I only half listened to him. I didn't want to. He and Dev were murmuring over me, and the sweetness of sleep beckoned.

"How are you going to kill him?" Dev asked.

If he was talking about Myrddin, I was sure it would be bloody. I yawned and wished they would stop their whispering.

"I think I might leave that to someone else. I don't think I can kill my own child, but it must be done."

I sat straight up in bed. "What?"

Yeah, he had my full attention now.

"I told you she was half asleep," Dev said.

Daniel groaned and let his head fall back.

"What the hell do you mean you're going to kill one of our children?" I nearly screeched the question.

Daniel sighed and started talking.

Chapter Nine

I gratefully took the coffee Albert offered me the next morning. I only allowed myself one mug in the morning during my pregnancies, but I was definitely going to savor this one. It had been days since I'd had coffee, and there hadn't been any of Albert's pastries on the planes we'd visited.

"Are the masters coming?" Albert moved around the dining room. I'd always wondered how such a large demon could move with such delicacy. He inspected the silver coffeepot and settled china cups on their saucers, his clawed hands looking incongruous against the fragile dishes.

But that was Albert. He was the definition of gentle giant.

"Yes. Dev was finishing getting dressed, and Daniel was taking a quick shower. They'll be here any moment." I'd been in shock the prior day. I hadn't taken a chance to talk to him privately, and if anyone deserved my thanks, it was this halfling who'd been so loyal and loving to my family over the years. "I wanted to talk to you."

He straightened up, his horns almost touching the ceiling. "Of course, Your Highness."

It had only been a few days since I'd seen him, but I felt the years between us in that moment, and it brought tears to my eyes. "I don't really want to talk to you. I only have one thing to say." I set my cup down, and there was a moment's panic in his eyes as I moved toward him and wrapped my arms around him. "I love you, old friend. Thank you for everything you've done."

A shuddering sigh went through him and he patted my back. "You are my family, Your Highness. You have been since the day you married the prince. You should understand that the children have become the light of my long existence. I bless the day you came into my life."

I stepped back, grateful he gave me that moment. "And I bless the day you came into mine." I did have one question I wanted to ask him. "That day we disappeared, Grayson Sloane asked if he could speak with you."

Albert nodded. "Yes, the dark prophet came up to the penthouse that morning."

"He warned you, didn't he?" I wasn't sure how I felt about the fact that Gray had known and not warned me. There are two prophets walking the Earth plane. I'd met the first many years before. His name was Jacob and he came from the Heavenly plane. Grayson was the Hell plane's prophet, and like his Heavenly counterpart there were rules that governed his existence. Gray could see all possible futures, but he couldn't clearly warn anyone. Instead he could only speak in terms that could be taken in any number of ways, so I wondered how he'd managed to warn Albert.

"He did, though I did not understand I would need to act so quickly," Albert admitted. "His warning was somewhat cryptic, but that is his nature. He tried. He tried very hard to get me to understand. He made himself sick, Your Highness."

The fact that Gray had been able to get a warning out at all was a miracle, and I tried to tamp down my irritation that Gray had known and not told us. Though even if he'd tried, it likely wouldn't have worked. "So he gave you his whole prophet spiel, and then when Myrddin came to the penthouse, you figured out it was time to move?"

"I understood that if anything happened to you and Daniel, I should run with the children. I should not allow anyone outside our household to gain access to them," Albert explained. "It was Sarah who warned us something was wrong. She came to the penthouse that morning looking for you. She'd heard unsettling rumors."

"Do you know what happened to Sarah?" I felt sick inside that I couldn't find my friend. At least we knew where Neil was.

Albert shook his head. "We realized that our cell phone service was unavailable, and she went to warn Neil and Chad. I did not see her again. Your father and I decided we should move the children. Eddie came with Trent."

"But Gray didn't come?"

"From what I understand, the dark prophet bought us time. He went to speak with the wizard while Eddie and I tried to make the children ready. Harry helped. It was during this time I also wiped the hard drives on all of the computer systems. I locked down the bank accounts as my master taught me, and I gathered the documents required to access the money left. We still have much of the cash Master Dev prepared for such an occasion. I am sorry we couldn't save your father."

He'd taken on such responsibility. "It wasn't your fault. You did what he wanted you to do, what we needed you to do. You were more than we could have hoped for."

Albert tilted his head. "I am happy to have done this duty. I will stay and look forward to welcoming the next member of our family. Congratulations, Your Highness. I'm glad you and Master Daniel had a chance to grace our world with your child. And Eddie is over the moon at the thought of Mistress Kelsey having a baby. Our dark times…well, we're not through them yet, but you bring light and life with you."

"Thank you." It still seemed surreal that I was pregnant. It reminded me of another pregnancy that had come at a bad time. That pregnancy and what happened to me in the catacombs of Paris had come full circle, and I had to face the choice I'd made that day. But I still had questions before I had to deal with what Daniel had told me the night before. "You said Gray was still there that morning. Is he all right? From what I heard last night he didn't stick with you and Trent."

"He could not," Albert explained as we heard someone walking down the hall. "We decided it was easier for Gray to stay away. He couldn't leave the inner planes. He must remain close to the Hell plane, and after he began his descents…well, Hell changes a person.

I'm worried at what Mistress Kelsey might find."

So was I, but the door opened and I had to let it go for now.

"Good morning, Mother. Albert, this looks lovely as always." Evan walked in and picked up her plate.

Albert gave her a nod. "I wanted something special for your parents' return. I'll be helping Eddie prepare for your journey if you need anything else."

"Thank you," Evan said, turning to me when the door closed again. "I hope this family meeting doesn't take too long. We're due to head to Atlanta in thirty minutes. I don't intend to hold Kelsey up."

So she was still in a good mood. "Where's Fen?"

There was a massive buffet laid out, and it couldn't all be for us. Daniel didn't eat, and I scarcely thought the platter of grilled meat was meant for my breakfast.

"I'm going to make him a plate." Evan moved to the buffet. "Dad asked that we make this a family meeting. Fen isn't blood."

I snorted at the thought. If we didn't understand our kids now that they were grown, they certainly didn't understand us. "Daniel isn't technically blood either, but I assure you he's family." I seriously doubted Danny had meant to leave Fenrir out. And if he had, then I was going over his head. I crossed the room and opened the door to the hallway. Sure enough, Fen was leaning against the wall, waiting. "Fenrir, there's half a cow in here for you. Is your mother with you? She's welcome as well."

He was absolutely adorable when he smiled. "Thanks, Your Highness. Mom is taking breakfast in her room. I was going to join her, but she's like super pregnant and apparently not enjoying it. Normally I can eat through anything, but that's some hefty vomit going on there."

"We'll need to make sure to pack some snacks because her morning sickness won't last, and I assure you she'll want food." I ushered him in, grateful this baby of mine didn't seem to have the same effect on me. "Where are the boys? And has anyone seen Grandad?"

I probably should have asked if they'd seen Shy, but in this case it was specifically my father who should be here.

"Shy's sleeping. She projected Grandad a lot yesterday. It takes something out of her. More recently, it's really left her exhausted.

She'll sleep until afternoon at least. As for the boys, they slept out with the trolls. They have a little encampment on the other side of the mountain." Evan passed Fen the plate she was holding and picked up a smaller one for herself. "The room we put you in was spelled to contain Fae sex magic, but Rhys wasn't taking any chances. Which is funny because he's the reason we had to spell the room. Did you know that Rhys doesn't need to actually have sex to infect a whole area with lust?"

"Things got real bad when Rhys figured out how to..." Fen started to giggle and then seemed to realize who he was talking to. "Sorry, Your Highness. I meant…"

"You meant when Rhys masturbates, so does everyone else." I sighed. "If his father had been around he would have taught him to control that."

"I told you Momma isn't a prude." Evan placed a Danish on her plate.

Ah, the first bit of movement after yesterday's debacle. "I've dealt with Rhys's issues for a long time. You try getting called into a school meeting where you have to explain why every teacher in your son's grade is suddenly pregnant. Including the one who'd gone through menopause."

"Yes, that was a fun time." Dev strode in looking as delicious as a man could look. He'd changed into the slacks and sweater Albert had found for him. "Good morning, Evangeline. Fenrir. I hope we didn't disturb you last night."

Fen shrugged even as he overloaded his plate with meat. "Nah, those dampeners work. Sasha made sure Rhys had some serious protections in place after Rhys started an orgy on the werewolf plane. We all saw way too much that night."

Rhys started to walk into the dining room with Lee behind him. The minute he heard Fen talking, he tried to turn and walk back out. Only his twin stopped him. Lee playfully pushed him back into the room.

"Do we have to talk about this?" Rhys's eyes rolled, but he turned and walked in again. "I would rather discuss battle plans. Please tell me this isn't what Dad called us in here to discuss."

Lee's smile went wide. "Goddess, I hope so."

"I promise I can help you control your magic." Dev put a hand on

Rhys's shoulder. "It will still go a bit crazy when you're truly emotional, but you'll be able to control it during sex. I haven't asked you this yet, but have you had children?"

Lee snorted, and Fen nearly lost his plate.

Rhys went a hearty shade of pink.

"Devinshea, maybe you and Rhys should talk about this privately." Sometimes Dev took his open-book policy when it came to sex way too far.

"No, Papa. I don't have children," Rhys replied.

"If you've had unprotected sex, it's entirely possible you could have impregnated a female partner." Dev was never one to back down from a hard talk, especially when it involved sex. "In fact, it's probable, son. You have to be very careful."

Rhys looked his father in the eyes. "I don't have children."

"Papa, he doesn't have children." Evan stepped in as though she thought Rhys might need her.

"Unless he's kept up with all of his female partners, how can he know?" Dev asked.

"Because I haven't had any, okay? I have not had sex with a female. Or a male, or anyone but my right hand," Rhys said through gritted teeth.

"His right hand gets a workout, though." Lee poured himself a glass of juice. "I mean it. That sucker is strong. It can go for hours."

"Remember that when I use it to stab you, brother," Rhys growled Lee's way.

Fen put his overly full plate on the table and couldn't contain his laughter. Evan sent him a dirty look. Fen held up his hands. "Sorry, baby. Hey, I can laugh. I'm absolutely one hundred percent as pure as Rhys. Lee's the slut here."

Lee simply shrugged. "Well, I'm human. You guys have plenty of time to get your freak on. I've got fifty years if I'm lucky."

"Uh, I have a human life-span, too," Evan pointed out. "And yet no one talks about poor Evan having to go without."

Rhys frowned her way. "You're seventeen. You can wait."

"Lee was sixteen when he nearly started a pack war by sleeping with that she-wolf," Evan said primly.

"Yeah, well, we all know that Lee probably won't make it past his twenties the way he's going," Rhys shot back. "He's the most reckless asshole ever to walk the Earth plane."

"Rhys, it's not normal for you to not have sex." Dev's jaw was hanging open in pure shock.

Evan had that prim look on her face I was coming to associate with her raging against the patriarchy. "But it's normal for me because I'm a girl."

"Your brother is a fertility god," Dev argued. "At his age I was quite experienced."

"He means he'd plowed through every female in the *sithein*, and many of the males." I could translate for the kids.

"Zoey, you are not helping," Dev replied.

"I disagree. Mom is helping my case a whole lot. Go Mom." Evan took a seat beside Fen.

I noticed Daniel had joined us. He moved in quietly, his eyes going straight to Lee. After what he'd told us the night before, it wasn't surprising. He'd likely been thinking about what he needed to tell Lee all night long.

I thought we should do it privately, but Daniel had convinced me it was a family issue. Rhys had never been able to hide what he was, nor had Evan had a choice in keeping her glow private.

"Lee turns out to take more after Papa than I do." Rhys sat down, his plate completely empty.

"Lee does not have your needs, Rhys." Dev still seemed to be reeling. "Sex isn't simply for fun when it comes to you. It's a necessity."

Rhys shook his head, his decision made long ago. "I am not in a place where I can take a goddess. I'm not going to risk my magic going wild and getting us all in trouble. You know Myrddin has spies, and an explosion of Fae fertility magic could get through the wards and potentially give away our position."

"See, all Lee risks when he spends the night with a lady is a venereal disease," Fen quipped. "Rhys could start our own personal apocalypse."

"We all know why he's waiting," Evan said quietly.

"Yes, it rhymes with the chick I want has my grandad inside her," Lee snarked.

"I will end you," Rhys vowed.

Evan sent Rhys a sympathetic look before looking back to Lee.

"Stop teasing Rhys. It's hard on him because he's right about the dangerous part. If there's a Fae-sex-magic bomb that goes off, any number of our enemies could come looking for him, including the ones who took Lee's eye."

"I want to know who was involved in that," Dev said, his tone quiet. Dev was often at his deadliest when he went still and quiet. "And son, I can teach you to control your magic. You have to funnel it off. In small bursts or controlled bursts, the wards will hold. Using your agricultural powers can help. When you're stressed or feel the pressure building, grow a couple of trees or a small crop of vegetables."

"Ooo, I've been craving strawberries," Evan offered.

A small smile played on Rhys's lips. "All right then. We can certainly talk about how to take the pressure off me in safe ways. And I'll have your strawberries when you get back."

Evan seemed excellent at calming her brothers down. She'd found her role in the family.

"So is this what we're supposed to talk about? Rhys's sexual disfunction?" Lee proved he could almost keep up with Fen. He'd downed a couple of Danishes and a whole lot of bacon. "Dad said we had family business."

"It's not business." I knew what he meant, but what Daniel was about to say was so personal to me. This was the rest of our lives, this choice we were about to ask the children to make—specifically one of my sons.

"No, it's not, but it's important." Daniel sat at the head of the table.

Fen's hand went over Evan's, as though he was afraid whatever was going to be said next might hurt her. They all suddenly looked like they were waiting for the axe to fall.

"We know Dad is going to take over," Rhys said. "We've always known that. What we will have a problem with is if he chooses to sideline us. We're not the young kids you left behind. We're good at this."

"I know that. But this is not about the war we find ourselves in." Daniel leaned forward, his hands on the table. "It's about something that happened a long time ago. It happened before any of you were born. We were warned about it, but we didn't know what the consequences would be until now. Zoey?"

I sat down next to Lee. We'd decided last night that this was my story to tell. I put a hand over his, and he went tense as he seemed to understand that this was all about him. "When I was pregnant with you and Rhys, we were at war with the old Council. I didn't take part in the last battle, but I was there at the beginning. Marcus tried to get me out, but we were caught. I was shot and your body was injured in utero. Technically we all died that day, but we were given a second chance."

"By the angels," Lee said. He'd heard part of the story before. "It's how I got Lee Owens's soul."

I nodded, tears clouding my eyes. "Yes, but there was something more. The angels told me that one of my babies had been changed, and that we would have to deal with the change down the line. I said I would take you no matter the circumstances."

"What's wrong with me, Mom?" Lee's hand had tightened around mine, and the air around us seemed charged.

"Though it was the angel's energy that sparked us all back to life, it was Daniel's blood that healed our bodies. It was vampire blood that restored your developing body. It was the king's blood that saved you and changed you," I explained.

Lee's jaw dropped, and his eye went wide with surprise and no small amount of joy. "Holy shit. I'm a motherfucking vampire."

I winced, but only a little. I would have to include that in his list of times he could curse around his mom.

Chapter Ten

"Lee, really? Motherfucking in front of our actual mother?" Rhys frowned his way. "That is rude, and none of us wants those two words used together."

Lee turned to his twin. "Are you serious? You find out I'm a latent and the only thing you comment on is my use of language?" Lee gasped as though a truth had hit him. "Dude, this is why I'm so good at languages. It's the dark demon inside me."

"I wouldn't exactly call it a dark demon," Daniel said, a frown on his face, too. "The vampire is a part of you. Son, this is serious. You are a latent vampire and you have a decision to make."

"Fen, you want to kill me? I don't trust Rhys to do it. He would be brutal about it, but you can just pop a claw or something." Lee was grinning from ear to ear. "Or Evan. How about shooting an arrow through the heart you claim I don't have."

"Oh, you have one. You simply don't use it when it comes to women," Evan shot back.

"I do, too. I love them all, which should mean I have the biggest heart of all," Lee replied. "It's huge. It'll be easy to hit."

Rhys held up a hand. "How do we know this? I understand the concept of a latent, but how on all the planes would we know until he died? He's been around vampires all of his life, and no one has ever looked at his dumb ass and said you're one of us."

It was everything I'd feared. When Daniel had explained that Lee was a latent vampire and must be given the same choice he gave all latents, I'd known what Lee would do. When Daniel identified a latent vampire, he offered the latent the choice as to whether he wanted to die in the natural course of time or begin his life as a vampire. Many chose to become a vampire in the prime of their human lives so they spent their "immortality" in a younger body rather than dying naturally. While the vampiric DNA would heal all wounds, it did not change age. The vampire was stuck in a perfect version of whatever body he'd died in. Lee would immediately want to end his human life and walk the night. He would do it so he could be a badass, so he could finally be more than human. So he could feel like he fit into our world. He wouldn't think for a second about what he was giving up.

"Your dad has always been able to tell when a new vampire rises," Dev explained. "It's a necessary but rare talent. In the beginning, that talent was one of the only reasons Daniel survived. Your father can feel when a vampire is going to rise, and oddly enough, we tend to be in a place where it's easy to get to the vampire before he rises the first time. I've always thought it was fate guiding us. Like when Sasha rose. He died in Munich. We were in Italy at the time. Daniel felt his death and we were able to get there before he rose and killed everyone in his general vicinity."

"We were lucky there hasn't been a vampire rising in the last twelve years." Daniel was studying Lee though he spoke to all of us. "I checked last night and the academics have seen no evidence that we've had a rising while I was gone."

"I think that might be fate, too," Dev said under his breath.

"But I haven't died," Lee pointed out. "I mean it was close a couple of times, but I'm still here. Do I get my eye back? I've missed peripheral vision. Think of all the women who escaped my notice simply because they walked by my left side."

Evan huffed, a frustrated sound. "Lee, this is serious."

"So is the fact that I might get my eye back," Lee countered. "My eye was taken with a magical weapon. Vampire blood couldn't save it."

Danny leaned Lee's way. "I assure you that you will have your eye back. The magic worked on human flesh, and when you rise, you will see the world again. You will see it perfectly, and you will be able to avenge all of your losses."

"I thought we weren't going to take a position on this." I sent Danny my harshest frown because we'd discussed this. I knew Danny would feel better if Lee wasn't vulnerable, but Dev and I had argued that there was a point to human life. There was a lot Lee gave up if he rose at this point in time. He was so young. He hadn't fallen in love and had a family. He hadn't gone to college or traveled the world for fun. He hadn't spent days and days in the sun, and he wouldn't if he died.

Danny sat back. "I'm sorry. I get upset when I think about what happened to him. Lee, you need to give this decision serious consideration. The reason I know you're a latent is that I can sometimes feel it before death. I had an inkling when you were a child, though I wasn't certain, which was why I never told your mom or your papa."

"You could feel it when I was a kid?" Lee seemed to have sobered, finally starting to process the news.

"Not exactly," Danny admitted. "It was more how you behaved. It was the connection I had to you. I was afraid it was me seeing what I wanted to see. I wanted a connection to you. I didn't want to lose you."

"You didn't want me to be human," Lee surmised.

Danny shook his head, and it was easy to see he was frustrated. "I didn't want to watch you age. I didn't want to think about you dying. Rhys has the protection of his Fae nature. Yes, he can die, but he'll probably outlive me. At the time I assumed one day Evan would marry a vampire and live a companion's life, which would also mean she outlives me."

But she wouldn't because she was in love with Fenrir. Fenrir, the wolf king, who was looking at two hundred years or so if he merely lived a normal werewolf life-span. Which he likely wouldn't. He was so much stronger than any other wolf that I had to believe he might live longer, too. A companion lived a human life-span without regular vampire blood from her partner. It was part of the exchange. Though Danny had fed from Dev the night before, he'd opened a vein and we'd both had a sip. The king's blood kept Dev and I young and healthy, protected us from injuries.

I would need to make sure Evan took her father's blood from here on out. I hoped she didn't fight me on it.

"What about my childhood made you consider that I could be a…" Lee went a little pale. "It was Mia. I clung to Mia when I was a child. Like you clung to Mom before you turned. I loved Mia. Even when I was a kid, even before I knew what it meant, I loved her. Because she was a companion."

"It's more complex than that." Yes, it was ironic that I was the one making that argument since in the beginning I'd stayed away from Daniel for that very reason, for the idea that our love for each other was a trick of biology. "Yes, you'll always be more attracted to a companion, even before you can see her glow. But that doesn't mean your feelings aren't real. I assure you, your dad has met companions he didn't fall in love with."

"Lee always protects Evan first," Rhys admitted quietly. "It's one of the reasons I split us up when I can. Lee can be even more unreasonable about Evan than Fenrir is."

Fen had gone quiet. More than that, he'd stopped eating.

"I'm glad to know Lee has a reason for being an asshole." Evan had a smile on her face but it was tight and didn't come close to reaching her eyes. "It also explains why he's the most reckless of all of us. That's part of it, right? The latent vampire tends to be reckless."

"Only if there's a companion around." Daniel winced slightly. "I think in the beginning it was about Mia, but if he's reckless now it's because he's been raised around them. There are several here at the base. Simply being around companions—even ones he would have no sexual desire for—would spark the urge to walk the night."

"But there are reasons not to," Dev pointed out. "The good news is, you're in control, Lee. You can make the decision. It might be good to talk to some vampires."

Lee waved that off. "I talk to vamps all the time. Let's kill me and get going."

"Lee, you're still young and you look it. Your dad turned at twenty-one and he had trouble for that very reason." Though Daniel never had real trouble getting into a bar since he used his mental powers to get the bouncer to let him in. It wasn't like he was drinking the liquor or anything. But I was grasping because I didn't think my other arguments would sway him.

"You haven't even had children yet." Dev gave him the argument I didn't think would work.

"I don't want kids. Trust me. There's enough of our DNA out there in the world," Lee argued. "I'm sure Rhys will eventually spread his Fae seed all over the place, and Evan will spit out lots of little wolves. I can be their vampire uncle."

Danny put up a hand. "Stop. You're going to take time to think about this. You cannot turn today."

"I wouldn't," Lee protested. "I promise that I'll let you guys make a big deal out of it. We should have a ceremony or something. I will definitely wait until Evan and Fen get back. We can talk about how to do it, but you have to understand I'm not going to change my mind. I want this. I've wanted it my whole life. And I'll be a better fighter."

"You'll be half a fighter because you'll be dead during the day." Fen put his napkin down. "We'll have to carry you around the way we do Sasha. You won't be able to do anything while the sun is out."

"We can't know that," Lee argued. "It depends on the class. I could end up being a daywalker if I'm an academic."

"The king's base class was warrior." Rhys seemed to know a lot. "Yes, our father is a king, but he would most likely produce warriors."

"Lee wasn't produced the way a vampire would normally be conceived." Dev looked to Rhys. "It's DNA that's passed on through human conception. Daniel's blood healed Lee while he was in utero. His organs were still in early developmental phases. That gave the blood a chance to change Lee. Rhys wasn't damaged so he didn't change at all. Honestly, we can't know Lee wasn't meant to be fully Fae before that moment. So we can't apply past knowledge to this situation."

"Maybe I'm a king, too," Lee said quietly.

"I think that is highly unlikely," Daniel replied. "Despite the odd nature of how you became a latent, there have only been two vampire kings in recorded history, and their rising came at important times. I believe there can be only one at a time. We have to assume your rising will be a normal one, and that means we have to control it."

"Or I'll go insane and eat everyone in sight." Lee's goofy grin was back.

"Yes. You need to be very aware of that and be careful," Daniel warned. "You need to think about how you want to die and who will feed you that night. You'll need blood and sex, and they should come from someone you trust. I'll take you through the part of the turn that restores your control, but the woman you choose will take you through your first feed both physically and sexually."

"Or man." I wasn't going to fence Lee in. He really was like Devinshea, and Dev had a sense of shame when it came to his sexual fluidity when he was younger. I wasn't putting that on my son. I couldn't help but think of the way Lee had looked at Dean. There had been something between them, and it wasn't mere curiosity.

Lee got serious again. "It should have been Mia." He took a long breath and looked back to Danny. "I promise to think about it, Dad. And I'm completely forgetting what we have to do. I can't plan my turn until Mom and I get the bag of holding. The Council is warded against vampires. It will be far easier to slip through as a human. Besides, I think it's either my status as a human or some unique trick of my DNA that allowed me to see the grimoire. Mom couldn't see it."

"Or it was because you were a child." I'd thought a bit about it. Myrddin certainly wouldn't consider a child any kind of threat.

"I've never heard of wards being placed based on age," Dev mused. "I don't know how magic would know a particular age. Perhaps there's a way to identify puberty."

"Or virginity. We know they've got lots of spells concerning the state of a being's purity," Danny said under his breath.

"Then everything in the world is now warded against Lee." Evan's braid shook as she pointed her brother's way.

"Ha, ha. But also fair. We have to hope it was because I'm human and Myrddin wouldn't worry about a human touching his precious," Lee said. "So I keep my human status until we get the job done. I'll think about it, Mom. I promise. I don't promise I'll change my mind, but I will listen to you. We can talk about it while we plan the job. I'm sure Granddad will have lots to say, too. For a dead dude, he does not stint on the advice."

Evan stood and went to Lee, her hand going to his shoulder. "I'm happy for you, brother. But you should eat all your favorite foods because there's no more Danishes for you after you go on the all-blood diet. And no more beer."

That got Lee to frowning. "I hadn't thought of that. Huh. I should do all the drugs before I die. I've got a list. I was waiting to try them when I was super old, but I should start now."

Rhys's head fell back. "I knew this would happen. Lee is already a ball of chaos. I don't see how giving him fangs and claws is going to help things."

They were off, all three siblings arguing playfully. Fen was the only quiet one, his eyes on Evan.

I knew we'd made the right decision to tell Lee, but I still hated the fact that we were discussing the end of his human life. He would spend an eternity without the sun.

I could fix it. I could find a way to go back and we would have his whole childhood to ease him into this, to make being human and having a family seem more…

I didn't know what I was thinking. I wasn't even really thinking of Lee in that moment. I was thinking of what I'd lost. What we'd lost as a family.

Still, I had to admit, they were close. We'd done something right. Our children loved each other. Though they were planning one of their deaths and having fun with it.

"It's going to be okay, my goddess." Dev leaned over and kissed my cheek. "I know you're worried, but you must eat. Do you remember what happened when you didn't?"

Danny stood up. "I do. I had a fainting spell, and Devinshea has never let me live it down. Rhys, be prepared to grow some potatoes because your mother craves them when she's pregnant. Goddess, I hope there's plenty of butter here."

"And cheese." I wouldn't need it. I meant to be back in the right timeline before this baby was born. I would have Albert prepare all those potatoes in our kitchen in the penthouse. Where we belonged.

Would this baby be born at all if I played around with the timeline? Did it matter if I brought her into this world where she would be hunted? How did I weigh one child against another? What did I owe each of them?

Danny was at the buffet loading it up with pretty much

everything I loved. Normally.

Rhys smiled as he looked over at me. "The trolls here make the best butter. Apparently the cows are enchanted. I think you'll be perfectly comfortable here, Mom."

Fen stood, leaving his half-eaten plate behind. "I can assure you the cheese is great, too. I'm going to check on my mom. We're supposed to leave soon. Evan, given what we've learned, if you would rather stay with Lee, I understand. Eddie and Casey are coming with us so Mom and I will be okay."

Fen walked out and Evan's jaw dropped.

"What the hell was that about?" Evan walked to the door.

"Is he mad because I'm a vamp?" Lee suddenly looked worried.

"I don't think so." I suspected it had to do with being reminded of Evan's life expectancy and how little he could do about it. It was likely something he didn't think about at all. Fen was young, and despite the circumstances of the last few years, there was privilege that came with being the biggest, strongest wolf on the plane. He didn't worry about death. "Evan, maybe you should talk to him, but don't leave without seeing me. You're going to start taking your father's blood."

Evan stopped, her eyes going wide. "I'm going to… You know we dose on vamp blood before we go on a mission. We're not careless. Sasha would never send us out without vampire blood in our systems."

"My blood is different than Sasha or the academics." Danny put the plate in front of me. "Even a little of my blood can slow your aging process and make you stronger than you are now. You should take some every day. You can put it in coffee or tea. If you think it's going to bother Fen, then I'll talk to him."

"I think Fen was reminded that he can't give her what a vampire can," Dev said.

"He can give me everything I need." Evan turned to Danny. "If you'll send some with me, I promise to take it. I'm going to talk to Fen. And Lee, do not die while I'm gone. I think we should have a whole ceremony and yes, I will totally put an arrow through your heart and take a video to share with all your bitter ex-lovers. It'll be fun."

"My ex-lovers aren't bitter," Lee complained. "I leave them all quite satisfied."

"Are you absolutely sure he's not Fae?" Rhys got up and grabbed a plate, his appetite seeming to come back.

"I'm all vamp, brother. I was just raised around a lot of Fae and it had an effect." Lee sat back, looking pleased with himself. "It explains a lot. I need to find a comfy daylight resting place. Sasha complains bitterly when he has to sleep in a body bag. We did that a lot when we were on the run."

The door opened again and Shy stood there dressed in a pretty yellow sweater, jeans, and knee-high boots. "I know this is a family thing. Can I grab some coffee?"

It was time to be the queen. Of all Vampire. Of this little base we found ourselves in. Of my family. "Please, join us Shahidi. You are more than welcome. I understand my father tired you out yesterday."

Rhys moved in, having gotten a cup of coffee in record time. He set it down at the place to his left, holding the chair for Shy. "It takes a lot out of her. She won't be able to let him out again probably until this evening."

"Can he still hear us?" I found my sense of humor was coming back online. And my cheekiness.

Shy sat down and reached for the sugar bowl and creamer. "Oh, yes. He's still with me, but it takes a lot out of both of us for him to be able to speak directly through me."

"Ah, well, we were discussing the fact that Lee's a latent vampire and wants to transition as soon as possible," I offered.

"Oh, that's so mean, Momma." Lee snorted and downed a slice of ham.

Shy went still for a moment. "Yes, he has feelings about this. Many feelings. I might need to make this coffee Irish."

Danny leaned over and kissed my cheek. "You are a cruel queen and an even meaner daughter. You eat and talk to our sons. I'm going to get Evan's care package ready. I'll meet you outside when they're ready to go."

He would bleed for her was what he meant. As he did for all of us. The least I could do was eat so we all kept our strength up. I nodded and picked up a muffin as Danny walked out.

"I'll make mine Irish, too," Lee announced. "After all, I'll only be able to drink for another couple of weeks."

"You will do nothing of the kind since you're supposed to be planning a heist with our mother." Rhys turned to Shy. "And I will not let grandfather drive you to drink."

"There are many things about this situation that drive me to drink," Shy admitted. But a little smile curved up her lips as she looked at Rhys. "It's not all bad though. Harry is happy, though he wants to have a long talk with Daniel."

I would let that conversation happen since Danny deserved it.

The three of them started talking and joking. Dev sat beside me and for a moment we enjoyed the morning.

* * * *

An hour later I watched as Evan waved and put a hand on Eddie's small shoulder. Eddie was transporting them to Atlanta. With Eddie included there were five of our group headed off to meet with Trent and the primals. Casey had packed up his laptop and everything he would need to communicate with the base. Fenrir had a backpack over one shoulder and a small cooler in his other hand. I happened to know it contained a whole bunch of sandwiches and a small thermos of blood for Evan's use. Kelsey had her own backpack, which most importantly contained that book she'd brought back from the outer planes. She'd hugged me and promised to find the weapon we needed to give Lee and Dean their best shot at taking out Myrddin. I'd promised to watch after Dean.

We'd made the decision to keep Dean here because he needed to get to know Lee. Now that we knew Lee had vampiric powers to look forward to, it made even more sense that he could possibly be the one to kill Myrddin. Dean hadn't argued. They were already talking, Lee telling him about his newfound vampire status as the slight hint of brimstone that accompanied Eddie's teleportation wafted through the air.

"I don't like leaving things with Evan like that." Dev had an arm around my shoulders.

"You'll have time to make it up to her," Daniel promised. "They'll be back in a few days, and it will be good to see Trent again. Maybe go easier on Fenrir. Those two have a lot of obstacles to get through. Don't be another one."

"Well, they have obstacles because it will be difficult for them," Dev argued. "At some point Fen will need to take his throne. It would be far better for all of us if he did. He can control the wolves. Well, for the most part. I don't know that he can force them to accept Evan as his mate. Any children they have won't be full-blooded wolves."

"We don't know what will happen. Our job as her parents is to give her good advice and support her." They needed to understand that not accepting Evan's relationship with Fen wouldn't break them up. It would break them off from our family, and then they would be alone. "I need to get ready for Neil. He's supposed to come by this afternoon."

I couldn't wait to see my old friend. It wasn't the first time he'd aged and I hadn't. Once he'd spent thirty years in Hell while a few days had passed here. I had to hope these years had been far happier than those.

There was a clanging sound and the ground shook slightly. I saw Lee start to run our way, Rhys at his side.

"What is that sound?" Daniel asked.

"It's the alarm." Lee had my elbow in his hand, starting to guide me away. "Someone is approaching the base. From the sound of it, a lot of someones. It could be an attack. I have to get you to safety."

It looked like the war was already beginning.

Chapter Eleven

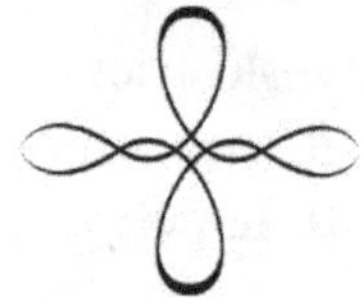

I pulled against Lee, trying to see what was going on. There were two groups moving. One was headed further into the base and the others were heavily armed and moving the opposite direction.

Guess which way my husbands were going.

"Is it Myrddin? Can he get in?" It did not escape my notice that our only way out had recently teleported to Atlanta.

"We're heavily fortified, but I don't know what Myrddin could do if he's at the gates." Lee didn't let up and frowned my way. "We have protocols in place, Mom. Don't make me carry you to the safe house. There's a house deep in the mountain that has extra protections on it. Myrddin shouldn't be able to find it, and if he gets close, you'll be able to sneak away via a set of magical portals. There's one that only opens from this side and leads to a cave where we keep a ship that will take you out to sea."

It was good to know they had a plan in place, but I wasn't sure how I felt about hiding when my husbands and sons were going to battle.

"I don't need to go to the safe house, Rhys," Shy insisted.

It looked like Shy was having the same problem I was. Rhys had picked her up and was striding resolutely our way.

"You do if we have an army at our gates," Rhys replied flatly. "Until the dead you can talk to can also hold a sword or wield some battle magic, you go to the safe house."

Shy stared up at him. "It's not a damn army. It's the wolves, and they're the ones who lost pack members. My dead might not be able to physically fight, but they can give me information so you don't hurt our allies."

I dug my heels in. "The wolves? Neil's pack? They're the ones on the outside?"

Rhys stopped, too, and suddenly Shy was on her feet. "You're sure?"

Shy nodded and pointed to her left at something…someone we couldn't see. "Unless this wolf is lying to me, which he assures me he is not. They were attacked this morning. They need help. Every second you leave them outside the mountain is another chance for them to be found. They have a witch with them who is giving them cover, but she's dying. She won't be able to hold out for long."

Lee's hand came off my elbow and I took the opportunity to turn and run for the main gates.

"It's Neil! Let him in," I yelled.

Shy was running next to me, Rhys at her side.

He held a hand up, waving it. "Turn off the alarms. Let them in quickly. They're safe."

It was good to know Rhys trusted Shy. He'd taken her word without question, and that made me trust her as well. Daniel nodded to the women standing near the doorway we'd come through. They were Fae and seemed to use their magic in a collective way since they held hands and formed a circle before the doorway shimmered and the tunnel appeared.

And so did my closest friend. Neil stood at the front of the group of wolves. A ragtag band, because they looked rough. Some of them were so young, barely teenagers. Some old and likely thrown out of a cruel pack. Neil had brought them together. A brown wolf bounded forward, rushing through the tunnel ahead of the others as the rest of the group struggled to help the wounded make it inside.

It was hard to see once they'd moved into the tunnel because it was dark in there. Now I realized how much Dean had lit our way the day before. Dean was standing with the women whose magic guarded our mountain base. His eyes were closed as though he was lending them his strength or perhaps studying the magic they made.

"That's our Circle," Lee whispered my way. "They're our witches, the ones who managed to get out and find their way here. Or they were already in Europe. There weren't many witches who didn't heed Myrddin's call, but there are a few who work with us, and the ones who live in Frelsi are beyond reproach."

One of those witches looked awfully familiar. "Is that Sarah's sister?"

"Yes," Lee acknowledged. "Lily showed up here long before we came. When Myrddin rose, she led a small band of witches here to take shelter. They've guarded the Huldrefólk ever since."

I saw the moment the witches went stiff. Lily Tucker opened her eyes.

"Your Highness, I feel something coming. It's not corporeal, but it's looking. Something is out there probing the mountainside. Myrddin's eye," she said, her voice tremulous. She was a few years older than Sarah and unlike her sister, she preferred her hair in its original color which was now a pretty brown with streaks of steel.

"Get those wards up," Rhys ordered. He'd taken the leadership role, Lee standing beside him, a sword in his hand.

"It's looking for wards, Prince Rhys," Lily insisted. "It's followed the pack. It's behind them but getting closer."

Myrddin had sent out an eye to search for us. If he found us, we could expect a battle long before we were ready.

"Close the wall," a deep voice said. "Close it now. I'll handle the eye."

Dean had said the words. He moved to the beginning of the tunnel, standing in the center, holding his palms open at his sides. The witches looked to Rhys for confirmation.

"Do it," Lee ordered.

"We trust him?" Rhys asked his twin.

"Yes," I said. "He's trustworthy, and he understands magic this plane has no knowledge of. Let him try. Kelsey trusts him with her life."

Rhys nodded. "Close the outer wall."

I felt a shimmer go through the air around me and knew we were closed off from the outer world again.

Then there was a shift in the air, power flowing from a new source. Dean. His hands glowed slightly and the whole base seemed to go silent as we waited, the very air around us stilling except for the buzz of power that seemed to come from Dean. Even the wolves in the tunnel went silent, covering their wounded with their bodies as they waited to see if we would be invaded.

It wouldn't come in that moment. Myrddin would need time to gather his forces.

Unless he simply planned to bombard us from afar. Were we about to be hit with a fireball? Or a magic bomb that would blow us all away?

Dev's hand found mine, squeezing as though he knew my thoughts. They were probably the same as his, but his face never changed from its stoic expression. We waited, Daniel standing at the front of the group, and I could see his claws out. He would throw himself into whatever fight came our way.

The witches relaxed, Lily looking to Rhys. "The threat has passed. I don't know how or why, but I can sense it moving on. I do not believe it found us."

"I put up a veil." Dean had gone paler than usual. "It's something we used to do when we were hiding out from, well, from everyone. The witches who were after Summer in particular had some spectacular ways to find hidden wards, so my old mentor taught me how to put up a veil. It's a thin coating that bounces the magic back at the probe spell. All it senses is itself. And the natural environment."

"You doing okay?" Lee moved in, offering support.

"I probably should eat something. Something felt weird about that magic. It was so oddly familiar," Dean admitted. "I don't know. Like I said, it was weird. I'm not used to the power I can tap on this plane."

"I'll make sure he gets back to the *brugh*." Lee let Dean lean on him. "I'll get him something to eat and then come back. We'll need to make a place for the wolves."

I nodded as they started back for the *brugh*.

The brown wolf had resumed her progress. She was in her wolf form and so slight and delicate, I didn't think she could be anything but female. She hit the end of the tunnel and stopped as though shocked at what she found. She lifted her nose and scented the air and then all of her focus was on Danny. The wolf bounded right toward him.

Dev held my hand and we ran to join him. The threat seemed to have passed, and I wanted to help those wolves. I could see shadowy figures in the tunnel, starting to make their way toward us now that the danger was over.

The wolf made it to Daniel and then she was a lithe young woman with a mass of brown hair and familiar eyes.

"Is that Courtney?" My heart felt like it would stop. When I'd left she'd been a little girl who was afraid of pretty much everything in the world. She'd been a tiny werewolf who'd played in my home, watching movies and pretending with her cousins. Because while her father wasn't my blood, he was my brother.

"I think so, my goddess." Dev picked up the pace.

Courtney Owens stood in front of Daniel, her brown eyes wide. "Uncle Dan…Your Highness."

"You had it right the first time," Daniel assured her. "Where is your father? I heard he was ill."

Tears fell from her eyes onto her cheeks and she pointed behind her. "He's with Mom. He's been getting weaker and weaker, but what happened today pushed him over the edge. I don't think he's going to last. We made our way here. We didn't know where else to go. I'm sorry. We didn't mean to put you in danger."

She was still a baby, and she had such responsibility on her shoulders. I moved in, my arms open to offer her a hug if she wanted it.

"Aunt Z." Courtney wrapped her arms around me. "You're here. You're really here."

Tears welled in my eyes in response to the relief in her voice. How hard had it been on my sweet niece? On all the wolves? "I am, sweetie, and your uncle Daniel is going to help your dad. Take us to him. He doesn't have to wait."

She nodded and started to turn, but the wolves were making their way out of the tunnels. Neil carried one end of a stretcher, a young wolf I didn't recognize carrying the other end. There were others trailing in, but my eyes were on that stretcher because I recognized the she-wolf walking next to it.

Lisa Owens, Zack's wife. She walked beside the stretcher and there was a sling around her body, a toddler clinging to her.

Neil held up a hand and they lowered the stretcher to the soft grass. He looked around and his eyes stopped on Danny, and I watched a shudder of relief go through him. "Daniel, he's dying. He needs you. Please."

Daniel was already rolling up his sleeve, moving in and kneeling down. Courtney held her mother's hand and watched.

Neil strode up to me and I found myself in a bear hug. "God, Z. What the fuck took you so long?"

"It's only been a couple of days for me," I admitted, holding him close.

He pulled away, looking back to Zack. "Bitch. I missed you. I'll break down and let you pamper me when we figure out if Zack is going to live or die. He's been weak, but whatever that asswipe sent through our camp damn near killed him. I'm sorry. I didn't know where else to go, and I couldn't leave the rest of them behind."

He took my hand and pulled me closer to where Zack lay.

He looked pale, and he'd lost so much weight. His brown hair was limp against his forehead. Zack took such pride in his clothes and took care with his appearance. He'd modeled himself after Devinshea, wearing slick suits and keeping up a meticulous grooming routine. He looked more wolfy than I'd ever seen him with a scraggly beard. I didn't like it. The years had not been kind to this man who'd become family so long ago.

"Your High…Dan…it's been so long. I thought you were gone," Zack whispered.

Danny put a hand on Zack's shoulder. "We got trapped and then something went wrong when we came back. We never meant to be gone so long."

"He needs blood, Dan." Lisa didn't prevaricate. "You can explain later. Save him now."

"Lisa…" Zack admonished.

Danny simply bit into his own wrist and started the flow. He put his wrist to Zack's mouth. "She's right, old friend. Take what you need. We'll sort it all out later."

As Zack began to heal, we all took a deep breath and realized what we'd managed to avoid.

* * * *

Two hours later, we sat at the big dining room table that also served as a conference room. Though because there were wolves involved there was also food. Lots of food. Albert had started cooking the minute he found out who our guests were. I happened to know he was planning yet another feast for this evening. Though the wolves would likely simply call it supper.

"How long has Zack been sick?" Daniel paced the floor. "How did you end up here? Why didn't you go with the kids? Is Chad sick, too?"

Neil set down the turkey leg he'd been eating. I'd helped him settle everyone into various shelters around the base before we'd come back here for the debrief. I'd watched in a bit of shocked wonder as Neil had capably handled his small pack. They'd all looked to him or Lisa, who'd introduced me to my nephew Justin who was three years old and looked like his father.

"Which question should I answer first?" Neil asked. "Do you want a rundown of what happened when you disappeared or my analysis of why Zack has been in decline? Chad is good. He hasn't had your blood in years, but he's kept himself under control."

That turkey leg was getting thin. I moved to serve him some of the enchiladas Albert had made. We'd asked for some privacy and I'd promised to pamper my dearest friend. "I think you should start with Zack. Danny's feeling guilty."

"And confused," Danny admitted. "I know after you stopped taking my blood, you lost the strength it had given you, but it didn't make you sick."

"Of course it did," Neil said softly. "You weren't around to see how it affected me."

When Daniel and Neil had broken off their working relationship, Neil had left us for over a year. He'd gone to the woods and kept mostly to wolf form. He'd been weak when we'd found him, but at the time we'd thought it was because he hadn't been in human form for such a long time. "You didn't need Danny's blood to bring you back."

Neil smiled my way. "No, I needed you and Sarah's tough love and these enchiladas. Some things never change." He looked back to

Daniel. "I was sick in the beginning. I was very weak. That was why I stayed in wolf form for as long as I did. Over time, the sickness went away, and then it was loneliness that kept me from turning the way I should have. But I never got as bad as Zack has been. I don't think Zack's sickness is all about not having access to the king's blood. I think it started years ago. When Myrddin took over the Council building, Zack fought. He fought hard." Neil sighed. "How much do you know about that day? Am I about to be the bearer of really shitty news?"

"We know very little." Dev sat next to where Daniel would sit had he not had so much nervous energy. "Last night was about getting the lay of the land. This evening we're scheduled to have a full debrief on everything Sasha and the academics know about that day."

"So I have to tell you because I don't want Zack to have to do it." Neil put his fork down, a sure sign that whatever he was going to say would be bad. "When Trent fled with the kids, Myrddin decided to lock the Council headquarters down. He called everyone together and told us the royals were dead and the academics had done it. He blamed Marcus."

"Yes, we know that, though I still don't understand his logic. Why would Marcus and the academics want to take me out?" Daniel asked.

"Because they wanted the throne. Everyone knows the academics have always been active in politics. It's easy for some people to believe they decided it was their time to rule. Especially among some of the vampire factions. According to Myrddin, Kelsey was in on it. Having a Hunter helped them decide this was the right time to move on the throne, as Hunters are connected to academics. She would be their *Nex Apparatus* when Marcus took the crown," Neil explained. "None of us close to the throne believed it, of course, and when Myrddin realized we didn't, he attacked. I believe he wanted to take out those closest to the royal family. They targeted me, Sarah, Zack, and some of the vampires in Daniel's circle. You have to understand. That day was chaotic. Sarah and I split up because we both had to protect our families. Most of the vampires were sleeping. Hugo helped me hide Chad's body until we could get out. By the time night fell, most of the damage was done."

"Who did we lose?" Daniel asked the question flatly, but I knew how much the answer would hurt him.

"We lost most of the vampires who were in the building at the time. The academics were able to hide because they're daywalkers. Hugo and Henri and Casey did what they could, but we still lost several," Neil said. "Including Justin. It's why Zack and Lisa named their surprise kid after him. We all loved Justin. Myrddin's group busted through the doors to their apartments and staked the vampires in their beds. Zack tried to save the rest. I was with him when Myrddin's group caught us trying to smuggle out a group of shifters. Zack held the line while I got them out. Myrddin hit him with something, a ball of darkness from his hands. I don't know. I only know Zack was never the same. I got him out, but he was sick after that. We managed to take the stash of king's blood we had. Casey snagged it when he realized Liv wasn't coming with us. We had enough for a couple of months, and that helped. I think if Casey hadn't saved it, Zack would have died."

"You got Chad out?" Daniel asked.

Neil nodded. "Yes, we used the tunnel under Ether."

Dev's brows rose. "What tunnel?"

"The one we didn't tell you about because it was obvious Myrddin had some kind of control over you." Neil frowned and turned to me. "Sarah and I decided when Myrddin showed up that we might need a secret way out. We didn't tell you, Z, because it was better you didn't know. I didn't want you keeping more secrets from them. I understand if this is considered treason…"

"It's considered smart because Myrddin had compromised us." Danny finally sat down. "I'm grateful you took precautions."

"There's a tunnel under Ether?" Dev seemed shocked at the idea.

"Yes. The kids didn't use it because they were already teleporting. We didn't want to risk giving it away if we didn't have to. And it's warded. Sarah protected it with her heart's blood. We weren't sure one of us wouldn't have to go with them. I know she allowed Zoey and I safe passage through." Neil's appetite seemed to pick back up.

"I want a list of the dead," Daniel said. "Justin. I turned him myself. He was a good kid. Damn it. Did they get Angelina?"

Angelina had been Justin's girlfriend. She'd fought her own pack to be with the vampire. She was also Lisa's sister.

"She was at her mom's that day. She was out of town with Lisa and Courtney. They'd gone to Denton to be with their pack and by the time they found out what had happened, it was over. I think they would have killed her, too, if she'd been home. I know she wouldn't have sat by and let them kill Justin," Neil explained. "We picked them up there and when we went on the run, Angelina came with us. She eventually met a wolf and mated with him. She's in France with his pack. It took us years to settle down because there was a bounty on our heads, but we found a few packs willing to hide us. When Trent and Sasha settled the kids here for the winter months, we took to the forests. We've been there ever since. Until today. I thought Myrddin had basically forgotten about us."

"Until we returned. Obviously he communicated with Liv, and he knows we're back and we got away. Neil, I'm sorry. We should have brought you in last night. I thought we would have more time," Daniel admitted. "What exactly happened?"

"I was getting ready to make the journey here. I wanted to ask you to heal Zack myself. I knew you would, but I wanted to explain the situation, to prepare you for it. A little after dawn it hit." Neil took a long drink of water before he continued. "It was like a slow wave of nausea at first. I thought I was getting sick until I realized Brendan and Cassie were feeling it, too. They're the kids Chad and I…well, it's not a formal adoption, of course, but they call us both Dad. Brendan's pack decided he would be an alpha one day and the current alpha doesn't like challenges. They left him on his own when he was six years old. Cassie was born with a genetic defect that makes it hard for her to turn. She was only three when her pack abandoned her. They're teens now and quite healthy, so I knew something was going wrong."

My heart clenched at the thought of Neil having kids. I'd met them briefly when he'd settled them into the small *brugh* Lee had made ready for them. The kids had carried Chad's sleeping body in and made him comfortable and promised to watch over their vampire dad while their wolf dad debriefed the royals.

"Was it a spell?" Dev asked.

"It was some kind of dark magic. I think it was probing us. I felt it move around, flicking like a sharp tail inside me." Neil's voice had gone deeper than normal. "Lily made sure we had some magical defenses and when they kicked in, we decided to run. It was Myrddin. I know because he spoke to me directly. I suppose he was looking specifically for me."

"And what did he have to say?" Daniel asked.

"He said I should tell you to turn yourselves in, to plan no rebellions, and all will be well. All you have to do is come to the Council building. Or you can contact him and he will meet you. He told me this was all a misunderstanding. I was the only one who heard his voice, so I have to think that eye of his recognized me. You have to know that he's lying. He will kill you. He'll kill you all, though I suspect he'll torture you first. The rumors are someone stole his grimoire."

"I'm sure you were in on that," Dev accused. "We didn't find out until much later."

"Until we had the thrall stones removed," Danny pointed out.

"I will need to hear all about the thrall stones, and I would like the whole story of how Daniel handled being human." Neil took a bite of the enchiladas and sighed. "So good. I'm staying close to Z because Albert goes into beast cooking mode when she's pregnant. Anyway, he suspects our favorite thief had something to do with his big book going missing, and it's killing him. The demons are willing to give him some time, but it's been over a decade, and even the immortal know that's too long. He needs that grimoire, and I worry now that you've returned, he's going to find a way to put pressure on you to talk."

"We're going to steal it back," I told him.

"Well, of course we are." Neil's lips curled into a smile. "And luckily I know exactly how to get in the building."

It looked like this would be a three-man job.

Chapter Twelve

I stared out over the party and wondered how long it would take to find my godmother. If anyone would know how to fix the situation I found myself in it would be Ingrid. Naturally, though my godparents had helped build the protections that allowed Frelsi to flourish, they didn't live in the city. They were somewhere in Iceland walking the bridges and living the way they had for millennia.

I wasn't sure I would be allowed to go looking for them. Well, I was fairly certain I wouldn't.

"Oh, Z, I was wondering where you would be brooding," a familiar voice said. Neil moved out of the shadows and sat beside me on the porch steps. He'd changed out of his earlier clothes and looked more like the Neil I knew in dark-wash jeans and a stylish shirt that brought out the stark blue of his eyes.

There was a huge bonfire going, and lively music sounded through the base. The Fae were dancing and feasting with the wolves and others inside Frelsi. Dev was sitting around the fire with Rhys at his side, holding court, while Daniel had closed himself up with the vampires. Chad had joined Sasha, the academics, and to my horror, Alexander Sharpe, who apparently loved playing the spy.

"I reserve the right to brood." I didn't look his way because I was pretty sure I was about to get a bestie tough-love talk and I didn't want it.

Neil was quiet for a moment. "I know you saw me a few days ago, but it's been over a decade for me, and I've missed you. I've missed you and Sarah. You have no idea how many times over the last few years I've had long conversations with the two of you in my head. I can't talk to Sarah. I won't ever see her again, but I had some hope for you."

I felt my heart constrict at the thought. There was so much loss in this place. "You really think Sarah's dead?"

He nodded, his eyes on the fire in the distance. "Yes. I know she didn't leave that building. Neither did Mia or Felix. No one saw them after noon the day after you disappeared. I have to believe if she'd lived she would have found a way to connect with me or Trent afterward. She wouldn't hide and not let anyone know where she was. But like I said, she didn't leave the building."

"How can you be sure?" I would way rather be upset with her that she hadn't called than know she was dead.

"Because I talked to everyone I could. I know she didn't use the tunnel because I had a CCTV on it. And I hired a team to look for her. They checked all CCTVs in the neighborhood and none of the Days show up on them. She hasn't used her bank account or credit cards. She hasn't gotten in touch with anyone, including her sister. We tried a locator spell and we got nothing," Neil said. "She was one of Myrddin's biggest targets that day. Even bigger than me because of how powerful her magic was."

Until I saw a body, I wouldn't believe it, but I felt Neil's pain. He'd had a long time to come to terms with the loss.

I didn't accept the loss at all. Not of Sarah or Justin or of time with my kids.

"I'm sorry you had to go through that. All of it."

"Z, you know it wasn't your fault."

I shrugged. "Maybe it was. Maybe I should have pushed harder all those years. I knew something was wrong with Danny and Dev. I knew it every time Myrddin was around."

"Yeah, well, I did, too, but I didn't think that asshole had shoved demon bones in their heads." Neil shivered. "It's a pretty clever trick, though. I bet Nimue has one, too. Though you should know no one's seen her in years. She used to be by his side, but according to our spies, she hasn't left the Council building or even her rooms for that matter."

Nimue had been there the day Danny and Dev had been infected. She had been vulnerable, too, and she'd changed shortly after that day. It had happened the day Myrddin had fixed Danny's heart. Nimue had held the stasis chamber that allowed the operation to take place. She'd been unconscious while she held the magic. After, she'd chosen to stay with Myrddin. The next time I'd seen her she'd been a different person.

"If she is, I don't know how to get the thrall stone out," I admitted. "Dean has been studying them though. He could try. He seems way more powerful on this plane."

"I noticed he and Lee seem to be getting along." Neil said the words with a cautious tone, like he wanted to get into something but thought he needed to ease me into the topic.

Well, it was my son's sexuality, and Neil had a lot of experience with parents struggling to accept the truth. I did not have that problem. "You mean they have a crackling sexual chemistry between them?"

Neil shrugged. "You have to admit Dean is pretty cute. He's got that silver-haired but-really-young thing going for him."

"And he has a thing for my kids. He was half in love with Summer." I'd told him a lot about what had happened with Summer and Marcus while we'd worked together this afternoon.

"So sexual fluidity is big in the outer planes, too," Neil mused. "You're handling this pretty well."

I snorted. "Am not. I've got one daughter in what's probably a hopeless relationship. One who's a sex god afraid of sex. And one who seems to have worked his way through most of the supernatural world. And who's ready to die, but only after he's tried a bunch of illicit drugs because as he puts it, he's going to die anyway and doesn't have to worry about getting addicted."

Neil's laugh rang out. "I love your kids."

I turned slightly so I could see Neil's profile. "Yours seem pretty cool."

His smile got bigger, the love he felt right there on his face. "They're awesome. I know it's not the way I thought I would start a family. I thought Chad and I would find a way to adopt a baby. That's what we're taught. You hold that baby in your hands and you're a parent. It wasn't like that for me."

"That's the easy way, I think. Not that any of it's easy. They put this tiny thing in your hands and you have a profound connection to this wriggling bundle and you're a parent. You had to choose. You had to look and see a need you didn't create and build that profound connection. You didn't get the perfectly clean ground to plant that garden in. You got all the mistakes and fuck-ups from someone else, and you had to start there. Do you understand how brave you are?"

He sighed, a soft sound. "I don't know about that. I couldn't leave them alone, you know. For a couple of years there I thought it had gotten better. I thought we'd fought the battle and my world was safer for wolves like me. Instead, it all just went underground. When Myrddin took over and the Council fractured, it came to the surface. Not all packs, but the brutal ones can do whatever they like again. They left Brendan to die in the woods alone. Chad found him one night while he was hunting. From what I can tell he'd been in wolf form for a long time. We had to teach him how to speak again. Cassie…they brutalized her, but she still had the sweetest smile. Somehow that little girl managed to survive with her soul intact. God, Z, I love them so much. I didn't know I could love the way I love them."

I reached out and held his hand. He'd become a parent. He'd chosen to love. "You've done a magnificent job with them."

His hand squeezed mine. "I hope so. I feel like I'm fumbling all the time. It came so naturally to you and Sarah."

"Hah. That's where you're wrong. It did not come naturally. We learned on the job. The biggest problem we had in the beginning was how to change a diaper and get them on a sleep schedule." Those times had been tough, but they'd eased me into motherhood, letting me dip my toe into what would become a vast ocean of emotion and decisions, teaching me how to handle what would be harder than I'd dreamed. "You were thrown right into the deep end and you swam. Neil, one of the things I've learned—and you were one of my teachers—is there is no one way. The world will try to set up a definition of what a parent should be. It's easier for the vast majority of beings to have this boxed-in definition that reflects their own experience, but it's false. There are two requirements for parenthood, and neither one of them has anything to do with biology. As you've learned, the fact that you donate sperm or manage to push one out of your vagina doesn't make you a mother or a father."

"Love and responsibility. They're the only things that can make you a parent," Neil said quietly. "Is it weird that the responsibility came first?"

"It always does, babe." I shifted so I could lean against him. "But the love that comes from it is a wild ride."

A ride I was thrown off of and had to figure a way to get back on.

"So you don't have a problem with Lee flirting with Dean?"

"Nope. I always knew my kids wouldn't be straitlaced when it came to their sexuality," I replied. "They have three parents who talk pretty openly. One of their dads is a sex god and the other is Fae."

Neil let out a loud laugh. "Danny's gotten that good, huh?"

It was easy to fall back into old patterns with Neil. Good patterns. "I'm just saying they weren't ever going to fall into the parameters of normal, and I'm okay with that. Though like I said, I'm worried about Rhys and Evan. If I'm worried about Lee, it's not about his sexual escapades. Those will probably get worse when he turns, but at least I won't have to worry about him getting a disease."

"He doesn't come into contact with humans often," Neil offered. "From what I can tell most of his exploits have been with Fae who understand he's not serious. Though I heard there was a barmaid."

"Yes, I heard that as well. Do you spend much time with them?" Somehow the thought that my kids had Neil in their lives helped ease my pain.

"Fen stays with us on full moons, so I spend time with him, and Evan usually comes with him. I see Rhys and Lee often. I know we should have moved in here, but for some of our wolves, it's better to be outside."

I had figured this out earlier. There had been a reason Neil wanted to come alone. He'd intended to find a way to take Danny to his pack home until Myrddin had screwed everything up. "You mean it was better for Zack."

"Yes. We tried staying in Frelsi as a pack, but it weakened him not being connected to the Earth plane. I checked on him earlier and the king's blood seems to be working," Neil explained. "His color is back and he was sleeping peacefully. He even looks younger already."

Zack had been Daniel's servant for such a long time. His need for king's blood seemed to have become an addiction, and one he couldn't come back from. That wouldn't be a problem normally since Danny was more than happy to give Zack blood. "I'd like to know what was in that spell of Myrddin's."

"I think it was supposed to be a killing blow."

"But Daniel's blood saved him initially." I'd thought about it, too. It made sense. "Myrddin's power packs a punch, though. Have you tried to clear it from his system?"

Neil huffed. "Honey, we've tried everything. Lily nearly killed herself trying to leach that poison from his system. Myrddin's magic is very different from hers. Most witches are Earth plane witches. They manipulate the forces of this plane to cast their magic. Some, like Sarah and her sister, are more closely attuned to the demonic."

Because Sarah and Lily had once been legacies. Like Gray Sloane, their births had been orchestrated to bring power to a coven, and their souls had been pledged to Hell. Sarah and Lily had been raised from Hell by Felix, who'd been a celestial angel at the time. He'd redeemed their souls before allowing himself to fall.

Gray's father had broken the contract and Gray had been released.

If what Myrddin had set on Zack was a spell or a curse, a caster of similar magic might be able to reverse the effects. He or she would certainly have an easier time figuring out how to deal with the effects.

"But Lily couldn't make a dent?"

Neil shook his head. "She got sick even trying."

"Myrddin is a weird mix of Hell and Earth, with a little Heaven plane thrown in. I don't know that there's a witch on all the planes with his kind of magic."

Neil seemed to think about that for a moment. "Maybe not on this plane. Dean seems to have picked up a lot from the outer planes."

"But he was conceived here," I countered. "He's from the Earth plane and his magic should reflect that. One of the things I want to do is look into his mom's family. I don't think they're known to the supernatural world. I'd like to know if he's got any magical relations. I'll make sure Dean takes a look at Zack in the morning. I would love for you to stay here with us. I know you'll want to go into the forest for the full moon, but I'll worry about you out there. Especially now that we're back and Myrddin's looking for you."

"It's been quiet the last few years. I think he got complacent," Neil admitted. "We had to be on the run in the beginning, but he hasn't been on the offensive for a while. Now that you're back he'll be scared again. He'll also think you might have his grimoire. He'll be looking, so I have to hope either Daniel's blood fixes Zack or the new wizardling can. You think Dean's the baby Myrddin sent off plane?"

"From what we can tell. We have a whole bunch of prophecies on several planes that say yes. From what I've seen him do here on this plane, I'm a believer." We'd talked endlessly about this during the days we'd spent with Summer. She'd believed Dean had a destiny, too. "It's kind of confusing, but this is what we've been able to piece together. Kelsey believes that Dean and Lee are at the heart of the prophecy about taking down Myrddin. And when I say Lee, I mean Lee's soul. Originally it would have been Lee Owens and Dean, who would have been thirty plus years younger than Lee."

"But Myrddin manipulated things so Lee died," Neil mused. "And then he was given the choice to have his soul rebooted, so to speak."

I nodded. "Yes. And honestly, his plan might have worked if he hadn't tried to use that stupid painting. Time moves differently on the outer planes. When we met Dean he was in his early twenties and Lee was here on the Earth plane."

"So if Dean had managed to somehow find his way here, there would still have been an age difference between them." Neil chuckled. "If Myrddin hadn't interfered, they wouldn't be the same age."

"Yes, and that seems to mean something. According to Kelsey, for Lee and Dean to be effective they have to be equals."

Of course she also thought that there was some magical third component to Dean and Lee's destiny. Some weapon we hadn't found yet. A weapon only the two of them could wield. Prime. That was the word she'd used. Only they could prime this mysterious weapon.

If the weapon needed youth and sexual chemistry, they were ready.

"It's certainly an interesting thought. He killed Lee. I guess he thought a fully grown werewolf was more dangerous than an unborn child," Neil mused. "It's kind of surprising he would leave that to chance though. He's ruthless, and he hasn't minded killing our children when it suits him."

"I don't know. He's ruthless, but he's also the kind of man who hedges his bets. If he thought there was any way he could use Dean down the line, turn him in some way, he would risk it. It certainly wasn't done out of kindness. I think a lot about the fact that Nimue could have put him back in his crystal coffin if I hadn't let him put those thrall stones in. I should have been more careful."

"Don't take that on yourself. You were up against a powerful supernatural being who had several thousand years on you. No one could have solved that problem. But you're the nexus point, so you have been placed right in the middle of the situation, and your decisions will make all the difference. You were so smart to steal that book. Do you have any idea what could have happened if you hadn't?"

I'd made the choice to steal the book that day, and I'd stolen Gladys on impulse. Not stolen. Taken her back. She was ours, mine and Kelsey's. She belonged to the companions. The Sword of Light had been given to us. It was a celestial battle weapon that soaked up the strength and power of whoever's blood it drew in. It then could unleash that power to the one who wielded it. The right one.

"Oh, shit. I know why he was studying Gladys."

Neil gave me his "duh" look. "He wants to close off the Heaven plane. I assumed he was studying Gladys's heavenly properties."

But he wasn't thinking of what had happened recently. Well, recently for me. "Neil, Gladys soaks up the power of those she kills. It was how Kelsey won her last battle in the arena. You know, the one against Jude."

Neil's eyes went wide. "Gladys soaked up the power of an angel. She's got celestial power inside her right now. That could work. He might actually be able to do it if he has the right spell. But he can't wield that sword. It never worked for Daniel."

"Myrddin's had years to solve that problem. Though he'll need a queen to call her." I'd had to bleed for that sword to work. Gladys required a sacrifice and it was my blood, my life if Daniel wasn't around to save me. "He needs me. He needs me and that sword. I don't know if he needs Kelsey to wield it or if anyone with companion blood will do. There were a lot of people who saw what we did that night."

"I hadn't thought about that," Neil mused. "We'll need to take this to the academics. They can sit down with our witches and try to figure out exactly what he can do if he gets his hands on Gladys."

I hated it when I figured out how much worse things could get. "They should be out of their meeting soon. I'll tell Danny and he can deal with the rest of it."

We sat there for a moment, the night soft around us.

"When are you going to break, Z?" He asked the question quietly, as though he knew he was opening up a door that might be better left closed.

"What do you mean?"

"You lost years with them. You're going to do one of two things. You're either going to break or you're going to try to do something stupid to get those years back."

I went quiet.

Neil's arm went around me, hugging me close. "So we're going the stupid route. You know if you do that, I won't meet Cassie or Brendan."

I didn't like the idea of that, but I also thought things would work out the way they were supposed to. I had to believe that. "Maybe you meet them a different way. If it's meant to be, then it will still be."

A chuckle came from him. "The fact that you can't see the irony of that statement lets me know you're still Z. It won't work, you know. It can't."

"But you'll help me, won't you?" I asked.

"Of course. I'm your best friend. But I'm helping you because I know it won't work," Neil said.

It had to work. I had to get back to my real life. I didn't understand this world I found myself in, and I couldn't find a place in it. My children didn't need me anymore. Not really. Sarah was gone. There was no guarantee we could win this war. The world had changed and I'd been left behind.

"I'll be here when you finally break, Z. I'll be here and we'll rebuild. That's what we do." Neil's head rested against mine, and we sat that way for the longest time.

* * * *

It was late into the night when I found myself sitting around the big bonfire. Most of the occupants of Frelsi had taken to their beds. Neil and I had talked to Danny and told him our revelations about Gladys. He'd gone straight back into the conference room to talk to the academics, though I'd noticed he hadn't invited Alexander to this meeting.

At least he was practical about the Victorian vampire. The serial killer vampire.

Neil and I had made the rounds, playing the queen and her favorite courtier. I'd plastered a smile on my face and even managed to dance with both of my sons. Rhys had been stilted and proper, and Lee had swung me around like he hadn't a care in the world.

I worried for both of them.

But for now I sat and contemplated the world I found myself in and how I was going to get out.

"Your Highness?"

I glanced to my left, expecting to see one of the brownies or the trolls who had made the effort to ensure I had anything I could need. Instead it was Lily Tucker. She wore a flowing skirt and a heavy cable-knit sweater, her salt and pepper hair flowing down her back. "Please. It's Zoey."

A ghost of a smile hit her face. "Maybe it was once. I remember when you were nothing more than my younger sister's odd friend. How far you've come."

"I don't know. Right now I feel like I'm back where I started." Maybe not exactly where I started, but pretty close. It hadn't been long after I figured out how powerful Danny really was that we'd started our play to put him on the throne and free the supernatural world from the tyranny of the old Council. We'd been hunted back then, too. The only difference was now our children were on the run with us.

They had been on the run without us for over a decade.

Lily settled herself on the bench next to mine. "Oh, I don't know about that. I remember the first time around. Most of it. I drank a lot back then. No matter how many times Felix tried to wipe away the memory of that stint in Hell, it lingered. It still does, though I can handle it better now."

Lily had been taken to Hell on her twenty-fifth birthday, payment for her mother's power. "I know it bothered Sarah."

Lily chuckled. "Sarah had Felix. I swear there must have been something in his dick because she moved right on. I'm sorry. I know that's not fair. She handled it better than I did. I think in a weird way she almost viewed that time as penance for what she did to you."

That felt like three lifetimes ago. Sarah had put me in a bad position years and years before. I'd forgiven Sarah's betrayal almost as soon as she'd committed it. She'd done it for Lily. "She did it to save you."

"She failed and then you saved us all." Lily sat back. "I don't think I ever properly thanked you for that. I'm afraid I was a bit lost then. And after I got my act together, you were the queen and it felt weird to talk to you. I'm sorry for that, too. It shouldn't have been. That was my problem, not yours."

"I didn't need thanks," I replied. "If Sarah had told me what was happening, I would have helped you."

"And that is why you're the queen," Lily pronounced somberly.

I had to laugh at the thought. "I'm queen because I'm married to Daniel. I don't know that I'm queen at all anymore."

"Oh, you're the queen. Myrddin is the pretender. Never doubt that," Lily said with a sigh. "I lost most of my coven to that asshole. Only three of us made it out. The rest…well, they drank that Kool-Aid right down."

"He's a legend in the witch world." There were entire covens who worshipped him when he hadn't walked the Earth plane, when he'd been trapped in his crystal coffin.

"Yes, he is, but we also used to be honest about him," Lily pointed out. "We knew he was a source of power, but we also knew he had ties to Hell many of us didn't want. He's convinced even some Earth witches that he's the way to save our kind. That this is our time to rule. Like witches were some sort of left-behind creature."

"I think all of the supernaturals have members who feel that way. For some, it's true. I mean there are entire populations of werecreatures who died out because the wolves and panthers and tigers ate them." Our world could be brutal, and the separate factions had been at war from time to time. "But witches had a place at the table with Daniel."

"And Myrddin offered them the whole table. For some that was intoxicating. They're not thinking about the balance. There will be a cost, but that's not important to them now. For all the power they have during these years, they will be serving demons for many more. Forever, since if Myrddin gets his way, there won't be a Heaven plane to escape to."

"Do they know what he's planning?" I asked.

Lily shrugged. "I don't see how they can't. They aren't thinking. They're caught up in power. I suspect the ones closest to him are also caught in his web. Myrddin has…you would probably call it charm or charisma. It works specifically on witches. Especially younger ones."

"But it didn't work on you?"

She shook her head. "No. Because I see him for who he is. I see the face that lies under the mask."

It was good to know there were some witches his power didn't work on. "Sarah never fell for his charm either."

"Because we both spent time on the Hell plane. I suspect that's why we were immune," Lily mused. "I often see through demonic guises. Sarah did from time to time, but I suspect being close to Felix healed a lot of her scars. I didn't have an angelic protector shielding me from the worst of it. It's funny that now I view that time as a strength. It prepared me for this moment. If I hadn't gone through what I did, I would likely be in the Council building kissing Myrddin's feet."

It was interesting that Myrddin's charm didn't work on Sarah or Lily. We might be able to use that in some way. "So do you think they can come back to our side?"

"Some of them, for sure. Some of them are already questioning," Lily allowed. "But they're trapped. I think with you back, there might be many who are willing to reconsider their choices. Without you, Myrddin seemed to be the better bet for witches. Though you should understand that there are many who are true believers."

"Like Olivia Carey?"

Lily nodded silently.

I took a deep breath, feeling sorry for Kelsey and Casey. I knew Casey still felt something for Liv because I'd heard him telling Daniel he thought Myrddin had influence over her. I hated the idea that someone I'd cared about would be on the other side of this war.

"I want you to know that I'm going to do everything I can to help you win this war, Your Highness," Lily promised. "I know my sister is gone, but I hope you understand that you can look to me if you need me."

"Is she really gone?" I'd asked the question all day, the answer becoming heartbreakingly clear.

"Yes. I don't feel her. If my sister was alive, she would make contact. I worked with Neil to try to find her. I don't think she ever left the building." Lily's eyes shone with tears. "I miss her. I miss Mia and Felix, too, but Sarah… I don't remember a time in my life when she wasn't there. I know there was, but even my oldest memories have her in them."

I let the moment sit between us, trying to decide if I could trust her. Lily had power. I needed a witch and magic if I was going fix this timeline. "What if you could get her back?"

Lily sniffled. "I would do anything to see my sister again."

Lily knew a lot about magic. She wasn't as talented as Sarah, but then almost no one on the Earth plane was. But she came from the same magical line.

"What do you know about the painting we fell through?"

"Only what Trent and Sasha's spies have told us." Lily sat up, wiping her tears. "Your Highness, you went through a slipstream, a magical wormhole of sorts."

"Is there a way back?"

She seemed to think about it for a moment. "I don't know. That particular wormhole is closed, but there are time spells. It depends on how you lost that time. What if the years you lost didn't happen because of the plane you were on? The king mentioned you were on several. Last night he told us some stories about a Vampire plane."

We hadn't actually set foot on the Vampire plane, but we'd heard enough about it to know how unique it was. "Yes. It's where Dean was raised."

"I don't understand the time differences, but I suspect they don't all line up," Lily said. "Not twelve years' worth, and you would pick up time on planes that run slower."

Finally I was getting somewhere. "Do you think we lost the time inside the wormhole?"

She nodded. "I think it's possible. And if it's possible to lose time in the wormhole, it could be possible to gain it back. That's not the right way to say it."

But I understood what she meant. "It's a form of time travel. The question is can I get back the same way?"

"If you got back, you could save Sarah." The words came out on a quiet gasp.

"Yes, I could save us all." A little hope lit through me because Lily was clearly thinking about the problem. And she wasn't telling me no. I pushed back thoughts of all the complications that could come from going through time again. I would deal with that later. I only wanted a chance to set things right. To go back to the world I understood. Even if we won this war, this wasn't my world.

"I need to think about this." Lily stood, straightening her skirt. There was purpose in her eyes, and I knew I'd found an ally. "I understand how to open a wormhole to get to another place. It's a form of teleportation, and I've gotten good at it. I would need to figure out the time element."

"I would appreciate anything you could do," I assured her.

Lily nodded. "I'll begin immediately. Like I've said since yesterday—your return brings us all hope."

She strode away, back to the eastern side of the base where there was a neighborhood of cottages.

I was warmed by more than the fire. If Lily could find a way, I might get my life back. I might get my children back. I would have to be careful. There were things that needed to happen. I would make a list and sort through all the issues.

"So the queen is not as placid as she seems," a silky voice said.

I turned to watch Alexander Sharpe peel away from the shadows, his long limbs moving with predatory grace. He wore all black—black slacks and a black collared shirt and loafers. The only other thing he wore was a gold ring that I didn't remember him wearing before. Unlike the rest of the group, he didn't bother with a jacket. He either didn't feel the cold at all or perhaps he preferred it.

I didn't like the fact that he'd been listening in to my conversation with Lily. If she was an ally then Alexander definitely qualified as a foe. He would use any information he had on me to leverage his position with Danny. "I don't think that's any of your concern."

"Oh, I think the fact that the Queen of all Vampire is considering time travel concerns all of us." Alexander moved in and took Lily's seat. "Though I should warn you I don't think that's going to turn out the way you think it will."

"Because Lily's lying to me?" I knew she wasn't, but I was interested in seeing what Alexander would say.

"Because our fair Lily is holding on to hope with both hands. She lost her precious sister, and you suggested a way to get her back." He tsked my way. "I'm surprised with you, Queen Zoey. I rather thought you were all about kindness. Giving her false hope isn't well done of you."

It was time to go to bed. Long past. I stood. "Good night, Alexander."

"Wait, my queen." His voice had gone softer. "I'm sorry. I didn't mean to upset you. I also wasn't hanging about eavesdropping on purpose. I hadn't had the chance to express my true joy at seeing you again."

I felt my brow arch. "That's good to hear."

"But you don't believe it?"

"I know you, Alexander. I trust you as long as you believe you're on the winning side. If you decide Myrddin is the better bet, you'll go with him." He'd been an ally of sorts in our war with the old Council, but I'd never truly trusted him.

"You don't think a man can change?"

"I don't think you're a man at all. I don't think you were a man even when you were human. I think you were born a predator and you'll die one."

His dark gaze turned thoughtful. "Perhaps. I've had a long time to reflect on my existence. Both the one today and my human life. I always find it fascinating how humans study serial killers. As if they can find answers in the past, some point in the killer's life when a trigger was pulled and they became deadly."

"Sometimes there was a trigger."

Alexander shrugged off my assertion. "And sometimes an apex predator is required by nature to thin the herd, so to speak. There was no one event that set me off. I had a perfectly lovely childhood. I had a mother and father who cared about me, a sibling who was kind. My father was what you would call a doctor, and we had a comfortable existence."

"So how did you end up killing prostitutes and terrorizing London?" I knew I shouldn't encourage him, but I wanted to know the answer.

His lips curved up in a smile that held no humor. I swear in the light from the fire, I could see a hint of fangs, and his smile looked too large, like his mouth could open far more than it should. Like he could swallow the world if he wanted. "Because I was born to. Because despite my ideal circumstances, I needed more than warm food and Mummy's love. I was only six when something deep inside me led me to slice open the local vermin to see what was underneath their skin. I looked normal from the outside. I married, you know."

Despite the fact that I knew I should follow my first instincts and walk away, I found myself sitting again. "No. I didn't know that."

He nodded, his left hand playing with the ring he wore on his right ring finger. "Yes, I was. At the ripe old age of seventeen. She was a slip of a girl. Good family, of course."

Not a smart family. They'd married their daughter to a monster. "Did you kill her?"

"Heavens, no. Why would I ever fuck where I ate? I think she had her suspicions, but she was a devout girl. She'd been taught the highest religion of our class—to look the other way as long as it didn't affect us," he said with a chuckle. "Some things never change, do they? It's why I find you fascinating. You could have had quite a good life. The Council would have offered you and Daniel anything you liked so long as you didn't cause trouble. I've thought a lot about it. You didn't do it because you thirsted for the crown."

"I did it because the old Council was threatening the world."

"Not your world. At least not as long as you stayed in line," Alexander pointed out.

"It's all my world. That's the thing, isn't it? Louis was going to subjugate the wolves." That time seemed so long ago and yet it had only been a little past a decade for me. "I'm not a wolf, but I knew what it meant to be under Louis's thumb. I could have stayed silent and it might have bought us time, but he would always have come for us. They always come for you in the end, no matter how compliant you are. A tyrant needs someone to crush. When he's crushed everyone else, it's your turn. So instead of waiting, it's better to stand and fight with those first targets. It's better to go down fighting with them than to wait your turn."

"Ah, but many of them didn't fight *with* you in the first place. You fought *for* them. Even when they didn't appreciate you."

"I'm not some saint."

"Of course not, but you are different. Which is why I'm surprised you're wilting in the face of this challenge, my queen. I'll be honest. I expected you to be all…peppy about it."

Not even the serial killer understood my plight. "I'm sorry I can't be happy I lost twelve years with my children. I can't be happy my friends are dead."

"There are always losses in war." Alexander stood again. "Well, I wish you luck finding your way back to the time when you didn't have to fight at all."

I didn't like the idea that I was trying to get out of a fight, but I deserved some peace. "I just wanted to raise my kids."

"Then you should have stayed silent. Then you never should have put on that crown. You should have refused Daniel, who was always going to be here, and run with your lover to the safety of a *sithein*."

They weren't as safe as people made them out to be. But he was right about one thing. Being the queen didn't mean safety. It meant sacrifice, and in that moment I resented the hell out of it. The truth of the matter was I hadn't been given a choice. If I loved Daniel and stood by him, I had to become the queen. In the years since, I'd been more than happy to let him and Dev run the supernatural world while I focused on being a wife and a mom and a friend. Every now and then I hosted a state dinner or smiled and waved.

I'd liked that life. Was it awful to want it back? To fight to get it back?

"These are interesting times, Your Highness. But if you want to return to a less complex time, I won't stop you. Or mention it to anyone else. There are a couple of acquaintances of mine who can perhaps even aid in your endeavors," he said smoothly. "But you should know that time travel is fraught with inconsistencies. And just because you manage to make it back to what you consider a proper timeline, it doesn't mean this one goes away. At least not theoretically."

"What is that supposed to mean?"

"Do you honestly believe I haven't thought about it?" Alexander asked. "Haven't thought about going back and warning my younger self that a Hunter would take down the greatest predator of all time? I've had a hundred plus years to fill, and I'm no longer allowed to practice my favorite hobby. I don't know if what you seek is possible at this point, but the likeliest positive outcome would be starting a new timeline. You would go back to when you left, but this timeline is already established. It can't be erased. You would merely split reality and go a different direction, leaving all of us without your presence."

Leaving my kids here without me? "You can't possibly know that."

He shrugged, a negligent gesture. "I can't know it for certain. I suppose you'll find out." He nodded. "Ah, the Green Man has come for his goddess. Your Grace."

Devinshea stepped into the circle of light, holding his hand out. "My goddess, you're all right? Daniel and I have been looking for you."

I stood and took his hand. "I'm fine. Sorry, I lost track of time."

"Good evening, Alexander." Dev started to walk me back to our *brugh*, and I could feel Alexander's eyes on me the whole way.

His words would haunt me for the longest time.

Chapter Thirteen

"Are you sure this is a good idea?" I stared at Daniel as he knotted his tie. I was sitting on the bed watching him get dressed. He'd only recently announced his plans for the day, and I wasn't particularly happy about them since they included leaving the safety of Frelsi.

"I can't have everyone we need to meet with file into town. Myrddin knows we're somewhere in Iceland. Until we can move to the New Zealand base, we're going to have to be careful. Honestly, even when we move we're going to have to meet our allies in neutral places. I'm flying to Edinburgh to meet with the Scottish alpha. It's not a long flight, and it will tell us a lot." He stopped and turned my way. "Do you want to come with me? Are you upset I'm taking Dev instead of you?"

Dev lived for things like this. He loved playing the political game, and he would be far more helpful to Danny than I would. I would mostly want to go and find the places where they filmed *Outlander*. "No, I don't want you to go at all. It's dangerous. Shouldn't we wait a few days? At least until Kelsey gets back?"

I'd talked to her briefly the night before through the mirror network the Fae had set up. She'd checked in, and I'd made sure Evan was all right. They were staying underground and the primals' nest was well protected according to Sasha. She should be safe, but I already missed my daughter. Kelsey was gung ho to get to work so she'd cut the call short. Well, she'd said that was the reason, but I'd also heard Trent whispering just out of sight, and the poor man hadn't gotten any in twelve years, so I could forgive them both for not wanting to talk.

"We can't wait, Z. Right now there are a million rumors running through the supernatural world, and I need to put some truth out there." The suit he was wearing didn't fit exactly right. It was one of Hugo's, and it strained a bit at the shoulders and was a tad too big in the waist. It was sad because he had a dozen suits at the penthouse that had been tailored to fit that hot bod of his. Devinshea had selected each one, so they were perfect. Myrddin probably wore them, and now they would have to be burned. "The Scottish alpha has a lot of influence over the European wolves. I also need to get somewhere I can safely call the new American alpha. They don't have a mirror so I have to use a cell phone, which means I need to be outside Frelsi for it to work. According to Sasha, John McKenzie died suddenly and mysteriously a few months after we disappeared."

McKenzie had been the alpha of the American packs. He'd sat on the Council and been a true friend and ally to us.

"By *suddenly* you mean he was murdered. Well, we all know that would have helped Myrddin because if the wolves are in chaos, then they can't challenge him." Dev strode into the room sighing in obvious despair at Daniel's suit. He immediately got into Danny's space and started to redo his tie. "It was one of several strategic assassinations we believe Myrddin ordered. All in all, though he started out fumbling, the wizard quickly found his feet. His main problem now is he hasn't made any progress on his promises to the demons, and they're getting weary of waiting. Come here. That tie is terrible. You should wear the blue."

Danny's left brow rose.

Dev simply shook his head. "You know appearances are important. I can't do anything about the suit, though you should know we're going shopping after the meeting. You need clothes, and not ones you've borrowed from Hugo. Sasha is closer to you in size but he's got terrible taste. I looked through his wardrobe. It's all tactical clothes and sweaters and combat boots."

"Yes, because it's cold here and he's a general," Danny pointed out, but there was a hint of a grin on his face.

Dev lifted the new tie over Danny's neck and started to knot it with an expert hand. "And you're a king and must look the part."

"With the wolves, shouldn't that mean I show up with fangs and claws out, covered in blood?" Danny asked.

I liked wolf society. It was way more laid back than Vampire, but even I knew better than to argue with Dev when it came to presenting an image.

Dev finished knotting the tie, and this time it lay perfectly against Danny's shirt. And brought out the blue in his eyes. "I think we want them to see you as a charming, reasonable alternative to Myrddin, not remind them you're a vicious predator who can sometimes take over their wills and force them to do your bidding." He sighed as he looked Danny over. "That will have to do."

Danny's eyes rolled but he brushed his lips over Dev's. "I long for the time you can dress me properly again."

Dev kissed him back, lingering long enough to make me wonder how much time we had. Then both men were turning my way, Dev's eyes on me. "Now what is this I hear about Zoey wanting to take my place? I don't think that's a good idea. I need to get a lay of the land, and we don't have a proper dress for her."

I laid back on the bed so they didn't see how hard my eyes rolled. "I wasn't saying I wanted to go. I'm fine here. I was worried about you going at all, but I can see you have it all planned out."

I was worried that they were enjoying this, that they kind of missed that time when we were on the run, having to play the game from behind. For the most part the last decade of our lives had been as quiet as they could be when one ruled over a supernatural world.

Dev had moved to the side of the bed, staring down at me. "My goddess, are you feeling all right? I know this has been a shock for us all, but I worry about you. Maybe we should sit down and talk about whether we should pursue this course."

I stared up at him. "Do we have a choice?"

"There's always some kind of choice," Dev allowed.

"Not if we want to stay on the Earth plane, there's not." Danny sat on the edge of the bed, his hand going to my leg. "And the kids have made it plain that they believe this is their fight. We'll have a hard time persuading them if we decide to run."

"Run where?" Dev asked. "I don't think we can safely go back to the Faery planes connected here. Not with all of our children. Back to the outer planes? I suppose we could try to find our way back to Summer and Marcus's kingdom."

"We don't know what closing off the Heaven plane will do to the outer planes," Danny pointed out. "It could upset some balance we don't understand."

"But Summer might," Dev countered. "I know she's still learning, but she's had years to get her power under control. She might be able to help us."

"Or we could try to open a wormhole and get back to our timeline," I said quietly.

The silence that followed weighed on me. I could feel them trying to figure out how to handle me.

"Is this what you were talking to Alexander about?" Dev asked.

I'd been thinking about my talks with Alexander and Lily all night long and all of this morning. I'd come to one conclusion. "Yes. I think we lost those twelve years when we came through the painting again. It would explain how the sonic weapons went dead."

Dev seemed to consider that. "Yes, that would be a reasonable explanation. They were both fully charged when we went through."

"Okay," Danny allowed. "Let's say we did lose them when we walked back into the painting. It would have been a good final strategy for Myrddin. I don't see how that changes anything."

"If it was a wormhole we walked through, and we lost time there, we could potentially reverse the effect," I explained.

Dev was quiet for a moment. "Did Alexander know anything useful?"

So he'd heard more than I thought he had. "He seems to think even if I can manage to add the time component to a wormhole spell, it won't change this timeline. It will simply start a new timeline. But he's not exactly an academic, and the ones we have here aren't into science."

I was wrong, of course. Henri was very much into science, but medical science and biology were his fields of expertise. And Hugo was a lawyer. Neither of them were experts on physics. And yes, neither was Alexander or Lily or anyone I'd talked to up until this point.

"You've been asking around about this?" Danny had sat up straighter.

I took the time to sit up as well, leaning back against the headboard. "I'm exploring possibilities."

"Zoey, if our allies find out we're trying to leave, it won't help us," Daniel said with a frustrated sigh. "I do know a bit about science, and I don't see how this possibly works out in our favor. The entire scenario is fraught with potholes, and you know it. If we go back, we probably make things worse. We can only play the cards we're dealt."

A bit of bitterness welled inside me. "Says the man whose cards made him all powerful and invulnerable."

Danny stood, his eyes going wide with anger.

Dev put a hand on his shoulder. "Don't. Don't make this worse. You know how she processes loss, and she's been handed a huge one. Let her do what she needs to do and trust her to make the right decision when the time comes."

Danny looked like he wanted to argue for a moment, but he seemed to calm down. He took a long breath and then held out a hand. "Okay, Z. I only ask that you talk to us before you do anything. Can you promise me?"

I nodded and took his hand, allowing him to pull me up and wrap his arms around me. "Okay. I won't do anything without telling you."

It wasn't like I would ever leave them behind.

Would I be leaving Lee and Rhys and Evan behind? Would these versions of them remain here?

I shoved the thought aside because Alexander was wrong. He was trying to throw me off. If I allowed this timeline to stand, I abandoned my children and Sarah and my father. I abandoned the vampires Myrddin had killed.

There was a brisk knock on the door and then it opened and Neil was walking through, a big tray in his hands.

"Good morning, royals. Ooo, that tie is perfect, though the suit needs some work." Neil crossed over and set the tray at the end of the bed. I could smell coffee, and it looked like Albert had made another glorious buffet of breakfast goodness, including his ridiculously indulgent potato hash. My stomach growled. Baby girl and I were hungry.

"That's what I said." Dev glanced at the clock on the mantel over the fireplace. "I would love to stay and steal some of that breakfast, but we need to get going. The flight's going to take us a couple of hours. We're using the portal to Reykjavík and flying from there. That should save us half an hour."

"There's a portal?" I probably should have paid attention to all the meetings we'd had.

Neil perked up. "There is. We've got a portal to Reykjavík and to Húsavík and Bolungarvík. All the viks."

"The Fae set up a small portal system long ago," Dev explained. "Reykjavík is the furthest we can go, but we've been told it's safe to use."

Neil's eyes lit. "Dev, there is shopping there. And the queen…oh, to see her in rags…"

"They aren't rags," I argued. Though I was already thinking that I had at least three towns I could search for my godparents. "They've just been through a lot."

"They're practically vintage." Neil looked at himself in the standing mirror. "And honestly, I don't look like the queen's bestie." He gasped. "Oh, my god. I look like a dad. I'm wearing dad jeans, and I haven't had a haircut in years." There was a little panic in his eyes as he turned my way. "I wouldn't do me, Z. I. Wouldn't. Do. Me. What is Chad thinking? I've turned into the kind of man who gets asked directions by families."

"Yes, everyone needs new clothes," Dev said with a chuckle. "I already put the wheels into motion, so to speak. Albert shut down most of our accounts, but they've been safely managed over the years. I've had a human security firm taking care of my company. A few million have been transferred to European banks. I think you'll find Rhys is going into the city to ensure that we have access to funds. He's picking up credit cards for everyone."

I didn't like the thought of that. "You're sure that's safe? Won't Myrddin be watching our accounts?"

"Which ones?" Danny asked. "I assure you Devinshea set up a network Myrddin hasn't untangled yet, and the security firm had instructions to move the money around on a regular basis. I've been in touch with them and they've released all of it back to us. It was weird. The Taggart on this plane sounds exactly like the one on the Vampire plane. And he's every bit as obnoxious."

"So we have money?" Neil asked.

"If by *we* you mean…" Danny began.

Dev stopped him. "Yes. We have money, and I expect you to buy the queen some clothes fit for her. And see if you can get Lee out of those tactical pants he wears all the time. We can deal with Evangeline when she gets home. She's going to need a completely new wardrobe."

"Good luck with that." Danny moved away, checking himself in the mirror. "I think our daughter is a tomboy."

"If you want Evan on board, get Fen into a suit." I already knew how to handle my daughter. She needed to be tough, needed to be one of the boys, right up to the point that Fenrir looked at her. And Fen was easy. If I asked him politely and pointed out how nice he would look and how it was important for he and Evan to dress properly for certain functions, he would trip over those overly large paws of his to get into that suit. "She'll say she doesn't want pretty clothes, but that's the warrior in her. She's been raised around men. She'll learn she's got weapons of her own."

Devinshea had been the one to teach me that lesson.

"I'll try with Fen. I promise." Dev leaned over and brushed his lips against mine. "We have to go. If you and Neil want to accompany Rhys into the city, I think that might be good for you. But you have to stay close to Rhys."

"Uhm, hello, still a bodyguard," Neil said with a sigh. "I know I look like a sad dad right now, but I can still bite a head off. I just try not to do it around the children."

"I trust you, Neil. Stay close to Z if you decide to go into town," Danny ordered. "And definitely if she decides to go searching the bridges on the outskirts since that's where I've heard our godparents are this time of year."

Well, I never said he didn't know me.

Neil groaned. "I think my amazing, beautiful day of shopping is going to turn into something terrible. I should eat a little breakfast to keep my strength up."

"How is Zack?" I hadn't had a chance to go by his room this morning.

"He's resting, and that's a good thing," Neil said, his tone more serious than it had been before. "He hasn't slept well in years, so I'm counting it as a win."

There was another knock on my door and then Lee was pressing through followed by his brother. Lee ignored his fathers and walked straight up to the bed, tossing his big body next to mine and putting his head on my lap. "I feel terrible, Momma."

"He's got a hangover," Rhys said.

"Hush. Our mom is back and she's going to take care of me and not be mad at me for drinking too much." He looked up at me. "I never learned how to moderate. But in my defense, I was told Papa's sperm actually had alcohol in it when I was conceived."

"Lies," Dev said with a sigh. "You two watch out for your mother today. If you have any instinct that tells you to get back to base, follow it. Your mother is your main priority."

"Of course. I've got a list of supplies, too, but we've got a crew who are going to bring them back. After I make sure the supplies are on their way, I'll be more than happy to escort Mom around," Rhys offered.

"Maybe you should stay in." I brushed back Lee's hair the way I used to when he was a kid. He'd always been my most affectionate child, climbing into my lap when he needed a cuddle. When he was sick he always wanted me to hold his hand and read him a story.

Who had comforted him all these years? Was my absence the reason for his reckless behavior? I knew part of it was his nature as a latent vampire, but I had to wonder if going from a coddled, beloved child to a soldier on the run had pushed him to do risky things.

He shook his head. "Not a chance. I'm not letting Rhys have all the fun." He sat up and reached for one of the croissants on the tray. "I might be exaggerating for attention. Also, I know I'll feel better once I eat. This looks delicious. I missed breakfast."

"Because you were still at Hildie's in bed," Rhys pointed out.

"Well, I like to leave them satisfied, brother," Lee shot back. "Sometimes that takes long into the night."

I looked to Dev and Danny. "You're really leaving me with them? You know they greatly resemble the two of you, right?"

Danny grinned, one of those sunny smiles he rarely graces us with. When he smiled and his dimples showed, I knew he was genuinely happy with the world. "That's how we know you'll be safe.

Take care, sons. And don't eat all of your mother's breakfast. Remember, she's pregnant."

Lee groaned. "I was trying to forget that part." He frowned. "Not that I'm unhappy about another sibling. I'm thrilled. We can do better this time. We'll take all the mistakes you made with Rhys and do the opposite."

"Yes, I'm the troublesome one." Rhys reached a hand out to Daniel. "I promise I'll protect Mom. You don't have to worry, sir."

"Oh, I'm going to worry about that *sir* a lot." But Danny shook his hand. "I'll worry about it until you remember I'm your father, not merely your king."

"You're both, Dad. I have to remember that at all times," Rhys said solemnly.

Danny glanced over at me, and I gave him my best "see, I told you time traveling back to save our kids from years on the run is the best way" look.

Danny and Dev left, promising to be home shortly after nightfall.

Rhys and Lee began to argue while Neil did his best to eat what Lee didn't.

It was going to be a long day.

* * * *

The portal turned out to be a door that led to a hallway that led to another unassuming door that opened into the back of a small shop.

The scent of old books and leather surrounded me as I walked in behind Rhys. The room I found myself in was illuminated only by a single light, throwing shadows all over and leaving most of it in gloom. It was a big change because we'd come through a long, well-lit hallway. It had been odd to go from the mountain trappings of Frelsi to that super-clean industrial-looking passage and then into this gloomy room.

Of course, that corridor that had taken roughly thirty seconds to traverse had taken us hundreds of miles from where we'd started.

Sometimes magic was fun.

"The hallway is there in case anyone ever tries to follow us through. According to the Fae who built it, originally it was door to door, but when we showed up, they decided to put a layer of security in. We can trap any interlopers in the hall," Rhys explained. "It's also why I needed a drop of blood to let the door know you're okay. It will work for you from now on. If you're ever chased, make sure to close it behind you so no one can get in."

"Has this ever happened?" I hated the thought of them running for their lives, getting to the door first being the only way to stay alive.

"Only a couple of times, and it's always fun to trap the bad guy," Lee offered with that devil-may-care grin of his. "At first they try to open the door to Frelsi, and then run back here and try to go through that door and find out it's locked, too. They yell a lot at that point and after a couple of days they start to beg. Fun times."

I didn't need to know about all of his hobbies. I definitely didn't need to know what they'd done to whoever had gotten trapped. "Is this a bookstore?"

We were a small party, and Shahidi and I were the only women. She was dressed for the cold in a winter-white parka over her jeans and sweater. She'd offered me her extra pair of warm boots, and I was grateful for them because even though we were inside, I could feel the chill. It reminded me how warm it was in Frelsi, how the Fae magic kept us safe from many things that might hurt us.

"Yes." Shy followed me through. "Though this is the back of the store where they keep the books on magic and the arcane artifacts. It's run by elves passing as humans. They have a perfectly normal-looking bookstore as a front. They live in Frelsi when they don't have the shop open."

It was how many of our citizens lived if they could pass for human. They had one foot in the human world and one in the supernatural. They had jobs or businesses that outwardly catered to humans, with hidden places for their supernatural brethren. I glanced around at the high shelves as I followed Rhys. There were books and jars and little boxes that might bite if one tried to open them. I'd learned not to open things in magical shops. It often went wrong.

"Hey, you don't want to do that." Lee moved in behind Dean, putting his hand over the book Dean had been about to open. "That one's a screamer. I mean it. She's really loud."

"Oh, yeah. *The History of Anna the Betrayed*." Neil shuddered. "She didn't like being betrayed. Also, if you're male, the pages give you paper cuts because she was betrayed by her husband. She screams at a pitch that's particularly bad for male witches. Because her husband was a male witch who sold her to the Hell plane."

Dean eased his hand away. "I will remember that in the future. No opening strange books."

Lee's lips curled up. "I'll show you the safe ones. There are some fun ones. Like the tale of Jayne, the Beloved. She was happy and liked to share."

"I'd love a tour. There's a lot to see, from what I've heard. So far, all I've seen of my home plane is the inside of a building and Frelsi," Dean replied, his tone deeper than normal.

Lee's smile was smooth, his invitation obvious. "Well, I hope you find some places that spark your interest today. I can show you a lot of fun things to explore."

Rhys made a barfing sound. "Could you take a break from thinking with your dick, brother? Remember that we're on a mission."

Lee waved him off. "We're picking up supplies and clothes for Mom, and I have to take her out to visit the trolls and listen to Uncle Neil complain about the mud while you and Shy go to the bank and pretend you're not all into each other. It's not some dangerous mission. We come here all the time."

Shy moved past Lee. "Your grandfather thinks you should have been spanked more often as a child, and I agree with him."

Rhys shook his head as he walked to the door that seemed to lead out of the back of the store. "I wouldn't spank him now. I think he likes it. And he needs to remember that our mother is here, and that means every mission is dangerous."

I didn't like the sound of that. "I'm not doing anything crazy. I only want to see my godparents."

"I didn't mean you were the danger." Rhys held the door open for Shy and then me.

"Then you don't know your mother well enough," Neil quipped.

Rhys ignored him. "I meant there are many powerful creatures who would love to use you as leverage against Dad. And Papa. And me, when I think about it. If the Fae took you, they would be able to force me into a bargaining position when it comes to using my Green Man powers. I might have to do something I don't want to do in order to free my queen."

"I would get you back because I love you, Mom." Lee wrinkled his nose his brother's way. "Asshole. Stuff the 'queen' nonsense. She's our mom, and she's always been trouble."

"I'll try to make sure you don't have to get me back at all." I didn't want to put my kids in a bad position. "Rhys said he thought Ingrid and Halle will be at one of two bridges this time of year. I'll take Neil and go to the closest one while you're getting the supplies. Albert promised me cell phones will work now. He gave me one so you can call me and I'll meet you back here."

Rhys's brow rose, and he looked so much like Dev it hurt. "I'm not sending you off to search for Ingrid and Halle with Uncle Neil alone. He's not your bodyguard. He's your accomplice. I know he would protect you, but he'll also let you run wild."

I started to argue but Neil held up a hand. "Come on, Z. You know he's right. So we'll take Lee with us."

Rhys snorted. "Or you'll shop in a very public place while Shy and I go to the bank and Lee picks up supplies. We're one block over from Laugavegur Street. There are lots of shops there. And if we take too long, there are cafés you can wait at. I'm serious, Mom. I need to know you'll stay in public places. The bridges are on the outer edges of town. You can't go there without a serious guard."

We moved into the more human section of the store. A tall, lithe woman with long hair stood at the cash register, a book open in front of her. She glanced up and nodded Rhys's way before going back to her book. If she was concerned at all with a bunch of people walking out of her back room, she didn't show it.

Lee shrugged his broad shoulders. "I'm with Rhys on this one, Mom. I would probably let you do crazy shit, too. It's been a long time since we did stupid things, and now that I know it's okay to die, I'll be even more reckless than I was before. Also, there are lots of Fae around those bridges, and some of them are not friendly, if you know what I mean."

I certainly knew what it meant to have my comings and goings decided by someone other than myself. It looked like it was starting all over again, but this time I would be herded around by my sons. Having my sons guard me made it hard for me to ignore the bodyguards' advice and do whatever I wanted. I had to set an example. "All right. Your Uncle Neil and I will go and do what I do best."

Lee groaned. "Mom, don't be mad. You don't just shop and look pretty. I know what a badass you are, but you don't understand this world yet. I promise when I get my fangs and claws, I'll take you tons of crazy places. We can steal things for fun."

"We'll have a long talk about that," Rhys promised. "And you'll only be able to take her places after night falls, so remember that when you race into your vampiric life. Now walk Mom and Uncle Neil down to the shops and then check in with Sonja. She's got our shipment. When you've checked it and approve, send them here and hike back to guard Mom. I'll text you when Shy and I are heading your way."

"Yes, sir, general sir." Lee gave his twin a jaunty salute before starting for the front door. "Dean? You want to come with me or stay with my mom?"

Dean had his silvery hair pulled back in a queue and hidden under a knit cap. "I'll go with you. You can tell me all about your escapades last night."

That got Lee's face falling fast. "Oh, that? That was nothing. I consider it a farewell to human sex. I'm going to hit the highlights."

I groaned and looked to Neil. "He's going to kill me."

"You have no idea how happy I am that Brendan and Cassie are such angels," Neil replied.

I heard Rhys cough, and when I turned Shy was slapping him on the back, a beatific look on her face. "Sorry. He got a throat tickle."

Rhys nodded and coughed again. "Yep. Sure did."

So Brendan and Cassie were normal, not-angelic teens. That was good to know since at least one of mine seemed to be trying to personify a couple of the deadly sins. Neil and I followed Lee and Dean out, and I felt the sun on my face for the first time in days. There was light in Frelsi, but it wasn't the sun I was used to, and I tipped my face up to it.

"Enjoy it while you can." Neil glanced down at his watch. "We've got three hours of this before it sets again. It's winter here in the northern hemisphere, so there's not a ton of daylight this close to the arctic."

"It's why we came here," Lee explained. "We chase the night. That's how Sasha puts it. We spend winter here, and then when the days get longer, we move to New Zealand as winter starts in the south. You'll like our Kiwi base. It's like the set of *Lord of the Rings*. But man, don't call the dwarves there hobbits. They get offended and they are quick with the axe. Come this way. There are some decent stores up ahead. I don't know if they're good enough for Papa, though. Iceland isn't like a fashion capital. But we can get you some warm clothes."

It sounded like I would need them if we were going to spend all our time in winter. It made sense to chase the night since Sasha wouldn't be effective during the daylight hours. Though he would be protected from UV rays while inside Frelsi, Sasha's body required a rest period that followed the Earth's sun. Winter would give him more time when he wasn't in a daytime stupor.

I loved summers. I loved taking my kids to the pool at my dad's house and having barbecues and going to see baseball games with my guys. I loved long vacations at the beach.

I loved spending mornings on my balcony with Dev and Danny, precious quiet time together before the kids were up and we needed to take them to school or soccer games.

"Hey, you've got your sad face on, and Lee's going to stop talking long enough to realize it soon," Neil whispered my way.

Lee was giving me and Dean the lowdown on the city, pointing out some of his favorite shops and cafés. I plastered a smile on my face because I didn't want him to think I wasn't enjoying my time with him. I definitely didn't want him to think I was wishing he was a younger version of himself, that he didn't have those scars and that eye patch covering his wound. That I wished he'd never had to come here at all.

"The bookstore is called Sun and Moon Books," Lee informed me. "It's kind of a meetup spot for the supernatural elements of this part of the world. It's considered a place of peace, but that stops at the door to Frelsi."

"Are there covens in this part of the world?" Dean asked.

"Most of the powerful covens are in Dallas now." Lee turned down a bustling street. "But there are some around this part of Iceland. I would be careful with any witch you meet. You can't know if they're working with Myrddin unless they're actually living in one of our safe spaces. You should talk to Lily. She knows a lot about the witches around here. She's got a little coven going."

"I would like that," Dean admitted. "I've been a solitary practitioner most of my life. I would like to work with a group."

It was only another couple of minutes before Neil and I were dropped off at a clothing store with strict instructions to not leave the block. We'd been told to put the things we wanted to buy on hold and Rhys would come by to pay and have it all hauled back to Frelsi.

It reminded me of the time I spent held by the old Council. I'd shopped, though I'd had no intention of actually wearing the clothes I'd bought since I'd been planning to break out.

I'd been pregnant then, too.

"Okay, does this sweater complement my eyes?" Neil asked me about thirty minutes into our shopping spree.

I nodded, though I'd barely glanced at what he was holding in his hand. "Sure."

He growled, an impatient sound. "You are so frustrating."

"I'm sorry. I'm not excited about buying clothes I won't be able to wear in a couple of months."

Neil frowned but seemed to consider the situation. "We can buy you some cute maternity clothes. Come on. Why don't we go down the street? I saw a baby store. I know you don't need it right now, but looking at adorable baby clothes will put you in a better mood. Or we can go into the juniors section. I was hoping you would help me find some clothes for Cassie."

He knew how to get to me. And the truth was I often like to shop for other people far more than myself. Neil hadn't been able to shop without worrying about money for years, so I was willing to indulge my old friend. I also was pretty interested in buying some clothes for Evan, and I did love to look at baby clothes.

Would I have this baby on the run? Would she be hunted like my other kids?

Or would I find a way back to the safety of my old timeline?

We started to walk out the door, and proof that my old timeline hadn't been safe at all stood right outside the door.

Myrddin was here, and Neil and I were in trouble.

Chapter Fourteen

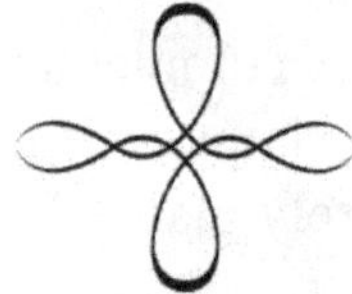

He wore all black, from the coat around his muscular body to the loafers on his feet. He was polished and yet menacing.

On the outside Myrddin appeared to be a man in his prime, and I supposed he was. He looked to be around forty in human years, with dark hair and eyes that could change with his intent. Normally they were dark, but from time to time the color would lighten and yet still stay cold. He was attractive, but there was no way to miss the ruthless will that always surrounded the male.

Neil immediately moved in front of me, ready to take whatever the wizard would throw at us. He'd seen what Myrddin had done to Zack and yet he didn't hesitate.

Myrddin sighed, a long-suffering sound. "Now there, Mr. Roberts. There's no need for such dramatics. I came for a friendly talk. Do I look like I'm about to rip Her Grace's throat out?"

"That's Your Highness to you," Neil growled back. "She's the Queen of All Vampire and you will treat her with respect."

"Vampire is fractured," Myrddin replied. "As are all of the supernatural tribes. It happened shortly after the queen and king disappeared and left their duties behind. It was up to me to bring them all back together. I'm afraid that while Zoey still holds her Fae titles, the rest of them are gone. Kingdoms are fragile things, Your Grace. They tend to fall apart if the king isn't around."

"And whose fault was that?" Neil shot back.

I was tired. And maybe I had some of that recklessness that charged Lee's every move. If Myrddin was going to kidnap me in broad daylight on a busy street, then he could go for it. There was a café next door and it looked warm and inviting and filled with a bunch of humans. I had to bet Myrddin was still holding the supernatural laws sacred for now, and our number one rule was—don't scare the humans.

"I need something warm." And it didn't hurt that I could smell cookies. I turned my back on Myrddin and walked to the small café.

"Zoey, we should get out of here." Neil was right behind me.

"And go where?" Myrddin was here, and I didn't know if I could shake him. I also didn't know how many guards he had hidden around the city, ready to pounce. If I was about to be taken, the least I could do was grab a snack.

"I don't know," Neil huffed. "Someplace that's not here surrounded by… Huh. I guess you're right. We're safer in a crowd. Humans having those pesky cell phones on them all the time helps us out. Ooo, try the chocolate cake of death. It's super rich. And meringue cookies. You know what? I could eat."

He always could eat. Neil had that good old werewolf metabolism I envied. I thought briefly about texting Lee or Rhys, but then the danger simply shifted from myself to my boys. I had to hope they would take their time getting their errands finished.

I glanced over and Myrddin was still standing outside, staring in like walking away was the last thing he'd expected me to do. He looked…almost confused. When a young woman opened the door and walked inside, he followed her.

"Zoey, I'm only here to talk to you." He held his hands up as though showing me he didn't have a weapon would make me feel better. Myrddin was a weapon. Ancient magic flowed through his veins. "You know there's an explanation for what happened. I'm going to assume your brain went to all the worst places since you seem to have a terrible impression of me."

I ordered a pot of tea and let Neil select our treats while I moved to a table at the front of the café. It was by the window and chilly, but it also allowed people walking on the sidewalk in front of the café to see anything the wizard might do. "Are you seriously going to try to play me this way?"

Myrddin sat down across from me. "I know you won't believe me but losing the king for over a decade was not my intent."

"Excellent. It was all a mistake. I'd like my crown back now. I'll let my husband know he can take his, too."

Myrddin stared at me for a moment. "That won't happen anytime soon. I've been forced to make certain deals in order to survive. Though I did not ever intend to banish Daniel, I've made the best of things, and your return could complicate my plans."

Neil moved in, putting a tray of sweets on the table. "I wish you would stop doing that. I'm supposed to be guarding you. Do not make me choose between this cake and your life." He sat down beside me. "The tea is on its way." He gave Myrddin the stink eye. "No wizards allowed. Buy your own cake."

Myrddin chuckled and sat back, his body leaning away from the table. "I should have known nothing would faze Zoey Donovan-Quinn."

"Oh, I assure you losing twelve years had an effect." I pulled my gloves off and set them aside. "Now what are you doing here? I won't ask how you found me because you would only lie."

"I've always known there was a base somewhere here in Iceland. I assume you have a network of portals," Myrddin mused. "It's what I would do, and your ties to the earthly Fae are legendary. I think it's somewhere up north in the mountains, but it's well shielded. I almost found it the other day."

"Yeah, fuck you very much," Neil said.

"I'm sorry I wasn't at the coven house when you returned." Myrddin studied me carefully. "I'd love to know how a painting that should have been on the Hell plane managed to end up in one of the offices. I've already had a long talk with the witch who runs that particular office."

I wasn't about to tell him about Christine. I hoped whoever we'd screwed over hadn't been one of our own. "Don't look at me for information, buddy. I just got here."

"And yet you've already caused much chaos. It will take weeks to get the wards back at full strength. That bomb your spawn set off was quite effective." Myrddin chuckled. "I should have known it wouldn't take Daniel long to find his group of loyal friends. That was my true trouble with Daniel. My other charges tended to be lonely and isolated. I should have gotten to this king earlier. I might have been able to save him."

I'd been Danny's best friend even when we were children. "You mean you might have been able to control him better than you have."

"Oh, I controlled Daniel perfectly well. You were the problem, and now I find your children very difficult," Myrddin admitted. "If I'd been allowed to influence them, they would be living happily in the safety of the coven. Poor…Lee, I believe his name is…he would still be whole. It was a terrible thing the Fae did to the boy. And with a magical weapon so the big Russian couldn't fix him. That certainly wouldn't have happened if he'd been in my care."

"Yes, because you would have taken my human son under your wing. He would have been so safe with you." The meringue cookies were delicious, and I was starting to have a suspicion that we were safer than I thought. The more I watched Myrddin, the more I thought something was wrong.

Myrddin's eyes narrowed. "He's not human though, is he? He's something more."

I set the cookie down because it suddenly tasted like ashes in my mouth. I'd only discovered the truth about Lee the day before. "How would you know that?"

"Because Daniel told me, of course." A sympathetic look hit the wizard's eyes, and he looked like he knew he was in control again. "You know how close we were. Daniel told me long ago that he had suspicions about Lee, but he couldn't be sure. Apparently the latency of a vampire is more easy for Daniel to discern after puberty. But I knew he was right. I knew Lee was a special child. I assure you I would have protected Lee until he came of age to make the decision to transition. I would have protected all the children."

He would have used them. They would have been chess pieces to this man, and if he'd known about the prophecy concerning Lee, he would have killed him immediately.

Daniel had told Myrddin what he hadn't bothered to tell me. Oh, I'd gotten the whole explanation that he hadn't been sure and didn't want to worry me, that he hadn't wanted to force me to keep the secret from Lee until he was able to process it. I'd heard all of that, but the fact that he'd shared something so private made me angry.

"Zoey, if he didn't tell you until recently it's certainly because he was trying to protect you," Myrddin said in a soothing voice.

He went silent as the server brought our tea. She set cups in front of me and Neil and settled the pretty pot in between us. She ignored the fact that we had a third person at the table.

I poured us two cups with a practiced hand. Because pouring tea and making small talk were things I was supposed to be good at now. They were my "place." Bitterness rose up like an old snake threatening to strike again. I had to remember that it was the thrall stone that had influenced Danny, and he didn't have it anymore.

I also needed to remember that Myrddin didn't know those stones had been discarded on another plane. I needed to save that so Danny and Dev could use it if they ever needed to.

"He tries to protect me from a lot of things I don't need protection from." I needed to get off this subject or I could screw things up. And the truth of the matter was I had some questions for the wizard. "Did you mean to get rid of me, too?"

Myrddin sighed. "No. Marcus was my target, and then I realized I could get rid of the Hunter, too. I stand by both decisions. Marcus wasn't going to be reasonable about our contracts with the demons. And the Hunter was a walking nightmare. She was going to be trouble for everyone, you know. You can't control her."

I didn't need to control Kelsey. I trusted her. If she ever came for us, it would be because we deserved it.

"But after the Hunter went through, I had to leave the painting where it was," Myrddin continued. "To take it down would have been suspicious. I'll be honest, I never thought Olivia could spell the pixie the way she did. Even then she was stronger than I believed. Once that was put into place, well, the rest is history. Perhaps it was over before that. Once Devinshea was gone, Daniel would never be persuaded to stop looking for him. I never meant to lose Devinshea. He wasn't a problem."

Because he'd been under Myrddin's spells, too. "Well, you certainly used it all to your advantage. I hear you told the world that Marcus and the academics had turned against us."

He shrugged slightly. "The academics have a long history of

unseating rulers they don't like. It was a useful tale. There has to be a villain, you know. That's what I've found. Talk of unity for unity's sake is all good and well, but nothing brings people together like giving them someone to hate, someone to blame all their problems on."

"Yes, it's always good to have someone to beat up on," Neil said, his bitterness obvious because he'd been that punching bag before. "Find someone different and point their way and you can be the hero."

I glanced around and saw a few people looking at us, but they seemed to focus on me and Neil. Like we were acting odd. There was something we were missing. "And now you plan on handing the plane over to demonkind. I guess you're going for the prize for ultimate villain, aren't you?"

Myrddin sighed as though he'd expected better from me. "Am I? I don't know about that. You seem to think the demons will invade and turn the whole place into another Hell plane."

"Won't they?" I asked, though I knew the answer to that question. No matter what they'd told Myrddin—even if they thought they were telling the truth—full-blooded demons ended up going one way. The worst way.

He chuckled in a manner that let me know he thought I was a naïve child. "Of course not. The demons I'm working with seek to enrich the Earth plane, not destroy it. For eternity Earth has been held back by Heaven's rules and laws and expectations. Earth has been a son of Heaven and never truly allowed to stand on its own. Imagine what it will be like without the influence of a suffocating father standing over it every minute of the day."

He was insane. I was pretty sure of that now. "So the demons are going to be what? The aggressive asshole big brother we've always longed for?"

"No, they're going to teach humans how to care for themselves, how to enjoy their limited lives. They will teach them to live for today and not weep and cry about tomorrow," Myrddin explained. "They will teach humans that Heaven's rules are ridiculous, that it's all right to be a physical being. Imagine a world where creatures like Mr. Roberts here aren't treated like lessors because of his sexual preference."

"I don't think that was Heaven." Neil sat back, setting his cup down again. "I think humans can do plenty of damage all on their own. From what I've met of celestial creatures they're pretty cool."

We'd met several, including Sarah's husband, Felix. We'd been told that the force at the center of the universe was far more tolerant than humans gave him or her or it credit for. Love, tolerance, kindness, those were the tenants of the angels I'd met. And a couple of them had real potty mouths.

"Really?" Myrddin huffed the question. "And the one who tried to kill the *Nex Apparatus* a few years ago? Was he…cool?"

Neil shook his head. "Nah, he was an asshole, and he's probably somewhere here on this plane or another starting over again. See, you took something different than I did from that story. I was actually there and I saw what happened. I saw celestial beings who could wipe us out with a single thought stand and allow one of their own to be subject to Earth's laws for the simple fact that it was just and right. And when he died—even though he'd betrayed them all—they gave him compassion and allowed him to begin again. That's the trouble with some immortals. You get this one life and when you screw it up, you don't start over and try to get it right. You tend to double down. You're mad at Daddy and want to show him how powerful you are."

Myrddin's jaw tightened, and I could easily see that had been a direct hit. "My father was an incubus."

According to the legends, Myrddin was the product of a sex demon's seduction of a pious woman. "I believe he's referring to our spiritual father or mother, depending on your beliefs. But you don't have any beliefs, do you? Not beyond your own power. Heaven's done nothing for you, and the Earth plane's been kind of a bust since your power is always tied to someone else. Why not give Hell a try? The problem is they'll promise you everything. And it's all a lie. You're screaming into the void, wizard. What you want isn't something Hell can give you. You want power? They'll give you the illusion of it. You want to be some kind of guru for all of Earth? They'll hand you the keys to the kingdom and they will take them back whenever they want to. Your best bet is to climb into that crystal coffin of yours to wait for another turn and do better next time because no one is truly immortal and those demons will prove it to you when you fail."

"I have no intentions of failing, bitch."

There he was. There was the real Myrddin, the one who lived beneath the courtesy and double-edged words. I always found it interesting that it was only women who could truly rankle this legendary male. "But whatever will you do without your book?"

Neil went still beside me. "Zoey…"

It was my turn to shrug because he already suspected me. Tiptoeing around the subject wouldn't change his mind. It didn't mean I couldn't lie about it. If Lucifer was the father of lies, then Myrddin was at least a first cousin, so he deserved it. "I can tell him, Neil. I can tell him everything. I stole your book, asshole. I had a magical wallet. You know, the kind you can stuff anything into and it fits perfectly. It was a present from my father. You remember him? The one you killed. I had it on me when I fell through your trap. I did not bring the fucker back. I traded it to some witches on another plane. Got a good deal."

I had done nothing of the sort, but it was worth it to watch his eyes go slightly red, to see his fists clench and know he couldn't do anything about it. Well, I suspected he couldn't. If I was wrong, I was probably looking at a good dose of pain.

Neil put a hand on mine. "I think we should go."

"Why?" I sat back and put my cards on the table. Figuratively, so to speak. "What's he going to do? Strangle me? Use those noncorporeal hands of his to curse me? He has to be close for that to work, and I suspect he's back in Dallas using some poor witchling over here to focus his image."

Neil sniffed the air. "I can smell him."

"Which only proves how good he is at this. But have you noticed? The server didn't bring us an extra plate or teacup. Myrddin couldn't follow us in here until someone held the door open. He's sitting on the chair, but he hasn't touched anything. He's using some sort of spell to give his illusion depth and sensory reality," I surmised. "But he's not here. He's all pretty and dressed up and completely impotent."

Myrddin's jaw tightened, and I could practically feel his frustration. "Watch yourself, Your Highness. I won't always be a thousand miles away."

No. Hopefully he would be on another plane trying to track down his grimoire. Or at least expending energy and resources to find out if I was lying. "But you are today, so you'll forgive me if I'm not terrified."

"There will be no forgiveness from me," he vowed. "Not unless you convince Daniel to turn himself in now and you get my grimoire and the sword back. Did you have that in your pocket as well?"

"What can I say? I like a buy one get one free deal," I admitted. "Besides, that sword didn't belong to you. Of course I took it. That magical wallet was a hell of a gift. My dad's still fucking with you even after you killed him."

"Well, next time I see that little medium he's hiding in, I'll make sure to eat her soul. They're sharing right now, so that can be my buy one get one free snack." He leaned toward me. "Don't think simply because I'm not physically here that I can't make your life hell, Your Highness. I know basically where you are. I'll send demon after demon until I get what I want back. Not even your witch friend will be able to help you. I'll get my revenge on her, too. She thinks her heart's blood can keep me out. She's wrong."

He'd had my full attention all along, but oh, he definitely had it times a hundred now. "Are you talking about Sarah?"

"You know exactly who I'm talking about, and I'll cut her heart out when I find her," he vowed. "You want the real me, Your Highness, you'll get it. No more playing around with you. I'm going to kill everyone you love, and in the end I'll still get what I need from you. You'll bleed for me and I'll close all the doors to Heaven. You'll die knowing your line dies with you."

Sarah might be alive. Or he could be lying to me the same way I'd lied to him. Lee had told us that Olivia had sworn Sarah and her family were dead. But Myrddin was flustered and I might have gotten the truth out of him.

"I'm shaking in my boots." Like that was the worst I'd ever heard. I'd stood before Lucifer Morningstar and come out of the experience whole and alive. "Now run along, Myrddin. You won't be getting your hands on my husbands again. And tell whichever woman has been playing around with my things that she should watch her back. Bitch better have my crown."

I could see the rage in his eyes, feel it across all those miles, and it did nothing but harden my resolve. We sat there for a moment, the anger an ocean between us.

Then there was a knock on the window that startled me out of my stare off.

"Hey, Mom." Lee was standing right outside the window, a bright smile on his face. He waved at me, seeming to take no notice of Myrddin at all. "Ooo, cookies. Nice."

"He's still human." Myrddin's lips curved up. "Isn't that interesting? So human and vulnerable. Not that all your children aren't vulnerable. I'll get them all in the…" Myrddin's voice trailed off and his eyes went wide. "Who is that?"

Dean had walked up and stood beside Lee. Unlike my son, who was making goofy faces, Dean could absolutely see Myrddin. He was staring at the wizard like he knew exactly who he was and how much danger we were all in now that he knew we were back.

"A friend from the outer planes," I said. "I dropped your book off and picked him up. You know the universe likes a good balance."

Myrddin stared at Dean for a moment as though trying to memorize his face and then he turned back to me. "So do I. Don't forget that I'll make sure you pay for every time you defy me. This could have gone easy for you. You're the one who made it hard, and everyone will pay for your crimes." He leaned over and even though I knew he was an illusion, I didn't like being so close to him. "You think you're the only one who can create a bit of chaos? I've told everyone who's ever looked for you to come to Iceland. Looks like at least one of them is already here. 'Til we meet again."

And then he was gone, disappearing like the illusion he'd been.

Lee pushed through the door. "Mom? What's going on? Dean said he could see some old dude but I couldn't."

Technically Myrddin's like a couple of thousand years old, but Dean couldn't know that. So Dean thought a forty-year-old hottie was ancient? Youth. It made me feel old. Still, I let it go. "Myrddin's made his appearance and he's screwed up my whole day because now I won't get to see Ingrid and Halle. We need to get back to base as soon as possible."

We couldn't stay out in the open. Despite the fact that Myrddin hadn't physically been here, he could still do damage from halfway around the world.

"That was Myrddin." Dean stared at the place where Myrddin's illusion had been. "I've dreamed of him."

"Like you dream about Lee?" I kind of thought those had been…pleasant dreams. Dean had talked a lot about the dreams he'd had about Lee and a woman he'd never met. I hadn't heard anything about Myrddin.

Dean's cheeks flushed. "No. Not exactly."

"I'd like to hear more about these dreams," Lee said and then he frowned. "Shit. Mom, I need you to make a run for the bookstore."

I glanced out the window and caught sight of what had my baby boy so upset. His papa was walking down the street. Well, the douchebag version was. Dev's hair was shorter and he'd left this morning wearing a suit, not the leather pants and long tunic this asshole was.

Declan Quinn.

He was looking up and down the street, and I knew exactly who he was searching for. He wanted his nephew. Well, the one he thought was important. And because it was that kind of day, Rhys chose that moment to round the corner. Rhys and Shy were talking and hadn't caught sight of Rhys's uncle, who'd likely come to kidnap him and take him back to Faery and force him to have sex with a whole bunch of gorgeous women he did not want to have sex with.

I was done with evil men for the day, and definitely done with ones who threatened my babies.

"Mom, I'll distract him," Lee offered. "Grab Rhys and run for the store."

It was time for me to show my boys that Momma was home and she could take care of business. It was sweet that they wanted to protect me, but I'd learned a long time ago how to protect myself.

"What are you going to do, Z?" Neil asked around a mouthful of cookie he wasn't about to leave behind.

"I'm going to explain the situation to my brother-in-law." I walked to the door and out onto the street, the boys following behind me.

Declan stopped, his eyes widening, and there was no way to mistake his shock. "Zoey? Zoey, is it truly you? I didn't believe it when they told me you'd returned. I had to come see for myself. Is Devinshea here? Where's my brother?"

He held his arms open like I was going to walk in for a hug, and hey, maybe we could totally forget about the time he refused to give one son shelter and all those times when he actively tried to kidnap the other.

"Mom, get back." Rhys had stepped in front of Shy.

I ignored him, smiling at Declan.

"Oh, Zoey, I can't tell you how happy I am…"

I walked straight up to that asshole and planted a knee in his groin, trying to shove his dick back up into his body. He groaned and fell to the ground because I was still good with a knee.

"Mom!" Rhys shouted. "What are you doing?"

I leaned over my brother-in-law even as he cupped himself and cried a little. "I am back, brother. Remember that. I'm back and I know everything you've done while I've been gone. You are not welcome here. Go back to Faery and stay away from my sons."

I stepped over his body and started for the bookstore.

It was time for a change of plans.

Chapter Fifteen

"Are we going to leave him in there?" Rhys watched the mirror that showed us the hallway between the door from Frelsi and the one that led to Reykjavík. It currently had one occupant—a very distressed future King of Faery who paced up and down the corridor and readjusted himself several times.

"I'm not about to let that asshole in." I was unconcerned with my brother-in-law's comfort. "Your papa should be back soon. He can deal with your uncle."

Declan was Devinshea's problem. I'd learned to leave him to Dev long ago.

Neil watched Declan pacing. "I think it's funny. Hope he used the bathroom before he left Faery. How do you think he got here so fast?"

"The Unseelie *sithein*," Lee replied. "It's how they all get to this part of the world. The door to the Unseelie *sithein* is in the Scottish Highlands. From there he likely caught an eddy wind, since he can't fly like Dad. I wonder how close they came to bumping into each other."

I wished they had since then I wouldn't be the one dealing with the brat prince.

Declan had followed us back to the bookstore, and I'd made the decision to trap him rather than leave him roaming around the city causing trouble.

"Zoey, could you hear me out? Could you at least listen to my side of the story?" Declan stood in front of the mirror that served as both monitor and communication device. I'd been assured it was one way when it came to the ability to see through, and Declan would only hear us if we allowed him to.

"I'm surprised he's able to walk." Lee saw the humor in the situation. Or my baby boy simply thought a guy getting kicked in the balls was funny. "Momma really got in there. I swear, Uncle Dec's eyes nearly bulged off his face."

"Well, I taught my darling girl how to put a man on his knees." My dad had made an appearance. Shy stood off to the side, her lips curled up in a way that wasn't natural to the pretty young woman's face. It was the same smile my father wore when a job went off without a hitch.

Unfortunately, there had been plenty of hitches today.

"I'm just glad the snackums got through before we had to trap him." Neil touched the boxes of food and supplies that had been waiting for us. Lee had done his job and we would have food even though I hadn't gotten the clothes I needed. "I wonder what Albert's making for dinner."

A wolf always thinks with his gut. Always.

"He looks like your father." Dean stood to the side. He'd been somewhat unsettled after running into the man he was supposed to kill.

But then Myrddin had been, too. He'd paid Lee little mind, but the sight of Dean had worried him. It was one more piece of information I needed to think about.

"They're twins, though Papa is mortal and our uncle is fully Fae," Rhys explained.

"So they're like you and Lee?" Dean asked.

"Well, except now I'm going to become a creature of the night when I die." Lee said it with a smirk. "An all-powerful vampire who lives on precious blood and protects those he loves."

"If you talk like this after your turn, I'm going to stake you," Rhys promised.

"Mom, Rhys is threatening to end my immortal life," Lee said with a fake whine.

"Rhys, you can't stake your brother." I had to draw the line somewhere. "But I will teach you all the ways to irritate the hell out of him while he sleeps."

"Your mom was so mean to your dad when he annoyed her. This was before he could daywalk, of course. He would be in that dead stupor and your mom had all the power then." Neil smiled like he was remembering good times. "She would put show tunes on repeat and he couldn't do anything but enjoy the ride."

The smirk disappeared off Lee's face. "That's not fair."

Rhys patted his brother's shoulder. "Maybe not, but it's going to be fun. I can think of lots of things to do during the day. Loudly."

"Boys, be serious for a moment," my father said. "Your mother needs to make a decision. Are you going to hold the bastard until Devinshea gets here, or should you kill him and no one needs to know?"

"I can't kill him." Even if I wanted to, and I kind of did. "I do have a few words to say though."

I nodded Rhys's way and he waved his hand over the bottom of the mirror. "He can hear you now."

I stood in front of the mirror, staring at my brother-in-law. Twelve years hadn't changed any single feature of Declan's face, but there was something different about him, some worry that seemed to have aged the immortal faery. I wasn't going to let that soften my heart toward him. "Did you or did you not refuse my son asylum when he needed it most?"

Declan's jaw tightened. "You do not understand. I did that for Lee. Do you think I wanted to refuse him? I know you won't believe me when I say this, but I love my nephews. I love my niece. It would have been dangerous to bring a human into my world. And the wolf child would have been in danger as well."

"But Rhys was fine?" I asked. "Rhys was so safe you've tried to kidnap him a couple of times?"

"You know why we need Rhys. With Devinshea gone there is no Green Man walking either the Seelie or the Unseelie planes. We've had trouble with uprisings. I had to protect my own son from mobs who claim our whole line is cursed," Declan said. "I had to send him to his mother in the Unseelie *sithein*. I have not laid eyes on him in over a year."

I didn't want to hear about Declan's sorrows. "My children didn't see their kin for twelve. Don't think I weep for you. I trusted you."

"And I told you a long time ago that you can never trust a king. I cannot make decisions based on my own will. I must always think of my people. Even when I would rather slaughter the lot of them," Declan shot back. "I could not risk Lee becoming a focal point of their anger. He was better off with Devinshea's butler and the vampire."

"I was," Lee whispered. "Albert's cooking is way better. Also, it was more fun to learn how to kill shit."

"Lee, watch your language around our mother," Rhys admonished.

Lee shrugged. "I think Mom proved she's not some dainty queen when she shoved our uncle's balls up into his throat."

Declan ignored them. "I have questions, sister. You were gone for years, and I did not know what had happened. You owe me the answers. I have come here in good faith. I did not even bring a full guard with me because I didn't want there to be misunderstandings. The one I do have will not show himself. I ordered him to not touch anyone no matter what happened. So I want my questions answered."

Ah, so he didn't want the guards to defend him because he'd known damn well how I would react.

I owed him nothing. "Ask your brother. He should return in a few hours. Until then, enjoy your stay in our hallway." I nodded to Rhys, who cut our side of the feed. Declan's head dropped, but I wasn't about to give him more of my time. I had other things to deal with. The wizard had given up some information. If I could trust it. I turned to my father. "You said you didn't see Sarah after you died."

"No. I didn't. What's happened?" he asked. "Did Myrddin say something?"

Neil was suddenly interested in our conversation. "He did. He acted like she was alive."

"He said I should warn her that he would have his revenge on her," I explained.

Lee had straightened up, too. "He didn't kill Aunt Sarah? Does that mean Mia's alive?"

I didn't want to get his hopes up. I shouldn't have said anything, but I wasn't thinking straight. "I don't know, but I intend to find out. Myrddin could be lying to me. He could be trying to throw me off."

"I don't think so," Neil mused. "You had him pretty riled up by that time. He forgot to play the polite courtier. I don't think he intended to end that conversation with threats."

"Well, my daughter knows how to irritate an asshole," my father said. "Tell me you didn't give him ammo, girl."

I waved off that worry. "He already knew I stole the grimoire. I might have implied I had it with me when I went through the painting. But don't worry. I didn't mention the bag of holding. I called it a magical wallet."

Shy's eyes rolled. "Damn it, Zoey. That's close enough. If he thinks about it…"

"He won't," Neil argued. "He'll be far too busy trying to figure out how to get someone over to the outer planes to look for his grimoire. He might even try to do it himself. He hasn't been able to sense it, right?"

"No, but he wouldn't, would he?" Dad countered. "It's in the bag of holding. Even if he found that bag, he wouldn't be able to open it. It's primed for two people, and one of us is dead. Zoey's the only one who can find it and open it."

"Then it's all right that I sent him on a wild-goose chase. If we get any kind of word that Myrddin isn't in Dallas, then we need to be ready to get into the building." I would love it if I didn't have to make my way around Myrddin. I was nervous enough taking my son in. If I could buy us an advantage, I would. "But I need to figure out what happened to Sarah and her family. And he said something else."

"He mentioned her heart's blood," Neil mused.

Lee frowned. "I know she had wards up around the building she used her own blood for. I'm not sure what heart's blood is."

I knew. "It's super dangerous since she would have to had literally taken the blood directly from her heart. For the warding to work the way it should, the blood has to be in the heart chamber when it's extracted. It's a very strong ward that has a lot to do with the intent of the witch who gave her blood. With it, Sarah could keep unwanted beings out. Not merely make them not want to go into a space. She could keep them out like she'd placed a metal gate across a door."

"But I thought she'd done that all over the Council building," Neil said. "If she did, how could Myrddin move in?"

"Because it wouldn't work that way on large, public spaces." Dean took over the explanation, and that was a good thing because I was at the end of my knowledge. "I'm going to suspect this had something to do with Myrddin, right?"

"Absolutely. I know she did it so she would be able to track Myrddin if she needed to. She thought he would be able to get through some of her wards and she wanted to know if he took them down." She'd told me this in one of the last conversations we'd had together.

"The wards to track him would be easy, and if she was subtle, he might not notice. To keep him physically out, it would work best on a smaller space. Like her home or some storage area she didn't want him to gain access to." Dean seemed to think about the problem. "She could also have used the warding to boost any spells she might need. Her heart's blood would have that effect."

"So if she'd suddenly needed to keep him out, she could have used the wards to boost say a spell to keep a door closed." I was thinking it through, too.

Dean nodded. "Yes. It would make the space uniquely attuned to her."

"So she would have had an advantage if Myrddin attacked her." I wanted to believe that she was out there and she was alive. "She could have gone to another plane."

"There are no doors in the Council building. Not to other planes," my father pointed out and then grimaced. "Excepting to the Hell plane. If she got trapped, she could have been desperate."

Sarah knew a little about the Hell plane, but I couldn't see her taking her daughter there. Still, if it had been the only way. "Have we heard anything about odd going-ons on the Hell plane?"

"No, but we wouldn't hear anything. We're on the outside. Sasha might know something, or Alexander," Lee replied. "And it would have been long ago. By the time we came back to the Earth plane and settled here in Frelsi, Mia had been gone for years. Maybe she went off plane, too. Maybe she's out there."

Neil shook his head. "Not unless she found a way to… Is there any way they could have used the painting and you missed them?"

Oh, I liked that thought quite a bit. "She could have figured it out. She could have made a run for it. By the time she would have gone through, we were probably all at the *brugh* Summer stayed in. It was hidden. Sarah wouldn't have been able to find us, and then we hopped all over the place."

"It's possible," Dean said in a way that made me think he didn't like the odds. "Though if she was half the witch you say she was, once we were outside our wards, she should have been able to find us with a locator spell. Or she could have tried to communicate some other way. The plane we were on was a dangerous place."

"I want to go." Lee's hands went to his hips, a stubborn stance. "I want to go to whatever plane you were on and I'll find her. I promise."

"Lee, we have no idea how to get there," Rhys said. "And we have things we need to do on this plane. I can't come with you. I know how much you miss her, but they've had a long time to try to get back. Her mother is a formidable witch. If there was a way to return or to communicate with us, she would have. We have to face the fact that we were probably right the first time. They are lost to us."

"I've let you tell me that for twelve years," Lee gritted out, getting in his brother's face. "What the hell turned you into such a pessimistic asshole? She could be out there. Do you even care? She was your friend, too. We used to eat dinner with them and play games with Uncle Felix. Why would you throw away a chance to find them?"

"Because I have to be the realist. Because you're far too busy playing the charming rogue and hanging on to all your ridiculous romantic dreams," Rhys shot back. "One of us has to be pragmatic. Remember what happened the last time you played the hero. I paid, Lee. My scars might have healed, but I assure you I remember the night. I dream about it. I wake up screaming because of it, so you know what…go and find her. It will be easier to win this war if I'm not constantly trying to keep you alive."

"Rhys," Lee began.

Rhys ignored him. "Mother, I'm going to get some people to help take this shipment in and deliver it where it needs to go. I'm sorry the day went poorly. We can try again tomorrow if you decide that's what you want to do."

"Rhys, I'm sorry," Lee practically begged.

"You always are." Rhys turned and walked off.

"I think Shy is needed here more than I am right now," my father said. And then Shy was in control again. "I'm going to help Rhys. I'll calm him down, Your Highness."

She jogged after him, and I was glad someone was with him.

"Dean, Neil, could I have a moment with my son?" I didn't think I should make this a public discussion.

Neil nodded and led Dean off.

I turned to Lee. "What was that about? What happened to your brother?"

Lee had paled, but he shook his head. "I'm sorry. That's his story to tell. I'm actually shocked he brought it up in front of anyone else. It's been a hard twelve years. I know I smile a lot but…it was hard and I miss Mia. I wasn't trying to be an asshole."

What had happened to Rhys? Would he even talk to me about it? Or had I lost that right by being gone so long? He'd become a man without his parents around, and despite the fact it hadn't been our choice, he might never look to us for comfort again. At least Lee seemed willing to accept my affection. I wrapped an arm around his waist. "I know, baby. But you need to apologize to your brother. He's worried about your transition, and not for the reason you think."

"I'm going to be fine. I'm not even worried about the pain," Lee countered.

"Rhys is worried. He's worried he's going to lose his brother. He's worried you're going to become a vampire and leave him behind. You throw yourself into things and forget he's around." He'd done it his whole childhood. Lee had been the force of nature and Rhys the dutiful child.

"No, I don't." His head dropped down, resting against mine. "I guess I do. I remember how he used to ask me to play, but I wanted to work with Kelsey. And then I wanted to study languages. The weird thing is it was all about trying to make myself special. Rhys…I mean the Fae have always bowed down to him, and Evan was the only girl."

"But you were special to Rhys. You were his brother, his twin. You think he didn't feel the distance? You didn't know it at the time, but you were drawn to Mia for a reason. The same way your dad and I bonded when we were kids. I'm not saying you did anything wrong. I'm just saying that Rhys has always felt you pulling away from him."

"I didn't mean to make him feel that way." Lee stepped back, a frown on his face. "I love my brother. I would die for him. We're closer now than we were as kids. Rhys and Evan and Fen are my crew."

He remembered the language of his childhood, the language of thieves. "Give him a little time to calm down and then maybe spend some of your evening with him. Let him know you're here, that you're still his brother," I advised.

"He missed you, too," Lee whispered. "I know he seems cold, but I think he's scared you won't like who he is now. Evan, too. All Evan needs is for you to be yourself around her, but Rhys might need a push. Oh, hey, it looks like the dads are back."

I glanced over at the mirror and sure enough, the door had come open and Daniel and Dev had walked through.

"Brother," Declan began with a sigh of obvious relief.

Dev simply growled, tackled him, and started to punch.

"I missed you guys so fucking much," Lee said, and the smile was back on his face. "Sorry. I'll try to curse less."

He could try, but it wouldn't work. It was in his blood.

"Oww, I don't think Uncle Declan is having more kids," Lee observed.

At least one dude was having a worse day than me.

* * * *

A few hours later I sat studying the Council building layout that Sasha had given me. One of our spies had made detailed notes on all the changes that had taken place over the years. There were also pictures that made my blood boil. Pictures of my gorgeous penthouse redecorated to look like a freaking mausoleum. Someone had a serious hard-on for red and black and thought leather was a reasonable drapery choice.

If the bag of holding was where I'd left it, it would be in my closet. I'd put it in a corner. Even if Myrddin had cleared out my closet to make room for his ceremonial robes, he wouldn't have found my bag. So the question was how did Lee and I make our way to the closet without being detected. Neil offered us an easy way into the building, but getting up to the penthouse was a problem. And Lee wasn't exactly tiny anymore. We both had to fit under the Mantle of Arthur in order to stay safe from anyone who happened to be walking around the building.

I felt someone move in behind me, and then there was a brushing of lips over my hair.

"Are you all right, my goddess? I'm sorry I missed dinner."

He'd been talking to his brother. After he'd beaten the crap out of him, he and Daniel had decided they had a few questions for Declan and brought him into Frelsi. They'd been holed up in the conference room for hours. I'd spent the time going over plans and making notes and trying not to think about all the pain my children had gone through. "I'm okay. Just trying to wrap my head around this job. I wish I hadn't left the bag in my closet now. Some paranoid asshole made it hard to get up to the penthouse."

He chuckled. "Well, it turned out someone actually was after me."

"Not according to Myrddin. You were a mistake."

He frowned and sat down across from me. "I don't like the sound of that. I can be dangerous. Far more dangerous than Marcus."

"Not while you had that stone in your head. Myrddin didn't see you as a threat. I think he still believes he could influence you and Danny if he could get physically near you. Unless he has some way to tell we got rid of the stone, he can't know it's not still there."

"Well, if that happens, I'll likely pretend. I worry though about Dan. He's not good with pretending. And he's cranky. He punched a wolf in the face during our meeting today. Lucky for him it was a Scottish wolf and now they're friends."

Wolves could be very tolerant. "You think he can work with the alpha?"

"Yes. It was a good meeting after we got the violence out of the way. The wolves want peace again. They'd forgotten what it was like without any kind of centralized government. And they definitely don't want to deal with demons."

"They know about Myrddin's plans?"

"They have their own spies, so they've heard whisperings of

what he's trying to do." He frowned down at the pictures of what used to be our family home. "I should kill him for those drapes alone." He sat down next to me. "I'm sorry you had to face him alone today."

I was glad I'd had the chance. If Dev had his way, he would have hustled me out, and then I wouldn't know that Myrddin believed Sarah was alive. "I think I got some good intel."

"Yes. I saw that you wrote it up for Sasha. Thank you for doing that."

"Devinshea, I remember how to play this game. I know I've been depressed, but I'm not going to hide in here forever. I've got a job to do."

He studied me for a moment. "I thought you wanted to find a way to get back."

I shrugged. "I haven't given up on that, but I have to help out where I can."

"I don't think you should go," Dev said with a frown. "If Myrddin gets his hands on you…"

"Then you need to rescue me." I'd thought a lot about this. "You have to know he won't kill me. If he wants to use the energy in Gladys to close off the doors to the celestial planes, he needs me alive so my blood can activate the sword. I'm the queen of the companions. No one else will do. And since he hasn't had his grimoire for years, I suspect he'll need a moment before he's ready. It won't be the first time I had to survive in enemy territory, and hey, I was pregnant then, too. At least I don't have to worry that Myrddin's going to want me to put out."

"Goddess," he breathed. Dev's jaw went tight, and I realized I'd touched a sore spot that had healed for me long ago. Dev, not so much.

I reached out and put a hand over his. "I'm sorry. I didn't mean to sound so cold. I'm only telling you that I can handle whatever he throws our way."

Dev stood, pulling away from me physically. "You shouldn't have had to do it the first time. I'll be damned if you do it again. Maybe you're right. Maybe we should put all of our efforts into getting out of this."

The door came open again and Daniel strode in. "Getting out of this war? Have you talked to your brother again? Is he willing to let us in? Once Lee turns, we won't have to worry about him as much."

He wasn't thinking straight, and that made me wonder if he'd heard me, too. It sucks to be surrounded by supernatural hearing. It makes gossiping and complaining under my breath hard, and those are two of my favorite hobbies. "Being in one of the *sitheins* attached to the Earth plane won't help us. The demons will merely find a way in once they're done playing here."

"It could buy us decades," Danny mused.

"And still end the same way. What happened today that has you both on edge?" It wasn't merely what I'd said. It couldn't be. "Was it the wolves? Or Declan?"

"It was both, and then we've got the issue with Zack." Danny sat on the edge of the bed. "The blood worked for a little while. Now he's feeling tired again. Worse than he was before. Lisa wants to take him back out to the woods, but I'm worried Myrddin would simply find him and finish the job. He knows where to look."

"He met me miles away in Reykjavík," I pointed out. "I wasn't strolling around the mountainside. But it does make me wonder how he knew. Especially since he suggested he was the one who sent Declan."

Dev nodded. "Declan received word shortly after we returned. According to him, he knew we were back within hours."

That meant one thing. "He's got spies at the Council building. I thought they got rid of all the Fae."

"All the ones they can see," Dev replied.

Ah, so Declan's hidden guard was hard at work. That could play in my favor if he ordered them to help me. If I could trust them. They would always work in the best interests of Faery. I would rather work with spies who Sasha trusted. "That explains how he knew we were back, but not where we are now. Has anyone checked Alexander's communications? Does he pop outside to use a cell?"

"Zoey, he's been here in Frelsi for a week and he hasn't left once, nor has he used the mirrors to communicate," Danny said with a sigh. "I understand that he's dangerous, but he's one of the best spies we've got."

"Well, either one of your spies is a double, or Myrddin's got some of his own here." I didn't buy that he simply guessed we were going to be in Reykjavík today. "He definitely had someone on the ground. He couldn't have sent that projection of himself without someone here helping him."

"I suspect we can easily explain how he knew. He does have spies in the cities," Danny said. "There are bounties on all of the kids' heads, and there are also rewards for information about us. Sasha's tried to shake up the scheduling for supplies, but word can always get out. We'll have to hide our tracks better. Maybe we all need glamours when we leave Frelsi."

"He can see through them." Danny and Dev weren't used to being suspicious of Myrddin one hundred percent of the time. I had to be the leader in this. "Myrddin won't be fooled by glamours. We need more than that. The Mantle of Arthur is the only thing that will work on him, and even then, we have to be careful. We can't run around the streets of the city in an invisibility cloak."

"I don't see why not. You're planning on doing it," Dev pointed out.

"For one very specific job. Should we worry that he's got something that can detect the cloak? After all, it was in his possession for a thousand years. He's got to guess it's how I stole the book in the first place." I was already poking holes every place I could. It was the only way to plan a job. "I would assume when he took over the council building he took an inventory."

The Mantle of Arthur was one of the Thirteen Treasures of Britain, and Myrddin had gifted it to Daniel on the day we were taken by the old council. It had been how Danny and Zack had gotten away. We'd kept it close ever since. I had to assume Myrddin would mark its absence. I also assumed Lee and the kids had played with it over the years since it had been his favorite toy as a child.

"It nullifies magic," Danny explained. "Zack and I made a study of the cloak, and it renders you invisible to everything, including magic. We tried it on several witches and a whole bunch of wards and spells. When you're under that cloak, no one can find you. It's like you drop off the map of the world. I'm not worried about Myrddin being able to sense you. I'm worried about the two of you being under there. It's going to make it hard to move. It was one thing when he was eleven."

"Well, we'll have to practice." It would be so much fun running around under a small cloak trying to coordinate our movements.

"Or we can find another way." Dev sank down beside Danny. "I have a bad feeling about this. I don't like the idea of her going in with only Lee."

"I can't fit three of us in there." And honestly, I didn't want to because I was already worried that Lee and I were going to have to talk about changing his clothes after spending the night with…whoever he spent the night with. Baby boy needed some hygiene lessons. He would likely change his lazy ways when he got supernatural senses. There was also the fact that I had a bad idea. One of those stupid ideas I get that I really shouldn't even talk about. "Besides, I think I need you to agree to meet with him in a neutral place. If you and Danny keep him busy while I'm robbing him blind, he can't capture me and skewer me with a sword to unleash the power of an angel."

When I thought about it, it kind of sucked. Kelsey had totally killed that fucker Jude, but here he was again, trying to screw up everything.

Danny's brow rose. "You want me to meet with him?"

I nodded. "Not only do I want you to meet him, I want you to play him for a while. Listen to his concerns. Tell him I'm not with you because I disagreed utterly with meeting him at all."

"So basically pretend we're still in thrall," Dev surmised. "I think that's a dangerous game, my goddess. If he knows the stones are gone, what is to prevent him from trying again?"

"Well, you would be conscious this time," I pointed out. "And you would also be in a place of peace, so we should be able to nullify Myrddin's magic."

"If he agrees to it, which he likely will not," Dev countered.

"I don't know about that." Danny's eyes met mine, and I knew when he'd been keeping something.

"He's already contacted you." That hadn't taken long. "When?"

Dev's glare could have roasted our whole dinner. "When he asked me to speak privately with the alpha about future locations for meetings with the other European packs. I should have realized something was going on when you disappeared with the she-wolf. Is she a spy?"

"No, she doesn't need to spy. Myrddin contacted her over the Dark Web. He sent the message out to the Irish wolves, too. There isn't a pack here in Iceland that isn't connected to me, so those were his two best bets." Danny stood and started to pace. "I didn't tell you because I wanted to discuss it with our wife, and you know damn well if the two of us talk we generally make a decision and then inform her. I'm not making the same mistakes this time around."

It was good to know that he was thinking about how the first time had gone. He and Dev had been excellent at making decisions that affected me without ever asking my opinion. But then I'd done the same to them. I had to learn from my mistakes, too. "What did Myrddin want?"

"He wanted to meet," Danny admitted. "I think he hoped I would be the one in the city today. He obviously had it all planned out. I have to think he's got a witch he can work with in most of the major cities. He waited until one of us was sighted and then he worked his magic. Like I said, I think he would have preferred me or Dev, but it's a sign of desperation that he was willing to try it with you."

"Not that you aren't the prettiest of us." Dev always tried to soften Danny's edges.

He didn't need to in this case. I wasn't offended that I was the last royal the asshole magician wanted to deal with. It was a point of pride that most people avoided dealing with me if they could. "Well, the witch must be good because Neil couldn't tell he wasn't corporeal. It was an excellent illusion. And he had it focused. Dean saw him. Lee couldn't, but Dean could. And by the way, he did mention that he was surprised Lee was still human."

Dev's gasp let me know he hadn't been in on that secret.

Danny's eyes widened, and it was obvious he knew he was in serious trouble. "Z, I was under the influence of that stone. It made me think I was safe with him."

Dev stood and faced him. "And you weren't safe with me? Lee is our son. You knew he was a latent and you didn't tell us but you talked to him?"

"I wasn't sure." Danny huffed as he tried to find a way out. "You can't tell before puberty. At least I've never been able to. Look, I started to suspect it because of his behavior, but then I thought maybe it was wishful thinking."

"What is that supposed to mean?" Dev asked.

I knew exactly what he meant and how Dev would take it.

Sometimes I could translate for both of them. "It means he didn't have a biological child, and while that didn't stop him from loving the ones we did have, a part of himself envied us. The boys look exactly like you, and Evan resembles me. He's not making light of our family. He's being honest with us about something he doesn't want to admit."

"Okay, I do understand that." Dev's tone softened.

Danny sent me a half smile. "Thanks, Z. I was afraid I was seeing something that might not be there. And then Lee said something to me. Not our Lee. This happened when his soul remembered that he'd been…well, our Lee, but older and more cranky. He told me he sensed something different about himself, that he thought something was wrong with him and he was worried. He asked me to watch him. I promised I would. Like I said, I had suspicions already."

"Suspicions you didn't bring to us," Dev accused.

"I had my reasons for that. I explained it to you. What you're really upset about is that I told Myrddin. I can't explain that except that he always felt like good counsel. When I would talk to him, I felt more at ease. I felt like I was getting sage advice," Danny said with a sigh.

"And I didn't give you…"

I stopped Dev there because we weren't doing this. "You talked to Myrddin all the time. You asked his advice, too. I'm not happy about this, but you of all people should understand how Myrddin could trick a man."

Dev took a deep breath. "All right."

I turned back to Danny. "Have you talked to him yet."

He shook his head. "To Myrddin? No. I don't have a thrall stone embedded in my brain anymore. I was going to sit down and talk to you two before I did anything. I thought I might be able to make a deal to heal Zack. Like I could use the meeting for leverage."

He was so worried about Zack. They'd been a unit for over a decade, Zack always at his side. Dev might hold half of Danny's heart, but Zack was his friend. It was an easy relationship and one Danny had come to rely on over the years. I moved in and wrapped my arms around him. "We need to find a way to heal Zack without giving you up."

"Well, to do that I need to meet with Myrddin, but it has to be somewhere safe, and I need to think about how to handle him. How much time are you and Lee going to need?" Danny rubbed his cheek against my head.

"It depends. I'm hoping I can get up to the penthouse and back out in less than a half an hour. But I don't know what kind of physical security he's put in," I admitted. "He'll have definitely changed the lock, so to speak."

"Will he?" Dev moved behind me, surrounding me and obviously letting go of his anger. He did that so much more quickly now. "Myrddin didn't like technology. He preferred to rely on his skills. Would he even know how to change the elevator codes?"

"She's not going in until we know," Daniel said. "I can put Myrddin off for a week or so."

"And then we guarantee he's changing the locks." I thought we should move as quickly as possible. Getting in and out as fast as we could was the only way to go in this case. And the truth of the matter was I wanted to know if Lee could still see that book. I hoped he could because then he might stay human a little while longer, to see that there was a reason to let himself enjoy his human life.

A low growl came from the back of Danny's throat, a sure sign that he was anxious.

"Hey, it's going to be okay." Dev crowded me, getting a hand on Daniel's neck. "We're going to be all right. Come here and I'll show you."

Danny leaned over and their lips brushed.

Dev knew how to calm the king down after a long day.

Danny went from kissing Dev to devouring me, his tongue surging in and dominating mine in the most delicious way possible. My body went electric.

And then there was a terrible slamming sound as the door came open and Neil rushed in. "Daniel, we need you. It's Zack. He's dying."

We rushed out and I prayed we could find a way to save him.

Chapter Sixteen

"He's stable again." Daniel walked out of the room where Zack lay on what I prayed wasn't his deathbed.

"Good." Dev stood up and straightened his shirt. "I'll go speak with Albert. Some food might do him good."

He kissed my cheek before striding out the door. It was good for him to have something to do. He'd been pacing outside the room, his worry evident in the grim look in his eyes.

Rhys and Shy had taken little Justin to the house Neil and Chad were staying at. Neil had promised Lisa he would watch over her son while she tried to take care of his father.

Courtney wiped tears from her eyes and stood. "Can I see him? Is Mom okay?"

No one had been able to convince Courtney to leave. She'd sat in a chair by the fire, silent the entire time.

Daniel put a hand on her shoulder. "I think he would like that very much. And your mom is being strong. Like I said, he's stable, but I'm still worried. He deteriorated very quickly. We're bringing someone in. I need you to understand that I will do everything I can."

She nodded and let Daniel lead her inside.

The door behind us opened and Lily walked through, a basket in her hand. She was followed by Lee, who'd gone to find her and Dean. Dean looked around the place like he wasn't sure of his welcome. I rather thought he missed Kelsey. She'd been the one he'd spent the most time with when we were on the outer planes. He'd been shoved into this brand-new world and then pushed to the side because we'd been in constant trauma mode since the moment we got here.

He was far from everything he knew, and the person he'd been closest to was gone. He'd followed Lee around, but he still looked so lost. I hoped Lily and the other witches were taking him under their wings. He stopped in the middle of the room and went still as though he was taking in his surroundings and finding them alarming.

"I have a couple of tonics we can try." Lily set her basket down on the coffee table. "But I also thought we could let Dean have a look. His magic is different from any I've ever felt."

"Different how?" I asked.

Lily stepped in close, her voice going low. "Magic has a texture to it. I know that sounds odd, but it's the only way I can explain it. You know how spells can leave a scent behind? Or how you can feel the air crackle around you when a powerful witch casts?"

I remembered how it felt when Sarah worked her magic. There was an electricity that surrounded her when she concentrated. "I do."

"Dean has an aura around him. Like he's not merely a witch. Like there's something inside him that's constantly giving off magic. It's weirdly soothing," Lily said. "When I get close to him, I feel…calmer than I was before. I would say he's working some kind of charm magic, but he's not. It's not a charm or a glamour. I think it's just who he is. Or what he is."

"Do you think it's dangerous?" We had no idea how strong he was. I felt comfortable with him because he seemed so genuine. He'd saved our butts on the outer planes when it would have been easier for him to leave us behind. He was facing his destiny despite the fact that he had a privileged existence on another plane.

And Summer had cared for him and he for her. Now Lee seemed drawn to him. I wanted another perspective, though. I wanted to know how a witch would feel around him.

"I think he has no idea what kind of power he could wield, so yes. He could be very dangerous if he was turned the wrong way," Lily replied quietly. "Or he could be the hero he wants to be. There's a goodness to him that's hard to deny."

Her answer eased my mind a bit. I knew any witch on Myrddin's team would be wary of Dean and his odd magic, but it was good to know our witches liked him. "And you think he might be able to help Zack?"

"Zack was hit by a curse. It was battle magic, but there was a curse aspect to it. That curse is what's killing him. We've tried clearing it, but it's Myrddin's magic. It's the single most powerful magic we've ever seen on the Earth plane. That's the problem. We're using Earth plane magic to combat it. Even our dark magic flows from the Earth plane." She glanced back to where Dean stood frowning. "I understand that Dean was conceived here on Earth, but he wasn't born here. He was taken off plane while his mother was pregnant. Unborn souls are tricky things. They can be influenced, especially by their environments, or in this case by the mother's environment or the things she experiences."

Didn't I know that truth? Mine was sitting quietly in the corner watching Dean. "You think the act of being taken to the outer planes might have changed Dean's magic?"

She nodded. "Yes. From what he's told me, his mother was transported by a Planeswalker. She was in the demon's company for at least a day. That demonic energy is powerful, especially when they go through the doorways. It's possible that energy changed what would have been normal Earth magic into something else. I'm going to check into his mother's line. I suspect she might be from one of the lost families."

That was what they called magical lines who'd chosen to ignore their talents in favor of living human lives. They allowed their magic to go unused and over time, they'd lost their power. Sometimes it flared again, but they usually quashed it wherever they could. "Okay. I think we should absolutely let him try. He needs to start testing the waters here."

"I'm going to show him the ropes. I've asked him to follow me around when I go on calls. I serve as Frelsi's healer." Lily nodded Dean's way. "He can start small and work on it. But I would like to see if he feels anything from Zack."

Dean stepped up. "Your Highness?"

I held out a hand. "Thanks for coming, Dean. Did Lily fill you in?"

"Yes," he replied. "I can feel the curse from here. It's dark and it kind of makes me nauseous. It smells like rotten eggs."

"Is it bothering you enough that you need to leave?" I wasn't sensitive to magic the way Dean would be. Of course some people would just say I wasn't sensitive at all. They're usually the ones who would rather deal with Danny or Dev.

"No. I want to see if I can help. My old mentor was a terrible person, but she taught me a lot about curses." Dean walked toward the door. "The myth is that a strong curse can only be reversed by the witch who cast it, but Erna taught me a few tricks. The witches of Arete really liked to curse men. Like a lot. Being able to reverse a curse was a necessary skill."

"Erna was the one who had you in thrall, correct?" Lily asked.

Dean nodded. "She was from the witch plane, and one of her favorite things was apparently siphoning off other people's magic. She used Summer's for years, and I didn't realize how much of mine she used until she accidently took the thrall stone out of my head. I'm finding more and more power deep inside."

"You should have kept it. The stone, I mean. Like a souvenir." Lee had planted himself on the sofa. "Like I kept my eye."

He could still surprise me. "You did not keep your eye."

"Oh, he did. He's got it in a jar. He already showed it to me," Dean admitted. "It's well preserved."

I shuddered. "You will get rid of that."

Lee's frown went mulish. "No way. Dean thinks he might be able spell it so I can carry it around and see with it. Like a spy cam. How cool would that be? I could leave it places and it could spy for us."

I had been away for far too long. I would deal with the fact that my son wanted to be able to carry an eyeball around later. For now, I wanted to see if Dean could use his newfound power to help us out. "Let's go in, if you're willing."

"Sorry about the eye thing. It probably won't work," Dean said under his breath.

"Come on. I miss peripheral vision." Lee followed behind us. "Hey, do you think when I turn, the eye will turn, too? And then I'd have three?"

I sent him a look that would have had his eleven-year-old self shaking.

"Sorry, Mom." Lee went serious, and when he walked through the door, he immediately went to his cousin and wrapped an arm around her. Courtney leaned into him with the ease of long familiarity.

My family had found a way to stick together even in the worst of circumstances. The love they had for each other was easy to see. I wasn't sure if that made me happy they were so strong together or sad that I hadn't been a part of it.

Lisa looked up from Zack's bedside. She was holding his hand. "Zoey. Thank you for coming. He looks better, doesn't he?"

He did. His color was back, and there was a brightness to his eyes that had been gone before. But then that had happened when Danny had given him blood yesterday, too. Still, I nodded and gave her a smile. "He does."

"And I'll look like shit again tomorrow." Zack squeezed his wife's hand. "Zoey, you always tell me the truth. I'm not going to lie to you now. I don't think I come out of this. I think that it was a blessing that I have these last days with my family. I can't tell you how much I've missed you all and how much comfort there is in knowing you'll take care of them."

Danny's expression was grim, and I wondered how long Zack had been talking like this.

Lisa stood up and shook her head. "I need to go and find him some food. He has to keep up his strength so he can continue playing the martyr."

"I'm not trying to be a martyr," Zack argued. "I'm trying to be realistic. I'm trying to prepare you."

Courtney was leaning against Lee, trying to hide her tears.

Everyone was focused on the family drama playing out. Everyone except Dean. He was looking around as though he could see something the rest of us couldn't. His fingers splayed as though he was testing some invisible water.

"Do you see what you're doing to your daughter?" Lisa asked.

"I'm trying to get her ready." Zack sat up, his back against the headboard. "We can't go on this way. She needs to be prepared for this."

"Maybe I should take Courtney back to Uncle Neil's," Lee said tentatively.

She shook her head. "I want to be here with my dad."

Dean was frowning.

I could feel the heavy weight of emotion. Sometimes a situation is so grim that you can feel the weight of the moment, the despair blanketing you and making you feel like you can't breathe.

And sometimes it was an asshole's magic that made everyone crazy. "This is part of the curse, isn't it?"

"Zack's health? Yes." Lily moved in, setting her basket on the nightstand. "He'll feel a bit better because of the king's blood, but he got worse today. Worse than he's been in a long time."

Zack put a hand on his chest. "I'm going to get weaker. I'll feel better for less and less time and get sicker. This is the last time I take the king's blood. It's better to go out on my own will."

"I can't believe you're saying that." Lisa had gone pale. "You have to stay with us. You can't give up."

I was paying more attention to Dean. "It's fighting, isn't it? It knows Daniel might be able to save him."

Dean shook his head, and his eyes seemed to sparkle in the low light. "It's not the king's blood it's afraid of."

"What are you talking about?" Lisa asked, wiping her eyes.

"The curse." It was odd because now that I was thinking about it, I could tell the difference. It wasn't even really subtle. It had been the night before, but now it was like a surge against my skin.

Lily gasped. "I can feel it now. I'm sorry, Zack. I've never noticed it before. I knew it was some kind of a curse, but this is a living thing. I've never felt a curse like this before. Something's changed. I would have felt this."

"It changed. It's scared, and that is what you feel," Dean said.

"I would bet Myrddin learned this on the Hell plane." I watched as Dean went perfectly still though I spoke to Lily. "I know your father had a demonic background, but you haven't actively used it." Sarah had from time to time. It was why she'd been so strong at some defensive spells.

Lily shook her head. "Not in magic. When I was on the Hell plane, they used me like a battery. I certainly wasn't taught in this fashion. It's like it's alive. Why now? I've been around Zack for years and I've never felt anything like this from him."

"Please, Lisa. I don't want it to end like this. I know you don't want to face it, but I'm dying." If Zack was listening to us, I couldn't tell. He seemed intent on convincing his wife he wasn't long for this plane.

Probably because the curse was working on his brain the same way it was his body.

Lisa had moved to her daughter, wrapping her in her arms as though she could protect her from what was happening. Lee stepped in front of them. My son was always putting his body between danger and others. He had since he was small.

"Dean, maybe you should go. I don't like how it feels in here," Lee said.

Dean's eyes shifted slightly, glancing to where Lee was. "But if I leave it won't be afraid anymore. It will sink back deep inside and hide like the coward it is. That curse will feed on his misery if I walk away. It's not scared the king's blood will save Zack. It knows I'm going to kill it. Stand back."

Dean shoved his hand against Zack's chest, and I struggled to stay on my feet when a blast of heat went through the room. Danny moved toward Zack like he was going to force Dean off of him.

"Don't," I yelled over the shouts coming from Zack. "Let him try."

Lisa was covering her daughter, and Lee suddenly had a knife in his hand.

Lily seemed to shake off her initial shock. "I can help him."

She closed her eyes and started to murmur a spell I knew well. It was an incantation of strength, to help power what Dean was doing.

And what it looked like Dean was doing was nothing short of sucking the evil out of Zack's soul. Where his hand touched Zack's chest, lines of black crept up Dean's arm, the skin going from healthy to pale and sick in a second.

Before I could start to tell him this was a bad idea, that he shouldn't take the curse inside him, it was over and Zack slumped back against the bed. Dean stood, but his eyes had gone from crystal to pure black.

Lily's eyes came open. "He's taken it inside him. Dean, you can clear it. Let it go. You're stronger than the curse. You mastered it. You own it now. It is yours to command."

Dean stood there, his feet planted to the ground and those obsidian eyes looking too alien to me.

"Hey, buddy." Lee stood right in front of him. "You saved the day. Time to let it out. Tell the bad shit it can't live inside you and let's go get a beer."

Dean simply stared at him, and then I saw a single tear fall. He was fighting something inside, something hateful and evil. "I dream about you at night."

"I'm pretty dreamy," Lee admitted with a hint of a smile.

"Lee, I don't think you should be so close to him," Danny warned.

"I think he saved my uncle and he needs to remember that he's stronger than Myrddin's curse." Lee reached out and put a hand on Dean's cheek, his thumb brushing the tear away. "I would hate for you to give in to this. So don't. Let it go. Stay here with me. We just met and it would suck to not get to know you. I think you could be someone special."

Dean's eyes shifted, the darkness fleeing, and his skin went a little green. He stumbled toward the door. "I'm going to be sick. Oh, that was awful."

Lee's face split in the widest smile. "Hey, Uncle Zack. Good to see you again. I'm going to go hold back Dean's hair. He's got a lot of it. It's hot, but in this case very problematic. I think this is going to be a long session. Try not to shed too much. I'm on cleaning duty this week."

I turned and saw what had my son smiling. There was a big gorgeous brown wolf sitting on the bed, his eyes shining and tail thumping.

"He hasn't been able to change in two years." Lisa was crying freely, holding Courtney's hand as they surrounded Zack.

"I'm going to go see if the boys need anything." Lily picked up her basket. "I've got some herbs that might help Dean clear the curse. Or at least make his stomach settle more quickly. Your Highness, he's extraordinary."

Yes, he was, and I was starting to wonder why. We'd talked about his mother's family, but I was interested in who his father was.

But I let that worry go for the moment. I let it go because a part of my family was whole again. They were also wolves, since Lisa and Courtney decided to change. Danny, Dev, and I watched as the wolves ran through Frelsi, and when they howled their joy my heart was as full as the moon above us.

Chapter Seventeen

"How do you tell them apart? I thought it was bad enough when the father came and he looks exactly like the son, but now the uncle is here. At least the other boy had the good sense to get his eye taken so we can tell the difference between him and his brother."

I bit back a smile as I sat listening in on the Fae talking around me. I sat in the communal dining area the morning after Zack's return to his wolfy glory. Danny, Dev, and Zack were going to see a man about buying a plane since all of Dev's credit cards were working once again. I rather thought the plane would be conspicuous, but Dev had pointed out that we only had one portal-opening tiny demon, and Danny could only fly one of us at a time, so unless we wanted to hoof it or take public transportation, we needed a plane.

I could have had breakfast in bed, but I didn't want to be alone. So that was how I ended up listening to a group of trolls try to figure out who was who in Dev world.

I didn't take the quip about Lee's eye as an insult. With the *sidhe* it might be since they worshipped perfection, but these were trolls, and Lee's lack of an eye would merely prove to them how tough he was.

"Oh, well we could always tell the twins apart by their smiles," a female said. "Or if you are close to them, by their eye color. But the smile always gives them away."

"Lee has the brightest smile." That was accompanied by a happy sigh.

"And the human one usually has that cantankerous pixie around him," a masculine voice pointed out. "Rhys is so serious, and Lee not at all. Though both of the twins are good males. I will admit 'tis harder to tell His Grace and the other one apart."

"I'm the other one?"

I looked up and realized I should have stayed in bed. Declan was frowning at the table of Fae, though he'd kept his voice low enough they didn't seem to have heard.

"Do they not realize I shall be their king one day?" Declan huffed and sat down on the bench across from me, the table between us.

This dining area was outside, a grouping of benches sitting on the greenest of grass, the sunlight soft across the town. There was a warm wind despite the fact that I knew outside the mountain it was winter. This was Fae magic at its finest, and I realized how much I'd missed Faery despite the man sitting in front of me.

I leaned back so the trolls could hear me. I could answer some of their questions. "You can tell His Grace and His Assholiness apart the minute they open their mouths. Also, for a few days you'll be able to tell them apart because the future King of Faery will be walking bowlegged because I kicked him in the balls."

The biggest of the trolls laughed heartily and slapped at the table. "Ah, 'tis a good one, Your Grace."

"They do not show enough respect." Declan seemed particularly broody this morning.

"And I don't think you're the royal who's looked after them all these years." If there was one thing my brother-in-law did consistently and with great talent it was to fail to read the room. Any room, really.

Declan shrugged. "Yes, I have noted that they treat Rhys with great respect. I suppose they'll come to love Devinshea as well. He was always beloved by the outliers."

"Probably because he doesn't refer to them as outliers."

"Well, it's what they are. The earthbound Fae have always been on the outside. They're more than welcome to join their brethren in our *sitheins*, but they stubbornly cling to the old ways."

I stared at him because he wasn't a man who should ever chide someone for clinging to the old ways. "Your mother has been queen for like three hundred years."

He nodded as though I'd made his point. "Yes, she is a very modern monarch, and she has trouble dragging some into the new world."

How do you argue with immortals? Their version of time is different from ours. "I think they're happy in this one. And I know the Earth plane is grateful for the continued blessings of the Fae here."

The trolls had gotten up, and they bowed my way.

"And we are happy to have a Green Man and his goddess counted amongst our people," the leader of the group said. "It was always told to us that the royal triad wasn't fussy like the other Seelies we knew."

"We've heard the stories for years," a slender troll explained. "They told your tale around our campfires and under our bridges. When times got rough, there was even talk of some who went looking for you. But we always knew you would return, and when our young Green Man saw Arkan Sonney, we knew you would be home soon and there would be no more need to look for you."

"Arkan Sonney?" Declan asked.

The trolls all huffed as though the future king had displeased them by not knowing local lore. Though in this case I rather thought the creature was Manx and not Icelandic. The northern European Fae lore wove in and out. Declan hadn't been forced to sit through Devinshea's very long and detailed course on Faery creatures of the Earth plane.

I'd had to sit through it twice when he realized I'd hidden a Sarah J. Maas book behind the text he'd given me.

But luckily I knew this one. "She's talking about a faery creature. It's a pretty white pig that's oddly enough actually a hedgehog. But when the hedgehog takes on the form of a white pig, it brings luck and fortune to the one who sees it. Are you telling me my son went against the orders of his commander because he saw a cute little piggy?"

The largest troll nodded. "Aye, a wise one is our Rhys. Good day, Your Grace."

Declan watched them stride away. "They did not even wish me well."

"I don't either." I stood because it looked like I wasn't going to eat breakfast at all.

Declan put on his pouty, woe-is-me face. "Zoey, please. I know you cannot forgive me, but I need to talk to you."

I no longer fell for anything my brother-in-law tried. My anger with him was tied to the fact that we'd gotten to a good place before Danny, Dev, and I had gone missing. He'd spent time at the Council building. He'd allowed his son, Sean, to be a part of our family. I thought we were good, and I'd been incredibly wrong. "Whatever you have to say, you can say to Dev. I'm not involved in any kind of political moves you want to make. And don't expect him to come to Faery anytime soon."

"That's where you're wrong. He will relent on that because he knows how much we're hurting," Declan insisted. "Devinshea never shirks his duties, and he will eventually get Rhys to see reason as well. But that is not what I want to talk to you about. I want to talk about how to fix this. You are the only one who will see this cannot be allowed to stand."

"What?" I asked. "I assure you I'm more than happy to support my son's decision concerning the Fae who tried to force him to do their will."

"That was the Unseelie," Declan argued. "One of the reasons Mother is in trouble is the fact that she wouldn't force Rhys to perform his duties. She is heartsick over the entire thing but you will not see it because despite the fact you have a crown, you have never sacrificed for it."

"Never sacrificed?" I'd pretty much died for that fucking crown. I sacrificed for it every single day, and I'd never truly wanted it in the first place.

A hard look came into Declan's eyes. "Not in the way we have. You've never been forced to choose between the crown and your children."

"I can promise you my crown would lose that battle."

Declan nodded as though I'd proved his point. "And that is why you are not a true queen. Damn it, Zoey. I did not come here to fight with you. I came here to ask what you are going to do about this situation. You have to fix it. Daniel and Devinshea would never take the chance, but you will. You will do anything to set this place right."

I sat again, shoving the anger to the back of my mind because he was saying something I was interested in. I'd shut down talking to Danny and Dev about my plans since I didn't really have any at this point. "What are you talking about?"

He glanced around as though making sure we were alone. "I am talking about finding a way out of this mess. You were taken out of time by something magical. There must be a way to fix it."

He was thinking along the same lines I was. The balance had been shifted by magical means, and that almost always meant it could be shifted back the same way.

Of course, there would be a price, but I was willing to pay it.

"The painting won't work. I've already thought about trying to go back through it, but I've been assured it no longer functions. Know any time traveling spells?"

"I don't know of spells, but I have researched some tricks we might incorporate," Declan allowed. "I've been looking for a way to get you back since the moment I realized what the wizard was doing."

"Why didn't you use that hidden guard of yours to protect your brother's kingdom?" That bothered me, too. We'd had powerful allies, and they seemed to have all failed.

"It happened very quickly, and the wizard was prepared." Declan's eyes trailed away. "He's far more formidable than I imagined. I thought he was a friend. Devinshea told me he was someone I could trust. By the time I realized it was going wrong, I went after the children. I didn't know they'd already been taken to safety. No one informed me there was some kind of plan in place. I assumed I was still in charge of getting the children to safety if anything happened."

"What safety? You turned them away. If you'd taken the children with you, what would you have done when they wouldn't allow Lee or Fen inside the *sithein*?"

"That didn't happen until later," Declan corrected. "I assure you if they had gone with me that day, they would have been inside, and once inside my mother wouldn't have allowed them to be taken. It was months later they showed up, and by then the damage had been done. I intended to do my duty. I wasn't allowed to."

"I wasn't the one who told Albert to take the kids. It was Gray who warned him." I'd like to have a talk with the dark prophet, but I was leaving it all to Kelsey. She was going to meet with her husband and report back to us about anything of concern.

"I wish he had warned me." Declan met my eyes, and his gaze alone told me how tired he was. "That day was so chaotic. After I got Sean out and many of our Fae contingent, I started to look for ways to find you. Then I looked for ways to warn your younger self."

"What did you try?"

He sat up straighter. "I attempted to send you several messengers. There are faery creatures who can travel across dimensions, and it's been said they may even traverse time. They are noncorporeal, of course, and can be difficult to deal with. I made deals with three such beings to find a time when you were younger and warn you. It seems none of them made their way to you."

"I did not get any notes from ghosts, no." Though I ignored a lot of weird shit. If they hadn't shown up right in my face, I likely wouldn't have paid attention.

"Perhaps it was because they came from a Fae plane," Declan said with a sigh. "I might have more luck here on this plane since they would only have to travel across the time dimension."

I didn't like that I only had three allies in this, and two of them were Jack the Ripper and my brother-in-law. "I'm trying to find a way to go back and reset things. I've been told if I do that, I might be forming a new timeline, not erasing this one."

He shook his head. "I don't believe that. There are not infinite versions of the same world. There might be different planes with different versions of the same souls, but then why would there be splits inside of splits. It makes no sense. The most logical outcome is that time will be reset and we can fix things. I thought to do it the easy way, but now I fear we must take a more dangerous path."

"And what would that be?" I didn't have to question who would be taking this path. I would be the one walking it.

"There is an amulet the oldest of the Fae use to speak with their ancestors," Declan explained. "It was given to us in the ancient times as a way to connect the past to the present. We could use the device to gain advice from our forefathers."

"Like a walkie-talkie to the past?"

"I do not know what that is. It is a way to reach through the years and speak to our first kings and queens."

I didn't see how that would help. "I don't need to speak to them. Unless you're suggesting that I call up some old Faery king and ask him to slip a little note somewhere for me to find millennia later. Do you think they had Western Union back then? Can they prepay for that message delivery?"

The tightness around Declan's eyes let me know he was sick of me, too. "No, Zoey. I am merely saying that I have in my possession something that your criminal brain might find a way to make useful for our current situation. If you find a way to warn yourself of what's coming, then we never have to deal with this. I never have to refuse my nephew entry and comfort. You don't have to miss twelve years with your children. Lee never needs to lose an eye. You can certainly keep Evangeline away from that wolf."

All I wanted was to make sure my kids never had to go through the pain they had. I didn't see how an amulet with a one-way call was going to help me. Unless I could convince the ancient Fae royals to ship a note through time, it would be useless to me.

But I never said never. "You have it on you?"

He reached into his pocket and drew out a golden disc attached to a chain. "I smuggled it out of Faery and will likely be in serious trouble when my mother and her council realize it's gone. But I am willing to risk anything to reset this timeline."

I reached out and took the amulet in my hand. It was roughly the size of my palm and heavier than it looked. "How do you use it?"

"It must be in proximity to one of the Seelie or Unseelie treasures. That is what we call the jewels our royals wear. For Mother it would work by attaching it to her crown. I have a jeweled sword it works with."

"So now I have to steal your mom's crown? Because you know I'm coming for the sword, so you should hand it over."

He rolled his emerald eyes. "You wear one of our treasures around your neck, Your Grace. You have to know the High Priest's goddess is considered royalty."

The Goddess Chain. It lay against my heart, and I almost never took it off. It was the same with my wedding ring. I'd been wearing both when we'd gone through that painting, so they were the only possessions I had from my former life. "So I put them together and make a time traveling phone call?"

"Something like that," Declan allowed. "You must wear it close to the Goddess Chain for several days before you can use it. The amulet will be primed by close proximity to the treasure, and you'll know it's ready when it glows."

"I have to think about it." I wasn't sure there was anything I could do with it, but the thought intrigued me. "Do you know how it works? Or rather why it works?"

He shrugged. "I only know that it does. Not that the ancients are all that helpful to me. They do not understand the complexities of the modern world. It is much harder to be a royal today than it was back then. But they do understand things we do not. They have knowledge that has been lost."

"Your Highness, would you like more tea?"

I looked down and a brownie stood at the end of our table, her small body in a shift dress and her scraggly hair adorned with a pink bow. I loved the brownies like I loved my pixie army. They were the sweetest of the Fae.

"Yes, servant," Declan said with a sigh. "I will take some tea, and you may fetch my breakfast. I will need meat, of course. And bread. I believe I smelled pastries. Hurry along now."

The brownies eyes went wide and the tea tray trembled. "Oh. I was speaking to…of course…"

"Nope." I picked up the creamer and dumped it over Declan's head. "She was talking to me, and as far as I'm concerned you are a prisoner here. Get your own breakfast."

He frowned fiercely and picked up a napkin. "One of these days, Zoey."

"Yes, one of these days, you will learn." I shook my head and took the tray from the brownie, setting it on the table before I stood and held out my hand. "Come now, my sweet friend. Can you show me to my son's *brugh*? I need to speak with him."

"Yes, Your Highness. Of course, I shall," the brownie said and began to lead me away.

"Zoey? You'll do the job, right?"

I pocketed the amulet. "Yes."

"Be careful with that," Declan called out. "It must stay in close contact with one of the treasures. If not, it will find its way back to Faery, and sometimes the effects are violent, to say the least."

That was good to know.

I would do the job, and it started with finding my son.

* * * *

I found Rhys walking out of the cottage Neil and Chad and their kids were staying at. I'd spent some time there the night before, catching up with Chad and getting to know Neil's kids. They were all kinds of awesome, and they looked at their dads like they were heroes. Which they were.

I would have to remember to add them on my list of things that had to happen when I put the world back to rights. They would still be out there, still need Neil and Chad.

Rhys took one look at me and then stopped and seemed to try to decide if he could turn another way or go back inside and maybe hide. I saw the moment he figured out he couldn't get away from me. "Good morning, Mother. How are you?"

Feeling distinctly unwanted was how I was. But then I remembered what Lee had said. He'd told me Rhys was nervous because he was unsure of his welcome. I thanked my brownie escort before turning to my son. "I'm good. I slept well. I think knowing your uncle is going to be all right helped a lot."

Rhys nodded. "Yes. It was good to see that wolf again. It's been years. And Courtney can finally be a kid for a while. She's spent all of her time worried about her father and taking care of her little brother so her mom could watch after Uncle Zack. It will be good to see her smile."

If we'd been there, Courtney wouldn't have been forced to take all that responsibility on herself. My little niece, who had been afraid of everything as a child, shouldn't have had to grow up so fast. And I barely knew my nephew. I hadn't been there when he'd been born, hadn't been a part of that particular miracle.

So much missed. So much loss.

"Have you checked in on Dean this morning?" I fell in beside him as he started back on the path toward the center of town.

Rhys nodded. "Lee took him to Lily's last night. Dean stayed over so the witches could watch him. I believe Lee was going to check on him this morning, but he told me Dean was already feeling much better. And you? Are you all right? I notice you didn't go with Papa and the others to buy the plane."

"No. I trust your fathers to buy the best plane they can find." I hated that our conversation felt stilted without Lee around to ease our way. "I know you probably don't remember it, but you rode on a lot of planes as a kid."

"I remember," Rhys said, his voice finally going soft. "I remember there were always cookies, and Papa set up movies for us. I remember when we would hit turbulence how you would try to make a game out of it so we wouldn't be scared. And you said that even if the plane fell apart, Dad would scoop us all up and fly us safely to the ground." He huffed. "And then Lee prayed for the plane to fall apart because he thought it sounded like fun."

Yes, that was my son. Lee had found a certain glee in turbulence. Evan had cried and clung to her dad, never once thinking of being "brave" because she was a baby and she needed comfort and had always received it. Rhys had been the one who'd sat silently, his hands on the arms of his chair, holding all of his fear inside. They'd all been loved and given our attention, but personality is something no parent can change. Rhys had been born with a core of reserve. I'd been the one to see it, the one to always ensure I sat beside him on the plane so if we hit strong winds, I could ask him to hold my hand because I was scared. "I'll make sure you have cookies when we use the new plane."

Rhys shook his head. "I don't think I'll be going anywhere soon. I'm needed here. Now that you're back, I'm going to pour my time and effort into Frelsi and the Fae here. Obviously, if I'm needed in battle I'll be there, but getting you and Dad and Papa back was the mission."

"I thought the mission was taking back our rightful places."

"Your place, Mother," he corrected softly.

I groaned. "I hate it when you call me Mother. It makes me sound like I'm eight hundred years old and holding something over your head."

He sighed. "I'm sorry. I'll try to call you Mom. I've been around too many formal Fae lately. I'll try to be more like Lee and Evan."

"That wasn't what I was saying either." He was definitely turning out to be my touchiest child. But then it had to be hard to be Rhys.

Evan had Fen and Lee had...well, apparently Lee had most of the supernatural world to comfort him. Rhys was alone, and it was obvious he felt it.

We needed an intervention, my son and I. Or perhaps an adventure.

Rhys started walking again, his long legs eating up the distance. "It's all right. I don't mind. I know I'm a little more uptight than Lee. I should call you what you want to be called. If you want to be called Mom, then Mom it is. I use the more formal term *mother* when talking to our allies. I tend to refer to you as the queen or my mother. Momma didn't have the gravity I thought it needed."

Had I been some political figure to him for the last few years? I wondered how much of our lives he'd forgotten during the time we'd been apart. I'd talked to Lee about how Rhys had felt when he would leave his brother in favor of working with Kelsey. What I hadn't told Lee was when he would do that, I would find a reason to spend time with Rhys. I would take him out for ice cream or ask him to teach me how to play his video games. We would sit on the balcony and work on his homework. While Kelsey had held Lee's attention, I'd tried my best to show Rhys he was wanted. "I would hope we could be less formal when we're with family."

"It wasn't merely you," Rhys assured me. "I referred to Dad as the king and Papa as His Grace. Always. It was a relief to hand all the political stuff back to them."

Oh, I didn't think he really meant that. Even as a kid, Rhys had little tells. His chin would come up slightly when he was lying, and there it was, that minute uptick that he likely thought made him look all upright and trustworthy.

What was going on in Rhys's head?

Before I could try to examine that line of thought, Lee was walking out of the door to the long house that served as one of Frelsi's common spaces. It was close to the dining area I'd been in for breakfast. Inside the long house there were kitchens and storage spaces, a little area that functioned as a general store, and several meeting rooms. Lee had a bag in his hand, and he waved our way.

"Hey, Mom. How's it going?" Lee asked as he caught up. "I can't wait to catch a ride on whatever plane Papa is buying. Do you think they'll have those cookies we used to like?"

I was sure it didn't help my case with Rhys that Lee immediately proved how charming he could be. "I'll make sure. Your brother and I are going to find my godparents. Can you check in on Dean while I'm gone?"

Rhys had stopped and turned my way. "We're what?"

Lee nodded and held up his bag. "Sure thing. Lily asked me to grab some herbs. She's got a whole treatment plan for Dean. He's doing great, but she wants him to rest for the day to make sure he's cleared the curse. I think he has. I watched him yack for a good hour. If there's more curse, I don't know where it's sitting."

"Good. I'm glad he's on the mend." I was planning on having a talk with Dean at some point, but I didn't want to crowd him when he wasn't feeling well. It looked like I would be talking to all the boys today. "Tell him hi for me. We'll be back before your dads get home. I hope."

"Wait. What are we doing?" Rhys asked.

"You promised yesterday that you would take me to find my godparents." I knew he'd been putting me off on that, but I wasn't going to let him out of the promise.

Rhys frowned. "That's not a good idea. With everything that happened yesterday I think we should wait until Dad can take you. Maybe with Sasha and a couple of the others. Yes, I'll put together a proper guard for you. I should have talked to the dads about that this morning."

So he could foist me off on someone else? Not a chance. I moved in beside him and threaded my arm through his. "All I need is my sweet son."

"Lee is going to take you, then?" Rhys said the words with a hint of desperation that absolutely offended me.

Lee shook his head and stepped back. "No can do, brother. Dad sat me down and had this whole long talk about how I can't die before he's ready to turn me. See, if I took Mom out and I died, then I would likely wake up and eat her, and that would be super bad for my psyche."

"Excuse me?" What had Daniel been putting in his brain?

Lee gave me a half shrug and his "what are you going to do" smile. "Mom, you're a companion. If I die and we're out there all alone, you're going to have to run because when I wake up I'll be all kinds of crazy psycho killer and you'll be a big old ball of light, and I won't remember you're my mom. You'll be dinner, and there's like a whole psychiatric thing Dad called an Oedipal complex that gets worse if you're a vamp and your mom is a companion. I don't know. He talked a lot. What I basically got out of it is killing my mom is bad. You know I could have told him I agreed with that without the long lecture. When did Dad get so chatty?"

Was Daniel trying to give Lee a complex? "You're not going to eat me."

"Correct. Which is why, alas, I cannot be the one to traipse around muddy bridges looking for Ingrid and Halle. I know all the old stories and I would definitely die," Lee announced. "The good news is Rhys is hard to kill, and he probably won't drink your blood. And if you talk about how long we breastfed, I'm leaving right now."

Rhys glared at his brother. "If you can't die while you're alone with Mom, how the hell are you going to run a heist with her?"

"Oh, I have to do that. I'm the only one who we know can actually see the grimoire," Lee replied.

"She doesn't need to see the grimoire. She needs to see the bag. She'll be able to see the bag," Rhys countered.

"What if she drops the bag and oops, the book falls out?" Lee faced off with Rhys. "She can be very clumsy. That's how she dropped you on your head as a small child."

"I did not." I mean maybe once, but it wasn't from very high.

"How do we know *I* wouldn't be able to see the book?" Rhys ignored me entirely.

"Uh, we only get one shot at this and we need to go with the sure thing," Lee replied. "Besides, we're going to be invisible, so I seriously doubt I'll die. Also, I've literally done this job before. I did it when I was eleven. I can do it now. And you can pull your weight and take our mother to see her godparents. It's been twelve years since she's seen them. How heartless are you?"

"I'm pretty sure from her point of view she saw them last Thursday," Rhys shot back before turning to me. "Why can't you wait for Dad?"

"I don't want to." I wasn't about to point out that I had actually seen my godparents shortly before the world exploded. Nor was I going to tell him I wanted to ask Ingrid about time travel. It was becoming very obvious that I might not win this fight, and I also wasn't going to break down in tears. Even though I wanted to. Rejection hurts, and rejection from someone I loved the way I did Rhys hurt like hell. I would need to regroup on this one. I stepped back. "I'll ask Neil to go with me."

I turned and started back toward Neil's house. I heard my sons whispering behind me.

"You made Mom cry." Lee's whisper wasn't much of a whisper.

"I didn't mean to." At least Rhys sounded like he felt guilty. "I just think it's a bad idea."

"Well, a worse idea is letting her run off on her own," Lee pointed out.

"She won't do…" Rhys groaned, a deeply frustrated sound.

"Yes, remember our childhood. If you think she won't go and do exactly what she wants, you do not remember our mother," Lee said.

"Then what do we do?" Rhys asked. "We can't allow her to run around the countryside."

It was my turn to argue. I turned and put my hands on my hips. I was still their mother. I didn't let their fathers tell me what to do, and I wasn't about to be shoved in a cage by my sons. "I've been taking care of myself for a long time. I'm not stupid. I won't go off on my own, but I assure you that Neil and I have handled many a dangerous situation. We were doing it long before you were born. I wanted to spend the afternoon with you, Rhys. If that's not what you want, then I understand, but if you think for a single instant that you can allow me to do something, you *have* forgotten your childhood. Go do what you need to do. Trust me. Your fathers won't blame you for whatever I do or I'll remind them who I am."

Lee sent his brother a shake of his head. "Now you have to do it, and she's pissed. So good luck with that."

Rhys had gone a bit pale. "Of course I would love to escort you, Mothe…Mom. It would be great."

There was a part of me that wanted to walk away, but I was his mom and I didn't get to put my ego over my relationship with him. I'd been gone for twelve years, and I needed to figure out how to reach the most reserved of my children.

Even if I was going to fix this thing. Even if it didn't matter that there was distance between us because when I fixed it he would be a child and I would have another chance.

I forced a sunny smile on my face and walked back his way, threading my arm through his. "We should take a picnic lunch. My breakfast was interrupted by your awful uncle. It's okay. I poured something over his head. It's my new plan. I'll make sure he leaves soon."

Lee waved, a huge smile on his face. "Have fun storming the castle, you two."

I could have sworn Rhys cried a little, but he marched on.

Chapter Eighteen

I sat by the fire Rhys had built and had to admit that if I wanted to have a picnic, I should have picked a country that wasn't so near the arctic in the middle of winter. While Frelsi was magically lit and the sun shined down during daylight hours, out here in the real world the day was already dying and giving way to what felt like endless night.

"Are you all right?" Rhys got to one knee and started to dig through the backpack he'd brought along.

I wasn't about to admit that I was incredibly cold and wanted to hike back into the city and find the nearest warm café and never leave it again. Instead I gave him a smile that I hoped didn't freeze on my face. "Great. Though I have to admit, I was hoping this was the one."

We'd been to four bridges on the outskirts of Reykjavík. Luckily Sasha kept a car with a friendly family in the city so we hadn't been forced to walk all the way. While Rhys had driven around the city, I'd managed to get him to admit that he liked movies, especially action movies, and enjoyed pizza when he went out in the city.

That was about it. I'd done most of the talking, and I was coming to believe that my son thought I was some sort of pampered princess queen who'd never done a day of work in my life, much less fought monsters the way he had. It wasn't that Rhys was acting superior. He'd been perfectly solicitous, but there was a distance between us that rankled.

What had Lee said? Rhys was worried I wouldn't like who he was now.

And I didn't like the fact that he was holding out on me. In more ways than one.

"Are you sure you want to keep going?" Rhys asked in a polite tone. He sat down on the rock across from me. "It's cold today. We could head back into the city and get lunch there."

Where I was certain he would find someone to join us so he didn't have to be alone with his mom. Neil and Cassie had come with us as far as the portal. They were doing some shopping and then heading back into Frelsi, but we could probably still catch them, and that would mean Rhys didn't have to sit and talk to me.

"Or you could take out that eternal flame in your backpack and make us comfortable."

He frowned. "And how did you know I had that?"

"I looked through your pack, of course. I wanted to make sure you had everything you needed," I replied primly. "You'll also discover I slipped a couple of notes in there so you can find them later and know your mom loves you."

His jaw went tight, and he managed to not let his lips curve up. "You are incorrigible." He sighed and reached back into his pack. "And I remember you used to do that. I would open my backpack and there would be a note about how special I was and how I should never forget that you love me."

It was good he remembered one of the things I did right. "I wanted to let you know I was with you. I know school was hard on you."

He nodded as he pulled out the small, enchanted stone I'd recognized earlier. "Yes, and it was made so much easier when the kids around me found all the notes you wrote."

I frowned as he dropped the stone into the fire. Someone—probably Lily—had enchanted the stone and it did its job, creating a warm bubble around us. I sighed in pure pleasure as our small encampment was suddenly comfortable. "I'm your mom. I do embarrassing stuff."

His expression softened as he settled back down. "I know. I liked the notes. I liked that those notes were for me and not Lee. I know that sounds shitty, but I liked that you did something for me you didn't do for him."

"He wouldn't have read them." Lee would have rolled his eyes and gagged. I knew my boys. "He had different struggles, but yours were every bit as difficult."

"It wasn't easy being the only fertility god at school. I know Lee was the only human, and some of the kids gave him hell about it, but you try being the kid in school who can pump up your chances to get pregnant. I never sat at the front of the class. Ever. They put me back as far as they could. I had not one teacher offer to hold my hand as we walked down the hall. They always held Lee's hand when we were young."

Once Rhys's powers had grown, it had been hard keeping him in school at all. Danny, Dev, and I had many a parent-teacher meeting where we had to advocate for our son. "I'm sorry, baby. It's hard to be the only one."

He shrugged and pulled his gloves off. We wouldn't need them now that the eternal flame was doing its job. "Papa was there, but he was in control and I wasn't. And I know other people have it hard. Being alive is hard. Everyone has their struggles, but my particular issue actively created more people. In some ways it was a relief to go on the run, to not have to worry about fitting in with a bunch of teens who wanted to be able to have sex with no consequences. The teen wolves hated me. I wasn't allowed anywhere near them."

My heart ached for him. "You never told me that."

"Well, it's also hard when your mom is the queen and anything she does can cause problems for the king," he said softly.

"We tried to keep you out of that. I know it's hard to believe, but your fathers and I tried to give you as normal a childhood as possible."

He chuckled at the thought. "As you have said on many an occasion, there is no such thing as normal. There is only what we know and what we are afraid of."

I had to blink back tears. "I didn't say that last part."

"No, but it's what I've learned over the last few years. Normal is a throwaway word, and yet it's something we cling to and use to force others to do our bidding. It's normal for the Fae to want fertility, so I should do my job whether I wish it or not. I should conform to their normal. It is normal to be immortal, so Lee was not welcome and we should conform to their normal. Well, we found our own, and damn the Fae."

"Not all of them," I pointed out. "You seem very popular in Frelsi."

A warm smile came over his face. "I've found earthbound Fae have a completely different view of normal. They must fit in on a plane where they're overwhelmed by humans, and therefore they're tolerant of all. I'm never going to be Papa. I'm never going to fit in with my pure relatives. I even hate that word. Pure. What is it supposed to mean?"

"I think it's another one of those words meant to separate us," I replied. Finally we were talking, and all it had taken was my nosiness and utter disregard for his privacy. "You must be careful with the Seelie. The Unseelie as well. You have your father's talents, but even he was only considered a proper Green Man when he ascended."

He was quiet for a moment. "I don't know that I want to ascend."

Had he even been thinking about it? There was no need for him to. Dev had done it to stabilize our alliance with the Fae. And to prove a point Rhys didn't need to prove. "Oh, baby, you don't have to. You never have to. That's up to you and you alone. I know it feels like you have this grand destiny, but you're in control."

He huffed. "It didn't feel that way when they attempted to kidnap me."

"Well, that was assault and nothing you could control, but in this, you can. You will learn how to control your powers, and you can give or withhold them, and you should understand that even if they succeeded, your family would come for you." I had no doubt even had we never gotten home that Rhys would not have been left alone.

"Yes. Lee would have led a charge into the Unseelie and gotten himself killed. It was what I worried about at the time," Rhys replied. "Of course, I would have felt better had I known he would rise again. You know, now that I think about it, I should have known none of us could ever escape the chaos Lee can bring. Not even death can stop him."

"Rhys," I began.

He shook his head. "No, Mom. He's my brother, and I have to put up with him in a way you do not. I get to throw all the shade I want his way."

"Fine. Though you should know there's a sensitive boy under all his bravado."

Rhys snorted and looked down to the ground. "There are some unforeseen consequences. The stone melted the snow, and now we have mud."

I glanced down, and he was right. The ground beneath us was getting messy, and we would likely sink into it when we rose. "You can fix it if you want."

He hesitated. "I shouldn't."

"How long has it been since you used your powers?"

"I can't not use them. It goes badly if I don't. I do grow things, but I tend to do it in a passive way. I take off my shoes and walk around Frelsi at least once a week."

And that was why the grass was so green. I wasn't going to argue with him about this. It was Dev's place to show Rhys how to control his powers. "I suspect you help in Lily's garden, too. Her herbs are beautiful. Well, I don't mind the mud. Do you want a sandwich?"

"I would love one. It's nice because if I was out with Lee, I would have to fight him for it. I don't know how he stays so fit because he eats like a wolf. And with Fen, well, he eats a lot. And so fast. A picnic like this would require Eddie to transport half a kitchen's worth of food."

I opened my bag and pulled out the sandwiches Albert had packed for us. They were ham with brown bread and butter. I'd been told they were Rhys's favorite. I started to pass him one and stopped when I saw him leaning over, his fingertips hovering above the ground. There was a look of deep concentration on his face as the ground around us gently began to change. The grass grew, pushing through the earth and blossoming to form a silky emerald carpet under our feet. It formed a circle around us, a patch of spring in the winter gloom.

He sat back up, and I didn't miss the satisfied expression that crossed his face. "It's easier with you around. I can feel the energy from the Goddess Chain."

"I didn't know it had energy," I admitted and passed him the sandwich and took out my own.

"Oh, yes. It soaks up the sexual energy from you and Papa's encounters." He frowned suddenly. "And now that I am saying those words, I wish I hadn't because it's pretty strong today. I wish I didn't know that."

I wished he didn't know it either, but this was one of those "normals" I needed to throw away. "Sex is healthy. It's a good thing to share when you truly care about someone."

Rhys's brows rose. "Has anyone told my brother that? He shares it all the time."

"Or when you and your partner simply want to have some fun and everyone consents."

He shuddered. "I don't need a sex talk, Mom. I get it. Sex is good for the sex god. The truth is being around Papa has already helped a lot. I had a long teaching session with him that was deeply disconcerting and oddly comforting, and then Bris gave me advice as well. I was afraid to have sex because of what could happen. I have a weird relationship with sex."

"Because it's who you are and it's why you've had trouble," I said. "I can understand that. I always found it odd that my life often revolves around something I can never see."

"Your glow?"

I nodded. "It's affected me all of my life, and I can't see it. I might have gone my entire life without knowing it existed. Some companions do since there are so few vampires."

"Do you wonder what that life might have been like? If your father had been someone with no ties to the supernatural world? What would your life have been like if Granddad had been a farmer somewhere isolated? You might never have met a vampire and had a… I was about to use that word again."

"Normal, yes. It's hard not to. I don't think about it anymore. If he had, then I would never have met your dad and never have fallen in love with your papa. No. I love the life I have." I even loved sitting here and talking to my son, despite the fact that there was awkwardness between us. "There is always a balance. That's what I've learned. It's kind of been beaten into me. I had hard things to get through, but I was also given extraordinary love."

"Were you given it? Or did you fight for it, too?" Rhys asked as though he'd thought about this a lot.

"I suppose that's true. I suppose we fight for everything." I sighed and took a drink from the thermos Albert had packed for me.

The water tasted faintly of citrus. At the penthouse there was always a pitcher of infused water around. We ate in silence for a moment before I decided to push him a little. "How long have Fen and Evan been together?"

I thought it would be easier for him to talk about his siblings.

He swallowed what appeared to be half a sandwich, and I realized my boy wasn't as self-aware as he thought he was. He could eat, too. "Forever, it feels like. They kind of clung together because they were younger than me and Lee. Sasha was easier on them training-wise in the beginning. Eddie and Albert took care of them while Lee and I trained, so they formed an attachment at a young age. At some point it went from friendship and comfort to something more. I don't know. You might not be able to understand."

I felt my eyes widen. "Excuse me?"

His lips curled up, and I realized he was fucking with me. It made me feel better.

I sighed and reached into my pack to get the cookies Albert had packed. "You know very well your dad and I had a similar story."

He shrugged. "Yes. I've heard it from Grandad many times over the years. I think hearing those stories did nothing but reassure Evan she was following in your footsteps. I know she was hard on you, but that was mostly about Papa. And you seemed very standoffish in the beginning."

"I was in shock. You were eleven a few days ago."

He nodded. "I know. We've had years to think about this moment, and like so many things it wasn't what we expected. Though you seem to be settling in. I'll be happy to tell Evan that her mother is already meddling, and she should expect many long and annoying conversations."

I wanted to argue with that, but I did have several conversations planned for my baby girl. I didn't think they would be annoying. I thought they would be charming and informative, but then I bet my dad had thought that, too, and he'd been wrong. So wrong. "Well, that's a mom's job. I feel like I have a lot of conversations to make up for."

"You would be surprised. Sasha's pretty good at talking to us about things that should be hard. He was good with Evan. He had a daughter he had to leave behind when he turned. I think he viewed us as a way to make up for that, or maybe a second chance to be a father figure. And Eddie read a lot of parenting books. There were many times I wished he'd read less. Trent mostly just tried to survive us all." His expression had softened as though fond memories were playing through his head.

Memories I had no part in. His formative years had come and gone, and I'd been a distant memory. "I'm sorry I missed it. Did it help at all to have your grandfather?"

"Like all things in this life I find myself leading, Grandad's reappearance was confusing. I'm glad it didn't happen until I was almost seventeen or I think my sexuality would be even more fucked up."

Now we were getting somewhere. "You like Shy?"

He'd eaten half of his second sandwich but seemed to lose his appetite. He wrapped it back up. "She's a beautiful woman. She's smart and kind, and she's been through a lot."

"And she carries your grandfather's soul around."

Rhys huffed, a frustrated sound. "He chooses the worst times to come out, Mom. Like the absolute worst. I almost managed to forget he was there once. Shy and I had been talking late into the night, and it was almost dawn. I lost my head and moved in to kiss her and Grandad shows up and tells me she's not ready. Couldn't she have told me that herself? Did she have to send my grandpa after me?"

I bit back a laugh because though he was joking, it was easy to see it hadn't been funny for him. "Was it the first time you tried to kiss a girl?"

He snorted as though I'd said something silly. "No. I've had some minor experiences. We visited some interesting planes. I've made out with a few women in bars, but I couldn't let it go far. Sasha made sure there were condoms around, but I didn't know if they would work on me. And I didn't know how to ask. I can't believe I told you that."

"I'm very easy to talk to. You know you used to tell me everything. As for the condoms, they work or you would have many more siblings."

"I shudder at the thought. I can't handle the ones I do have. That's good to know though. Condoms, however, don't stop my magic from going crazy. One of the pubs we were in, one of the ones

I made out in, it got covered in ivy. We had to hack our way out. The owner was not happy."

"You'll get better with that, though you're already far more powerful than your papa was at your age. He could only explode a single houseplant when we would make out."

"You don't have to talk about it. Trust me, Papa talks far too much about it. I don't remember him being this forthcoming," Rhys admitted. "I know we had talks about how to control my powers, but they did not include stories of how he has to control them around you and Dad."

I felt my jaw drop. "He does not."

"And he gives examples."

"Well, he's Fae. I happen to know his mother is very open about her sexuality. Including hitting on your dad once."

Rhys winced. "Are you serious?"

I nodded. "And I will talk to your papa. He needs to know where your boundaries are."

If we'd been here all along, would those boundaries be as tight as they seemed to be now?

"Anyway, Shy and I have a nice friendship," he continued. "It's good we didn't confuse things."

I'd seen the way Shy looked at my son, the way her eyes followed him anywhere he went. "You never tried again? You haven't talked to her about how you feel?"

"I told you how I feel," Rhys replied, his expression shuttering. "It would have been complicated. Besides, she doesn't want that kind of relationship."

"That's not what she said. At least that's not how you said it," I replied.

Rhys shrugged. "She didn't say anything at all. Granddad did."

"I suspect your grandfather was protecting Shy. Not from you. He said she wasn't ready. That doesn't mean she'll never be ready. You said yourself that Shy's been through a lot. How early was this in your relationship with her?" I asked.

"A few weeks after she showed up in Frelsi."

"And you haven't talked to her about it since?" I thought he might be too timid around her.

"I respected her wishes," Rhys said firmly.

"What are her wishes now?"

"She seems happy with the way things are." Rhys sighed and stood up. "We should go. We're losing what little daylight we have. I'm beginning to suspect Ingrid and Halle have moved on. We'll check deeper into the countryside tomorrow. I can send out someone to find them and then we don't have to repeat this."

I had pushed him too far. I suspected Rhys was the one who was truly satisfied with not having to deepen the relationship. He'd tried and gotten shot down and wouldn't try again. My son was locked in routine, and that could be hard to get out of. "I don't mean to pry."

A brow arched over his emerald eyes, an expression I'd seen many times on his father's face. "Really?"

"Okay, maybe I do, but I'm your mother."

"Well, I've done okay without you for years. I don't need you to tell me what to do." He stopped and took a long breath. "I'm sorry. I didn't mean to hurt you."

I forced myself to stay steady when emotion rushed through me. "But you did mean what you said."

"I should have been more politic," my son allowed.

I needed to make him see the truth. "Rhys, I didn't mean to leave you. I never meant to leave you."

"I understand that."

"On a logical level you do, but there's still a little boy inside you who wonders why I lied. Who wonders why I would have promised him I would see him in the morning and then disappear. I can understand why it might be easier to be angry with me."

"I am not angry with you." He stood and slid his gloves on again.

It was so plain to me that he was angry. "Baby, I can't even start to deal with the problem if you don't acknowledge that it's real."

He leaned over and waved a hand over our fire, the eternal flame going out like he'd hit a switch. "Let's talk about it in the car if you insist on pushing the subject. I believe we have a storm coming in. I want to avoid it if I can."

I was what he wanted to avoid, but then I was getting the suspicion that Rhys avoided anything vaguely emotional. "Not talking to me won't help the problem."

He placed the eternal flame back in his pack. "I'm talking to you. I wouldn't dream of not talking to you. That would be impolite."

He stood and bit back a growl. He was so much like his fathers. He had all of Dev's courtly ways of letting me know he was upset, combined with Danny's stubborn will to not acknowledge there was a problem at all.

The wind rushed back in, and I felt the cold again. I was standing in that patch of spring Rhys had made, but there was no doubt it was wintertime again. Rhys stalked off toward the car and I stood there, watching him walk away from me.

How could I get him to open up? How could we heal if we didn't acknowledge the wound?

I started after him, my boots crunching against the snow. My rage needed a place to go. I worried if I got into that car with him right this second I would say something I shouldn't. I needed to let off some steam.

I screamed. I let it out, let go of some small part of my rage and fear, let it spread across that snowy white field.

"Mom!" Rhys's eyes had gone wide.

I made a quick snowball and held it in my hand. Maybe if we lobbed snowballs at each other we could find some balance.

"Do not throw that, Mother." Rhys started my way. "I am not joking. Put it down this instant or there could be hell to pay."

"Come on. Pick one up and throw it at me. You're mad. I'm right here and you're still angry. Take it out on me."

I could handle a couple of snowballs way more easily than I could not speaking to him, not feeling connected to him. Rhys had been the one to bottle things up. If I let him, he would shut me out forever.

Rhys pointed a finger my way. "Put it down. Put it down right now, Mother."

Yeah, he should have known me better than that. I reached back and lobbed that sucker his way.

It was going to thud straight into the center of his chest. Well, it should have. Something stopped it in midair. It hit something invisible and then slid to the ground.

Rhys's face had gone a chalky white. "I wasn't scared of you hitting me with a snowball. I was scared of you hitting one of them."

Before I had a chance to ask what he'd meant, I felt something grab my arm and I knew we were in trouble.

Chapter Nineteen

"Could you stop wiggling? It's annoying."

"My wiggling is more annoying than being tied up and staked out under a bridge?" I didn't understand my son's thought process.

We were bound by some sort of invisible rope, back to back, sitting on the frozen ground. It had taken mere seconds for whatever thing had captured us to get us tied up and left under the bridge, probably as a sacrifice to whatever troll would show up first.

"I find the entire thing annoying. Is this what you used to do?" Rhys asked. "I've heard some tales of your adventures, and you always made them sound charming. Now I wonder if most of those adventures could have been avoided if you had simply not."

"Not what?"

"Not done whatever it is you did to piss off every supernatural creature you come in contact with," my son replied. "Like that frost giant that Dad killed in Faery. Maybe if you hadn't pissed Dad off you could have gotten in and out very quickly and the giant could have lived."

Oh, I had not been the problem that day. "Or your father could have listened to me and we wouldn't have been in the situation in the first place. Tell me something, Rhys. Are you this rude to your fathers? Is it because they're men and men don't make the silly mistakes women do?"

He went quiet. "It's because I'm far more afraid of you than I am of them. I'm sorry. I should have told you that field is a known place for the invisible ones. Are you cold?"

I was still irritated with him. "Yes, I'm cold. I'm sitting on a foot of snow. And I don't know why you would be afraid of me."

He went silent. Maybe I didn't want the answer to that question.

"What are the invisible ones?" I could at least find out something about our captors.

"They prefer the term Hidden Folk," Rhys said with a sigh. "They're a group of Fae who exist on a parallel plane. They don't like it when you hit them. They've got a thing about it. It's a good sign that they didn't show themselves."

I disagreed. "I wish they had. I would have liked a word."

"No, you wouldn't. Look, Mom, I know this is annoying, but you broke one of their rules, and this is punishment of sorts. Just stay calm and Lee will come looking for us," Rhys promised.

"Or we can figure a way out of these bindings and leave." A frustrating day had gotten even worse and everyone was going to blame me, but how was I supposed to know where invisible people were standing?

"Please don't listen to her," Rhys said in a calm voice. "She didn't mean to offend."

"I didn't know they were there," I insisted. "Are they still here?"

"I don't know. Probably. Maybe." He went silent for a moment. "I should have told you to be careful out here. I'm sorry. I take it for granted that everyone knows how to behave."

I could have told him I almost never behaved, but it seemed like that might make things worse. "If they exist on a parallel plane, how did I hit them? And how did they manage to manhandle us because I could totally feel them."

"In the places where the Hidden Ones exist, think of them as being slightly out of phase with our plane." Rhys's voice had taken on an academic tone. "There are many theories as to why. I personally believe that they were Fae who chose not to leave this plane during the great retreat. When humans got to be too much, they used magic to hide from them and got caught in an in-between place. Over the years they've figured out how to make themselves corporeal on this side of the veil. So they technically exist in both worlds."

I didn't see why they would want to be in both worlds. Like pick a side, people, but I often didn't understand the hows and whys of what any being does. "So some human accidently hits one of these guys and they get punished?"

"Yeah, but if it had been a human, they wouldn't have tied up the offender. They would have done something more subtle. Like pushing the poor dude into traffic or tripping him so he fell off a cliff."

"Are you serious?"

"Like I said, they're on the vengeful side. It doesn't happen often," Rhys admitted. "In this case, they will honor my Fae nature and not attempt to kill us."

I rather thought he wasn't thinking big enough. "Baby, you're a Green Man. You do know you rank pretty high in the world of the Fae, right? Tell them to let us go."

He went silent again, and I got the feeling we were in for a superlong punishment.

If he wasn't willing to deal with the situation, then it was time for me to take control. "Hey, Hidden Folk, I'm the goddess of the High Priest of Faery and this is my Green Man son. You want fertility? Let me out. I'm very sorry you got your butt hurt by a snowball, which considering where we are, you should be more used to."

"Mother, please stop." It was easy to hear Rhys's frustration.

"You can't rule a kingdom if you're skittish about ordering people around."

"I don't intend to rule anything at all, and the longer you talk the longer this will likely take. I pray Lee is smart enough to bring Lily with him or he'll have to figure out how to deal with invisible rope. I'm fairly certain it's magical."

So we were stuck. We were supposed to meet Neil in an hour or so, but I worried I would freeze to death before then.

We sat there in silence for the moment. They'd looped the rope around our torsos so we sat back to back, unable to see each other. I had a lovely view of a half-frozen stream. Slushy ice made its way downriver, and the bridge over our heads was a rickety wooden contraption that no one with any sense would actually try to traverse. I could have told Rhys that my godparents would never have considered it a proper bridge. Maybe back in the 1800s when it had been constructed it had been a luxurious place, but not now. It was a murder bridge.

And I couldn't even get to my gun. Not that I would have known where to point it. Also, if the grand invisible ones had been upset about a snowball, I can't imagine what they would do if I shot one of the fuckers.

"I thought silence would be more comfortable, but I was wrong. Now I wonder if you're plotting." Rhys managed to make each word an accusation.

My son had a bad impression of me. "I promise, I'll sit here and freeze to death and then you won't have to talk to me again."

His head dropped back slightly, leaning against mine. "I don't understand what you want. Why did you think throwing a snowball at me would make me… See, I don't even know what you were trying to do."

I sighed and wished I could see his face. "When you were young and you would shut down because you couldn't handle what you were feeling, sometimes your dad would make you hit the punching bag in the gym. You would punch and kick and yell, and it seemed to help you."

He chuckled. "Yes, I do remember that. But you should understand I don't do that anymore. I fight enough these days. I don't need to hit things that don't hit back."

I thought he kind of did. Rhys was wound tight, but he didn't seem willing to admit it. Every word I said seemed to make things worse. "So you're perfectly fine and don't need any help from anyone. It would have been easier if we'd never shown back up again."

"I didn't say that. I've been looking for you for years. It was logical to bring the king back so we can free the supernatural world from the wizard. Through careful studies and much discussion I came to the conclusion that Dad is the only one who can deal with the problem."

"Not according to the prophecies." The academics had been studying the prophecies for years. Sasha had whole notebooks of different interpretations, almost all of which led back to Lee and some mysterious other—who we now believed was Dean—to be the ones who could save the plane.

"Lee can't take out Myrddin on his own. And now I'm even happier we have Dad back since Lee's turn will be easier with Dad close. King's blood will calm him and help him find his footing, so to speak. The goddess only knows what would have happen if he'd turned without any of us knowing what was going on. Human Lee can be chaotic. I can't imagine what he could do as a newly risen vampire." He paused and then continued in a lower voice. "It was also good to get you and Papa back. I'm sorry it's been so awkward."

"It's going to continue to be if you won't even allow me to apologize." We needed to get to the heart of the matter.

"I don't need an apology. I'm not angry with you." He bit off every word like he had to make sure he got them all out. "Why should I be? You didn't make the choice to leave us. I knew that. I wasn't sure what had happened, but I knew you wouldn't leave me willingly."

He'd been so young, and there was no way he'd processed the loss as an adult would. "But I was still gone. You still woke up the next morning without a mother, and you had no idea where I was."

He was silent again, and I was left listening to the chattering sound of my own teeth.

"I'm sorry about the cold. Lee should be here soon. Somehow he always knows when I'm in trouble."

"It's a twins thing. You and Lee were very connected when you were younger." It was part of why it had hurt Rhys when Lee had started spending more and more time with Kelsey.

"I don't think Papa and Uncle Declan had it," Rhys said. "But I do remember being very close to Lee when we were young. It changed when Kelsey came on the scene."

I had to wonder how much Rhys knew about Lee's connection to the *Nex Apparatus*. "You know I named him after my guard, Lee Owens. He was Kelsey's biological father."

"Yes, I knew that."

"Do you remember when Lee got sick and he sounded different? He was young. Maybe ten. There were several days when he acted very weird."

"When he kept asking for a beer and telling me off for all the things I did?" Rhys sighed. "Yes. I remember and I remember that it was something weird and no one would tell us what was going on."

We might have mishandled that situation, but at the time it seemed better to tell them Lee was sick. "Sweetie, Lee has old Lee's soul. I know that sounds odd but a long time ago, I went to Faery and I was pregnant with you. Someone poisoned my drink and the result was I lost the pregnancy that should have resulted in you. Only you. You were what's called a new soul."

"Okay, now you sound like a crazy person."

"Of course I do, but I'm also telling you the truth and you know it. You might not have seen an angel in a long time, but you know they exist and our family has had dealings with them. After I lost that first pregnancy, you were on the Heaven plane and you were given a choice. You could be born to someone else or you could wait for your brother." Even thinking about that time made me tear up. "You chose to wait. I found out I was pregnant around the time Lee died. And then things got weirder."

"Really?" Rhys asked. "You're going to get weirder than knowing my soul before I was born?"

"Yes. I died the day we took over the Council."

Rhys was silent for a moment as though this wasn't something he wanted to think about. "You got shot, but Dad brought you back."

"Technically, he did. The truth is more complicated. When I died I found myself on the Heaven plane and I was given a choice. I had done my job. I was finished and I could stay there or I could go back and have my babies. I saw you that day. I saw you, and Lee was there. He was teaching you how to play cards. Your connection to Lee started long before you were born. But he has a connection to Kelsey that you cannot understand."

He was quiet for a moment. "So what you're saying is Lee's soul recognizes that Kelsey is his daughter. And they didn't have a relationship when old Lee was alive. His soul has unfinished business with her."

"I think we meet the same souls over and over again as we move through existence. Kelsey and Lee recognize each other. You are something different. You've just started your journey. We're the first souls yours has ever encountered, and the one you trusted most in all the world left you."

"You can't know I trusted you most."

He wasn't remembering our circumstances. "Yes, I can because I was with you last week, Rhys. You were eleven and you had a bad day at school and you didn't want to talk about it. So I watched some anime show with you and you leaned against me and after a while you got tired and laid down with your head on my lap and you finally told me that some of the kids were bullying you. I'm your mom. If I'm not the person you trusted most in the world when you were a child, then I did something terribly wrong."

He went quiet for a moment. "I remember that day. And if you had gone through my other pack, the one I take with me when we go on missions, well, you would have found the last note you left me. It was in the backpack I had on me when we went on the run. I've kept it all these years."

I had slipped the note into his backpack because they were serving pizza in the cafeteria and he liked to buy lunch on pizza days. "The funny thing is I don't remember exactly what I wrote. It was something about standing up to them, right?"

"'I love you and I'm proud to call you my son. You are a prince and a brother. A son and a friend. You have power and you will use it for good.'" He sighed. "It was a lot for an eleven-year-old, but I needed it then. I still do."

"I never meant to leave you. If I could change it, I would. If I could go back and stay there, I would change everything to stay with you. I would send your dad through and survive these years with you and Lee and Evan." I sniffled because I meant every word. I would give up that time with Summer, give it to Daniel and Dev not because I didn't hold it precious, but because my other children had been so young. They'd needed one of us. "I hope Lee gets here soon because my tears are freezing as they come out and it's uncomfortable."

"I'm sorry. I shouldn't have brought you here until I was sure. Though you are the one who pushed the matter. Is it so important you talk to them?"

"I had another reason to look for them. It was important to spend time with you," I admitted. "I can't spend time with Evan, and Lee seems to be surprisingly all right. You're the one who shuts me out. I know I should be patient, but that has never been my strong point."

"I'm not trying to shut you out, but you have to understand that I'm not a little boy anymore. And I would think you would need to spend more time with Lee. After all, you have a heist to plan with him. I'm surprised you haven't holed up with Lee and Grandad. They do that from time to time. They go off on fishing trips."

"And they don't take you?" That would bug Rhys on several levels. He would be upset that he'd been left out and that Shy was spending time with Lee and not him. Even if it wasn't really Shy.

"They've offered, but I find my relationship with Grandad uncomfortable, to say the least," Rhys admitted. "I'm attracted to Shy in a way I never have been with another woman. And honestly, Grandad never has known what to do with me. I'm not half the thief Lee is. He always liked those lessons of Grandad's, and I was happier helping Christine with her garden. I will admit that all those lessons came in handy. Lee is a good thief. He'll make you proud."

"He taught Lee because he thought Lee was human."

"He did that because he saw himself in Lee," Rhys corrected. "He saw Papa in me. It's fine. I dealt with the fact that I was on the outside a very long time ago. Lee was the fragile human and Evan was the daughter you always wanted."

"Rhys, you can't think that way."

"I don't see why not," he replied. "It's the truth. Everyone worried about Lee not fitting in and Evan walking around like a glowing ball of light for any vampire to find. I was the easy one to forget because one day I would be given to the Fae."

Surprise jolted through me. "What? You can't possibly think that we meant to give you to Faery."

I felt him shrug behind me. "It's what my uncle told me. He told me one day I would go with him to Faery and I would like the prince I am there. I believe he thought I would find it comforting, but I had nightmares about it."

"I will kick your uncle's ass, and this time I won't leave his balls on his body, I swear."

There was a long sigh from my son. "In some ways it made sense. What would I do here on the Earth plane?"

"What you're doing now. Lead the earthly Fae. They were left behind by the more powerful, and the oldest among them choose a solitary life." Like my godparents. Ingrid should have been a queen but she'd never wanted to rule. "The Fae seat on the Council was held by your uncle, and he placed no importance on the earthly Fae.

They've been left behind, truly caught in between worlds, and Frelsi proves they can thrive with a good leader. You can help them. That's your place if you choose it."

"I never thought of it that way. I was just helping out."

I had watched him for days, and I'd seen how the Fae came to him with their problems. They liked Lee, but they deferred to Rhys. "Sometimes it starts that way, but you can't deny that they look to you. They come to you with their questions and to settle their differences. You could do that on the Council. You could represent them and help them find ways to make their lives better. You could be a real voice for the Fae here, not merely a figurehead who only cares for the Fae in their safe *sitheins*. The Fae here need a king."

"What would you know about what the Fae need?" There was suddenly a tall, elegant *sidhe* standing in front of me. She had long blonde hair and a fierce frown. She stared down at me.

"Like I told you before, I've been the goddess of the High Priest of the Fae for years." The cold was starting to get to me. It wasn't truly dangerous because I had Daniel's blood, but it made me uncomfortable.

"The Seelie and Unseelie of the Fae planes mean nothing to us," she replied. "They left us long ago."

"My son was born on the Earth plane, and he never plans to live in Faery. He values the Fae here. He helped found a whole city of Fae," I announced like he'd come home with an excellent report card.

"He doesn't leave it often. You know there are more of us here," she said.

"It's dangerous for him to leave. I don't know if you've heard but there's a war on this plane." I had no idea how much the Hidden Folk kept up with Earth plane events.

"What good is a leader if he's in hiding?" That deep voice had not come from the female. I really hated not being able to see. "You call yourself a Green Man, but it's a boy I see in front of me. He can't even protect his family."

"Well, I rather thought I was being politic," Rhys said, and I could hear the tension in his voice. "I was trying to honor your traditions."

"One of our traditions is strength, boy," the male returned with a derisive snort. "You have none, Green Man. I've listened to you whine to your mother. She's got more fire than you. And if you thought for a second we were leaving you here as some inconvenience, let me assure you no one insults me without consequences."

"Magnus, perhaps we should rethink. I have heard of this female, and she does have power." The female had turned her frown to the man who was standing behind me. "You know we could use a true Green Man. His father is one. He's been gone for over a decade."

"Then his father should have trained him better. Ah, there's justice coming," the masculine voice said.

I felt the earth rumble under me.

"What was that?" I asked.

The Hidden Folk were gone, vanishing like a shadow in the gloom.

Rhys shushed me and then his voice went low. "Be quiet and maybe it will pass us by."

"What will pass us by?" I whispered the question.

"Mom, we're in a place covered in Fae, and they set us under a bridge. What do you think is coming?"

I heard a rattling sound, and then a low growl filled the air around me.

"Sweet meats. Someone has left me some delicious treats."

"What is it? We should turn around so I can see." Whatever was coming for us was coming from the wrong side. Although, might I point out that I didn't need to actually see it to know it was going to be bad. In the supernatural world, when one gets called a delicious treat by anyone who you're not in a relationship with, the best advice is to run. Because it probably is going to eat you in a non-erotic fashion. Unfortunately, I wasn't able to run because of the freaking invisible rope that bound me to Rhys.

"Mother, I am not turning us around so you can see the incredibly large troll that is coming to eat us."

That was what I was afraid of. I was even more pissed at the Hidden Assholes. "Really? I mistakenly hit you with a snowball meant to unleash some of my son's reasonable anger at me and you try to feed us to trolls?"

"If your boy is who he says he is, he'll get you out of it. If he isn't, then he's only good for troll meat." The male's voice whispered across my ears.

"Rhys, I think you should do something." It was one thing to get super cold, but I wasn't about to be eaten by a troll. I had things to do, and I couldn't save the world from the inside of a troll's belly.

"Do what?" Rhys asked, clearly exasperated.

"I don't know. This is the point where your father would use plants as a weapon or something." Dev would already have us out of the rope and he would be trying to use it on me in some weird sex way.

I caught the scent of really righteous BO and knew this particular troll didn't keep up the fastidious grooming routine some did.

"You can handle this, Green Man." The female's voice was quiet as though she had moved and was now closer to Rhys than to me. "My partner has what the humans would call a short fuse. He's stubborn, too, or we would be having this conversation in a civilized manner. I can sense your power. I believe your mother is correct, and you could be all she says you are. The Hidden Ones need help. We've been apart from our fellow Fae for so long we cannot connect anymore. We cling to shadows and old grudges, and it is killing us. But they will not listen to you until you prove yourself. So I will step away. You will live and be our hope, or you will die and we will know there is none."

There was something desperate and plaintive in her plea. Something that made my heart ache because I'd heard that plea before. I'd heard it in the leaders who were trying to save their people—even from themselves.

"You look tasty."

I turned my head enough to get a look-see at the troll who was planning to make us a snack. "I'm not. I think you'll find I'm very gamey."

"Mother," Rhys hissed.

"Lee isn't coming, baby. I need you to be ready to run if we can get out of this rope." My adrenaline was up. It pulsed through my body and reminded me that I could get out of this. I could save Rhys, and maybe if I was fast enough I could save myself, too.

"Or you can unleash all that power," the Hidden One said. "I can feel it. Why are you so afraid? Are you so afraid you will let yourself die, Green Man?"

I was starting to panic because Rhys truly was afraid of his power. He was terrified of it, of what it could do, of what it could cost him. "I did it. I hit your asshole husband or whatever he is. Rhys did nothing. I want a judgment. You have rules? Well, then you have to have justice, and killing my son isn't justice. I demand a trial."

It had worked for me before. If they took me to some weird hidden realm to be judged, I would go with them. I would trust that Danny and Dev would find a way to get me out if I couldn't do it myself. The one thing I couldn't do was watch some troll take my son's life.

I planted my feet in the snow and started to push against Rhys, trying to move so I was in front of the troll.

"You want a piece of me?" I yelled the troll's way. I was ready to kick and bite and fight. Anything to give my son time to get away.

And then the ropes came off and I felt a wave of warmth, a strong wind that blew the cap off my head. The snow beneath us melted and grass sprang under me. The strong body that had balanced me shifted, and I was on my back in the grass. It was a silky carpet beneath me.

I looked up and Rhys stood over me, reaching out his hand. His hair had come undone, flowing dark and long around his shoulders, and his eyes bled to green. Like his father's, but not the same shade. Dev's eyes were emerald, and Rhys's had become a bright shade, like someone had taken green and mixed light blue in. Like spring was there in his eyes.

I had witnessed a Green Man come into his full power. Rhys didn't have to ascend. He didn't need an ancient god to give him power. He held it all within himself.

"You are a menace, Mom." The sound of his voice reminded me that this was still my son.

"Am not." I took his hand and allowed him to haul me up. I looked around and saw the extent of his power. "Oh, Rhys, it's beautiful."

All around us spring had come, pushing out the winter's gloom. It was as though someone had put a dome over the valley we were in and locked out the cold. Trees had sprung where there had been none before, and there were swaths of white and purple flowers.

"Uhm, I would like to point out that I wasn't actually going to eat anyone," a far more cultured voice said. The troll suddenly didn't sound so savage. "I have a deal with the Hidden Folk. I help them with their system of justice and they help keep the humans away from my bridge. I'm actually a vegetarian."

I glanced to my right, and the troll who'd called me a sweet meat was wrapped in thick vines, his head the only part of him visible. "Sure you are."

"No, I truly am, Your Grace. Had I known who they were asking me to frighten, I would have explained that Her Grace, Queen Zoey, cannot be frightened by such a little thing as a troll. And good day to you, Prince of Spring. You seem to have finally come into your powers."

I stood in front of the troll, hands on my hips. He was at least five nine, with a roughhewn face and a head of scraggly hair. "Oh, you are not complimenting your way out of this, mister."

"He's not lying." The female was corporeal again, her legs tied up in long threads of grass. "He's there to scare people away from our field, and we try to do the same for his bridge. The humans have many meetings about demolishing the only home he's ever known. We persuade them not to. We whisper to them at night and seed doubt or convince them to forget this place exists. He would not have truly eaten you. Like I said, my mate is a stubborn male, and you pricked his pride."

"Well, he needs therapy," I announced. It had done wonders for Danny.

"What we need is the spring," she replied. If she was upset she'd been trapped by grass, she didn't show it. "Green Man, my name is Asta and my husband and I lead this tribe. We've been pushed to these fields, and they are fallow, my lord. We are starving and sorely in need of your help. I beg you to look past your anger with us and see that we are Fae, too. We are yours, too."

My son stood at my side as we saw what we hadn't before. The Hidden Ones shimmered to life before us—all thin and hollow. The shadows they pretended to be had become the truth of their existence.

I saw mostly adults, with a few children clinging to the hands of their weary parents.

"Sweetie, I'm afraid you can't take out your vengeance on them. No matter how much you want to," I said quietly.

"And there is the mother I remember." He stepped in front of me, a flick of his hand releasing both troll and *sidhe*. He turned toward Asta. "If I do this, the Hidden Folk must change. I understand the old ways taught us to torment humans, that it was our right to play with them because they are mortal, but that stops now."

"And you can't like stand by a person's bed while they sleep and whisper to them," I added. "It's creepy and weird."

"But then they will take my bridge," the troll lamented, fat tears welling in his eyes.

"I will handle it," Rhys promised. "The only thing my father grows better than plants is money, and you will find the humans understand that particular language well. If I grant you fruitful fields, how will you hide them from the humans?"

A big old field of spring crops in a place that didn't normally grow much more than moss would probably cause someone to have questions.

"We can hide our fields the way we do our homes." Asta's words held a note of hope.

"And you may punish me in any way you see fit, Green Man." Magnus moved to stand beside his mate. He got down to one knee. "I will take the punishment in exchange for food for my people, for that place at the table your mother spoke of. We have been voiceless for eons. My death will be a good exchange."

I groaned. "Do you people know what a drama llama is?"

Rhys's seafoam eyes narrowed. "There is a reason you do not deal with politics."

I shrugged because truth matters. I preferred to shoot things. Especially when I could see them.

"Until now I have not used my power because I've always been afraid of it. I worry if I use it, it will overtake me and I'll be further from everything I love," Rhys explained. "But my mother was right many years ago, and she's right today. I have power and if I choose not to use it for good, then who am I?"

Rhys leaned over and touched the ground, whispering something in Gaelic, and then he bent down and breathed over the dirt. Crops sprang up around us, crops and arbors of fruit trees. Warm winds shifted through what had once been cold and icy. Spring washed over the fallow fields, bringing life and hope.

"This is my gift to you, Hidden Ones," Rhys said, his tone steady and deep. "I give it to you willingly and with no request but to live in our world and follow our laws. You cannot hide from the world and then punish it when it accidently touches you. I do ask that you send a representative to Frelsi so we might open talks about how to best be allies, but make no mistake. You are earthbound Fae and I am your Green Man. I am walking spring."

They surrounded him like he was a messiah, and to them I supposed he was. To the Fae my son was a god of sorts, but I remembered when he was a child who wanted his brother to play with him, who clung to me when the world seemed unfair.

He'd stepped into his power when he needed to, when to not step into it would have been an act of selfishness he wasn't capable of.

"Hey! Rhys? Mom!"

I turned and Lee was standing at the edge of the field, and I realized the Hidden Ones had already proven they could keep their secrets from the world. Lee couldn't see us. Shy stood there with him, looking over what I suspected seemed to be a snowy, empty field. There was a look of pure fear on her face as she tried to figure out where we were.

I strode over to them, unwilling to leave them on the outside. I had to hope physical connection would pull them in. I reached out and grabbed their arms, pulling them close.

"Hey!" Lee yelled, and then his expression changed. "Mom. Whoa. What the hell? Where did all those people come from?"

"The Hidden Ones," Shy said. "They showed themselves to Rhys? And he did this? Oh, it's beautiful."

Flowers popped up around Shy's feet, making a circle around her. One sprouted up to the level of her hand, offering itself to her.

Rhys stared at her across the field, nodding her way as though acknowledging that she was here.

I watched the moment my son fell hopelessly in love with a woman, when he found his goddess.

"I think I want to vomit," Lee said. "I do not get the romantic stuff."

I pointed his way. "Don't you tease your brother."

"I won't now. Now he can like shove a tree up my ass," Lee countered. "I'll probably be way more polite to him from here on out, but the flower stuff is gross. So how did you manage to get Rhys to loosen up and unleash the god within?"

"You know how it goes. We had a nice talk, almost got eaten by a troll, and then your brother became walking spring."

All in all just another day in the life of a mom.

I stood in the warmth of spring, hidden from the world, and wondered if our new allies couldn't help with my problem, too. After all, they breached space. Could they do the same for time? The celebration went on around us, but I was stuck with a world of questions.

Chapter Twenty

"According to Alexander, they know something happened with Rhys today." Daniel paced in front of the fire.

"Yes, something happened. Daniel, our son is an elemental." Devinshea was still reeling from the news.

"There hasn't been a new elemental born to the Fae in a thousand years." Declan sat at the small table by the window, nursing his beer and his nose, since I'd punched him upon our return to Frelsi.

Then Dev had done the same after I told him what Rhys had said. I wasn't sure why the asshole was still here except that he wanted a piece of Rhys, too. He always had, but learning that Rhys's power had manifested in such a unique way seemed to have made my brother-in-law even more desperate.

"All right, I'll bite. What's an elemental?" I had my suspicions, but I liked to have it all laid out for me.

"It means that his powers are defined by an element of the natural world, and he has mastery over it." Dev sat across from me. He'd been watching Daniel pace as I'd told them my version of what had happened this afternoon. "There's a fire elemental in the Unseelie *sithein*. His powers are obvious. There are couple of water elementals here on the Earth plane. From the stories I've heard, in the beginning they were more common. They helped form the Earth. Rhys's powers come from a season. It's far more rare."

"Abbas Hiberna was an elemental. He was winter," Daniel pointed out. "He was incredibly powerful. Is Rhys like that?"

Kelsey had been the one to save us from the duke. He'd frozen the city over and tried to execute Danny. "He was a demon from the Hell plane."

"The different planes all have their versions of elementals," Declan explained. "We haven't seen a seasonal elemental in…I don't think my mother has even met one."

I didn't care what Declan said, my momma-in-law is old. She didn't look it. She looked like a young Cate Blanchett, if she'd never moved on from the *Lord of the Rings* trilogy, but the truth was she was old in Earth years.

"What does it mean for the plane?" Danny asked.

"It means our springs will likely be more productive anywhere Rhys goes. He'll have some control over wind and rain. I'm not sure exactly what it means since I have never met one," Dev admitted.

"It means life and fertility for the Fae. The fact that Rhys comes along at a moment when we are on the brink means the Fae can thrive again," Declan pronounced. "He must come home with me."

"He isn't going anywhere with you, you asshole," I shot back his way.

"Brother, I think you should be silent when it comes to Rhys," Dev added, his eyes narrowing. "You gave up all rights to him when you told him you would kidnap him and force him to do your bidding."

"I never said anything of the kind." Declan seemed genuinely confused at how we'd reacted.

"You told a scared little boy that he would someday have to live in Faery forever." And now I knew that fear had been with Rhys until this afternoon.

Declan sighed and sat back. "It's a beautiful place. I didn't think I was scaring the boy. I thought I was offering him something wonderful. He would seem sad because he wasn't getting as much attention as Lee or Evan and I would explain to him that one day things would be different. He would be worshipped in Faery. He would be valued."

"He was beloved by his family," Daniel replied. "All children think their siblings get more attention. I assure you we spent plenty of time with Rhys. If you asked Lee, he was on the outside because we thought he was human. Evan was too young to be annoyed with us, but it would have come."

Dev shook his head. "Declan, you forget our childhood. You were jealous of me because Mother worried about me. I was jealous of you because she spent time teaching you how to be king. She could not win. I assure you I remember it, and I took pains to pay attention to all my children and I still failed in their eyes."

"I don't think I was wrong to offer the boy a look at the future he could have," Declan argued.

Dev pointed his way. "You didn't offer him anything. You told him what he would do and where he would live."

"He is important." Declan stood and got in his brother's face.

"Yes, he is important, and he has choices." Dev looked ready to start another beatdown.

Daniel got between them with a weary sigh. I could understand. We'd had a lot of family drama in a week. "Dev, Zoey, I understand that you're angry with him. I am, too, but we're right back in the same position we were before."

We needed allies, and the Fae had helped us in the past. Still… "I am not giving him my son."

Danny stopped in front of me, his hands going to my shoulders. "And I would never allow anyone to force Rhys to do something he didn't want to, but we have to consider that leaving the Seelie and the Unseelie without a Green Man could do far more harm than good."

"I will go," Dev promised. "I'll go and prove to them that I'm back and they'll calm down. Bris and I will walk the fields and give them a show of strength."

"In the middle of a war?" Danny ran a hand over his head, a sure sign that he was frustrated. "I don't like the thought of sending you in alone, and I can't leave the plane right now. It's a delicate time."

"It's a delicate time in my kingdom, too," Declan declared before turning my way. His eyes narrowed as he focused on me. "I'm glad that my nephew is taking his place as a leader here among the earthly Fae. He must remember that the rest of us need him as well. And don't tell me you don't understand duty, Your Grace. After all, from what I have been able to ascertain, you gave up your daughter to her duty. Allow your son to do his or give me the second chance you promised."

His boots thudded across the floor as he stomped out, carrying his beer. I could feel the amulet he'd given me in my pocket. I'd been told to keep it close to the Goddess Chain or it might make its way back to Faery in an explosive manner.

I frowned at my Fae husband. "Is there a reason he's not locked up? He literally tried to kidnap our son. Rhys is afraid of him."

"I'm not afraid of him." Rhys sighed as he entered from the kitchen, Lee right behind him. "I apologize for eavesdropping. But my uncle's probably right that I should make an appearance in the *sitheins*. If Papa would be willing to come with me, I would consider it."

Rhys seemed more relaxed after expending all that magic, and it made me wonder how long he'd kept it bottled up. It also made me worry that he would now want the other things that went with being a fertility god. Would he feel more comfortable about sex now that he had control of his magic? Would he need it more than he had before?

Shy still housed my father's soul, and from what I understood about how they worked, it wasn't like she could shut him out. They experienced things together. If Rhys kissed her and followed the path that would lead to, my father would be there, too.

It wasn't something I thought a relationship could survive, and it was so obvious to me that Rhys was crazy about Shy and she had a thing for him. I worried he might take the Lee route rather than wait, and that could hurt him forever.

I needed to find another home for my father's soul.

"You know I'll be by your side," Dev said. "We all will, but this is not about pleasing your uncle or grandmother anymore."

"No, it's about power and responsibility," Rhys said in that sober way of his. "If the Seelie and the Unseelie destabilize, a war could bleed over to the Earth plane. The earthly Fae are my biggest concern. I will do everything I need to do in order to protect them. And we already have interesting allies."

"Yeah, the Hidden Folk are pretty cool." Lee slung his big body down on the sofa. "I still don't know if they're going to be able to see the bag of holding, though."

"I don't see why not. A pocket universe is out of phase with this one, and they can see those. They've always known where Frelsi was and how to get in. I count it as a good thing that despite being able to spy on us, it seems they've honored our city by staying out of it until now." Rhys leaned in, his eyes lit with the same excitement he used to get when he was playing a game and winning. He looked my way because in this he knew I was the boss. "Mom, I talked to Magnus and Asta, and they're willing to go to the Council building to make sure the bag is still where it's supposed to be. If it isn't, they'll look for it. I don't want you going in without being absolutely sure as to where the bag is."

"It's there. No one could move it." Of that I was sure. "Only Grandad and I can physically touch it."

"But we know Sarah did something that day," Rhys said gravely. "We know she told Neil she had something to do before she went missing."

"She had to get her family." At least that was what I thought she'd meant.

"That shouldn't have taken her long." Daniel seemed to think about the situation. "She knew about the bag, knew what it held. She knew it was in the closet, and she had to know that if Myrddin was taking over, he would likely end up in the penthouse."

"But he can't touch it." I didn't like the thought that Sarah might have lost her life trying to save that bag. "She knew that."

"She also knew that Myrddin is the greatest magical power the planes have ever seen," Dev mused. "It might have been one thing to leave it there when she thought you were coming back, but if she had even an inkling that things could go wrong, would she try to move it?"

I didn't know. I couldn't possibly know what had gone through her head that day. I only knew that she was missing and if she'd had any chance, she would have found my kids and watched over them.

"Rhys, I like this plan." Dev sat back down.

"Yes, I do, too," Danny agreed. "If they can touch the bag and move it, please tell them to walk out with it, and then your brother and mother never need to go in."

"I never get to have any fun," Lee groaned.

I shook my head. "They won't be able to. I know that spell, and

I'm the only one walking the Earth plane now who can physically move the bag. Once I touch it, the Hidden can take it, but I have to be there."

"They're willing to go in?" Danny looked to Rhys.

Rhys nodded. "Yes. The Hidden feast tonight because of me. They're happy to return the favor. They will go in tomorrow and bring us back information."

"We already have intelligence on the building." Sasha had made sure of it. The big Russian vampire had gone over everything he knew about the Council building now. If Danny and Dev had their way, they would push this heist off forever. "We need to move soon. You said Myrddin already knows about what happened with Rhys today. How?"

"Alexander left for Dallas two nights ago. Earlier, he sent a message to Sasha about a meeting Myrddin called with his closest advisors. Alexander isn't among them, but he's close to one of the witches," Daniel began.

"Does she know about the whole Jack the Ripper thing?" Some women are not smart.

"I think for some women that's part of his charm, my goddess." Dev reached out and threaded his fingers through mine. "They enjoy the danger."

Like I said—dumbasses.

"Anyway, the witch told him they'd heard from some of their spies here in Iceland that someone used a whole lot of Fae magic today," Danny continued. "Myrddin is worried something has happened here, and he's specifically concerned that Rhys has gained more power. I think Myrddin's witches here are experts on you, son. According to Alexander, they claimed to know what your magic feels like."

"Well, we knew Myrddin studied us." Rhys was the one pacing now. "What does he think Myrddin's going to do about it? He shouldn't be able to track me back here. And the Hidden Ones promised me that a witch might be able to feel their magic, but she can't touch them unless they allow it. She might track the magic to the field, but everything I did today is now protected by the Hidden Ones."

"I don't know what Myrddin can do about it, and that's what

worries me," Danny admitted. "I don't like how much he knows about my children. And some of his knowledge came directly from me."

"You were under thrall," Lee countered. "Don't worry about it. All is forgiven. I would be a terrible hypocrite if I didn't forgive you. I did a lot of things I shouldn't have when I was under the thrall of that mermaid on Lagoon world."

"You weren't under thrall. You were on mushrooms." Rhys rolled his eyes. "And I know you didn't know they were psychedelic, but neither did I, and I didn't end up in a mermaid orgy. Fen didn't either. Evan was smart enough to hate mushrooms and refuse to eat them."

"I don't want to know what happened, do I?" It seemed to me my children had too many adventures.

"Only with Lee," Rhys replied. "I merely sat in a forest and talked to what I firmly believed at the time was Papa Smurf. He was every bit as wise as one would think. And all Fen wanted was endless belly rubs. He immediately changed to wolf form and spent hours doing that thing where he rubs his back on the floors and his legs flail. He drooled a lot. Lee was the only one who ended up servicing horny mermaids."

"Ah, yes. I remember a day I spent in a mermaid grotto," Dev began.

I pointed a finger his way. "No. Absolutely not. This is not going to degrade into a session where you and my son, who was eleven a few days ago, do a top-ten list of supernatural creatures you've fucked."

"It's way more than ten." Lee's mouth shut suddenly and then he grimaced. "Sorry, Mom. So back to the subject. Rhys did a little magic today."

"Off the charts magic that was felt all the way in Germany," Danny corrected.

Lee gave his brother a thumbs-up, seemingly happy to get the attention off himself. "I always said you would explode someday."

"I did not explode," Rhys argued. "I merely unleashed a bit of my power."

"He grew flowers all around Shy. It was disgustingly romantic," Lee said, his nose wrinkling. "Did you even think about it? Like now she's going to expect that all the time. She'll want an orange and you'll have to grow an orange tree for her. You need to learn to lower their expectations, brother. None of my women expect anything from me but an orgasm."

"Lee!" He had to remember his mother was in the room.

"It's because you don't have anything to give them but an orgasm." Rhys completely ignored me. "All of the blood in your body is constantly in your dick."

"Boys, can we argue about Lee's private life another time?" Danny asked. "Though you should know we're having a long talk, son. A long talk."

Lee frowned. "I'm not going to like this talk, am I? I would like to point out that I was denied maternal affection at a time when it was so important. Can I be blamed for seeking out love and care?"

I pointed my baby boy's way. "Don't you blame that on me. Your brother is practically a saint and he missed me, too. You will not blame your degenerate ways on me."

"I did get a big dose of Papa's DNA," Lee attempted.

"Lee," Dev began.

Lee stood and straightened his shirt, his chin coming up. "Well, I can see Rhys is now the golden child simply because he can make the seasons change. I shall go and check on supper. I can still do that."

I reached up and gripped his wrist with my free hand. "Will you check on Dean?"

His lips kicked up in a grin that let me know he was utterly unaffected by the events of the day. "That's what I was going to do. He was doing great earlier. I'm going to call him the Curse Eater from now on."

"I need you to ask him a couple of questions, but I want you to do it without making a big deal out of it."

"You want me to gather intel. I'm good at that," Lee promised.

"He actually is," Rhys acknowledged. "No one suspects he has any ulterior motives. Not when he acts like a moron most of the time. It's an effective tactic."

Lee shrugged that off. "My sunny nature puts people at ease. People want to talk to you when you're not a morose bastard all the time."

"I'm worried he got that from me," Danny said under his breath.

I was absolutely certain he'd gotten that from Danny, but I wasn't going to point that out. "Ask Dean what he knows about his father. I don't think it's much, but if anyone can get something more out of him, it's you."

"Done," Lee vowed. "Trust me. I can talk about parents for a long time. See you at supper, Mom."

He strode away. I watched from the big windows as he walked out the kitchen doors and toward Lily's part of town. Rhys and Dev told me good-bye until supper as well. They were going to find Declan to discuss the situation in Faery in depth. I was left with Daniel.

"What are you thinking, baby?" Danny moved in behind me. His arms came around me, drawing me against him. "Note that I didn't ask what were you thinking when you left the safety of the city with no other protection than Rhys, who didn't like to use his powers. I know exactly what you were doing there."

"I was trying to reach him." I leaned back against his strength.

"You were trying to push him so he realized he could trust himself," Danny whispered. "I should know. After all, I remember a woman who believed so much in me she jumped off a building to prove I could fly."

Tears pierced my eyes because the memory was sweet now. Though at the time there had been a lot of screaming and praying I was right. It was one of those moments that seemed so far away, like it happened in another lifetime. "He was scared like you were."

Danny's lips brushed my head. "And you were right to push him. The same way you were right to push me." He was silent for a moment. "Z, I don't want you to do this job."

I sighed, but his words didn't upset me since they weren't surprising. "You don't ever want me to do a job."

"I know, but I really don't want you to do this one. I wish you and Harry had left us another way out. I don't suppose Shy could do it."

Now that suggestion did surprise me. I turned and faced him. "You would send a young woman like Shy in instead of me. That's not fair of you, Danny. She's done enough for our family, and Rhys would be devastated if anything happened to her. I think there's something profound between them."

Danny sighed and drew me back in. "I wasn't thinking about her so much as Harry. Harry has more experience than anyone on the planet. Harry's not still adjusting to this world. And Harry's not pregnant."

I wasn't going to remind him that I'd pulled off another job while I was pregnant and I'd been surrounded by our enemies then, too. I didn't need to. I was sure he remembered every day. "Unfortunately, Harry's basically a ghost. He can't bleed on the bag. Shy's blood won't work."

I would have to give a drop of blood to open the bag, to bring it back into phase with our plane. No more than a prick of my finger would do it.

And that was when I knew Sarah had gone after the bag.

"Oh, shit." I stepped back, tears in my eyes. "Sarah kept my blood on hand. She needed it for some of the wards she used. She warded certain spots in the building to keep people out but allow me and Neil in. It wasn't a long-term spell, so she needed to redo it a couple of times a year. There were some other spells related to health and well-being she used my blood for. She could have found it. She could have tried to move it."

Danny hugged me tight. "We can't know that."

"She knew how important it was to keep the grimoire away from him. She knew. We had just had a conversation about it. What if going for the bag cost her her life?"

"We can't know that," Danny repeated. His hands rubbed over my back. "Baby, we don't know anything except Myrddin doesn't have it, and if we can do this safely, he never will. I'm sorry. I was expressing my fear. I trust you to do this. And whatever did happen back then, it wasn't your fault."

I couldn't help the guilt I felt. It weighed on me like a millstone, pressing on every aspect of my life. Watching Rhys come into his own had briefly allowed me to forget about the hell I found myself in.

"I want it all back. I want to take it all back," I whispered against his chest. "I want to do this all over again. One moment in time shouldn't ruin everyone's lives. It shouldn't ruin our family and everything we worked for."

"But that's how it works, Z. It's literally how it works. One moment, one mistake, can change everything. Didn't we learn that when we were kids? I died. I took my eyes off the road for one second and it was over. I didn't want it to be, but it was. We don't get to choose, and it's not what happens to us that matters. It's how we deal with it."

"These are our kids. Danny, Lee is out of control, and Rhys has spent years so wound up he can't even show affection properly. Something happened to him and he won't talk about it. I haven't spent enough time with Evan because she ran out of here as fast as she could. They are in pain and you would have me do nothing about it."

"No, I would have you do exactly what you did today." Danny stepped back, obviously frustrated with me. "You walked Rhys through an experience that along with everything else he's learned, will make him into a leader. Don't you think Harry would have turned back time and made sure I didn't get into that car if he could have? Would you have gone back to save me that night?"

At the time I would have done anything to stop Danny from getting into that car. But then he wouldn't have risen. We wouldn't have met Devinshea, and there would be no Rhys and Lee and Evan. Kelsey would have been taken by the Council and twisted into what they required or killed when she refused to comply.

Summer wouldn't have been born, and the outer planes would be lost.

So much depended on that one terrible moment.

"It's not the same. What we went through…they shouldn't have to go through that pain. We took it for them. They shouldn't be traumatized. They should have had a good life," I insisted.

"It isn't so bad." Lee stood in the doorway. He held a bag. "Sorry. I forgot the herbs Lily wanted me to bring her. Unlike my brother, I happily admit that I like to eavesdrop. I've found I learn a lot. It's not such a terrible life, Mother."

Oh, shit. Now he was calling me mother. "Lee, I wasn't saying something bad about you."

"No, you're just sad about how I turned out," he said quietly and with absolutely none of his devil-may-care air. This was the Lee who hid behind his smile, the one who felt all the hurt.

"I think you shouldn't have had to go through any of it at all," I replied.

"Your mother didn't mean anything," Daniel tried.

"But she did. She wants to try to change things, to go and fix the world. You see, nothing happens here in the city that I don't end up hearing about. Some of the brownies overheard your conversation this morning." Lee stared at me, more serious than I'd seen him before. "I know I act like an idiot. Sasha taught me that. He taught me that people tend to see what you want them to see. I kind of thought you would see more."

"I see that you're not happy, baby. You think I'm fooled by the arrogance?"

"I earned some of the arrogance, you know," Lee said. "I earned it by being the absolute toughest son of a bitch in our group. I earned it by never quitting. They took my eye and I still saved my brother. Dad knows the story because he's asked me. Papa sat down and told me how proud he is of the man I've become. But what my mother has done…my beloved mother, the one I held above everyone else…what you've done with your time is plotted with my uncle about how to fix us, how to go back to the time when we were children and easy to love. The funny thing is we would always have grown up. We always would have become more complex. You know Papa said we judged our parents when we were kids, and he's right. Now that I have space, I can see honestly how much love and care I was given, and so can Rhys and Evan. Not a one of us truly blamed you for what happened to us. But I do blame you for this. You want to erase who I am because looking at me hurts you?"

My heart ached because now I was the one who was hurting him. He didn't understand what I was trying to do. "I didn't say that. You can't expect me to be happy that you had to go through the kind of pain you and your brother and sister have."

Lee chuckled, but there was no humor to the sound. "Life is pain, Mother. You know that. You know that even if you had been here with us, there would have been pain. You can't control the world. Even the great and grand nexus point can't control everything."

"I didn't control any of it," I shot back. "Don't make me out to be some manipulative bitch."

"Hey, we need to bring the temperature down," Danny said.

"But the world really does revolve around you," Lee pointed out, ignoring his father. "And now that you don't like the consequences, you want a do-over. The rest of us have to fall in line because you don't like the outcome."

He was deliberately misunderstanding me. "I want to take away the pain that happened to you over the last twelve years."

"But then you take away the joy, and there was joy. A lot of it. You take away the bonds we've formed. Do you know what the man beside you talked to me about?" Lee asked, the challenge in his voice unmistakable.

"Lee, I told you she needs time," Daniel began.

"He talked about family," Lee continued. "He said he was proud that we'd kept our family together, that we hadn't broken. He was proud his children stuck together. Even when our parents were gone, we looked after each other."

"You think I don't feel that way?" I loved them. I loved how close they were.

Lee stared down at me. "I think you've spent so much time thinking about how to get back what you lost, you haven't considered what you have in front of you. I don't know what will happen if you manage to use that artifact Declan gave you. I don't know if this version of me will cease to exist or if we'll simply be without our parents again, stuck in a war without you."

"I'm not going anywhere, Lee," Danny promised.

"Yes, you're the perfect parent," I said under my breath, angry that he wasn't backing me up.

"No, I'm not, and neither is Dev." Danny turned his attention to our son. "And Lee isn't giving you the time you need. You're being impatient, son. She's built her life around the three of you. You are her whole world, and you can't expect her to come to terms with this loss in a day or two. She had dreams for you, for our family, and I know they might seem selfish to you, but they weren't. She loved the life we had, and it's hard for her to let go. She fully believes she's the reason this happened. She's drowning in guilt, and she does not need this from you."

"I should have known you would defend her." Lee stepped back. "Well, I hope you let me know what you're planning to do, Mother. I'd like a heads-up if I'm going to cease to exist. I have a couple of things left on my bucket list."

"Lee," Danny said.

Lee put up a hand. "No, it's fine. It's not like I'm going to run off. And I'm not going to tell Rhys what I found out about that artifact and that Mother is plotting behind our backs. He doesn't need that kind of heartbreak. I'll be ready to run the heist with or without you. I hope you'll at least do me the courtesy of leaving a little blood behind so we have a chance against Myrddin in case we're still here after you find your way back to paradise."

"I didn't mean to hurt you." I couldn't hold back the tears now, and I watched my son look at me with a blank expression.

He shrugged. "Hey, I didn't mean to hurt you either. I guess it's what we do. I'll report back to you with what I learn from Dean. You'll find I'm a good soldier. I get the job done no matter how much it hurts. I'm pretty sure I get that from my mom, so I have no doubt you'll succeed."

He turned and walked out.

"Zoey, what did you take from Declan?" Danny's mouth was a flat line as he stared at me for a moment.

"It's nothing. It's a way to talk to the ancient ones. I wanted to study how it connects the present to the past." I could feel tears pouring from my eyes, but I felt oddly numb, and I knew in that moment that if I could have gone back, I wouldn't have blinked an eye. I would have shredded the universe to go back and have one moment when my baby looked up at me and I was the sun in the sky, the one who could never betray him.

I should have had years with him, should have had at least a decade before he decided to hate me. And it was all gone. He'd been a tiny baby in my arms yesterday, and now he was a man and he didn't need me anymore.

"Damn it. Come here." Danny huffed and dragged me into his arms. "Baby, he didn't mean it. You're both in bad places. He was a child yesterday for you, and you were the perfect mother for years for him. He didn't get the chance to grow and change with us. God, he's so damn much like you. It was inevitable that you would spark off each other, but you didn't get the time to learn how to fight with him."

I didn't want to fight with him at all. I didn't want to fight with any of them. "He doesn't understand."

"Baby, none of us understands," Danny whispered. "We all need time to adjust. I promise you we will get through this."

There was a knock and I looked up, praying it wasn't another child of mine come to accuse me of not loving him.

Sasha stood in the doorway, a grim look on his face. "I'm sorry to interrupt, Your Highness. You have to know I wouldn't unless it was an emergency."

I stepped away from Danny and tried to wipe my eyes. We seemed to move from one crisis to another, with no time to breathe in between.

Danny reached for my hand, but I avoided him. I couldn't accept his affection. The guilt I'd felt moments before had tripled. Danny and Dev had been giving our sons attention and building relationships with them, and I'd held myself back because I couldn't handle the idea of this place.

I was the problem.

My husband gave me the look that meant he wasn't done with me, but he turned his attention to Sasha. "What is it?"

"Myrddin sent us a message," Sasha said. "And a dead body."

I forced back my pain because we had a job to do.

Chapter Twenty-One

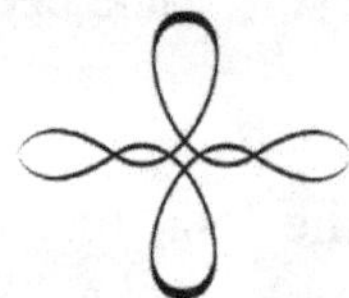

I felt so numb as Dev sat down beside me. Rhys and Dev had been found quickly, but Lee was still out in the village. Sasha sat in his place across from Danny. Zack sat where he always had—at Danny's side. He looked healthy and whole. He was back in a suit, and though it was big on him, the way he was eating it would soon fit him perfectly again.

It was good to see Zack smiling, but I couldn't feel the joy I should.

"Are you all right, Mom?" Rhys placed a mug of tea in front of me. "You look like you could use some food. I could have Albert make something for you."

I shook my head. "Dinner's almost ready. I can wait. Thank you for the tea."

Would he be so solicitous if he knew what Lee did? Would he ever forgive me?

"You're welcome." Rhys sank down to the chair beside mine before turning Sasha's way. "What's happened? Who did he kill? Does this have anything to do with what I did this afternoon?"

I reached for his hand. "Sweetie, you didn't do anything wrong."

He gave my hand a squeeze before letting go. "I know, but it seems a coincidence. And I know Alexander contacted Sasha about it earlier. Myrddin hasn't made a real move on us in months. Lately, he's been satisfied with putting bounties on our heads."

"Well, we knew he would likely make a move now that the king has returned," Sasha said.

"Who did we lose?" Danny wanted to get right to the bad news. It was his way. He took the hit and moved forward.

"The body of Nancy Luthor was left behind the bookstore in Reykjavík. She was a witch I recruited a few years back. She wasn't one of my higher-level spies, but she was solid," Sasha stated. "She had been stabbed, but the wizard hexed her so she was able to give us a message."

Zack had been among the group that had used the portal to Reykjavík. Now that he was healthy again, he was taking his place as one of Daniel's generals. "Her body was dead, but Myrddin used it to speak through her. Lily went with us, and she's ensured that Myrddin can't use the body in such a fashion again. She's at rest."

I was glad I hadn't been there to witness this message of his. "What does he want?"

"A meeting, of course," Sasha replied. "He wants the king, the queen, and Devinshea to come to Dallas. He's promising a neutral place. He's allowing you four guards and will submit to wards around the meeting place if that will make you feel more secure."

"Sending a body doesn't instill a lot of hope in me," Danny said tightly.

"Yes, well, I believe the body was meant for me, and it's possible Myrddin plans on throwing me under the bus, to use an American saying." Sasha wore a grim expression. "First he's telling me that he knows more about my network than I think he does. Second, I believe he's going to try to convince you I was always the problem and that he's tried to hold everything together. He will do this in an attempt to ascertain if he still has control over you."

"But what he truly wants is to keep the throne." Dev knew the truth of the matter.

"He has to in order to fulfill his agreement with the demons," Rhys replied. "He doesn't get a do-over with them. They won't simply allow him to hand the throne back to you and go on as we did before. They want what he promised them. So you have to understand that no matter what Myrddin says about wanting to meet with the dads, he really wants Mom."

"I concur," Sasha agreed. "Myrddin's plan will involve getting his hands on the queen. He believes she's the key to finally doing what he promised."

"Well, I'm certainly not going to put my wife in the same room with him," Danny announced. "So I don't think I'll be taking any meetings."

But I needed him to take that meeting. He was forgetting one of the rules of thievery. It was always better to steal from someone who wasn't there. "It would help me to have Myrddin out of the Council building. I would assume this neutral place isn't the Council building."

"No, Your Highness," Sasha replied. "He's proposing to meet at a park in public in the afternoon. This particular park is small and highly visible."

"I wouldn't even consider meeting him in private." Danny sat back. "If we meet in the daylight, in a public place with humans around us, it could work. I'm going to assume nothing's changed in the last twelve years concerning humans and their knowledge of the supernatural."

"It remains the one thing all of the supernatural world agrees on," Zack replied.

"It is still our highest law." Sasha's words were tinged with the grief he still felt for his daughter. Tasha was human, and though I was sure he checked in on her, he couldn't ever be near her again. He couldn't talk to her or get to know who she was now. She was lost to him.

My children weren't lost. I'd found them again. I did have the chance to get to know them.

Sasha would kill to have only lost twelve years with his daughter.

"So we have to assume Myrddin will follow it," Danny continued. "Otherwise, even he can be punished."

"I thought the whole point was to give the Earth plane over to the demons." I didn't trust Myrddin to follow anyone's rules.

"He can't do that until he can lock the celestial planes out. I can assure you the angels will do something if the humans are at risk. At least I would hope so," Dev said.

I had to shrug. I was the one who had dealt with angels the most. "They have odd rules. We can't predict what they'll do. I have to think they have some knowledge of what Myrddin wants. They'll likely leave it up to us to save the plane."

By us, I didn't mean humanity as a whole or some giant supernatural army. I meant those of us sitting around the table. I had done Heaven's work more than once.

"We can't count on angels to do the work here on the Earth plane," Danny agreed. "So that means we have to move forward with our own plans, and that includes Zoey getting her hands on the grimoire and Gladys. If I take this meeting, she would have some time without Myrddin in the building."

Dev looked Sasha's way. "By doing this in the daylight hours, it takes you off the board. I believe that's his point. It means our guard will have to be made up of shifters. He will bring his strongest witches."

"Will he even meet with us if we refuse to bring Zoey?" Danny asked.

"I would certainly say we don't tell him she's not coming," Sasha advised. "He needs to find that out at the very last moment possible."

"He'll know I'm in town." This could be very good for my heist. Knowing Myrddin and his strongest witches would be out of the building gave me the perfect time to get in. "We take someone with us, put a Zoey glamour on him or her, and make sure I'm seen around. They won't be able to tell unless they get close, and by then it's hopefully too late. Neil could do it. Or he can run around shopping with whoever plays me."

The big Russian nodded. "This could work. I believe Myrddin might actually prefer this scenario. He can't try to take Zoey if she's in that meeting. It would be much easier to pick her up somewhere else."

"Myrddin's played this game many times," Daniel said with a sigh. "He knows what he's doing and how to manipulate a situation. He would ask for something he knows we won't give. He'll maneuver us into a situation where we compromise. The compromise is exactly what he wants."

"He'll think I'm an easy target," I pointed out. "He'll believe that I would be out shopping while Danny and Dev are handling him."

"I don't know about that." Dev seemed uneasy with the whole situation. "I think Myrddin knows exactly how competent Zoey is. He certainly knows she's a thief."

I had an ace up my sleeve. "But he doesn't know the grimoire is in the building. He won't expect that I'll try to get in."

"My network has told me that he's torn up the penthouse." Sasha seemed even grimmer than usual, and I wondered how close he'd been to the witch who'd died. Or perhaps he was a male who'd seen more death than he'd wanted and yet refused to allow himself to become numb to it. "He's looked for the book around the globe, and he hasn't been able to find it."

Because it wasn't on the globe.

"If he believes the queen is the one who stole the book, he has to think about the timing," Zack mused. "There were only a few hours between when Myrddin would have last seen the book and when Zoey and Daniel disappeared. The book would have to be somewhere Zoey could have stashed it quickly."

Sasha shook his head. "Eddie was in the building that day. He could have teleported the book anywhere. I assure you Myrddin has done his due diligence. He's mapped out every single place that book could be and he's searched it. He has to believe that the queen alone knows where the book is or he would have found it."

"When is this meeting supposed to take place?" Danny asked.

"He would like to meet tomorrow," Zack replied.

Danny shook his head. "He can't expect us to be in the States by tomorrow."

"It's his way of testing to see if we'll use Eddie," Sasha surmised. "He's likely trying to figure out where everyone is. He's getting his chess pieces lined up, and this will help him."

Danny looked my way. "Zoey, how long do you need to be ready, and how big a crew are we talking?"

"I'm going to keep it to a minimum. It's me and Lee and Neil." I wished I didn't have to bring Lee into it, didn't have to put him in more danger, but he really was our best shot at pulling this thing off. There was also the chance that if I left him out, he would find something far more dangerous to get into. He truly was my son. "The Hidden Ones have agreed to go in first and make sure we know where the bag is. I have to assume that Myrddin has the penthouse warded to the nth degree, so if they can make sure it's still there, that would be helpful."

Rhys leaned in. "Asta has assured me she can have an answer for us before Mom ever gets on the plane. The Hidden Ones have a network they use to move across the globe. It will take them a few hours to get there, search the building, and get back. We'll at the very least know if there's a reason to go in at all."

"Do we have a reason to believe it wouldn't be there? The way you and Harry have described the bag of holding, there should be no way for Myrddin to have found it." Sasha looked through his notes.

"Zoey thinks Sarah might have found a way to move it." Danny's fingers tapped along the table, a sure sign he was anxious about the whole thing. "If she did, she likely disappeared with it. If Asta doesn't find anything, then we won't show for the meeting with Myrddin at all. If she does, we'll follow through on the plan. How compromised do you think your network is, Sasha?"

"I think Myrddin would kill them all if he could, or he would use them to send me bad intelligence. That hasn't happened so far," Sasha replied. "Up until now, all of my intelligence has been solid. He might have gotten lucky. I'll be careful over the next few weeks, but we'll need someone to help the queen and Lee."

I was happy that spy couldn't be Alexander. I would be going in during the daylight hours, so they couldn't foist him on me. "I would rather work with Christine if I could."

"Myrddin won't take her along," Sasha assured me. "She's not the strongest of his witches. She's been a very valuable source. Rhys, you need to confer with the Hidden Ones. Take our maps and make sure they know where to look first."

"Is there any way they could take some of Zoey's blood and grab the bag?" Danny asked.

"Not unless she knows some witchcraft I don't," a familiar voice said. Shy stood in the doorway, but it was my father who was speaking. "Sarah might have. She was an amazing witch. If she had some of Zoey's blood, she might have been able to do it, but I wouldn't know how to replicate it."

"She told me she had something to do," Zack said quietly. "That last day, I saw her in the hall and she was scared. I tried to get her to follow me. I already knew the kids were out of the building. I was trying to find Neil to get the rest of our people out. Sarah said she would meet me later, but she had something to do. I didn't see her again."

"And Neil firmly believes she didn't leave the building." I hated to even think about this, but I had to. "Do we know who lives in Sarah's apartment now?"

Sasha stared down at his notes. "She was on the floor below the penthouse, correct?"

"Yes, it was one of the floors that was separated into four residences," Dev explained. "Neil and Chad had one. Sarah and her family. Zack and his. For years we kept the last open for visiting VIPs. Myrddin took it over when he came to live at the compound. He and Nimue stayed there."

"Of course, he's now in the penthouse," my father said, sliding into a seat close to Rhys. "But the floor Sarah used to live on is considered a high-security area. From what I learned when I hung out at the Council building, he doesn't allow anyone but his most trusted witches on that floor. Some say it's because he doesn't want anyone too close to his domicile."

Sasha nodded as though Dad had prodded his memory. "Yes, we have several theories about why he did this. Some believe it's for security purposes. Others think he's doing some kind of research he doesn't want anyone to know about. He allows very few up there. Christine gave us what we hope is a complete list of wards used to keep witches out."

"The cloak is very effective against wards," Rhys explained. "We've tested it against everything we could and it always beats the wards. Certain cats are another thing entirely. Most won't notice a thing, but a strong familiar knows something is wrong."

"Yes, but even a strong familiar can be distracted." I remembered how the pixie Dannan had taken on Myrddin's familiar so Lee and I had time.

"I think this could work." Sasha closed his notes and looked Daniel's way. "Your Highness, I know you're worried about the queen, but I think with the proper reconnaissance, she can run this op with confidence. I will find someone to play the part of the queen and be seen around town with Neil. You and Devinshea will meet with Myrddin. Zack, I need you to make contact with the shifter groups in the area. We're still close allies with the big cats there and they can provide security."

Zack held up a hand. "Uhm, hello. I don't know why I should call someone. I'm one hundred percent good to go."

Danny shook his head. "No. You're not coming. I don't want Myrddin to know we've healed you. It's better to let him think the curse is still working on you or he might have questions we don't want to answer."

"Yes, this is how it must go," Sasha agreed. "I will also remain here in Frelsi in case this is some kind of trick to leave us unprotected."

"Sasha, I know you couldn't be at the actual meeting, but I would rather have you with us," Danny began.

The Russian was quiet for a moment. "I can't, Your Highness. It's too close. The temptation to see her… I cannot risk that my heart would overrule my head."

"Your daughter." Danny sighed. He'd forgotten where Sasha's daughter lived. "I'm sorry. She's in Dallas. You're right. We need to protect Frelsi. If you don't mind my asking, have you been able to keep up with her at all? Her name is Tasha, right?"

The saddest smile crossed the Russian's handsome face. "Yes, Natasha, but she still goes by Tasha. She is well. She's a freshman in college and very beloved. Her guardi…her parents adore her and she's happy with her siblings. She would not even remember what I look like after all this time, but I fear there are many in Dallas who would. I have watched them all, you know. Watched the men who became my brothers, watched them marry and build families. Whatever we went through, it was worth it because there was a good life on the other side. I struggled in the beginning, but I have hope now."

Rhys turned Sasha's way. "I know what you sacrificed. I am grateful to the goddess for sending you to us."

"So very grateful," Daniel said.

"It has been my honor, but I will say that I'll be happy when this war is over." Sasha pushed his chair back. "I would like to know what proper vampire society looks like. And I would like to travel a bit. In style this time. We did not do first class when we were running across the planes."

"Trust me. You'll have all the first class you can get," Dev promised as he pushed back from the table. "I'm going to call and make sure our plane is going to be ready. That means taking the portal to the outside world. I might be late for supper."

Daniel stood. "I'll go with you."

One by one they left, eager to get to work. Dinner would come soon, and I was thinking seriously about asking for a tray in my room. I didn't know if I could sit at the table with Lee and not break down in tears. Then Rhys would want to know what had happened, and he would hate me, too.

"Are you all right, my darlin'?"

My father was the only one left at the table. I gave him a wan smile. "I'm as good as I can possibly be."

"Something's happened," he said. Shy's big brown eyes seemed to look into my soul. It was odd to be talking to my father and looking at the gorgeous woman my son was infatuated with. "I saw Lee earlier. He told me he was good, too."

I thought seriously about getting up and basically running to my bedroom, but knowing my dad he would simply follow me. If he truly thought something was wrong, he wouldn't care about privacy. "Lee found out I've been investigating ways to change the timeline."

Shy's head dropped back as my father unleashed a frustrated groan. "Damn it, Zoey. I was hoping you would keep that nonsense to yourself."

"It's not nonsense, and I tried to. It turns out Lee's still excellent at eavesdropping and spying. I suspect someone's given him a charm or a spell of some kind or Danny would have known he was coming." I wasn't used to anything getting through Danny's senses, but even as a child Lee had found ways around anything in his path.

"They've been working on some spells that fool supernatural senses. Lee tries them out all the time. He's always looking for an advantage in a fight. It's what happens when a human has to survive in the supernatural world. I should know. Like you and Lee, I grew up in this world. I wasn't a child, but I was young when I first learned there was something beyond the human world we knew, and I was eager to explore it. I learned quickly how dangerous it could be."

I knew most of his stories. He'd fallen into this world. Even when he'd been young, he'd had a reputation in the human world as an expert safecracker. My grandfather had been a locksmith, and my father had grown up surrounded by them. He probably should have taken over the business, but Dad had rebelled. One day a mysterious man had hired Dad to crack a safe. That man had turned out to be a vampire who worked for the Council. They'd taken a vote and decided Harry Wharton was trustworthy and had skills the supernatural world could use, and thus began his career. "That was why you needed a fierce reputation."

"I needed more than that. I needed friends. I needed protection. Like Lee, I took every advantage I could get," my dad admitted. "Lee feels his vulnerability every day. I wish he hadn't heard that. He's been looking forward to your homecoming for years and years. He's missed his mother."

"Are you sure it wasn't Kelsey he missed?" I couldn't help it. The question was out of my mouth before I could think to disregard the impulse. "I'm sorry. I shouldn't have said that. I know why they're so close."

"Yes, but it still had to hurt when he would choose to spend time with her instead of you," my dad said, sympathy plain in his tone.

"I don't truly resent them for it. I'm glad they got to spend time together." But I was self-aware enough to admit that it hurt. Now that I looked back, I could see that mere months ago Lee was already pulling away from me. Not in a bad way. He was growing up and finding a place for himself. Finding spaces that didn't include me. It was the painful part of parenting. If you're successful, they leave you behind.

"I like Kelsey, but it hurt the first time Lee told me he couldn't go out for ice cream because he was working for Kelsey," my dad admitted. "I had to tempt him with lessons to get him to spend time with me."

"I'm sorry. Their relationship was new." And on a level most of us couldn't truly understand.

"Well, we've had a good time together now," my dad said. "These last few years with the kids… I wouldn't take them back for the world."

"Not even if you could get more? Not even if you could have been alive all this time?"

"My darlin', not even if I could have spent those years with you."

Tears swelled in Shy's eyes. They shimmered in the soft light that illuminated the *brugh*. "It's not that I don't love you, that I didn't miss you. It's that these years with them were precious, and I've learned that we cannot change the past. We take what we're given and we do the best we can. Watching my grandchildren become what they have…"

"They've struggled, Dad." I had to argue with him. It wasn't like they'd had some amazing time. "They've had to fight for their lives."

"And so did you, and you wouldn't take a moment of that heartache and hurt and pain back because it made you who you are. I know what you went through with Marini. Do you think I don't cry about it? Don't wish with all my heart you didn't have to? It plagued me for a long time, thinking about what you went through. I had dreams about it at night, and I would wake up and sit there in the dark wondering if I could have done something to save you. Would you take it back?"

"It was the only way to save us all. No." Now I was the one who was crying. I'd dealt with this a long time ago. At least I thought I had. Maybe we never get over the kind of violation I survived. I'd joined a club no one wants to be a part of, and yet there are so many of us. There are probably more of us in that club than are not. Women understand how fragile we are, how our bodies and souls are protected by the thinnest of armor. And yet we are resilient. We somehow pull ourselves back together and move forward, the great and grand majority of us still finding a way to live and love and open ourselves again.

It's what women do. In the human world. In the supernatural world.

If this had only happened to me, I would be moving on, trying to weave my life back together. But it had happened to my children. How did I let it go?

And then I realized I was sitting with the man who had the answer to that question. Danny and Dev had tried to talk to me. Declan had pleaded his own case. Lee had accused me. But my father knew what it meant to be in my position. "How did you stop thinking about it?"

"I didn't. Never, daughter. Not a day goes by that I don't have some thought about what you went through. It's a scar on my heart that I couldn't protect you," he said. "But it's the joy of my life that you came through it, that you survived. You are my pride and my joy, Zoey. I might not have been the best father in the world, but I did some things right by you."

It no longer mattered that my father looked like a gorgeous woman in her twenties. I saw my dad standing there in front of me. I saw him in his slightly wrinkled suit, his silver hair slicked back with that one piece that could never be tamed. I saw his hazel eyes, so much like mine. I looked far more like my mother, with the exception of my dad's eyes. I saw the man who'd raised me when he'd had no idea what to do with a little girl. My mother had walked away. We'd both been scared that day, both emotional and sad and betrayed, and he'd shoved aside his own pain to comfort me.

I stood and so did he, as though he knew I needed to be in his arms. My dad hugged me and I was six again, desperate to know that he would be here, that he wouldn't leave like my mother had.

"I wouldn't have anyone else, Dad. No one. No matter what we went through. If I could pick a thousand times I would always pick you."

He had been thoughtless and reckless at times. He'd allowed Danny and I to do things no other parent would. I'd been angry with him. No one could make me feel as small as my dad could when he ignored me. He'd also been my everything, and he'd done as well as any imperfect, flawed human being could do.

He'd loved me with every fiber of his being, and that was all I could ask, all I could truly wish for.

"And I would pick you, girl. Every single time." He stepped back, his thumb wiping away my tears. "Zoey, you forgave me for my mistakes. You have to forgive yourself for something that wasn't a mistake at all. You didn't mean to leave them. You didn't have a choice. They grew up without you physically there, but they didn't grow up alone. Albert told them stories. Trent did, too. When they came back from the other planes, Neil wouldn't stop telling them about their mom. And you were there in their hearts and souls. No amount of time could erase the love you gave them for the eleven years you were there. Stop wishing for what could have been and see what you have. I know that you will eventually wake up and be the mom they need. It's what you do. But, my darlin', I won't be here to see it."

I'd known. I'd known from the moment that flower had risen from the ground at Rhys's command and bloomed for Shahidi that my father's time was up. He wouldn't stand between them, and staying inside Shy meant they couldn't be together, couldn't explore their feelings for one another. My dad would sacrifice for them. But there were other ways. "We'll find another vessel."

He shook his head, calm as I'd ever seen him. He was at peace with the decision he'd made. "No. My life was done a long time ago, my love. These last years have been a gift. They were a gift from Heaven, and a gift from this young woman who welcomed me inside her soul. She's carried all of my burdens for years now. She carried them and shared herself with me in a way I can't imagine. I honor her by letting her go. She's going to be my granddaughter-in-law one day, if she's brave enough. She's been a joy to me, too. Getting to see the world through her eyes was a revelation, and she has so much to offer. She can do great things."

He wasn't merely talking to me. He was talking to Shy. He was letting her know he approved of her feelings and that he loved her, too.

"Dad, we still need you." I wasn't sure I could handle this. The ground beneath me wasn't stable, and I needed my dad.

But wouldn't I always? Wasn't that the sad truth of this relationship of ours? I would never be okay with losing my father.

"And I'll be here." He put a hand right above my heart. "I'll always live here. I'll be with you the way my mum and dad were with me. This is the natural way of things. It's time to take my place. That door is open. It's been with me the whole time, you know. It hovers close, always there if I want to use it, but it's open wide now. It's telling me it's time. I'm not afraid of it. That's the funny thing. I'm afraid to not go through it."

I wanted to beg him to stay. I wanted to tell him that I wasn't ready to lose him, wasn't ready to be without my dad. I could do it. I could plead with him, guilt him into staying with me.

"Are you sure?" was the only question that came out of my mouth.

He nodded slowly. "You're safe. My grandkids are safe. I know you've got a battle ahead of you, but if there is one thing I've learned it's that you will win. You and Danny and Devinshea. You won't stop, and you three will make things right. No one can stop my girl when she decides to fight. And you'll figure out which battle is worth fighting and which one is futile."

He was telling me what they all had been, and yet somehow when he said it, I felt the truth.

"You don't think I can go back and fix it, do you, Daddy?" I could barely see for the tears streaming down my face.

"No, my love, you cannot, and deep inside you know it. You can't fix it any more than I could fix what you had to go through. And your children—the ones you're trying to save—they wouldn't have you go back, either. They know there is only one way to move and that is forward. Love them for the amazing people they are now. You gave them a family even when you were gone. You had people who were so loyal to you that they gave years of their lives to love and support your children. You were there. You were there every time Albert tucked them in. Every time Sasha taught them a lesson on how to survive. You were there when Neil played games with them and when Trent fought for them. If Sarah could have, she would have mothered your children with every piece of her soul. Even when Zack and Lisa were aching with what happened to him, they took your children in and gave them everything they had. You built that network, and it was there when your children needed it. You will never get over the loss of those years. But don't cost yourself a day more with regret."

I had to let it go. I didn't want to. I wanted to fool myself that I could fix it, but some things can't be made "right." I had been in a haze of guilt and loss, but my father's words pierced that veil. I couldn't go back. If I did I threatened the whole world, including my children. My grief seemed endless, but my joy could be, too, if I only held on and got through the pain.

My children were alive. They'd survived. They'd stayed a family. I couldn't protect them from pain, couldn't wrap them up and ensure nothing bad ever happened to them. If I did, I also kept them from a real life because no one got out pain free.

I would honor their resilience, their survival. I would look to the future, to what we could build from here. Myrddin had taken the building that housed us happily for years, but that wasn't our home.

Home was wherever we were together, and he couldn't take that from us.

"I wish you could have known this baby." I put my hand to my belly where my child with Daniel was growing.

My dad's lips curved up. "Oh, I know her. She's strong like her mum. She's smart and loyal and true. She's going to have Daniel's eyes and that razor-sharp mind of his. She's going to be as kind as Devinshea, and as witty as you. She's going to bring light into the world. And she'll be every bit as lucky as her grandad. I won't be here for her, but you have to know that I'll be watching that little girl grow."

"And I'll tell her stories of her grandfather. The best thief the supernatural world has ever seen." I took a long breath, some odd sense of peace settling over me. He was good. He was going to someplace good. He was finally complete. "How will you do it? Will you just be gone? Should we bring everyone together?"

"Walk with me." He threaded his fingers through mine.

He led me through to the door and out into the village where night had taken control. A warm wind brushed over my skin and I could see Rhys had been at work because our *brugh* had night-blooming jasmine all around the front porch. There were big groves in the distance where only this morning there had been nothing but grass.

"He's going to be magnificent," my dad said as we started down the cobblestone walkway. "Never would have thought my grandchildren would be so magnificent. I just hoped they wouldn't go to jail."

I had to laugh at that because I'd kind of had the same thoughts. "We had a fund, you know."

"Course, you did. I taught you that," he said with a grin. "I left them all notes, even Fenrir, because he's become one of mine, too. I sat down this afternoon and wrote everyone a letter. Shy knows where they are. Everyone but you. Couldn't find the words."

I squeezed his hand. The moment was both surreal and right. I realized in that moment how few people got this. I got to hold his hand. I got to say good-bye, to know how loved I was.

This was a blessing I wouldn't have gotten if I hadn't fallen through that damn painting. If I hadn't, I would have gotten a call someday that he was gone, that he'd had a heart attack on some golf course or a stroke while he was working in the yard.

I couldn't fix what had gone wrong, but I could find the joy in today. I could embrace the fact that my heart was only breaking because it was so full.

"I don't need a letter. But I could bring the kids together. I could call Evan and have her come back. I'm sure they want to see you," I offered, still wanting to put the moment off. Wanting these last minutes to stretch out.

"Please, I just want this. Just you and me one last time." He pulled on my hand, leading me toward where the nightly bonfire had started. Some of the Fae were already enjoying supper on the common grounds, and a little band was playing.

He stopped before we got to the actual dining area. The music had switched to an old Celtic song, and he pulled me close. "I always wished you'd had a wedding where I could have walked you down the aisle and had that dance with you."

My weddings hadn't been regular human-style affairs, and my father hadn't attended either. Danny and I had followed the vampire rituals, and my Fae wedding hadn't been anything my dad should ever see.

I knew we were an odd pair. From the outside we were two women dancing under the moonlight, one weeping openly with her head on the other's shoulder, but I was dancing with my father. The sweetness of the moment pierced through me.

"I left a letter for Christine," he said quietly. "I know she wasn't your favorite…"

"I'll do anything for her." I'd left behind any bad will I had for the witch long ago, and even if I hadn't I would have walked through fire for the woman if my dad had asked me.

"Take it to her when you can," he said. "Let her know that she was a good wife. She was…well, that little witch was my soul mate somehow. I loved her."

"Then I love her, too." I was glad he'd found her, glad she'd made him happy. That was all that mattered. Not her age or anything else. She'd made him happy. She'd been good for him.

"Tell her I'll see her at the end. She won't be alone. That's what she's afraid of. She's terrified there won't be anyone waiting for her," he whispered. "Don't let her be afraid."

"I won't."

We danced for a moment, a father and daughter swaying to the music, holding on to each other the way we had all of our lives, and I understood why he'd wanted his dance at the wedding. It was a goodbye of sorts, a sending off. It was a loving memory of a childhood that was ending and a new chapter to open.

This man had taught me how to love. How to dream. How to crack a safe. How to live.

I am who I am because Harry Wharton was my father.

We danced, the moment lengthening into a time I will never forget, never regret. That one song stretched out, encompassing our lives together, and I relived it all.

I was a child who sat on Daddy's lap and listened to his stories.

I was held as I cried because my mother left us. *I won't leave. I won't ever leave you, girl.*

My father takes in Danny because his best friend is gone, and he can't let that boy go into foster care. Somehow the man who'd never been ready for a child had two to raise.

My father snaps pictures at our graduation, and he's so proud we're going off to college.

My father stands with me as we realize Danny's gone.

My dad fights with Dev and finally accepts him as his son.

My father plays with his grandkids, his smile wider than I can ever remember.

My father gives his life to save them and then fights death itself to watch over them.

The music changed, a bright rhythm starting up, and he kissed my forehead and I felt the moment he leaves. I felt a shudder go through Shy and a breeze lifted my hair up. I looked up and the sky was full of a million stars.

My father walked through the door we all walk through one day, the stars shining down on everyone he loved.

"Your Highness?" Tears flowed down Shy's face. "He's gone."

I nodded. "I know."

"He…he loved you so much." She was shaking, and I realized how much she had lost, too.

He was my father, but they shared a body for years. "He loved you, too, Shy."

"I know. I'm going to miss him."

She hugged me, but it had changed. Where before she had been the one giving comfort, she was Shy again, and I would bet she felt alone. I held her tight, this kind young woman who offered my father's soul refuge. Who'd made this moment possible.

We held each other under the stars, and I whispered the words that were in my heart. I whispered them to Shy and to my father. I whispered them to the goddess and the Heaven plane and the universe around us.

"Thank you."

Chapter Twenty-Two

"I can't believe he's gone." Daniel's arms tightened around me hours later. It was deep in the night and I'd cried so much my chest hurt, but there was a feeling of peace, too.

My father was happy. My father had completed his journey and he could rest now. There was something good in that knowledge.

And I'd let go of my dreams of the past. I'd made the decision to live in the now, and that meant fighting for our future.

"I can't believe he named our unborn child." Dev held up the letter that had been written by my father. Shy had explained how he'd spent the whole afternoon writing his good-byes. There was one for all the children—including one who hadn't been born. "*To Harriet on her Eighteenth Birthday*. I am not naming my sweet daughter Harriet. I learned my lesson with Evangeline. If we name our perfect baby girl Harriet, Daniel will inevitably call her Harry."

"I think that was Harry's point," Danny said, rubbing his cheek against mine.

Dev set the letter down and joined us on the bed. "I was planning on convincing you to name her Rosalind. No one can make that name masculine."

"I'm afraid she's a Harriet." It was a good name. It would always remind her that she had a grandfather who loved her, who fought for her even before she was born. "Did you read the letter he left you?"

"Yes, he told me to get a haircut, and there was a twenty dollar bill. What does he expect me to do with that? I can't get my hair cut for that," Dev said.

Danny laughed. "God, I'm going to miss that old man."

"He also told me he loved me." Dev sighed and leaned against me, surrounding me in their warmth and love. "I never imagined Harry would even think those words about me."

"I think you grew on him." Danny's arm moved to encompass Dev. "I wish I could have talked to him."

"He didn't want to make a big deal out of it. I think he did that for Shy. She was pretty torn up. I think he wanted to make it as private for her as he could." That young woman had become part of our family. Even if she never returned Rhys's affection, she would be my daughter and I would watch out for her. I'd held her as we'd both cried, and my instinct to care for her had been overwhelming to say the least. She was alone again, her soul once more on its own, but she would find she had a home among us forever.

I'd settled her in her room before I went to find my boys and Dev and Danny. I'd given them their letters and held Evan and Fen's for their return. Then I'd cried some more.

"You should know I'm giving Declan back the amulet," I said quietly. I hadn't announced my decision to the boys because I didn't think Lee would believe me. And nothing should interrupt his grief tonight. Asta and Magnus were already at work. They would check out the Council building and make sure my bag was where I'd left it. Then we would make the meeting with Myrddin, and Lee and I would go in using the tunnels.

"I knew you would, baby. You just needed some time." Danny sighed against the back of my neck.

"And you're not giving it back. That amulet is powerful. We might need it." Dev laid his head down on my lap.

"You want to consult with the ancients?" Danny asked.

"Perhaps." Dev sighed against me. "Or it can be used as a small bomb if she needs it. I would like for her to have all the tools we can give her while she's in the Council building."

"A bomb? Declan mentioned something about it being

destructive if not properly used." It was around my neck. I didn't think carrying a bomb around was good for the baby.

"It's perfectly stable as long as it's close to the Goddess Chain," Dev explained. "If it's not within a few yards of it, it dematerializes here and goes back to its base, which is my mother's palace in the Seelie *sithein*. The transfer is a bit on the violent side. I'm not sure why, but when it opens the veil it tends to start fires or blow up whatever it happens to be sitting on. But it has to be apart from the chain for fifteen minutes or so before it will return home."

"So she can't just leave it on Myrddin's pillow and hope it blows his head off?" Danny was a little bloodthirsty when it came to his old mentor.

"Not unless she managed to sneak in while he was sleeping," Dev explained. "Otherwise all she would do is blow up his pillow"

I wasn't interested in anything but getting my bag back. "Did you set up the meeting?"

"Yes, we'll need to be in Dallas soon. We're still negotiating the time. I've already been in contact with Jamie and Nate Atwood," Dev explained.

"Kelsey's brothers?" They were technically Kelsey's half brothers, but she didn't make the distinction. Nate and Daniel had been in the same game group for years, and Jamie worked with the Texas Rangers on their weirder cases. At least he had twelve years ago. "Are they still in the area?"

"Yes. Both married. Jamie has two kids and Nate has one on the way. Kelsey's already been in touch with her family," Dev announced. "Nate finished college and he's working with his brother. Since Gray left the Rangers, they haven't had anyone to investigate the supernatural cases. The Atwood brothers are who they shift those to now. Jamie's going to find us a safe house, though we'll only use it if we have to. My intention is to leave as quickly as we can after the meeting with Myrddin."

"Do we know what happened to my dad's house?" Danny and I had spent our teen years in the house in North Dallas.

"He told me he left it to Christine," Danny said.

"Good." She'd lived there longer than I had. It was right that he had the place where she and my dad had been happy together.

"How long do you need us to distract Myrddin?" Dev's hand

moved over my leg, stroking and giving me comfort.

"I'm hoping Lee and I can do the whole job from start to finish in an hour. Hour and a half tops." It was surreal to be sitting there talking about a job when my father was gone. The boys had taken the news hard. They'd gone off to the other side of the mountain where I was sure they would drink and mourn their grandfather.

I had to hope the loss brought us together. I worried that after we got the grimoire and the sword, my kids would relegate me to the royal role. Daniel and Dev would have so many political moves to make and I would be needed for some of those meetings, but I mostly wanted to stay here in Frelsi and get to know my kids again.

I needed time with them, but I feared I'd lost Lee. He would transition as soon as he could, and then he would involve himself in the vampire world. One day he would find a companion and we might see him every now and then.

Like I'd seen my dad.

"I'll make sure you have at least three," Danny promised. "Myrddin enjoys listening to himself speak. I'll ask him some questions and let him give me a history lesson on demon politics or some shit."

"You have to be careful. If he thinks for a second you're covering for me, he'll unleash the hounds." Or the cats. I bet there were a lot of cats in the Council building now. Or the coven house.

There was a knock on the door and Dev sat up. "I'll get it."

Danny kissed my cheek and his hand went to my belly. "You will get that bag and nothing else. No matter how tempted you are."

There were a couple of pairs of shoes I'd been thinking about nabbing. "If I see my crown I'm taking it."

"I'll get you another one," Danny promised.

But I wanted that one. I wanted the one he'd placed on my head on the day of my coronation, the one that was rumored to have been worn by the first companion to marry a vampire millennia ago.

"Z, are you okay?"

I sniffled, trying not to lose it again. "As okay as I can be. I'm going to miss him."

"Me, too," Danny whispered. "I loved that old man."

Tears pierced my eyes again. I thought I didn't have any more tears left, but there they were. I might always cry when I think of those precious moments with my father. "He loved you, too. I'm sorry you didn't get to see him."

"He wanted time with you, baby. And he wanted to protect Shy. We've got to make sure she understands that she's part of us no matter how any relationship with Rhys plays out."

Oh, my vampire husband and I were so in synch. "I agree."

"Zoey, the Hidden Ones are back." Dev looked grave. "And they've brought a friend with them. Well, part of her."

"Part?" I didn't like the sound of that.

"They found a head." Dev had seen a lot of crazy shit, but even he was a little pale now. "And she apparently wants to talk to you."

It looked like I was going to have an interesting conversation.

* * * *

I stared at the head in the box and while the simple act of staring at a head in a box is weird, it is made infinitely weirder when the head stares back at you.

"Where the hell have you been, Zoey? Do you have any idea how long I've been in this fucking box? And I blame you. What the hell were you thinking? How could you not know what was happening? Do I look like a woman who hates a dude one day and the next is like hey, I think I'll spend decades with an asshole who would love some revenge on me?"

The legendary Lady of the Lake had some issues she wanted to work through. And she wasn't wrong, exactly. "I didn't know what a thrall stone was back then. You know Danny and Dev had them, too, and I only recently managed to get them out of their heads. How did you get yours out? Is that when you got the…you know…axe?"

"I don't know. That line is quite straight. I'm thinking guillotine." Dev stood next to me.

"Nah, I could totally do that with an axe. Or a sword," Danny mused. "Hey, Nim, do you have any idea where my sword is? I know Z's all up in arms about getting Gladys back, but I think I'd like Excalibur back as well. Is that what he used?"

"He's a witch. He used a damn spell, and this box keeps my body from growing back." Nimue's violet eyes flashed with irritation. "As to how I got rid of the thrall stone, my body eventually rejected it. Oh, it took fifteen years, but it finally came out, and I was pissed."

"How long have you been in there? Also, how are you talking without vocal cords? Don't look at me like that. I have questions." I got that she was upset, and I would be, too. But I definitely had questions.

I did some quick math in my head. Myrddin had placed the thrall stone in her head when he'd healed Danny's heart—the same time he'd placed the stones in Danny and Dev. After that, Nimue had announced she would stay with Myrddin while he traveled the plane, learning about this new age. They'd been gone for roughly ten years and then they'd started showing up at the Council house. So the thrall stone had come out of Nim's head years after we'd fallen through the painting.

Nim's eyes narrowed, and then she somehow managed to sigh. "I'm not human, Zoey. I never was. I'm made of magic, so you can't expect me to follow the rules of the physical world. As to how long I've been here, I think it's been at least eight years. My body processed the thrall stone sometime after you fell through the painting. And yes, I knew about it. I'm sorry."

"I'm sure at the time it seemed like a reasonable thing to do," Daniel allowed. "Nim, I know what it feels like to be in thrall. You do things you wouldn't normally do."

"Yeah, well, at least you didn't sleep with him."

I sobered because I knew what that felt like. "No one blames you. I'm glad you're alive. Is Myrddin going to miss you?"

I had to consider the fact that she might have to go back. If something important went missing, it might tip the wizard off that I had plans.

"I don't think so. He hasn't opened this box in a very long time. I can't be certain, but the last time has to have been years. I can sometimes hear people talking. I know seasons have changed many times since the last time I saw the light," Nim said. "I think he feels like I'm a failed experiment, and he can't bear to look at his failures."

"The box was deep inside the closet." Asta stood back as though being too close to corporeal beings was odd for her even when she was in her solid form. The Hidden One had been busy this evening. She'd managed to make her way to Dallas and back here in the course of a day. She was planning on having a debrief with Sasha when she finished with us. "I went there looking for the bag, but this is what I found."

A pit threatened to open deep in my gut. "The bag wasn't there?"

Asta was slightly translucent. I could see the outline of the bookcase behind her. I'd been told that the Hidden Ones hadn't been prepared for the fact that there was a door to the Hell plane in the building, and it had made them sick. They'd done their job, but Asta was still weak and Magnus was back in their field recovering. They would not be able to go in a second time. "It was not in the place you told me I would find it. There were many shoes though."

At least my shoes were still there. Myrddin probably didn't need much closet space for his robes.

"Bag? What kind of bag are you talking about?" Nim asked.

Frustration welled inside me, but the truth was I couldn't have the Hidden Ones take Nim back. I couldn't sentence her to more time in Myrddin's care. Not even to get the bag. "I had a bag of holding. It was in the closet when I left."

Nim's eyes went wide and a smile lit her face. "You did it. You stole his grimoire. Oh, sweetie, you should have seen his face when he realized it was gone. He was in a rage for days. It was lovely."

All I felt was sheer panic. And arrogance. I'd really thought my plan would work. "I left it in my closet in the penthouse. No one could have moved it."

"That's why the witch showed up that morning," Nim said, her gaze seeming to go inward. "When Myrddin realized he'd lost the king, he panicked. We went to the dark temple to confer with our demonic allies and that was when he decided to take over the crown himself. When we came out, it was morning and he had to put his plans in motion. He started by taking out as many vampires as he could. The academics were too fast. They got away, and so Myrddin went after the wolves. While he was trying to take out your allies, Sarah Day was in the penthouse. The children were gone by then."

"And my father was dead." His body had died that morning, and I'd said good-bye to his soul mere hours before.

Not good-bye. I'd hugged him like he was going on a long trip, one I would take someday, and he would be waiting to welcome me.

"Yes. Zoey, I'm so sorry..." Nim began. "I promise I wasn't involved in that. He could make me think things were more normal than they were, but he couldn't force me to do something that ran counter to my true soul. I have never killed for him."

I shook my head because my emotional state was far too fragile, and we couldn't lose time to my grief. "I can't right now. Just tell me what happened. The kids were gone and my father was dead. I thought Sarah tried to get away, too."

"Myrddin told me to get upstairs to ward the penthouse as quickly as possible," Nim recalled. "He didn't want any of your allies to get in and possibly lock him out. It was important to secure the cash he knew Devinshea kept. Though I believe he thought he would have access to the bank accounts, too. He was so angry that Albert had secured them before he left. He had to find different sources of income."

"I'm sure the Fae gold I kept helped him out," Dev said bitterly. "He knew the combination to my safe because I thought it was a good idea in case he ever needed anything from it. Goddess, those stones can do a number on your brain."

"You're telling me." Nim was every bit as bitter. "Anyway, Olivia and I went up to do Myrddin's bidding, and once we got there, I realized we weren't alone. Sarah Day was in the penthouse and she was holding something. A small tote bag. It looked like she'd gotten some blood on it. It was weird because later on I realized there were little drops of blood all over the closet. Now it makes sense. Was the bag primed by you?"

I nodded. "Yes. Only me or my father could see it. Sarah could use my blood to make it visible in this world. So she figured out something had gone terribly wrong and she went to find the bag. What happened to her?"

"I don't know. She knocked Liv out, and Myrddin hadn't told me to specifically hurt Sarah. When I wasn't directly under his influence, I could still think for myself. Sarah was a friend. She told me she had to get out, and I didn't know what was in the bag so I let her go. I stood there and watched her run away. About ten minutes later something happened. The whole building shook, and there was this blinding light. When we went down to the floor she lived on, that was when we discovered she'd locked her apartment away. Myrddin's tried to get in but nothing's worked. He's tried to physically knock the door down. Nothing. He tried to go up through the floor below or down through the ceiling, but he hasn't been able to get through. There's an utterly impenetrable ward on that apartment."

I looked to Daniel, my heart beating faster.

"How would she survive all this time in that apartment?" Danny knew exactly what had gone through my head. "She has to eat."

I wasn't sure, but I knew my friend. "She's a powerful witch. If someone can figure a way around it, she could."

"Or she got trapped," Dev offered. "We don't know what we'll find in there. Zoey, maybe you shouldn't go into that apartment."

"She has to. It's where the bag is," Asta explained. "The head is right. That space is sealed off tight even to me, which means the wards hold on an interdimensional level. But I can feel the energy coming from the pocket universe inside the bag. The Hidden Ones can always sense the interdimensional energies from pocket worlds. The bag is in there, and there's something else, something old. A remanent of energy. Like something ripped a hole in the veil. It's closed now, but it was powerful enough to leave a scar in the physical world."

So she could have gotten out. "She could have opened an interdimensional doorway. She could still be alive. I need to get into that apartment."

If the door was still open, we might find a way to get Sarah, Felix, and Mia back. She might have left me instructions.

"You can't, Zoey. She warded it with her heart's blood. It's the only explanation. Her heart's blood and something else. Wasn't her husband an angel once?" Nim asked.

"Felix. Yes, he fell and took a human body to be with her."

"She used his heart's blood, too," Nim explained. "It doesn't matter that his body was human. A fallen angel still has celestial blood running through his veins. No wonder Myrddin couldn't find a way in."

"Why wouldn't she take the bag of holding with her? Why leave it in the apartment?" I was trying to make sense of her actions.

"Because she was going to a place she might not be able to come back from," Nim said quietly. "Because she worried if she took it with her, you would never get it back. She was too worried to leave it close to Myrddin. And with good cause. That book contains a piece of his soul. You couldn't hide it from him forever. No matter how powerful the bag was. He would have found the bag and would have found a way to open it. The book itself wants to be with him. Sarah built a safe around it with her family's blood. She sealed it off so it was waiting for you when you returned. I'm going to assume you can get in. It was your blood in the closet. She had a supply for spells?"

"Sarah was our healer." Dev sat on the edge of the bed, his hands on his knees.

"Then she could have spelled that locked down ward to drop when you show up. It's what I would have done," Nim admitted. "Zoey, you can't let Myrddin near that book. Or the sword. You know what he wants to do, right?"

"He wants to close the door to the celestial planes. No more heavenly interference, and then he'll let the demons in." It was good to remind myself what was at stake. "He thinks he can do it by using the energy stored in Gladys from the fight with the angel Jude."

"The power in that sword is immense," Nim agreed.

Nim didn't need to tell me that. I'd been pierced by that sword. "He can't wield it."

"No. It takes someone with companion blood, but that's easy enough to find," Nim replied.

She hadn't been in the arena that day. "And it takes me. That weapon has to be primed, and not with some little drop of my blood. I'm the queen of the companions. I have to basically die for that sword to work."

"That would serve his goals well enough." Nim's eyes closed briefly, and when she opened them again they had gone a deeper shade of purple. "No matter how well Sarah protected that door, the wards require updating. They will eventually erode, and he will get in. I don't think she understood how long you would be gone. She was trying to protect it, but she never dreamed the wards would have to hold for over a decade. He'll get in. It might not be tomorrow or even this year, but he won't stop trying."

"They still felt strong to me," Asta said. "But I didn't test it. If he can poke even a small hole in those walls, he can bring them down. I suspect the bag is visible, so he won't have any trouble seeing it."

The situation was worse than that. "If Sarah used my blood, it's also likely open. He'll be able to immediately extract everything he needs."

"No, he won't be able to get his hands on you if we don't send you in." Dev frowned my way. "Zoey, this changes things. If anyone can see the bag, we don't need you."

"But no one else can get through the door." He wasn't thinking properly. It was getting very real for my husbands, and that meant I had to keep up the pressure until they came around. "And I still need Lee in case something happens and the book falls out. He could see it as a child. I have to hope he still can."

"Humans can see the book," Nim explained. "It takes too much energy to ward the book from human eyes. The particular spell he uses takes into account how many eyes could potentially see. So he keeps the grimoire in the supernatural world and wards against other supernatural creatures. He has other ways to keep humans away. If your son could see it, it's because he's human. Myrddin is careful with his book. Other witches can't see it either. I couldn't see it. The only human he specifically warded it against was your father, and you know why he did that."

Because my father was an excellent thief. He would be the single human Myrddin worried about. So Lee was our only hope if something went wrong.

"I don't know, Zoey. Dev has a point." Daniel had started pacing. "I don't like the idea of all three pieces he needs being in one place at one time."

"If Myrddin gets the sword and the grimoire, he might not need Zoey. He's brilliant. He'll find a way to release the power and Hell will reign on the Earth plane," Nim said, her tone grim. "Everything changes if demons are allowed to roam freely. All the rules will be gone, and this plane will never be the same. Once they take this plane, they'll look to take others, and Myrddin will be the bridge."

"We're not going to have a better time than this meeting. We'll know where he is. If we give him longer, he'll figure out Nim is gone, and he'll likely find a way to blame me. He'll definitely know we have a way in, and he'll plug that hole in his security. He'll also take a closer look at everyone around him, and that means we could lose our spies. If we wait too long, the wards could fail." I wanted to get this job done and fast. I didn't want to give him a single extra second to find a way out of Sarah's trap.

And I wanted to get in that apartment to see if I could find her. I wanted to see if she'd left me anything more than the bag. If she'd had any time at all, she would have left clues, a note, anything that would help me find her.

I'd once saved her from the Hell plane. I wasn't about to let a little thing like her disappearing into time and space stop me, and she would know that.

I'd lost my father, but I had a chance to save my friend and her family, to bring back the girl my son had always loved.

I wasn't going to fuck it up.

"So how do we grow that body of yours back?" It would be weird to have her head hang around. A fully limbed Nimue would likely be more effective an ally. If we couldn't grow it back for some reason, I would have to find a nice mannequin body for her. I could dress her up.

"So you'll go get the bag?" Nim asked. I nodded and a sigh of relief huffed from her lips. "Thank the goddess. I don't want to see what a bunch of demons would do with my head. They like to bowl, you know. Now let's talk about getting me to a nice chilly lake. I need it isolated and deep because I do not want someone coming across my body while it's growing back and starting some true crime documentary. Toss me in the deepest part, and in a few months I should be ready to fight."

"First, you can answer a couple of questions for me." I had been thinking about this since the moment Myrddin had stared out of the window in the café. He'd looked at Dean with…some unnamed emotion. It wasn't fear, but I thought fear was in there. "What do you know about Myrddin sending a pregnant woman off the plane?"

Before Nim could answer, Lee strode in, Dean at his side.

"Mom, I know you're in… Whoa." Lee stopped in front of Nim. "That is a head in a box."

"You look exactly like your father." Nim's face had lit up. "Well, except the eye. You must be the little human one. Lee, right?"

Lee's eye widened and it stayed on Nim. "Mom, why is the head talking to me?"

It was good to know something could still freak my boy out. "The Hidden Ones brought me back a present. Meet Nimue."

Lee took a step back as if the head might attack. "But she's with Myrddin."

"Nope. She was being controlled like your dads, and when she got out of thrall, he cut her head off and put it in this box." I gave Nim a sympathetic shrug. "It's a nice box."

"Is it?" Nim asked. "I didn't see it. I kind of woke up here. It's very plain on the inside. Tell me he didn't just shove me in a basic brown box."

It was pretty ornate and painted a nice midnight blue. "Nah, it's got some bling. And a bunch of ancient writing that's done in a very elegant hand. It's quite tasteful."

"Zoey, focus," Daniel said.

Lee was studying the box. "This says it keeps magic from…I think the word is growing. Is this somehow keeping your body from growing back?"

"Yes, and that is a complete crime because my boobs are truly fabulous." Nim's lips had curled up. "You grew up really well, honey."

"Nim, that is my son." I should have known. She was right. It was my fault. The minute she'd gotten all serious and shit I should have pointed and done that Donald Sutherland scream thing because horny Nim had definitely been replaced with a pod person.

"Yes, and he's very adult now. And don't tell me I should find someone my own age. I'm ten thousand five hundred and fifty something years old. The last dude even close to my age gave me a magical roofie and then cut my head off, so you'll have to forgive me for wanting some youth," Nim shot back.

"I've never…" Lee began.

"No. Absolutely not. Do not complete that sentence." I pointed a finger my son's way because I wasn't about to listen to him talk about how he'd never done a bodyless head before. Boundaries. We needed some, my son and I. "What did you need, baby?"

"Lee asked about my biological dad." Dean managed to stop staring at the head. "I told him what my mother told me. I was conceived during a summer ritual here on the Earth plane. I believe that is why I have the power I have."

"You were conceived at a midsummer ritual?" Dev asked. We'd gone to many of those because fertility rituals were powerful when held within those rites.

Lee shook his head. "Nope."

"I was conceived at the ritual known as Burning Man," Dean said with absolutely not an ounce of irony. "My mother was into spiritualism at the time."

His mom had likely been into pot and the festival circuit.

"Oh, shit." That had come from Nim and answered a whole lot of my questions. "Was your mom a cute brunette with a nice rack?"

"What is this about?" Dean looked to me, seeming to know Nim couldn't be too serious.

"I wanted to get the 'Luke, I am your father' moment out of the way," I admitted. "Dean, I'm pretty sure Myrddin's your dad."

Chapter Twenty-Three

"So Myrddin knocked up a human at a music festival. I knew he and Nim planned to explore the world, but I thought they would go to museums or something. They were out in the world for ten years. How many little wizards did he manage to make?" The next day Dev still seemed to be mulling over everything we'd learned. He was in his seat on the new plane and we'd been in the air for an hour or so. When I looked out the window all I could see was ice and tundra far below.

Danny had spent the rest of the previous night with Sasha, the academics, and the Nimhead, as I had taken to calling her. She'd vowed revenge, but she was a head. What was she going to do?

Dev had stayed behind with me. He'd held me while I cried again and let me sleep against his chest. I'd somehow gotten through the night.

I was certain Myrddin had caused lots of problems during those years he and Nim had walked the planes before he'd returned to fuck up our lives. "I suspect going to a music festival was one of his less nefarious adventures."

"It's more than a music festival. It's also a place where you can not bathe for like a week and everyone's so high they don't care. Lots of wolves attend those things. So many smells." Neil sat back down in the comfy chair next to me. Naturally he'd found the snacks and had a whole tray in front of him. "Have I mentioned how much I adore private planes? I'm so happy I have my wealth and privilege back."

Apparently the last twelve years had sucked because Neil had to take public transportation.

They'd sucked for a lot of reasons.

I missed my dad, but that deep mourning had to wait because I had a job to do. I was doing it sometime today. I intended to be back in Frelsi with the book and Gladys before tomorrow evening.

"I went to a music festival on a faery plane once. I don't think it was a music festival as much as an orgy where they had musicians playing." My son sat across the aisle from me.

"Lee, I need you to seriously think about what you say around me." I did not want to know what my precious son had been doing all these years. There are some things that a mother should never know.

"I was just going to say I understand how it could have happened." Lee wore all black, and his backpack was filled with the things we would need for the job we were about to do, including the Mantle of Arthur. "Dean seemed pretty freaked out by the idea of being conceived at a giant sex party. Apparently the Vampire plane is actually pretty staid when it comes to sex. Or rather they value their privacy when it comes to their companions. Consorts. That was what he called them. He was pretty freaked out that his mom would have had a three-way with Myrddin and Nim. I tried to ease his mind by telling him you and Papa regularly perform in front of a crowd."

"That is a sacred fertility ritual," Dev said with a frown. "Although I will admit I can be a bit of an exhibitionist."

"Devinshea." And there were things our son didn't need to know.

Lee snorted and tried to cover up his laughter. "Anyway, I was glad to have a job for him to do while we're gone. He doesn't need to think about that for too long. Also, I think it's good for his mom that he doesn't have a way to call her on the Vampire plane because he would be asking some questions. Awkward questions."

Dean, Rhys, and Shy would be working on a project while we were gone. They would be taking Nim to Lagarfljót Lake in eastern Iceland. It was deep and cold, and according to legend was home to a big-ass serpent that Nim assured me would keep her company over the weeks as her body regenerated.

"We can't be certain Dean is the child of Myrddin." Danny was always the logical one. He had to look at all sides of a situation.

I personally knew that the answer that would fuck us over the most was always the correct one. The universe liked to screw with us.

Dev and Danny sat directly across from Neil and me. The jet Dev had purchased was a twelve seater and boasted a kitchen, bathroom, and small bedroom. Dev called it basic comfort and promised a better one when he could find the time to shop.

It was just the five of us and a pilot who'd passed Sasha's tests. We were running a tight crew this time. We needed to be able to move very quickly once Lee and I finished the job. We wanted to be on our way back to Frelsi before Myrddin realized what we'd done. I had high hopes that he would simply think the wards had finally failed and wouldn't realize his book had been in the apartment at all.

Though there was a part of me that longed for confrontation.

My hand went to the amulet that lay against my chest. I wished there was some way to get that sucker around Myrddin's neck and then walk away. "Nim seemed pretty sure."

"It was a long time ago," Danny pointed out. "I was unaware Myrddin had ever produced a child."

"Well, he's way better at keeping secrets than you are." It wasn't fair, but I was still pissed about how much they'd talked to Myrddin. And done dumbass things like giving him the combo to our safe. I'd customized that sucker myself, and Dev had handed over the keys to the kingdom. "I think Nim's right. I've always wondered why he would make it a point to put Lee in a situation where he died, but he sent Dean's mother off plane when he could easily have done the same. He could have ensured Dean was never born in the first place. I don't think it's his soft heart about kiddos that did it."

"They don't look much alike." Danny's whole body was tense, and nothing I said seemed to ease his anxiety.

"We can't be certain we've ever seen his true form." Lee looked more serious now. "I mean he's like Nim in that way. He doesn't look as old as he is. We have to think he might have looked different at one point. Or we might consider that Dean is an aspect of Myrddin. DNA isn't always a through line. We know Myrddin's DNA includes at the very least incubus demon. The legend has always been that he was the product of a virtuous woman and an incubus. However, we can't possibly know if that virtuous woman didn't have, say, companion blood or a hint of Fae. Dean looks a little Fae to me."

When Lee wanted to show his smarty-pants side, he could bring it. Dean's hair alone made me think Fae. Faeries—*sidhe* especially—sometimes came in extreme colors. Raven dark, like Devinshea and our twins. I'd seen some with hair the color of the purest snow as well, with crystal eyes to match. Like Dean's.

If that was true then Dean, like Myrddin himself, was a child of all three of the inner planes. His DNA came from Heaven, Hell, and he was conceived here on the Earth plane.

Rather like my Lee. Lee should have been like his brother—the genetic product of a companion and a Fae. Both are closer to celestial beings. Being conceived and born on the Earth plane centered him here.

But Danny's vampire DNA had taken root in his body. Lee was truly a child of all three planes.

"Not all children are carbon copies of their parents. I think I'm right about this. I saw the shock in his eyes when he caught sight of Dean at the café." Myrddin had been genuinely taken aback. "And I think Liv recognized Dean's magic. She said something about it being familiar."

"It would also explain why he was able to clear the curse Myrddin placed on Zack when no other witch could." Dev sipped one of the martinis he'd made for us. Naturally the plane came with a full bar.

We were set to land in Dallas two hours before Danny and Dev's meeting with Myrddin at Klyde Warren Park. It would be daylight out so we could be sure Myrddin wasn't bringing vampires with him. On our side it would only be Danny and Dev and the shifter guards we'd been allowed. I had to pray Danny could handle everything.

He had express orders to fly he and Dev away if anything started to go wrong.

The park wasn't far from Ether. Or whatever they were calling it these days. The Coven house, I assumed. I have to admit that the idea someone else was living in the home Dev had built for us rankled. Would I ever feel safe there again? This was the place where I'd given birth to our children, and I worried even if we got it back, it would feel wrong to me.

"Dean told me he dreams about Myrddin," Lee revealed. "And a woman. I think he might be dreaming about Mia. I don't know. He says she's blonde. I don't know how I feel about him dreaming of her. I get the feeling these are not merely friendly dreams."

"You don't know it's Mia. Lee, you have to be careful." Danny leaned toward our son. "I know you're hoping you'll open that door and Mia will be standing there waiting for you, but that's not the likeliest outcome."

"You think she's dead," Lee said softly.

Danny nodded. "I think that's a definite possibility. I think she died or she's gone. If she's on another plane, we'll likely never see her again, or she could have aged or not, given how time works on the plane she's been on."

"If she's much younger, then it's good I'm a vampire." Lee's gaze was steady on his father, as though challenging him to continue. "I mean if a two-thousand-year-old was good enough for Evan, then me waiting for Mia to grow up shouldn't be a problem."

"And if she's much older?" Danny never shied away from a challenge. I could have told him he wasn't going to win this one, but he wouldn't have listened to me anyway. "If she's in her eighties?"

"If Mia's alive, I'll spend her last days taking care of her. But at least we would have had those days," Lee said with determination.

"Believe me, I understand where you're coming from, son. I just don't see this ending happily for you, and I can't tell you how that makes me ache." Danny knew how Lee would feel if he lost Mia, how Lee already felt. Danny was worried we were giving Lee false hope.

"We'll see." Lee sat back, a stubborn look on his face.

My son was still processing everything he'd lost in the last few days. His grandfather. His faith in me. I had to find a way to get that back. He was saying all the right things, smiling when he needed to, but I could tell he was pulling away from all of us. He was going someplace deep inside where nothing could touch him.

"I thought Dean was having dreams about you." I wanted to reach him so badly.

"He is. He's had them for a long time. Or so he says. You know I won't touch him, right? I'll flirt all day long, but I'm not starting some kind of relationship with him." Lee took a drag off the beer he'd found in the kitchen.

I liked Dean. I thought he could potentially be a good influence on Lee. "I don't see why not. You know we would never judge you for who you choose to love."

A chuckle came from his mouth, though there wasn't humor in it. "I choose to love no one. I don't want that. If I can't have her, I'll be alone."

Danny and Dev exchanged a look that made me think they'd game-planned this particular conversation. Danny turned back to Lee. "You're going to have to be with someone when you transition, and you'll absolutely need someone afterward. I understand the impulse. I didn't want to have anything to do with another woman after I turned, and I couldn't be with your mother. But we're in the middle of a war, and you're going to need a companion. I've already got Henri and Hugo working on it. There are a few out there who are living in a protected state but are willing to meet with a vampire to see if it could work. Until we pair you up, you'll have to feed from the women or men in Frelsi. It will be infinitely easier once we find you a companion."

"Until you pair me up?" A brow had risen on Lee's face. "You're going to put together an arranged marriage for me, Dad?"

"No, he's not." I had heard nothing of this and would have put the kibosh on it if I had. Which was very likely why they hadn't mentioned it to me.

"He did for Evan," Lee pointed out.

"I never arranged anything for Evan." Danny sat up straighter. "There was a prophecy concerning Marcus, and Evan fit. I merely wasn't going to stand in the way if it happened."

"Well, the good news is there's not a prophecy about my sex life, so you can stay out of it," Lee shot back.

Danny's jaw went tight. "I'm trying to make this easy on you. Your transition will take a while, and a new vampire is weak for years. Decades, sometimes. According to Sasha the vampire world has taken a step back when it comes to how it treats younger vampires. They're constantly challenged, and as my son, you have to know they'll come for you. You'll likely have to fight from time to time, and in a young, weaker state, that could go poorly," Danny explained. "You can fix that by taking a companion. You have to know how vulnerable you're going to be. You'll have to sleep during the day, and older vampires will be far more powerful than you are. Myrddin has a few on his side. A companion will help level the playing field."

"Lee, Dad is only trying to look out for you." Dev weighed in, and I wondered how long they'd been thinking about this dumbass plan. "You need to be strong for the fight. And we don't have clubs anymore. At least not where we are. If you start frequenting the clubs that are left, that could be dangerous, too."

Vampire clubs were located in most major cities. They were a place where a vampire could find sanctuary and a meal for the night. A bloody B&B, so to speak. I wasn't aware how they worked since Myrddin had taken over. "Is Myrddin in control of the network?"

"He's in control of pretty much everything in the supernatural world," Danny confirmed. "He doesn't personally control the vampire clubs that are left, but he almost certainly has spies. I would prefer we keep Lee's transition a secret for as long as possible."

"Lee's not getting married so he can have the wife equivalent of a power bar." I wasn't about to let them bully our son so they would be more comfortable. I wouldn't let them do it to Lee any more than I would allow them to force Evan and Fen apart for the sake of politics. Rhys would select his own goddess, and the Seelie Fae could go to hell.

"Really, Mother? I would have expected you to be on their side."

Yeah, I bet he did. "I know you're upset with me because I had a perfectly reasonable freak-out over losing twelve years with my kids. And I get to be shocked by your sexual escapades because a week ago you thought girls were icky and you played with action figures. I know you're being all self-righteous—you get that from Dad, too—and think I'm looking down on you or I'm disappointed that you turned into a reckless manwhore who drinks too much. You were always going to turn into that. It's in your DNA. Judgment works two ways, my son. You wanted me to walk in and immediately accept every loss I'd been handed. Guess what? As the humans would say, I'm only human, and I have feelings, too. So no, I am not going to sell you to some companion you don't even know so your dads can feel better. Also, I suspect they're thinking you'll be a better fighter on companion blood. Your dads aren't all huggy when it comes to things like this. They're ruthless, and while they love you, if they can solve three problems with one companion, they'll do it."

"Zoey, he's not in love with anyone," Danny pointed out.

"Yes, he is. He's in love with Mia, and until we're one hundred percent sure he won't see her again, he can't even think about taking a companion. And when he does, it will be his choice." I was putting my foot down.

"I'm not trying to…" Dev began and stopped at the stare I gave him.

"All right. Lee's choice." Danny knew when I couldn't be moved.

Lee finally looked at me, his expression softening. "Thanks, Mom."

It was time to lay everything out for my son. I had made my decision. "Also, I'm informing you now that I will no longer be pursuing a separate timeline. I'll look for Sarah from this timeline and this plane. So you should get used to seeing me, and you should understand that I'll likely disappoint you again."

Lee reached out and his hand found mine, his lips turning up in a half grin. "I doubt you could ever truly disappoint me, Momma. I'm glad to have you back. And perhaps someday I'll let Dad parade a host of lovely companions by me, but I need some time. I'll make you a deal. Dad can find someone to help me through the turn. Not a companion. I don't want a permanent relationship, and I definitely don't want to deal with the addiction. Female. Male. It doesn't matter."

He was talking casually, but I heard the pain behind the words. "Sweetie, why not Dean? I think he would be okay with feeding your needs."

"He won't do it because he feels for Dean." Neil had put down his fork. He'd managed to finish the whole tray of food while we were having our family drama. "He's not ready for that kind of a relationship, and he doesn't want to hurt Dean."

"Uncle Neil shoots and scores." Lee sighed. "I'm not ready. I do feel something for him, but it's not right. Something inside me says it's not time."

I squeezed his hand. "Okay. We'll find someone."

"Hey, if I wait a couple of months, maybe Nim'll get her body back," Lee said with smirk.

I shuddered and released his hand.

Lee stood, chuckling. "I'm going to grab another beer and then I'll take a nice nap. I hear these fold down."

"There's a small bedroom," Neil said.

Lee shook his head. "Nah. Dad hasn't fed, so I think they'll be using that. See, I do know you, Mom, and I personally think it's gross. Uncle Neil, do you need another sandwich? You seem to have gone through the three you just made."

Neil nodded. "I can totally eat."

Lee gave him a thumbs-up. "Then we can feast while pretending my parents aren't doing freaky stuff."

"You have summed up much of my life with your mom," Neil agreed. "I'll come with you. I think I saw some cookies."

Danny stopped Lee. "I'm only trying to watch out for you."

Lee nodded slowly. "And I'm your son, and you should understand no one's going to force me into a marriage. Give me time. Hell, I'm not even sure of when I'm going to transition. I might put it off for a couple of weeks and see how I feel. Rhys convinced me I'm going too fast. I get that from my other dad."

Dev shook his head. "You get that from your mother. And you can transition when you want."

"As long as we can control it," Danny said. "That's why I need you to be careful. You've never seen what can happen when a vampire turns. It's violent, and the vampire can't control himself. It's why it's incredibly important that I oversee your turn."

"I'm not going to do anything reckless on this mission, if that's what you're asking," Lee said. "I promise, we're going to get in and get out as quickly as possible. If Mom tries to go for her shoes, I'll carry her out."

"I don't see that I have much use for them in Frelsi," I countered. Although I had a gorgeous pair of Gucci booties I'd never been able to wear.

"I'll buy you more shoes, my goddess," Dev promised. "And Lee, we're just worried about you. Your mother isn't the only one who's having problems with this change. It doesn't mean we don't love you. It's the opposite."

"I've been thinking about this and I suspect I should give you the same amount of time it took for me to get over losing you," Lee said softly.

"How long was that?" I asked.

"Twelve years one month and three days. Pretty much until the moment I saw you walk into Ether again. And like all things we pray for, it wasn't entirely what I expected and yet it's everything I needed. I'm not happy you're back. That would be a silly thing to say. We're…complete in a way we haven't been since we were kids. So let's take all this as growing pains and move on," Lee said. "But try to work faster than we did. I'd like to get back to happy family dinners. Oh, speaking of, I need to plan my good-bye to solid food tour."

"I can help you with that, nephew of mine," Neil promised as they walked off toward the kitchen at the front of the plane.

I looked to my husbands. "Seriously? You were going to set him up?"

Dev frowned my way. "I was going to be subtle about it."

Danny simply sighed. "It wasn't a firm plan. And we're not going to hold a stake to his heart. The truth is he will do much better if he has a companion. I'll worry about him less if he's better protected."

"Have you thought about the fact that Evan and I can donate?" I was absolutely certain my daughter would have no problem giving a little blood to keep her brother strong.

"I don't think Lee will be as reasonable about that as you think, though it's not a terrible plan," Danny agreed. "It would solve some problems, though I worry your blood is… It's high-octane fuel versus low-grade unleaded. I would bet Evan's is, too. It could be an all new level of addiction and put him off other companions. And then we're back to the whole Oedipal complex thing."

"That's a human problem." Dev shook that worry off. "Lee was raised in the supernatural world. He never expected his mother to age. He's perfectly disturbed by the fact that his parents still have sex. So let's have sex and disturb our son."

Dev was on his feet, his hand in mine, and he gently started leading me toward the back of the plane.

"I don't think that's a good idea." Neil might be used to freaky stuff happening right next door, but Lee was…apparently Lee was usually the one freaky things were happening to.

"I do need to feed." Danny crowded me from behind. "And you know you work better when you're loose. Harry always told us…"

Grief hit me fresh and hard, but it was okay because I was with them. Maybe we did need to spend this time together. I turned and Danny's face had fallen. I reached up and cupped his cheeks. "He taught us to always stretch before a job, to go in as relaxed as possible. There would be time to worry after a job was over, especially if anxiety got us put in jail."

My dad had been full of helpful advice for the teenaged thief.

I was so glad he'd gotten to spend time with my kids. That had been a blessing. I'd been gone, but my kids had their grandfather. They hadn't been alone.

And they would never be. I would make sure of it.

Danny leaned over and brushed his lips against mine. His hands found my hips and he kissed me, his emotions flowing. I wasn't alone either. I hadn't been for a long time, but every now and then I needed a reminder. I needed to know that no matter what happened, we would be together.

Dev kissed the back of my neck and his hands found my breasts, even as he began to maneuver us toward the bedroom. "Come with me, my loves. I think you'll like this new space I made for us. When our vampire doesn't want to do things old school, we can fly anywhere we like."

This was what Dev did best. He made us all comfortable. He made a home for us. Wherever we were.

I should never have doubted that I could make a home here. I had everything I needed.

I had my family.

Dev led us to the small bedroom and closed us in. "I need a few hours with you before I spend the rest of my day in complete terror."

"I'll be okay. I promise there's nothing to worry about on my end." But I knew he would. I would worry about them being with Myrddin. I worried about Myrddin finding a way to influence them again, to take a piece of them away from me.

Danny pulled his shirt over his head, his eyes going dark sapphire. "Oh, we'll worry the whole time. I'm pretty sure I won't breathe until we're safely back in Frelsi. All of us."

He was worried about Lee, but I happened to know Lee was a

damn good partner. I sighed as Dev cupped my breasts. We'd held each other the night before, but in our grief we'd only wept and slept in each other's arms. We'd needed this, too. We needed the reminder that we were alive and together.

Danny stood in front of me, looming over me. "I'm glad you decided to stay here with us."

He wasn't making fun of me, though now that I'd had some perspective put on it, I knew it had been a crazy plan in the first place. "We'll be all right. All of us."

He nodded and his fingers sank into my hair. "All of us."

"Well, Harriet might not. She might hate us for calling her Harri," Dev pointed out.

Danny groaned, but there was the sexiest smile on his face as he reached behind me and caught Dev's head with one big hand. "You are incorrigible."

I moved out of the way and watched them kiss. I loved watching them, loved how masculine they were pressed against each other. There would come a time in this pregnancy when I would be uncomfortable having the kind of athletic sex they craved, but I would be happy to watch them fuck.

Danny's fangs were out, and he grazed them over Dev's lower lip, nipping hard enough to draw blood. A low groan went through my vampire, and I watched my faery prince shudder.

I stepped in behind Dev since he hadn't managed to get out of his slacks yet, and that was a damn shame. Both of my men were stunning, and I wanted to see them in all their glory. I unbuckled his belt and undid the button, lowering the zipper around that monstrosity of a cock. It was a gorgeous monster and I let my hand curl around it. He was hard and ready to go, though I have to admit Devinshea usually is. His cock was warm and solid in my hand. I stroked him from base to tip, my hand lubricated by the arousal I found there.

"Yes, my goddess. That's what I need. Daniel, do your worst. You didn't feed at all yesterday. Take us both." Dev let his head fall to the side.

I saw Danny's fangs flash right before they sank into Dev's flesh.

His cock swelled in my hand and I stroked him, loving how hot the room had gone. I'd been promised the room had been properly warded so the pilot wouldn't go all lust crazy midair. He was a member of the Order, a human organization created long ago by the Heavenly prophet Jacob to counter Myrddin's threat. They were actively working against him now, and thankfully they had pilots who were above suspicion and who knew how to secure a cockpit against secondhand lust.

Dev's whole body shuddered, and I felt him come in my hand.

We were lucky Dev prepared for everything and there were extra clothes for all of us, because he was going to need new slacks.

On a normal man, this would mean he would be down for the count for at least a couple of minutes, but not my sex god. His cock was already swelling in my palm, letting me know he could take care of me, too.

Danny let go of Dev's vein, his tongue coming out to lick at those fangs of his. Every inch of my skin lit up at the sight of it. Danny was never hotter than when he let his inner beast out. Those sapphire orbs of his found mine, and I could feel his magic pull at me. He didn't need to pull me in to make me want to feed him. He did it because he knew exactly how good it made me feel. When Danny's magic pulled at me, I was surrounded by his love, his desire and adoration. Combined with Dev's lust magic, it was a heady concoction.

Dev let himself fall to the bed, clearing the way for Danny to get to me. He pulled my shirt off and made quick work of my bra. "You're going to be careful today."

I kicked off my shoes and Danny dragged my pants down, tossing them and my undies aside. No matter how many times I was naked with them, I always sighed like this was how we should be. "I promise. I'll have Lee with me. I won't do anything that could endanger him."

Well, endanger him any more than what we were already doing. I couldn't say walking into the enemy's stronghold to steal the most valuable thing in the world to a man who wanted to kill us was a particularly good mother/son activity.

"I love you," Danny said as he kissed me again. Our tongues tangled and his big hands maneuvered me to the bed. "Wear that like armor."

"I love you." He was going into danger, too. He had to face the man who'd held him in thrall for years. "When you want to kill him, remember that I love you and you can't. Unless you can do it where the humans can't see, and then, baby, go for it."

His lips kicked up in the sexiest grin. "I'll remember that."

He maneuvered me to the bed where Dev had shucked his slacks and now sat naked with his back against the wall. His cock was already hard again, and he held out a hand to me. I went to him, allowed him to turn me so I was lying against him, his erection against my back.

Danny's fangs were still out, so it was easy to discern he wasn't going for my neck. Dev's legs tangled with mine, holding them open for our vampire. Danny dispersed with the rest of his clothes and then climbed onto the bed, lowering himself down so his mouth hovered over my pussy.

Dev's hands cupped my breasts, and I could feel his lips on my neck. "I'm so glad you decided to stay here with us, my goddess."

"Like I would have left you behind." I barely managed to get the words out because my whole being was focused on their hands and mouths on my body.

"I wouldn't let you. We're together forever. No matter what some evil wizard tries to do to us." Danny lowered his head down and then I wasn't thinking anymore. I was feeling. I was floating.

Danny's tongue worked me over, laving my pussy with affection as Dev played with my breasts, tugging gently at my nipples.

It wasn't long before my eyes rolled back and I couldn't stop the orgasm. That was the moment Daniel sank his fangs into my thigh and that orgasm went supersonic. I was flying far higher than any plane could take me.

I was barely starting to come down when Danny released the vein and brought his big body up. With flawless accuracy he thrust inside my pussy and I sighed at the feeling. I wrapped my legs around him and let him take me where only these two men had ever taken me before.

* * * *

Hours later, I stood at the entrance to the tunnel under Ether and marveled at what Neil had managed to do.

"I can't believe you didn't tell me about this." He wasn't a good liar. In fact, he was a terrible one. He could keep a secret if he absolutely had to—like life and death had to. But Neil liked to talk. "This had to take months of planning and work."

"Oh, I had Chad put a whammy on me. Also, Sarah took care of most of the planning. She's very organized, and she does not mind yelling at contractors. God, I hope the lights still work." He fumbled around and suddenly a thin trail of lights illuminated the gloom.

"What kind of whammy?" Lee looked around the space we found ourselves in.

We'd only left Dev and Danny a few moments before. The park they were meeting Myrddin in wasn't far from the Council building. A group of shifters had agreed to provide security. This was the North Texas Pride, and they'd always been close to the royals. Danny was talking to the leader on the way to the meet.

Neil had led us to a building on Pearl Street a couple of blocks from Ether. The entrance to the tunnel was on the lowest level of the parking garage. The door was in the stairwell, behind the stairs. It was hard to tell there was a door there at all, but Neil had found it.

Neil stood back to allow us in. "When I need to do something that I do not want to do—like keep a secret from your mom—Chad kind of digs around in my brain and plants a suggestion that my metabolism will die if I do that thing. No more werewolf physique. All I have to do is make one wrong move and I've got the gut I truly deserve."

Naturally that's where he would go. "How did you build it? Is it magic?"

"It doesn't feel that way. It looks like it's solid." Lee stepped inside and then put a hand to his stomach. "Well, except for that. Wow. That ward is rough. I'm not sure I can get through. Not without vomiting. Aunt Sarah was serious about keeping other people out."

"Here, sweetie." I reached into my backpack and pulled out the charm Lily had made. "Lily was one of the people who could get through. She helped Sarah on the project. This should make the ward think you're her."

I placed the small charm in his hand, and his whole body seemed to relax. "Thank the goddess. That's better. So that's what any human would feel if they tried to walk through? That was some powerful dread. I'm going to be honest. If I didn't know what I know, I would have walked away and never come back."

That's what a really good ward could do to a person.

"You should see what happens to a witch who isn't allowed through," Neil said. "I'm sorry it affects you. Sarah was slowly working on the wards when she could. I guess she hadn't gotten to the kids yet. And it's a physical tunnel. Chad worked his magic on a construction crew."

"Danny is Chad's vampire master. How did he keep this from him?" I was sure it was one of the reasons Myrddin hadn't wanted to let Danny go through the painting. Danny's blood could influence any vampire or werewolf who took it.

Neil chuckled. "Oh, Chad will tell Daniel anything he thinks the king needs to know. He genuinely thought this was in his master's best interest, so he kept it from him. Chad is pragmatic when it comes to his servitude. It's the difference between a vampire and a wolf. After all those years, Zack would have told Danny no matter what. Which is why he was left out of this project. I always thought we should have made it prettier though. It's got a very latter-day mine vibe about it."

The walls looked solid, though the whole thing was way too confining. Lee could barely walk without hunching over, and his shoulders nearly brushed the sides. "So this will take us all the way to the basement under Ether?"

"Yes. From there you'll need to sneak up the back stairwell. Sorry, Z. I'm afraid you can't use the elevator," Neil announced with a frown. "They wouldn't be able to see you, but they would see the doors opening and closing, and that might attract attention. They'll be less likely to see the stairwell doors open and close."

It looked like I was getting a workout in. "All right. We should get going. I won't be able to call you. Believe it or not, cell service doesn't work under the cloak. Are you meeting the fake me?"

The lions were giving us a lioness who didn't mind wearing a Zoey glamour and shopping with my bestie in case the witches were on the lookout.

Neil glanced down at his watch. "Yep. She should be up in the lobby right now. The human security company who works for Dev's legitimate businesses is providing us with an escort so things look good."

"You put the tunnel under our human security team's building?" I asked, shocked at his audacity.

Neil shrugged. "They're willing to do some pretty crazy stuff for their clients, and Neiman Marcus is a block over. I thought it would be a good shortcut for us when it was done. Freaking Myrddin screws up everything. I thought I would have a shortcut to designer wear. Instead, I've got a shortcut to an Icelandic bookstore that smells like patchouli and smoked fish. Call me when you're out."

"It could be an hour or two," Lee said. "We're going to be careful about this. I promised the dads I wouldn't get Mom murdered."

It was good they all had faith in my skills. "You know I pulled off the first part of this job about two weeks ago in my time. And my partner was eleven, so I think we'll be okay."

"You better be, Z. I'll meet you back here in a couple of hours. If something goes wrong, I'll text you, though I know you won't get it until you get back to the tunnel," Neil promised. "Be careful when you come out. Our intelligence puts all of Dev's old playthings in the basement. Myrddin doesn't like human weapons, so he shoved the whole armory there and hasn't looked at it since."

Lee's eye lit with excitement. "Oh, I will be stealing some fun shit on my way out then."

Neil nodded and then closed the door behind us, and I was left alone with my son. Rhys had offered to come along, but I'd wanted to keep the group as tight as I could. So I'd convinced him Shy needed him. She was still working through losing Harry.

The last time I'd seen them, Rhys had been holding her hand, so it looked like my dad's plan was working.

Rhys was safe in Iceland. Evan had promised me she was securely in the primal nest.

I just had to make sure this son of mine survived.

"You have a gun. Two, I believe, and I don't want to know how many knives you have on you." I had a pistol on me and my kit. I probably wouldn't need it because I also had a key to Sarah's apartment.

"I have four knives. And yeah, we've got plenty of guns, but C-4's been hard to come by," my son admitted as he started down the tunnel. "And I think we left a metric shit ton here. I would get brownie points with Sasha if I brought him back some."

I followed behind him. It wasn't that I minded if Lee wanted to steal a little something extra, but I wanted this to go as easy as it could. "That C-4's been down here for years. How do we know it's even good?"

"We know because Sasha taught us whole lessons on weapons and how to use them. C-4's a stable explosive. It's easy to transport, and with the right amount you can take down a whole building easy-peasy. Papa always bought the good stuff. If there's C-4 in the basement, it's still good. I promise I'll only take some if we're not busting ass to get out of there."

My son's education wasn't what I'd planned, but it seemed like Sasha and Trent had done their best to prepare them for the world they lived in rather than the one I'd wanted for them. But then I'd probably been naïve about that in the first place. "Papa had some P-90s delivered a couple of weeks…well, twelve years ago. He hadn't had a chance to use them yet. I'll grab one or two of those if I can. I didn't ask you earlier, but how do you think Dean is handling the whole I have to kill my dad thing?"

One big shoulder shrugged. "He told me JT Malone is his dad. Did you know there's a JT Malone here on the Earth plane? He's like a billionaire oil guy. I showed Dean a picture of him on the Internet. He said that dude looked exactly like his dad, but on the Vampire plane he's married to Dean's mom and here it's some woman named Nina. I feel bad because according to what we were able to look up, they still don't know what happened to Dean's mom. Though apparently there are a couple of true crime podcasts about her."

"They can't ever know." I wished I could send the poor man a letter explaining that the woman he'd known as Dana Johnson was happily married to a vampire version of himself on another plane of existence. Her family had to wonder what happened to her. They would never know she'd had a son and he was here to save them all.

"It makes you wonder how many of those people who vanished off the face of the earth actually vanished off the face of the Earth plane," Lee mused. "That would be an interesting true crime series. Anyway, I think it shook him, but he doesn't consider Myrddin to be his father in any real sense of the word. I'll keep an eye on him. And hey, when I turn, I'll be able to keep two eyes on him."

My son was ever the sarcastic one. He'd come by it honestly. "Did anyone deal with the Fae who took your eye?"

He kept walking. "It doesn't matter. I'm not looking for revenge. In some ways they were simply doing their jobs. I injured them enough that I was able to do mine and get Rhys out of there. That's what mattered. Also I'm going to be honest again, Momma. Ogres pretty much all look alike to me, so it would be hard for me to be sure I was getting revenge on the right one. Evan tells me that's speciest of me, but I thought that even before I lost my eye to one of them. Don't get me wrong. I know maybe somewhere out there is a happy, nonviolent ogre commune, but I haven't found it yet. Every last one of those fuckers I've met have tried to eat me."

"I'm proud of you for saving your brother," I said quietly.

"Well, you taught us to watch out for each other," he replied. "Rhys and Evan and Fen have all saved me at one point. I know it was rough, but some of it was good. I think all childhoods are like that. I know most kids don't have to fight demons and ogres, but they all have bad shit happen. They have bullies and losses and anxiety. All children have to learn to survive in the real world."

His real world was a dangerous one, but then it always had been. "I'm so glad you had each other."

"And I'm glad you had Dad and Grandad when you were growing up. I'm going to miss that old man, but I think Rhys and Shy have a shot now. I can give him hell about the romantic crap."

"Don't you dare. You let them find their way." I used my best mom voice on him. I could be worse than any ogre.

"I'm joking. You have to let us give each other shit," he said and then fell silent. "How did Kelsey handle Marcus staying behind? I didn't get much of a chance to talk to her before she left."

I had wondered if he felt like she'd left him again just as she'd gotten back. "She wasn't trying to ignore you. She needed to see Trent."

"I know that. She asked me to go with her."

Now it was my turn to be silent. I hadn't realized she'd asked him. I understood why Evan had gone. Fenrir needed to get to know his mom again and he needed Evan. But it felt wrong to try to take Lee, too.

"Don't go all jealous on me. I chose to stay with you. I worry about her though. She and Marcus were close for a lot of years, and well, I worry about her because Gray's different since he started descending. I don't know how she'll handle it."

We kept hiking along, and I could faintly hear the hum of the road above us. "Different how?"

"Darker." Lee's voice softened as though he knew we were getting closer to our destination. "He started his descents because he wanted to know what was happening on the Hell plane, and for a few years he was open about it. In the last couple, he's started missing meetings with Trent. We know he's alive and walking the plane, but I think it's been at least eighteen months since Trent's seen him."

Kelsey was pregnant with Gray's baby. What was regularly visiting Hell doing to Grayson Sloane? He was a half demon, and being forced to live on the Hell plane had been something that Gray had feared all his life. "Does Trent have any way to contact him?"

"He has a cell phone when he's on the Earth plane, but I don't think he and Trent have talked much lately. I know it's hurt Trent, though he tries not to show it. It's been a hard twelve years on that wolf. I worry about how Kelsey's going to handle it," Lee replied and then stopped. "There's the entrance. I'm going to put the cloak on and do recon. I want you to stay here until I make sure the room's clear."

It was right there on the tip of my tongue to tell him that he was the son and I was the mom and I would go in, but the truth of the matter was Lee had more experience at this than I did. He was a soldier. He might have some skills when it came to thievery, but over the course of this war, he'd become a soldier and I had to honor that. "All right. Be careful."

I didn't want to send him in there. I'd been calm to this point, but as Lee put the cloak on and disappeared in front of me, it hit me that we were walking into the place where I'd lost him before. This was the last place I'd seen him as a child. I'd pulled the covers up around him and promised I would see him in the morning. I'd smoothed back his hair and told him good night.

And then I'd disappeared.

The hood came off and my son looked at me. "Momma, it's going to be all right. I promise."

"You're a floating head. That is never all right." I reached up and ruffled his hair the way I used to when he was a kid. "I'm sorry. I'm always going to worry about you. Now let's get this done. I want to get back to your dads. The less time we take the less they have to spend with Myrddin."

"Got it. Be back in a flash," Lee promised.

He flipped the hood down and disappeared. I watched as the door opened and then closed again.

There was a pit in my stomach that told me this was a bad idea. A very bad idea.

I took a deep breath and thought seriously about calling the whole thing off. This was why my father never worked with family. He worked with other professionals, and while he might have enjoyed their company, he'd had no real feelings for the people on his crew. Emotion is a dangerous thing to a thief.

I wanted to follow that instinct and take Lee back to Frelsi where he would be safe.

And what if Sarah's wards fell? I would be handing Myrddin the keys to a kingdom that would suddenly be filled with demons. If they were allowed on the Earth plane, everything changed. A war unlike anything we'd ever seen would break out with humans on one side and demons on the other, and I wasn't sure they wouldn't view most of my family as demons. Humans aren't known for being able to discern who the real enemy is. They would come for all supernaturals. Myrddin was simply thinking he could enslave the humans, could overcome them with his skill and the Hell plane's armies.

He was underestimating the humans. They would put up a fight, and their sheer numbers would give them the advantage.

I didn't want to fight at all. I wanted us to live in harmony, even if that meant we kept our world a secret.

The door opened again. "We're good. And there's so much C-4. What was Papa planning?"

"You know your dads like to be prepared." I stepped through the door and into the basement. "He probably had a coupon or something."

It was dark but Lee had his flashlight out, giving us some illumination. "Are we sure there's not a guard on the door?"

"Not according to our spies," Lee replied quietly. "According to the message Christine got out an hour ago, the building is very quiet today. There are only forty witches who live here full time. Some of them went with Liv on a top secret mission. She wasn't sure where, but it means we shouldn't have to worry about too many being around today. The basement is locked, but the witches don't seem to care about what's down here. Like I said, they don't use human weapons at all. I'm surprised he hasn't sold any of this. That's what I would have done if I wasn't going to use them."

"I suspect Myrddin isn't as comfortable dealing with the human world as you are." I looked around the space I found myself in. Lee was right. There was a lot of C-4. "You know the bag of holding can carry all of this and we won't even feel the weight."

It wasn't even stealing since Dev had paid for it. I wished Sarah had left the bag in my closet because I could have shoved a good deal of my clothes in there. And my shoes.

"Awesome. Let's get moving because I think I saw a flamethrower. Sasha thought buying one was a bad idea," Lee admitted. "Probably because of the whole peripheral vision thing. All right. The staircase is to our left, and then we've got a long haul up."

The thought did not make me happy. "No one can hear me whine, right? Because I need you to understand that I don't get a ton of cardio in."

Although I had run for my life several times when we'd been on the outer planes.

"I'll be able to." Lee frowned my way. "The cloak might keep in sound, but I will be in there with you."

"You know your namesake would have given me a piggyback ride." He would have, and then he would have taken the stairs in a dead run and I would have barely noticed the floors flying by.

"My namesake was a werewolf with super speed," Lee shot back. "As has been pointed out numerous times, I'm human right now. You're walking."

And he was true to his word. He made me walk up all those stairs. I think it was his revenge. It was odd to be back here. It had only been a few weeks, but I could feel that time had moved in this place. I couldn't even see anything with the exception of the stairs, but the building had a heavy feeling to it that it hadn't before.

There was a part of me that wanted to walk the halls, to see what he'd done with Dev's baby. Dev had bought this building long ago, and much of our lives together had played out here. The first night we'd met, he'd brought me to Ether and shown me a whole new world. It had been in his office upstairs that he and Danny and I had first made our bargain—a pretend relationship that had become the center of our lives. All three of our children had been born here, and we'd intended this to always be their home.

We'd brought the supernatural world together right here in this building, and Myrddin had taken it from us, had twisted it. This place had become infested with all the wrongs he'd done, and I hated that.

"You okay?" Lee asked as we reached the nineteenth floor.

This stairwell only went to nineteen. The penthouse had another escape that didn't connect to the other floors. It was part of Dev's security. He'd worked so hard to protect us, and it had still failed.

"I'm good." My legs had held up pretty well. Vampire blood gave a girl a nice boost. "But we need to be very careful from here on out."

We hadn't seen anyone in the stairwell. It had been eerily quiet the whole time. But we were about to go into what should be an occupied floor. According to Sasha's intelligence, Olivia Carey lived on this level along with a couple of other witches. Liv might have gone on some mysterious mission, but her neighbors could be around.

It was harder to fit two adults under the cloak than it had been me and a kid. We would have to move cautiously, but first we had to get through the door.

I was in front of Lee. His bigger body draped the cloak over me and he could still see, though "seeing" in the cloak was an odd thing. It was like looking at the world through a filter. Everything seemed muffled and slightly distorted. I opened the door as slowly as I could, not wanting to make a sound.

That was the moment I realized we weren't even close to being alone.

Chapter Twenty-Four

"Zoey?" The woman who stood in the hallway kept her voice low. "It's okay. This floor is empty for now, but we need to hurry."

I went completely still for a moment. Christine stood in front of the door I'd opened. I'd seen her just days before, but she'd changed. She would be fifty now, and it struck me that I'd known her for half her life. Or rather she'd known me and had to take my family into consideration. According to my father, she'd been good to him, but there was a part of me that still wondered.

Christine hesitated, staring into the stairwell as though she should be able to catch a glimpse of something. She wore khaki slacks and a button-down blouse. Her hair was shorter than it had been years ago, and there were fine lines on her face where before had been only the smooth perfection of youth.

"Please, Zoey. I'm worried something is wrong," she whispered. "I know you've still got the cloak. Harry told me Lee got it out of the building. There aren't cameras anymore. Myrddin got rid of them. You can come out."

"She's been with us the whole way, Mom. She's been one hundred percent true," Lee said quietly.

I had to make a decision one way or another. I either trusted the woman my father had loved or I had to take her out so I could do the job. I went on instinct, or rather I chose to honor my father's. I nodded and Lee lowered the cloak.

Christine's blue eyes went wide, and a sheen of tears covered them. "It's really you. Oh, Zoey, it's really you."

She reached out for my hand, and I wasn't sure I could tell her what I needed to tell her.

"Lee, you look so much like your dad." Tears fell on her cheeks. "You have no idea how much I've missed you all. Being here… I needed to do it, but I've missed you."

She'd seemed like such a silly thing when I'd first met her. She'd been far too young for my father, but somehow she'd been his soul's mate.

"Christine, I have to…"

She nodded and squeezed my hand. "It's okay. I know he's gone. Shy contacted me a couple of hours ago. We have a safe way to communicate. She let me know that Harry moved on and that he loved me. I lost him a long time ago. I've always known that. We have to do this now because it's too quiet around here."

"How did you know we'd be here?" Lee asked. "Did Sasha send you a note? Or did Shy tell you?"

"Shy would never say a word, even though we're close. And Sasha's far too paranoid." She sniffled but her eyes rolled slightly. "As if I haven't been doing this long enough to know when something's going down. I know that Myrddin is meeting with the king and Olivia is off doing something at his behest, as usual. She took three of our most powerful witches with her days ago. I'm trying to find out where she went. Anyway, I knew when he set up that meeting that you would take the time to try to get into Sarah's place. Is that where you hid the grimoire?"

I nodded, trying to suck up my emotions. "It might be. Sarah had it that last day."

Christine's brows rose. "You've seen Sarah?"

"No, but I have intel from a trusted source that puts the bag of holding in her hands before she disappeared." I wasn't sure what Christine knew about Nimue, and now wasn't the time to go into it. This was the time for me to let Sasha decide how he wanted to roll out information.

"If you do find her, she needs to be careful. Myrddin hates her.

Her heart's blood has kept him out of places he wants to go. She warded this whole building in it. It's wrapped up so tight sometimes it can be hard for demons who leave to get back in," Christine said. "Those wards of hers do some crazy things. Did you know if you break a window from the inside, the glass shatters back?"

"She wanted the building to be as insular as possible," I explained. "She was still working on it when everything went down. It's a weird function of the spell she used."

"Well, I'm glad it's still fucking with Myrddin," Lee admitted.

"Oh, he would love to get his hands on Sarah." Christine took a deep breath and seemed to steady herself. "All right. Let's see if you can get through the wards she put on her place. I think you should move fast, Zoey. Myrddin has plans, too. He doesn't know where the book is, but he has his suspicions. If I figured out you'll go for it, he could, too."

"Okay, we'll be quick," I promised.

"You're lucky that bomb the kids set off is still causing chaos with Myrddin's protection spells or it would have been hard for you to get on this floor. It's the only reason I was able to make it. Myrddin only allows his most trusted witches up here because it's so close to the penthouse. He'll get them up again soon. I'll keep lookout. If I knock on the door, you'll know not to come out." She turned and started toward Sarah's apartment.

"Are you okay?" I asked as we walked down the hall that should be so familiar to me. Neil and Chad had lived in the apartment to my left, and Zack and Lisa's home had been at the far end of this hall.

"I haven't been okay since the day that bastard killed my husband, and twelve years of pretending to worship that fucker have taken their toll. I had to convince him I'd used Harry to get more power. It was kind of awful how easy that was for him to believe," Christine said quietly. "This place is…it's evil, Zoey. He's infested the whole building. What he wants, it chills me to my soul, and I hate the fact that I once really did hold him in regard. I thought magic made us better than anyone else."

Once she'd been all in on the witch sisterhood, but it was easy to see she'd changed. She'd seen what that kind of selfishness could lead to.

"Do you want to come with us? When we leave, you can come

home." I was calling an audible, but I didn't like the thought of leaving her here. If Myrddin found out she'd helped us in any way, she would be dead in a heartbeat. Or worse.

She stopped and turned, a look of surprise on her face. "I could come with you?"

"Of course, Grandma Chris." Lee had the cloak over his arm. "You've done enough."

It was my turn to reach out to her. "Come back with us. Take your place in our little town. It's time to let Dev and Danny handle this." I wasn't going to explain that it would likely be Lee and Dean doing the hard work. "We can be back by tomorrow."

She nodded and a shudder went through her. "Yes. I want to see the kids again. I want to be with Harry's family."

"With *your* family," Lee corrected.

A smile came across her face. "With my family. We can leave from here. I don't need anything. All I need are my memories. Let's do this."

Her eyes had lit in a way that I'd never seen before. It's funny how we meet these people and never quite understand how they'll affect our lives decades down the line. We'd had a contentious relationship in the beginning, and now my kids called her Grandma Chris and I was happy to be able to take her home with us.

I would be happy to have her know Harriet and to be close to her.

So much emotion when I needed to be cool.

She stopped in front of Sarah's door, and I was surprised that it was still just a door. It was still painted green, and the bell was a gold color. It looked exactly like it had when I'd last stood in front of it. I reached out and touched the bell like I would have days before. I would have rung it and Sarah would yell that she was coming or Felix would open it and give me his sunny smile before inviting me in. Lee had rung that doorbell a thousand times asking if he could see Mia or if she could come out to play.

"It's so normal." Lee was feeling exactly what I was.

"It's not normal at all. You can't feel the wards. She must have protected you." Christine stood back. "There's also a light emitting from around the door, though you should know that over the years it's dimmed quite a bit. It's one of the reasons I recommended that we extract whatever's in there as quickly as possible."

It was time to find out exactly what Sarah had left behind. I looked back at Christine. "Be careful out here. Remember we've got the cloak. If someone shows up, give us a knock, and then run. We'll find a way out. If we get separated, meet us down in the basement."

"I don't intend to leave my post, but I'll warn you if I'm forced to," she promised me. "I'll be surprised if anyone even comes onto this floor. The other witches who live here went with Liv. There's a small security team monitoring Myrddin's wards, but they're on the fifth floor. And there's some kind of meeting down in the temple. That's what's worrying me. I don't know what that meeting is about. I don't like being on the outside."

"We'll be as fast as we can." Lee took a deep breath and started to reach for the door.

I moved in front of him. "I should do that. We know I'll be able to get in."

I unlocked the door with my key and it opened with a slight hiss. I stepped inside and Lee was next. He had no problem moving into the hallway. It made me worry that perhaps we'd brought the wards down simply by walking through. "Christine, do you still feel the warding?"

She nodded. "Oh, yes. I can't go in there. Shut the door and you'll be safe."

"Be careful." I wished she could come in with us, but our best bet was to get in and out quickly.

The door closed and I was left in a time capsule. For me it all looked normal, but like the rest of the building I could somehow feel the passage of time that had gone through here. Late afternoon light filtered through the balcony windows, and I held a breath because it was hard to believe Sarah wasn't about to walk in from the kitchen and ask me where I'd been.

"It's exactly how I remember it." Lee stepped into the living room. "Goddess, we were working on that stupid project."

There was a half-finished papier-mâché globe sitting on a table in front of the windows that opened onto the balcony.

"It was supposed to be the earth, right?" Sarah and I often switched off helping the kids with their projects. She took the more artsy ones and I edited book reports.

He nodded, standing over it and staring down like he could still see Mia sitting there, working on their geography homework. "Yeah, Mia picked it because it was the hardest one, and we would get extra credit. She didn't need it."

"But you did." Mia looked after Lee in a way most kids wouldn't think to.

I took a long breath and glanced around the living room where I'd so often sat and drank wine with Sarah and Neil.

It looked like they'd just vanished. Felix's reading glasses were sitting on the kitchen table along with a now old copy of a psychology magazine. There was a big platter of pancakes that looked freshly made. I could even smell them and the coffee in the pot.

"Are they still here?" Lee glanced around.

I watched as the pancakes seemed to shrink. Mold grew, and in seconds they were nothing more than a desiccated husk. The coffee that had smelled so fresh only seconds before suddenly smelled loamy, and even the paper of the magazine seemed to shrink in a bit.

"The wards might still be up, but we unsealed this place," I said. "Time is catching up here now. We should look for the bag. They're not here, Lee. I'm sorry. I hoped they were, too."

"But their bodies aren't here either." Lee sighed and started for the back of the apartment. "If they were, we would see them. So somehow they got out." He turned down the hall and stopped. "Whoa."

I raced to catch up to him and I stopped, too.

There were scorch marks down the hall. Where we stood they were merely tendrils, but I could see that they got bigger as they moved toward the bedrooms. At the ends they were ashy looking, but they lightened up as we moved down, a wave that went from gray to gold to an almost sunlit color.

"This leads to their bedroom. Lee, please let me go first. If they're…" I began.

My son was stubborn. He jogged ahead of me.

The scorch marks reminded me of the corona of the sun, curling out from the center, and there was no question where the center was.

Lee threw open the bedroom door, and despite the fact that the lights were off, there was an ambient glow that came from the ceiling.

"What is that?" Lee stood in the middle of Sarah's big bedroom and looked up.

There was the center. It was the lightest part of the marking, and I could feel a warmth coming from it. "I think that's how they got out. What did Asta tell us?"

"She said there was a scar here." Lee was staring up as though he could see through that yellow and orange light.

"She said someone ripped open the veil." I thought that might be what we were standing under. "I think that's the rip."

Lee looked my way, a big smile on his face. "She's alive. She's out there somewhere."

I hoped she was. Anything could have happened to them. If Sarah was out there then she would have tried to find a way back to this plane. The time changes could mean in her timeline she'd just left. Or she could have grown old somewhere, trying to get back.

I had more work to do when we got back to Frelsi. "We need to find the bag. We have our lead. We'll figure out what happened and where they are."

"But we need to move now." Lee pointed to his left. "I believe that's what we're looking for."

The bag of holding sat on Sarah's dresser, next to the ceramic dish where she normally put her rings at night. For some reason the fact that those little rings she always wore were gone gave me comfort. She'd gotten dressed for the day, and she'd made the choice to save herself and her family.

She was out there, and I would find her.

I breathed a sigh of relief when I got the bag in my hands. Like Nim and I had discussed, Sarah had broken the seal when she'd moved the bag. Anyone would be able to see it and open it now. I pulled the sides apart and sure enough, I could see Gladys in her silvery glory. Her light was contrasted by the grimoire's darkness. But those two things weren't the only contents. There was something there I hadn't left behind.

I reached into the bag and decided to take the chance because I recognized Sarah's handwriting.

READ ME NOW

She knew how to get my attention.

"What is it?" Lee moved in behind me.

"It" was a single piece of paper, the kind Felix took notes on. I glanced over and sure enough, there was a legal pad that had been tossed on one of the nightstands along with the pen Sarah had almost certainly used. Sarah loved stationary and had a ton of it. She had beautiful pens in every color. What this told me was she'd written it very quickly. "She left us a note."

Zoey,

We had to do it. We couldn't let her fall into his hands. The portal is one way, but if he comes through, all is lost. Destroy the portal any way you can.

I'm so sorry.

"Fall into his hands? Is she talking about Mia?" Lee asked, reading over my shoulder.

"I have to think so. Mia was already showing signs of her power back then. Perhaps Sarah figured out something we don't know yet. Or she's talking about Gladys. We always refer to the sword as a *she*. Sarah could have left a more descriptive note. Like how am I supposed to close some portal? Does she remember who I am? I know how to blow shit up. I don't know how to close a portal. And she could have left a map." There was a spark of panic threatening to well inside me. I wasn't good at magic. We all joked about how bad I was at it. How the hell would I close the portal?

And the *all will be lost* thing kind of freaked me out, too.

"Mom, calm down." Lee put his hands on my shoulders and stared down at me. "We don't have to do this right this second. We do the job we're supposed to do. The wards are holding for now. We get home and talk to our witches about how to close the portal. There might even be something in that grimoire that will help. But first we need to get out of here."

He was right and he was calmer than I was, likely a function of the fact that he'd spent twelve years at war and I'd been a stay-at-home mom. The weight of the world was back on my shoulders, and I felt it all.

But this was a twist we would have to deal with later. I wasn't going to figure out how to close that portal in the next hour, so it was best we booked it out of here. I grabbed the bag and looked to my son.

"We will find them."

He nodded. "I know you will. You found her in Hell. You'll find Sarah again, and when you do, we'll get Mia back. Let's get out of here. If we move fast enough we won't even have to use the cloak. It's crowded in there."

I wasn't sure about that. "I think we should still use it. I know it was hard to climb the stairs, but going down them should be easier."

We strode through the hallway and the lights were starting to die, the lamps aging and burning out around us. Lucky for us, Sarah had opened the curtains and the late afternoon light illuminated the living room. All around us time was catching up in Sarah's sunny apartment, and that made me worry, but I had to hope the wards held until I could find a way to close off the portal.

"And what is Grandma Chris supposed to do?" Lee argued.

It was always weird to hear her called that. Probably because when the kids had started she was barely thirty. Even now at fifty she looked too young to be a grandma. I was sure I would get a big-time lecture from Sasha about extracting one of his spies without permission. He should get used to it. I rarely asked permission and only asked forgiveness when I really needed it. I didn't here. She was in danger and she'd done her job. She could give us everything she knew and live out the rest of her days in the comfort of Frelsi, doing happy witch things and being part of the family.

After all, knowing what I knew in that moment, it was all she'd ever truly wanted.

I had the bag in my hand when I opened the door and stepped out into the hallway. "Christine?"

I gasped because she was face first on the floor, and what I did next was nothing more than instinct. I moved to her, dropping to my knees, the bag falling to the floor. I gently turned her over and there was blood everywhere. It was coming from the hole someone had punched into her gut.

"Zoey," she said softly.

"Mom, we need to get her out of here." Lee stood over me, and his gun had already made an appearance.

Christine shook her head. "You need to run. He's here. Thought he was on our side. He's contacting Myrddin. Couldn't get through the door."

I wasn't sure who *he* was. "Lee, get under that cloak now."

I didn't think I could save Christine. I had to think about Lee. In that moment I wasn't even thinking about the fact that I had the grimoire. I was thinking about my son, and I couldn't lose him again. I was panicking because my heart was engaged in this.

"Christine, we have to go. I'm so sorry. Dad…he told me he would be waiting." Tears blurred my eyes because I'd failed her. I'd failed my father, and I had to get his last message to her. "He said you won't be alone."

Her lips curved slightly even as a trickle of blood came from her mouth and she was seeing something I couldn't. "He's here now. Oh, it's good to see him. Don't be afraid, Zoey. What happens next…don't be afraid. He'll see the light and know. He'll see it…he was born in it…"

"Who is *he*?" I asked.

But the light died in her eyes.

"Mom?"

I turned and horror spilled through my veins because there was something sticking out of Lee's chest, something pointed and bloody. Lee's good eye was wide, and I could see the fear on his face. And then that blade disappeared and Lee started to fall to his knees.

"I do believe she was talking about me, dear."

Alexander Sharpe pulled the short sword in his hand up and dragged his thumb over it before bringing it to his lips.

"And thank you for bringing me that bag."

Chapter Twenty-Five

Lee hit his knees and groaned, his head coming up. "Mom? What do I do?"

My heart threatened to seize. His skin had already gone pale.

Alexander chuckled. "You die, boy."

I reached for my pistol, and I hated the way my hands shook as I leveled it at the vampire who really fucking shouldn't be walking around because it was still light outside. Alexander was a warrior. His vampiric talents were strength and speed. Academics were the ones who got to walk around in the daylight. Daniel could walk in the daylight because of Dev's unique magic. Alexander should be safely tucked away in his resting place, unable to even move when the sun was out.

"That's what happens when you send a child to do a man's job," Alexander said, staring down at my son with those reptile eyes of his.

I should have fought harder to have him executed before. I'd always known he would turn on us, but he'd been so patient. For years and years he'd been a useful tool, convincing my husbands, the academics, and Sasha that he was worth keeping around.

But a snake will always strike.

I fired and his shoulder flew back. "Lee, get inside that

apartment. Now."

We needed cover because that one bullet wasn't going to stop a vampire as old as Alexander. It wouldn't stop any vampire at all, but it could slow him down. The silver might kill him eventually if he didn't get the bullets out, but if I didn't hit him directly in the heart he could still fight.

I had to get Lee some cover. If his body was left out here…I had no idea what they would do with it. He needed time for the vampire blood in his system to heal the wound. It would if I could keep his heart going long enough, if I could keep Alexander from doing more damage.

I fired again but he was ready, twisting his body and moving faster than my eye could track.

"Silly bitch," Alexander said, brushing off the bullet like it was nothing more than a mosquito bite. It seemed to have gone through and hadn't lodged inside him like I needed it to. He kicked out and pain flared in my wrist as the gun flew out of my hand. There was a thud as it hit the floor somewhere behind me. Alexander stood over me like the elegant death bringer he was in his tailored suit and thousand dollar shoes. He'd likely worn only the best Victorian clothes back in the day, the genteel garments covering the monster he truly was. "That wasn't ever going to stop me."

I had to buy Lee a little time. He was moving, though slowly. I didn't think I could pick him up or even drag him inside the apartment where he would be protected. The good news was I happened to know I was a much bigger target. I knew what this predator liked to prey on. Women. At his core, he hated all women.

It should have been no surprise he would follow Myrddin.

And I bet he was a talker. Lee's chest was still moving. I needed time, and goddess, I needed a freaking stake. "How are you daywalking?"

I pushed myself back away from where my son was dying, tempting the beast to follow me. I dragged the bag along and had to hope I could get the gun in my hands again. If I could take out both lungs, I might have a shot at getting Lee behind the wards. When he was safely locked away, I would run like hell and get my husbands. We would do whatever it took to get Lee out, safe and whole. Surely Myrddin wouldn't want a crazed newbie vamp running around the

Council building.

Or the wizard would simply find a way to kill Lee the minute he left the safety of the wards, and that was a sure thing. If he turned here, he would rise and he would need to feed. He wouldn't think of anything beyond blood, and that would leave him vulnerable.

I couldn't let Myrddin kill him again. Oh, I knew it hadn't been Myrddin who fired the shots, but he'd led Lee to that first devastating death. I couldn't give him another chance.

Alexander held up his left hand, showing off the heavy gold ring there. It was wide and ornate, covering his ring finger almost up to the knuckle. It was the one he'd seemed fascinated with when we'd talked before. "A gift from the Dark One. Myrddin has all kinds of gifts for vampires. He's done what Donovan should have done years ago. He's made a deal with our brethren."

"You mean with the demons." I didn't know how much time Lee had. The vampire blood he took on a regular basis should start to work soon. "He's been making deals with demons."

"Of course. They're our family, so to speak. Our cousins. Donovan tried to find some supernatural utopia. He was naïve but strong. It's why I supported him the first time around. When he disappeared, I hedged my bets. Myrddin fumbled at first, and I decided to play both sides in this war. I like to come out on top, you see. I knew something was going to happen during this meeting. I wasn't sure what since our spymaster played it close to the vest. I decided it would be a good time to follow poor old Christine. She didn't seem to want to go with the rest of the group to help protect our leader. Sure enough, her instincts were right and so were mine. You should know I've already told Myrddin you're here. Now, I'll take that bag and then you and I can go somewhere quiet. There are lessons I've longed to teach you."

I was sure there were. I was surely the whore of his world now. That was what women were to a thing like Sharpe. Jack the Ripper had been the mask he'd worn once, but the beast underneath had never truly gone away. "He lets you kill, doesn't he?"

"Myrddin understands that humans are less than worthless. Human females are responsible for covering the planet with their mewling, wasteful spawn." Every word out of his mouth sounded toxic and poisonous. "When we close the gates to the celestial planes,

I will be given free rein to kill as I will. The Earth plane will be my hunting grounds, and I will live as I should."

My dumbass son wasn't moving toward the apartment. He was starting to crawl my way. Like he could kill the vampire while he had a hole in his chest and blood pouring out of his body. Why wasn't the vampire blood he'd taken earlier working? Danny had made sure he had it. He'd taken an extra shot. He should be healing.

"Oh, my dear, you look worried." Alexander glanced back at Lee, a sly smile spreading across his face. "Is the king's blood not working? Were you counting on that? It's so handy to have him back, I'm sure. Real vampire blood works well, but king's blood is something else entirely. It's so sad when there's an antidote." He held up the blade. "This is a present from the Hell plane. There are only two in existence. Forged from Lucifer's own bones. I'm afraid the vampire blood in your son's system will do nothing but speed up his death, and the fact that it's king's blood will make it all the more painful. We're coming for all of you, and there's nothing the king can do. I can't wait to see what this blade will do when I shove it through the king's heart." He pointed the sword my way. It still had my son's blood on it. "The bag. Now. Or we'll see what it can do to his queen."

Lee reached out and grabbed at Alexander's ankles, but it was obvious his strength was waning.

What if that blade could hurt Lee's turn?

I managed to get the gun back in my hand, and I fired before he could stab Lee again. Alexander moved, and I only managed to nick his side.

His eyes went black as night, and he raised that weapon over my son's body. "I'll take his head next, Your Highness. Drop that gun or I'll present your son to the Dark One in two pieces."

"Mom, don't," Lee gasped.

But I knew damn well that cutting off his head would stop any possibility of his turn. I couldn't let that happen. I dropped the gun. I had to find a way to get both of us behind the wards. Lee was so close. We needed to get into the apartment, and I had to figure out a way to let Danny know we were in trouble.

I held my hands up. "I'm doing what you want. I don't have any weapon on me that could kill you, so lower yours."

"Want your baby boy to be pretty in death, eh? Because he's not going to heal. The pain must be excruciating." Alexander turned his attention back to me. "The bag, now, Your Highness. And then we'll wait for Myrddin. He needs you alive, apparently, but I think he'll give me some time with you. After this, I'll be his right-hand man, so to speak."

I wasn't sure about that. Especially when I realized that I'd lied. I did have a weapon that could kill him. I picked up the bag.

I did have a play to make. One shot.

I held it open. "It's in here."

He wouldn't care about the Sword of Light. No. He would go straight for the book because he thought he had me on the ropes. It didn't matter that I was the queen, that I'd faced down demons and won wars against legions of Fae. I was a female and weak in his mind. I was broken when I was born. I was nothing a mighty predator should worry about.

He should have remembered that Hunter who'd taken his heart the first time.

His eyes lit and he reached in to grab the book. "Myrddin's grimoire. It's beautiful."

It was covered in what I was certain was some kind of flesh and written in blood. I bet that killer thought it was pretty. Unfortunately for him, he wasn't Myrddin. He pulled the book out of the bag of holding and it disappeared in his hands.

"What?" Alexander asked, confusion lighting his face.

I pushed him back, connecting with his arm hard, and the action did what I wanted it to. His arm came up and his hand released the now invisible book.

He immediately fell to his knees, trying to feel for it.

I let the bag drop, my hand firmly around Gladys. She hummed for me. I could feel her joy at being held by one of her sisters again. The Sword of Light is the traditional weapon of my people—originally named Amazon and now called Companion. She was a gift from the Heaven plane, from *my* brethren. She guided my hand because she recognized the man in front of her, recognized the pit that was his soul, the piece of him that sought to destroy that which he could not make submit.

In that moment, the Sword of Light and I were one, and I was stronger than I'd been before. She was made of the silver found threaded through angel wings, and she weighed nothing in my hands as we moved in an arc that descended on Alexander Sharpe's neck and sliced through his body like it moved through water.

Everything went still for a moment and then the legendary Ripper turned to ash and fell apart with a single breath.

The sword's blade was covered with his ash but only for a second as she proved she didn't need blood to soak in an enemy's power. The ash shimmered and then sank into her silver.

Gladys hummed again as though trying to wake me from that moment of connection between us. She knew I still had a job to do.

The only thing left of Alexander was that gold ring. I pocketed it and picked up that dark sword he'd tried to kill my son with. Unlike Gladys, this one didn't hum for me. This sword felt wrong in my hands and I tossed it inside the apartment. I didn't want to touch it but I wasn't going to leave it behind for Myrddin to use against us again.

"Mom, I can see it." Lee was on his belly, his head turned my way. "The book. I can see the book."

He was still breathing. I could salvage this. Maybe Alexander had been lying and it was just taking a while for the blood to work. Maybe vampire blood worked differently on latent vampires. I didn't know. I did know I had to get him behind those wards and then I would figure something out. I tossed Gladys into the apartment and gripped Lee's ankles. "Where is it?"

"It fell. It's near Grandma Chris. It's touching her foot," he managed. "Mom, you have to run. Take the book and run. You have to leave me."

I couldn't leave him. He was my baby. "We'll be fine. When we don't show up on time, your dads will come for us. We can go out on the balcony and he'll fly up and get us."

It wasn't a terrible plan. Unless Sarah had warded the balcony. Danny would look for us. Dev would move all the planes to find us. We had to hold on. I gritted my teeth and started to pull him in.

"No, Mom. You have to go."

"The king's blood in your system is going to work." I had to believe Alexander was lying.

It was hard to get Lee over the carpet, but once he hit the marble of the foyer, he slid easily.

Because of all the blood he'd lost. I slid my baby over the floor in his own blood.

But he was inside the wards. He was safe.

"I'm going to get the book. I'll be right back."

"No, run. Put the cloak on and run, Momma. Please." His words were slurred.

I wouldn't listen to them anyway. I wasn't leaving him here. He wasn't healing. There was so much blood.

If he turned, he wouldn't know to stay behind the wards. He would need blood. I tried to remember everything I knew about how a vampire turned. It took different times for the turn to begin. Danny had taken hours to wake. Chad had taken mere moments. Chad had been reasonable for a few minutes before the blood lust took over. Maybe I could talk to Lee. Maybe I could reason with him.

I'd turned Daniel. My blood had stabilized Danny.

I knew I should run, but he was my child.

As carefully as I could I stepped around the blood and started toward the book. I would use the bag of holding to find it. Lee had given me a place to start. I would slip the bag over that spot and close it and then I would have the book.

It would give me leverage in case it all went to hell. Went to hell? It had already gone there, but I might be able to salvage it.

I'd made it almost to the outside when I realized all really was lost.

Five witches stood in the hallway, staring my way. I recognized a few of them. Once these women had been friendly, had waved at me as we passed each other in the halls or met up at some school function. Now they belonged to Myrddin.

They all wore black robes, and there was some kind of symbol on their foreheads. Their eyes were vast night, a vacant black that told me they were being controlled.

And then the one in the center, the tallest of them, began to smile. She held her hands over her heart as though clutching something to her breast.

I would bet the book was no longer on the ground. He'd found a way.

"Hello, Your Highness. I wondered if you would make an appearance."

"Myrddin?"

"Not in the flesh, of course. My body is back at the park. I'm listening to your husband drone on and on about how we should be careful around demons. He's talking a lot. That told me he was probably covering for you. So the turncoat witch took my book and hid it here. Tell me—where did she go?"

He was still looking for Sarah. "I don't know."

"Of course you don't, dear. Is the boy dead? I should have known that butcher couldn't properly handle a job. I'm surprised at Christine. I guess she actually did love the old boy. She seemed so eager to learn. A pity, but we move on." Those eyes stared behind me. "Sharpe used the Dark Dagger on the boy?"

"If that's what you call it." A numbness descended over me. I was so overcome, I couldn't handle the emotions. The horror. The pain. The shame. The guilt.

The fear.

I shut down and went into survival mode, though I'd started to worry I wouldn't survive. Not at all.

An almost sympathetic expression crossed the witch's face. "Then it's over for his human life. That's your human son, right? Not the faery? If you brought the faery son along then I'm sorry. He's gone, and I'm going to have to spin that with the Fae in some way. Tell me that idiot didn't kill the Green Man?"

"Why would you care?"

"Because I don't need the Fae involved," Myrddin admitted. "But I don't think you brought him. You brought the other one."

"His name is Lee."

"The latent vampire." The witch Myrddin spoke through sighed. "Well, that could get messy. Come along then, Zoey. There's nothing that can be done for him. My witches will take you to a secure location. I promise you'll be treated well. We'll deal with…well, we'll handle what happens next."

I knew exactly how he would handle my son. They would wait for him to come out and then he would turn to ash alongside Alexander. "I'm not going anywhere."

"He will not care that you're his mother," Myrddin said. "He'll see your light and rip you apart."

And then maybe he would have a chance at the long life that should have been his. I knew I should think about the baby I was carrying, but Myrddin wouldn't care about her. I knew what he would do to us. That safe place he offered was a prison he would keep me in until he killed me. "He doesn't have to remember that I am his mother to make it true."

The witch stopped for a moment as though Myrddin was shocked at the turn of events. "Zoey, come out. I know you feel for the child. Come out and perhaps we'll negotiate with Daniel for his release."

"You would let Lee go?"

Pure calculation lit the witch's expression, and I could see Myrddin thought he could get even more out of this situation. "In exchange for the boy you brought back."

He was a greedy bastard. "In exchange for your son."

"Figured that out, did you? See, I have emotions, too. His conception was the result of my indulgence of Nimue. She has particular fantasies. I should have killed his mother when I learned of the prophecy concerning him, but I felt something when I realized he was my flesh and blood. I've never had a child before. I hate that I have to destroy him. I might try to turn the boy first."

He wouldn't be able to. Dean had been raised to do the right thing. He believed in his destiny. So I would be exchanging Lee for Dean, and I couldn't believe a word this man said. "And me?"

"Well, Zoey, I need you." He managed to say the words like they were something good he was offering me. "You know I need both you and Kelsey. My witches felt no power surge this evening. The ritual wasn't done, so the Sword of Light still contains the angel's power. And now the vampire's, though his is not important for my purposes."

He was forgetting something. "I have to die to prime that sword."

A single shoulder shrugged off that worry. "You didn't the first time."

"But you're not going to have Daniel there to save me."

He stared at me through the witch's eyes. "No. I will not. Sacrifices must be made."

I chuckled, a bitter sound. "Just not by you."

"Well, dear, that is why I'm the true king. I've hidden behind puppets for too long. It's my turn to wear the crown."

I took a step back, my hand on the door. "I think I'll stay here."

"The wards won't hold forever."

"They'll hold long enough. I'll give my son a chance. You're right. Sacrifices must be made, but if I'm going to die, it won't be for you. I think I'll keep the sword." As long as it was safe behind the wards, so was Kelsey. He would come for her, too. That might be what Liv was doing as we spoke.

The witch's lips formed a flat line. "Damn it, Zoey. This is preposterous. You know what he will do to you when he rises. He will feed on anyone, much less a companion. You're going to be a bright light calling him in. You think Daniel will show up. You think he'll feel the rising and he'll save you, but those wards will shield everything that happens inside them."

"It doesn't matter." I'd already thought of that. My mind had run through every possible scenario.

They all led to one place.

"What about the child you carry?" Myrddin proved his spies liked to talk, too.

I had to wonder if it had been Alexander who'd heard that rumor and passed it on or if there were others in our group. I put my free hand on my belly. "She was going to die with me one way or another."

"She could be another Fae goddess, Zoey." He obviously wasn't going to admit he would kill us both, and likely very soon. "I could be persuaded to wait until she's born. I could give her to her Fae relatives. All you have to do is come out."

At least I could shake him up a bit. Any Fae healer would be able to tell I was carrying a human child. "You think she's Devinshea's? One of the gifts we received from you sending us across the planes was Daniel turning human for a few days. Just long enough for me to carry his child."

And she would die with me.

The witch standing in for Myrddin went silent and then her eyes grew wide. "Tell me you are joking, Zoey."

"Maybe I am. Maybe I'm not. It doesn't matter, does it?"

"If you are telling me the truth then you carry a child who is the product of a latent vampire king and companion queen. The first in thousands and thousands of years."

"You going to try to sell her off to someone?"

The witch had paled considerably. "No. I will kill her the first chance I get. She is an abomination and cannot be allowed breath. She will be able to destroy worlds. Close the door, companion. Lock yourself away with your son and let him save the planes from that thing in your belly."

A chill went through me. He seemed to want to kill all of my children. Or he was testing me. "You'll have neither the sword nor me. The plane will be safe."

The witch's hands curled over the book I couldn't see. She'd stepped back as though Myrddin wanted more space between us. "I have the book. I'll get the sword. And you have another daughter. Evangeline should work. Good-bye, Queen Zoey. I think it is a good thing you came. Your death and that of the thing you carry inside you will save the planes so much pain."

The witch turned and walked away, toward the elevator that I assumed would take her to wherever Myrddin wanted to store the book.

The others remained, their blank stares telling me they still had a job to do—to ensure we never left this apartment.

I closed the door, a heavy feeling in my heart as I turned back to my son. I sank to my knees and stroked his hair like I had when he'd been a child.

"Mom, please," he whispered, all strength gone now. He was left with only the will to plead with me not to do this to him.

But there wasn't anything else I could do. I couldn't run. I couldn't call up Danny and ask him for a save. I was trapped, and all I could do was give this son I loved a fighting chance. "You need to get out of this building as soon as you can. Your dad will feel your turn once you're out of here and he'll come for you."

"Not before I kill you."

"I love you. It's okay, baby. I need you to remember that." I would shove those words into his soul. "It's okay. Whatever happens, I still love you. I love you so much. I've loved this soul of yours from the moment I met you."

Maybe the very first moment, because there had always been something about Lee, some easy camaraderie between us. We'd fit in that odd way people sometimes do, as though a piece that had been missing had somehow slipped into place.

"It doesn't hurt now. I think I'm dying."

I knew he was. Tears slipped from my eyes and I felt my heart breaking because these would be our last moments together, and I wished so very much that I hadn't wasted the days we'd had on looking for a way back. We only had the now, and I should have spent it with all of them. I should have sat them all down and learned every little detail I could.

"It's going to be all right. I'm going to be here for you."

"I'm afraid," he whispered. "I didn't think I would be afraid."

"Don't be. I'll be here, and then your dads will take care of you. All you have to do is get out of the building."

"Don't...don't want to hurt...please, Momma." He begged me.

I simply took his hand in mine and told him I loved him over and over so his last human moments would be surround with love.

I saw him as he'd been, a grumpy wolf who secretly wanted a family. He'd been my protector and one of my truest friends.

Then he'd been my son, a light in my life. Always curious. A force of nature.

I prayed our souls would meet again because I felt the moment he died.

It was time for me to save him. No matter what it cost.

Chapter Twenty-Six

I sat there as the light outside turned to late afternoon and wondered how long it would take. I didn't move. There wasn't a reason. I simply sat on the floor and held his hand, my mind going over our lives together.

I wondered if my dad would be waiting for me. I hoped so. I hoped he would be holding open that door he'd spoken of.

I even tried to call Oliver Day to me. I hadn't seen my so-called guardian angel in a while. I supposed he was out of practice when it came to me. My life had been boring the last several years.

Good. It had been good. I'd gotten to raise my babies for eleven years, and now I was so grateful for every single one of them. For every day. For every stinky diaper and mess I'd cleaned up. For every breakfast we'd had and dinner where we'd sat around the table. I was grateful for sleepless nights and soccer games.

I was grateful that they would be okay.

I don't know how long I sat there. I seemed to float on memory until I finally felt his hand move against mine.

He took his first breath as the day died—as the night began.

My son reborn.

He would be magnificent, and I wished I could see him when his father took him through his turn.

Lee's chest moved, and his hand slid from mine.

"What happened? Goddess, that's a lot... Okay that's weird." Lee turned over and got to his knees, his hand sliding the eye patch off his face. "Wow. Peripheral vision, how I missed you." He sat back, a look of wonder on his face as he stared at me. "Momma, you are so beautiful."

I glowed for him now. He could see something I could not. I reached out and cupped his cheeks. "Your scars are gone."

We might have a minute or two before the blood lust kicked in. I wanted to stop time and stay right here. We could stay in this moment forever.

"I know this light." He reached out as though he could touch the glow that surrounded us.

It was already starting. He wouldn't be able to help himself. This was why it was dangerous to be a companion. "Sweetie, I need you to know that whatever happens, it's okay. I love you. I will love you no matter what. I need you to listen to me. When I'm gone, you're going to have to run."

"Where are you going?"

"Don't joke. We don't have much time."

He frowned and then he was the one touching my face, his thumbs brushing away my tears. "Momma, don't cry. Don't be afraid of me."

I wasn't. I was. I didn't know what I was. "You have to get out of the building for your dads to find you."

"We're meeting Uncle Neil, and then we'll go home to Frelsi. It's going to be okay. I'm sorry I scared you like that. But I'm good now."

I watched him carefully. "You don't feel it? You're going to lose control soon."

He seemed to think about that for a moment. "No. I'm not. Though I really do need to eat."

I took a long breath. "Lee, I'm here for you. When it happens and you can't resist the light, it's okay."

He stood, his hands on his hips. He was covered in blood, and I didn't know if he realized it but his fangs were out and they were huge. "Are you telling me it's okay to eat you?"

I looked up at him. "You won't be able to help yourself. No new vampire can resist the light."

"This light?" He took a long breath as though he could smell the light around him, sense it, feel it on his skin. "I was born in this light. It's funny. I grew up feeling it but I didn't realize what it was. I thought it was affection, love, and it is, but it's the light, too. I was raised in this light, Momma. I would never dishonor it. And that hunger I should have is there, but I'm certainly not going to kill my mom. Do you have any idea what that would do to my psyche?"

I managed to get to my feet. I had no idea what was happening. "Are you all right?"

"He's fine, Your Highness."

I practically screamed as that deep voice spoke and I turned. Lee stepped in front of me but then I realized who it was.

Grayson Sloane stood in the living room dressed in jeans and a T-shirt, his dark hair curling slightly at the base of his head. The dark prophet looked like any guy walking the streets of Dallas below us with the exception of his pitch black eyes. It let me know he was here in a fully professional capacity.

"How did you get in?" Panic threatened to take over. "Did the wards fail?"

"The wards can't keep a prophet out," Gray explained. "You know we watch history's more interesting moments. This particular moment was one of my first prophecies."

I frowned and managed to move around my son who might not have to drain me since now Gray was here and hopefully he still had some blood. Lee could eat him instead. "Yeah, I remember some of those. A freaking trick and a trap? You could have mentioned I would lose twelve years."

Gray was a handsome man, built on big lines. "I lost them, too, Your Highness. I lost a lot. I cannot change what I see. But this, this, was one of the good things."

We had two different versions of good, Gray and I. "Excuse me? He just got murdered by Jack the Ripper and now we're stuck here and he's going to lose his shit at some point because all newbies do."

"Kings don't," Gray said.

"And this was my favorite shirt." Lee had some complaints of his own. "If I'd known…" Lee stopped. "*Don't believe the myth that there can be only one.*"

Gray's lips curved up slightly. "*There is strength in numbers. So much strength in the blood. Don't let them forget. History plays itself out again and again, mothers and fathers giving more than mere advice to their children.*"

"*They give blood so the story continues*," Lee finished. "That prophecy was about me. Dad's blood. Dad's DNA. I'm a king." He said the words solemnly. "I'm the first vampire in a long time who was raised by a companion, aren't I? It's why the light feels so familiar."

"Even as a child you would have felt her light," Gray said with a sigh. "It would soothe you. You were raised with your father's strength and your mother's light. You are truly a king for a new generation of vampires. Though don't count your father out. The plane still needs him. All of the planes do. And you weren't the only one who received his father's…gifts."

Something had changed in my son. He stood taller, his shoulders broad and straight, and there was not an ounce of self-doubt in him. "Dean. He's Myrddin's son but he was raised by a companion, too. We are darkness loved by the light."

"And that, we all pray, will make the difference. You are a king, Lee Donovan-Quinn, and if you were anyone but your father's son you would immediately challenge him for the crown." Gray's brow rose and his eyes shifted back to their violet color, and his body seemed to relax as though he'd gotten the hard part over. "You could win, you know. Even now, you might be able to take him down."

"He's not fighting Daniel." I couldn't even stand to hear that.

"Uh, what Mom said. Why would I fight my dad? Also, I don't really want a crown. I'm good with the whole all-the-superpowers, none-of-the-responsibility thing." His lips quirked up. "Can I fly?"

"You won't know until you try," Gray replied.

I got a hand on his jacket because he was not going to throw himself off the balcony. "Stop it. He needs to find some dinner and then we need to get out of here. He can try out all of his superpowers when we're safe at home."

We might get out of this. We might survive.

Lee's hand found mine. "Okay, Mom. You've had a day. Let's get the bag and get out of here."

"Myrddin has the book." I was going to have to own up to how much I'd fucked up this mission. "I have the sword, but Myrddin sent a version of himself to get his grimoire back. I would bet it's in the penthouse. I could…"

"Goddess, no. We are not going to Myrddin's. I might not murder my own mother in a blood lust rage, but I'm also not fully in control," Lee announced. "We already lost Grandma Chris. We're done, Mom. Are those witches I sense outside the door?"

"Four of them now." I'd thought they were going to be something we had to survive, but now I saw the upside. They were expecting a regular newbie, not a king. "You can try out some of those superpowers on them and get that first blood in."

Lee's eyes changed, going from brown to a golden amber that covered the whites. "Yeah, that hunger is kicking in now."

I probably should have been worried about sending my newly risen baby boy out with a bunch of trained witches, but I was going with my gut. He could handle it. "Have fun, baby."

He was gone before I could take another breath, and all I heard was the door slamming.

Then the screaming started, but honestly I'd heard worse. I looked up at our guest. "There's a rumor going around that you're visiting Hell and have not paid attention to your son."

The only dark prophet in existence blushed nicely. "I didn't mean to ignore Fenrir. I descended to protect him. You know I didn't come here for a lecture, Your Highness."

"The lecture is free." There was a gurgling sound, and Lee and I were going to have to have a talk about table manners. I leaned over and picked up the Sword of Light. "Have you talked to your wife? And what about Trent? Don't look at me like that. You know I'm nosy."

I wondered how long Lee was going to take. I hoped he didn't overfeed and get a tummy ache. He used to do that when he'd been a werewolf. He would eat the weirdest things just to prove he could.

"Yes, I have talked to Kelsey, and she's incredibly irritated with me," Gray admitted. "She's…she was gone for so long and a lot happened. I don't know if I should disrupt her life."

I pointed the sword his way because he should get used to it if he was going to continue down this path. "She's pregnant. Her life's already disrupted. Look, I can see that you're all dark and broody and bad shit happened to you. Get over it because you have a family."

"Get over it?"

"Five minutes ago I had prepared myself for a bloody death that would send my son into a shame spiral the likes of which the world has never seen before," I replied. "And now he's fine and I'm alive and I'm over it. I'm a mom. I have to be because two minutes from now something else is going to go wrong and I have to be ready."

The door opened again and Lee stood there, a hand on his belly. If the wards bothered him now that he was a vampire, he didn't show it. "I think I ate too much."

I nodded. "Yep, see, now I have a baby vampire king with indigestion and Myrddin has his freaking grimoire and I don't know where Sarah is and we still have to get out of here."

Lee held up his favorite toy. "He left us the invisibility cloak and the bag. So we're still ahead. Oh, shit. I don't need the cloak anymore. I can be invisible all on my own." His eyes narrowed. "Can you see me?"

He would have to work on that. "Yes, honey. I can see you. I'm sure Dad will start lessons tomorrow." The sword was humming in my hand, and I had a vision flash through my mind. Kelsey. She wanted to be with Kelsey. Good. It would give Gray a reason to see his wife. I turned it around and offered him the hilt. "She wants to see Kelsey."

"She?" Gray asked.

"Gladys."

Gray looked at the sword like it would bite him. "Uh, I don't think I should touch that."

Sure she tended to burn the flesh of men, especially those with some Hell plane DNA, but I expected him to be braver than that. Still, at least I had a way to transport her. I put her in the bag of holding and offered her to Gray. "She's Kelsey's. Please take her to your wife, and maybe you can bring her a sandwich or two. She'll forgive a lot if you bring her Gladys and some food."

Gray took the bag. "All right. I can try again. And, Zoey, it's good you're back. You'll figure this out."

"Do you know where Sarah is?" I had questions before he left. I knew we should take off, but I needed to know.

Gray shook his head. "She's beyond my sight."

Then she was far away indeed.

"Now ask me what you truly want to ask me, Your Highness," Gray offered.

"What Myrddin said about my daughter…" It seemed the dark prophet knew everything that had happened here.

"What did he say about Evan?" Lee asked. He'd been too busy dying to listen in on my conversation with Myrddin.

Gray ignored him, staring at me. "What Harriet will become is up to you, but remember what happened here today wasn't merely DNA. Raise your children in the light and even the darkest days won't seem so bad. And what Myrddin sees as destruction could be exactly what the planes need."

He was right. Why was I letting that fucker tell me my kid was bad? I'd made it through Rhys's formative years and Lee's turn. I was certain Evan was going to give me hell, too. Summer had nearly brought down the outer planes with her stubbornness. I could handle one little destroyer of worlds.

I could handle anything.

"I'm glad you're back, Your Highness." Gray tipped his head. "We've missed your chaos. Welcome home. I'll tell Kelsey hello."

He shimmered away.

That was new.

"How long's he been doing that?" I looked up at Lee. His color was back to almost normal and his eyes were brown again. Only the blood covering his shirt gave away the fact that anything had happened at all. Well, and his eye had grown back.

"As long as I can remember," he admitted and then sobered. "Grandma Chris's body is gone. The witches did something to her."

"I'm sorry. I can't tell you how sorry I am. But she was happy at the end. She's with Grandad." She'd been able to see that everything would be all right. I hugged him, not caring about the blood at all. "But, sweetie, we need to move. I know you're strong, but Myrddin will return soon, and I don't want you to go up against him yet. He's got his grimoire back."

He had his book and it was nestled upstairs in the home Devinshea had built for us.

Lee had moved to stand over what Myrddin had called the Dark Dagger. He reached down and picked it. "Yeah, but we have this. I didn't like it when it killed me, but I have to admit it's pretty cool now. We should take it with us."

"As long as you carry it because I'm not touching that thing," I said.

"Let's move. I'm just sad you gave away the bag because I still think it would be good to bring back some of that C-4," Lee said, starting for the door.

Chaos. Gray had said the plane had missed my chaos.

I'd come to get back what I'd stolen from Myrddin, and I'd only been partially successful. Why should he get to keep what he'd stolen from me?

"Hey, I do have superspeed now," Lee said with a half smile. "How about a ride down, Mom?"

In that moment I saw him as he'd been, with that scruffy smile he used to give me. My Lee. Always. "I think that's a great idea."

I hopped on his broad back and did not look at the hallway. I didn't need to see what a messy eater he was at this stage of his vampire life.

He was right about his speed. It came to him as naturally as breathing. I'd heard stories of how strong Danny had been after his turn, but his powers had made him nervous. He'd shied away from them because they reminded him he wasn't human anymore.

Lee embraced them. This was what he'd always wanted, and the power flowed and flowed.

If we passed someone on our way down, we were moving too fast for them to register. Before I knew it we were walking into the basement again.

Into all those weapons.

"Okay, Mom, hear me out. I run back and forth and save all these precious babies from going unused," Lee proposed.

I pulled the amulet Declan had given me from around my neck. He'd been right about the glow. It pulsed with energy, letting me know it was ready for me to use. But I wouldn't be making that phone call. I didn't need the ancients to tell me what came next.

War. It would be bloody and long and costly.

And we would win.

Starting now.

"Uh, Mom, whatcha doing there? Because it seems like maybe

you're going to put a magical amulet that's known to be volatile right next to the C-4." Lee frowned my way. "You're going to blow up all these pretty weapons, aren't you?"

I was going to blow it all to hell. Most of the witches were out of the building. I probably wouldn't even get Myrddin. The wards would keep the explosion from destroying the other buildings around us.

And the portal would close.

All in all, I was calling it a win. I placed the amulet directly in the middle of all that explosive goodness.

"I'm sending Myrddin a message. Don't fuck with the queen."

I walked away, knowing Lee would follow. Probably after stuffing his pockets with guns. I couldn't even blame him, but I walked away from that building that had been my home for so long. I walked away because we didn't need it. We would find another home, build another Ether.

We would be okay because we had each other.

Lee caught up and sure enough, he was carrying a flamethrower over his shoulder. "How much time before she blows?"

"Declan said it should be ten to fifteen minutes before it goes back to Faery." By blowing a hole through time and space, and thereby setting off my explosion. I jogged along. I was pretty sure Lee didn't even have to walk faster to keep up with me.

It's been my fate to be the only one with sad human strength and speed.

I pushed through the door that led to the parking garage of the MT building. Or I thought that was what Neil had called it.

"Daniel, she's here. What the hell happened? Lee, are you all right?" Neil rushed my way.

Danny was faster, though he stopped in front of Lee.

Lee gave him a grin. "Hey, Dad. Uhm, a funny thing happened on the way to the job."

"You turned." Danny breathed the words like they were sacred.

"And I didn't even eat Mom, although she did this whole drama thing where she was sacrificing herself. I would never have heard the end of that so I decided to just be a king…" He lost his sarcastic expression. "Like my dad. Is that okay?"

What Gray had said was messing with him, though I doubt he'd meant it to. The idea that there could be only one vampire king was built into our world.

A long, deeply relieved sigh went through Daniel, and he wrapped Lee up in a bear hug. "You have no idea how happy this makes me. I was so worried about you and your mom. What happened? You should have been done hours ago. We kept the meeting going as long as we could."

"And I was just here freaking out. I thought about looking for you," Neil began.

I hugged my bestie. "It's best that you didn't. We got caught and someone killed Lee. Would you like to guess who? And also, I told you so."

Danny had his cell out but he looked my way. "Who? How?"

"It was Alexander freaking Sharpe." Yes, there was a whole lot of righteousness in my tone.

"Shit." Danny pulled me in close, keeping an arm around Lee. "You both are still here."

"Zoey." Devinshea jogged around the corner. "I was about to walk to Ether to find you. Lee. Oh, thank the goddess."

Dev wrapped his arms around us and Neil worked his way in because he did not like being left out of any kind of physical affection.

I sighed in relief because I was with them again, and we were all okay for now.

"You'll have to tell us everything on our way home," Dev whispered. "And Lee will have to change. Dare I ask who he killed?"

"Oh, like a bunch of witches, but the blood is all mine. I didn't miss a drop of the witch blood." Lee was back to his jaunty self. "Dad, I got a little heartburn."

"Because you drank too much," Danny admonished as we broke away and started walking toward the car. "You have to moderate."

"Is Lee a vampire?" Dev asked, his emerald eyes wide in shock.

"Catch up, buddy," Neil said.

"We will explain everything on our way home," I promised. "Hey, is there any way Myrddin's in the Council building right now?"

"He left at the same time we did." Danny got out the keys to our rental. "So he should be."

The ground beneath us shook.

"Excellent." It wouldn't kill the fucker, but it would hurt him.

And he could dig for his book.

Dev had stopped. "What the hell was that?"

"Uhm, Mom might have blown up the Council building," Lee said with a sigh. "And that is why I had to save the flamethrower. Also, we got this cool sword thing that killed me. It's a souvenir."

"She did what?" Dev asked.

But Danny was already laughing.

I walked to the car. It was time to go home.

Chapter Twenty-Seven

"They're calling it a planned demolition." Sasha put a newspaper in front of me two mornings later. The ring I'd stolen from Alexander had found a new home, and I had to admit, the vampire looked good in the morning light. "What else can they call it given how the building fell? It didn't touch any of the structures around it."

I glanced down at the paper at the picture of all that rubble. It made me happy. And sad. But mostly happy because Myrddin had gotten caught in it according to our intelligence. He was at an undisclosed location healing.

I hoped it hurt.

Sasha shook his head. "I thought you would like to know your plan worked. Lily managed to get on site last night, and she said there is no more portal. Sarah's location is safe."

"She could have sent me a change of address notice," I groused. I didn't know how I was going to find her. I only knew I was.

"And you, my goddess, could have found another way." Dev stared down at the paper. "My beautiful club."

"Babe, trust me. I did us a favor. He'd done terrible things with the place," I promised him.

Danny walked in. He put a hand on the back of Dev's neck.

"Devinshea, think about how much fun you'll have building something new."

Dev's eyes lit up. "Actually, I had been thinking about renovations. I'll just have to do it from the ground up."

They were optimistic that we would get back to Dallas again. I was okay with wherever we ended up, as long as we were together.

The night before Danny had formally turned Lee. It was a ritual and nothing more because Lee didn't need the mystical gifts that came with king's blood. He had his own.

And he was already enjoying his vampiric life. A couple of times a night. With multiple partners.

Zack strode in looking dapper in a suit that fit him perfectly. "Morning, all. Boss, we need to get a move on. We're supposed to be in London to meet with the Order at one."

They were already busy bringing our coalition back together.

Danny leaned over and kissed me. "See you tonight, Z. Try not to blow anything up."

Dev took his turn, brushing his lips over mine. "Yes, my goddess. I expect this place to be standing when we return. And you have a shipment coming in today. From Paris. We're going to need bigger closets."

I could only imagine. Devinshea was back, and Europe's economy would get a big boost.

They walked out, taking Sasha with them. For the first time the vampire could join them in the daytime meetings. It wasn't more than a minute before the door swung open again and my sons were walking through, followed by Shy and Dean.

"Don't you even act all high and mighty, brother." Rhys was grinning as he grabbed a plate. "You got killed by Jack the Ripper. You're a trivia question now."

Lee put a hand to his chest, obviously offended. "I was murdered by a professional and guess who's still standing? Damn, why does food still smell good?"

Because he was a weirdo. He was already testing his limits, one of which had been easily overcome with a dose of high-charged energy from Bris. Lee daywalked from the beginning.

"He's been complaining about not having one last pizza," Dean said as he hit the buffet.

"He's complaining about everything." Shy shook her head. "And now that he's invulnerable they punch each other constantly."

"Oh, get used to that. The experiments will start soon," I promised. I knew how that went.

"I hope Evan gets home soon," Shy said, turning over her coffee mug. "I need more feminine energy around."

She was due home in a few days and I couldn't wait. I was hoping Kelsey brought Gray home, too. It seemed he'd been away far too long.

"Mom, Rhys is taunting me with a Danish. He knows I can't eat them." Lee sank to his seat. He might not be able to eat, but he didn't miss mealtimes. He sat around the table and joined in on the conversation always.

Like his father did.

Like family did.

"Stop taunting your brother," I said with a smile, and then I was surrounded with happy chaos as Neil walked in talking about all the things Dev had bought. Cassie and Brendan joined him, and Lisa and Courtney and the baby weren't far behind. The boys started to argue about who would have to take me to the bridges this afternoon since I still wanted to see my godparents.

I was surrounded by them, and I sat back and listened, happy to be with my family.

I just hoped Kelsey had an easier time than I had…

* * * *

Kelsey

Spoiler alert. I did not, in fact, have an easier time. But that's another story…

Kelsey, Trent, Gray, and the whole Thieves family will return in *The Rebel Guardian.*

Author's Note

I'm often asked by generous readers how they can help get the word out about a book they enjoyed. There are so many ways to help an author you like. Leave a review. If your e-reader allows you to lend a book to a friend, please share it. Go to Goodreads and connect with others. Recommend the books you love because stories are meant to be shared. Thank you so much for reading this book and for supporting all the authors you love!

Sign up for Lexi Blake's newsletter
and be entered to win a $25 gift certificate
to the bookseller of your choice.

Join us for news, fun, and exclusive content
including free short stories.

There's a new contest every month!

Go to www.LexiBlake.net to subscribe.

Discover the Faery Story Trilogy

By Lexi Blake
Now available

Bound
Book 1

A stranger in a strange land

Megan Starke has given up believing in knights in shining armor. With an unrewarding job and a failed marriage, no one would confuse her life with a fairy tale. No one is coming to save the day or carry her off to a romantic fantasy. So when she wakes up in a magical world and discovers she is to be the grand prize in a fierce and bloody tournament, she isn't sure if she's having a sexy dream or a horrible nightmare.

Two kings without a kingdom

Beckett and Cian were raised to be the saviors of their people. Prepared all their lives to lead the Seelie Fae, prophecy proclaimed they would find a bondmate whose love would complete them and unleash their magical powers. But the thrust of a traitor's blade stole that future and now it threatens to take their lives. Struggling in exile, their glorious destiny has become a curse. Unless they can find the perfect woman to save them, they will descend into madness and ruin. When all hope seems lost, Beck sees Meg and knows she's the key to their salvation.

An epic battle begins

In a world filled with dethroned kings, upwardly mobile vampires, and dangerous, feline-loving hags, Meg will need all her strength to survive. Finding herself caught between Beck and Cian, she's willing to do whatever it takes to claim her happily ever after.

* * * *

Beast
Book 2

A playboy who needs to grow up

Fresh from his latest tabloid scandal, vampire playboy Dante Dellacourt has been given an ultimatum. Either he takes a consort and settles down, or his family will disown him. Unwilling to lose everything he has, he reluctantly agrees to find a wife. Marriage is just another kind of contract, after all. No one said anything about love being a part of the bargain.

An outcast who has only known hardship

Exiled by her pack, Kaja is a werewolf without a home. Her life was never easy in the frozen tundra she grew up in, but it was familiar. Waking up in a foreign landscape, surrounded by bright lights, loud noises, and far too many people has left her overwhelmed. Frightened and with no one to trust, she savagely fights to get free of this strange new world.

A passion strong enough to change them both

Called to defend the gnomes of the marketplace, Dante is almost blinded by the radiant light coming off the fierce werewolf. Kaja glows like no consort he has ever seen. Gorgeous and wild, she calls to him in ways he had not dreamed possible. For Kaja, she finds in Dante a man unlike any she has ever known. They could not be more different, but she finds him irresistible.

In order to claim his werewolf bride, Dante must first discover how to overcome their differences. Will he tame his ferocious beauty, or will she unleash his inner beast?

* * * *

Beauty
Book 3

The princess in the tower

In one horrifying night, Bronwyn Finn lost her family, her kingdom, and the princes who had haunted her dreams for years. Left alone, years pass as she fights for survival and craves revenge against the uncle who took everything from her. But she's never forgotten her Dark Ones. Now she hides along with her guardian, but the war rages ever closer.

Two dark princes

A tragedy marred Lach and Shim's lives. The future kings of the Unseelie Fae are obsessed with finding their promised wife—Bronwyn. Lach and Shim have never stopped believing that Bronwyn is their mate. She is the bond that connects the halves of their shared soul.

A destiny that will change a kingdom

With the blessing of the renegade kings, Beck and Cian Finn, Lach and Shim begin a dangerous quest to find their bride before Torin and his hags take her life.

Across two planes, a war will rage. Lives will be lost. Love will be found. And the Seelie Fae will welcome their true kings home.

Treasured

A Masters and Mercenaries Novella
By Lexi Blake
Coming June 22, 2021

David Hawthorne has a great life. His job as a professor at a prestigious Dallas college is everything he hoped for. Now that his brother is back from the Navy, life seems to be settling down. All he needs to do is finish the book he's working on and his tenure will be assured. When he gets invited to interview a reclusive expert, he knows he's gotten lucky. But being the stepson of Sean Taggart comes with its drawbacks, including an overprotective mom who sends a security detail to keep him safe. He doesn't need a bodyguard, but when Tessa Santiago shows up on his doorstep, the idea of her giving him close cover doesn't seem so bad.

Tessa has always excelled at most anything she tried, except romance. The whole relationship thing just didn't work out for her. She's not looking for love, and she's certainly not looking for it with an academic who happens to be connected to her boss's family. The last thing she wants is to escort an overly pampered pretentious man-child around South America to ensure he doesn't get into trouble. Still, there's something about David that calls to her. In addition to watching his back, she will have to avoid falling into the trap of soulful eyes and a deep voice that gets her heart racing.

But when the seemingly simple mission turns into a treacherous race for a hidden artifact, David and Tess know this assignment could cost them far more than their jobs. If they can overcome the odds, the lost treasure might not be their most valuable reward.

About Lexi Blake

New York Times bestselling author Lexi Blake lives in North Texas with her husband and three kids. Since starting her publishing journey in 2010, she's sold over three million copies of her books. She began writing at a young age, concentrating on plays and journalism. It wasn't until she started writing romance that she found success. She likes to find humor in the strangest places and believes in happy endings.

Connect with Lexi online:

Facebook: www.facebook.com/authorlexiblake
Instagram: www.instagram.com/lexiblakeauthor
Twitter: authorlexiblake
Website: www.LexiBlake.net

CPSIA information can be obtained
at www.ICGtesting.com
Printed in the USA
LVHW090108050621
689459LV00003B/25